The Independence

The Independence of Claire

by Mrs. George de Horne Vaizey

Copyright © 1/30/2016
Jefferson Publication

ISBN-13: 978-1523789672

Printed in the United States of America

All rights reserved. No part of this book may be reprinted or reproduced or utilized in any form or by any electronic, mechanical, or other means, now known or hereafter invented, including photocopying and recording, or in any form of storage or retrieval system, without prior permission in writing from the publisher.'

Table of Contents

Chapter One. 3
Chapter Two. 9
Chapter Three. 15
Chapter Four. 17
Chapter Five. 26
Chapter Six. 32
Chapter Seven. 37
Chapter Eight. 41
Chapter Nine. 50
Chapter Ten. 56
Chapter Eleven. 62
Chapter Twelve. 77
Chapter Thirteen. 81
Chapter Fourteen. 88
Chapter Fifteen. 94
Chapter Sixteen. 99
Chapter Seventeen. 106
Chapter Eighteen. 112
Chapter Nineteen. 117
Chapter Twenty. 121
Chapter Twenty One 124
Chapter Twenty Two. 127
Chapter Twenty Three. 132
Chapter Twenty Four. 135
Chapter Twenty Five. 140
Chapter Twenty Six. 143
Chapter Twenty Seven 145

Chapter One.

"I'll have to do it."

Claire Gifford stood in the salon of the Brussels pension which had been her home for the last three years, and bent her brows in consideration of an all-absorbing problem. "Can I marry him?" she asked herself once and again, with the baffling result that every single time her brain answered instantly, "*You must!*" the while her heart rose up in rebellion, and cried, "I won't!" Many girls have found themselves in the same predicament before and since, but few have had stronger reasons for sacrificing personal inclination on the altar of filial duty than Claire knew at this minute.

To begin with, the relationship between herself and her mother was more intimate than is usually the case, for Claire was an only child, and Mrs Gifford a widow only eighteen years older than herself. Briefly stated, the family history was as follows—Eleanor Guyther had been the only child of stern, old-world parents, and at seventeen had run away from the house which had been more like a prison than a home, to marry a handsome young artist who had been painting in the neighbourhood during the summer months; a handsome merry-faced boy of twenty-one, whose portrait Claire treasured in an old-fashioned gold locket, long since discarded by her mother, who followed the fashion in jewellery as well as in dress. It was strange to look at the face of a father who was no older than oneself, and Claire had spent many hours gazing at the pictured face, and trying to gain from it some idea of the personality of the man of whom her mother persistently refused to speak.

Mrs Gifford shrank from all disagreeables, great and small, and systematically turned her back on anything which was disturbing or painful, so that it was only from chance remarks that her daughter had gained any information about the past. She knew that her father had been a successful artist, although not in the highest sense of the term. He had a trick of turning out pretty domestic pictures which appealed to the taste of the million, and which, being purchased by enterprising dealers, were reproduced in cheap prints to deck the walls of suburban parlours. While he lived he made a sufficient income, and before his death a formal reconciliation had taken place between the runaway daughter and her north-country parents, from whom she later inherited the money which had supported herself and her daughter throughout the years of her widowhood.

Claire had the vaguest idea as to the amount of her mother's means, for until the last few years the question of money had never arisen, they had simply decided what they wished to do, without considering the cost, but of late there had been seasons of financial tightness, and the morning on which this history begins had brought a most disagreeable awakening.

Mrs Gifford was seated in the salon staring disconsolately at a note which had just arrived by the afternoon post. It was a very disagreeable note, for it stated in brief and callous terms that her account at the bank was overdrawn to the extent of three hundred francs, and politely requested that the deficit should be made good. Claire looked flushed and angry; Mrs Gifford looked pathetic and pale.

It seemed, in the first place, quite ludicrous that such a relationship as that of mother and daughter should exist between two women who looked so nearly of an age, and Mrs Gifford's youthful appearance was a standing joke in the Pension. Every new visitor was questioned by Madame as to the relationship between the two English ladies, and never had one of the number failed to reply "sisters," and to be convulsed with astonishment when corrected; and in good truth Mrs Gifford was a wonderful specimen of the prolonged youth which is a phenomenon of the present day.

She was slight, she was graceful, her waving brown hair was as naturally luxuriant as that of a girl, her complexion was smooth and fair, her pretty features were unchanged, she dressed with good taste, and, though secretly proud of her youthful looks, was never so foolish as to adopt kittenish airs to match. Her manner was quiet, gracious, appealing; a little air of pathos enveloped her like a mist; on strangers she made the impression of a lovely creature who had known suffering. Everybody was kind to Mrs Gifford, and she in return had never been known to utter an unkind word. She had been born with the faculty of loving everybody a little, and no one very much, which—if one comes to think of it—is the most powerful of all factors towards securing an easy life, since it secures the owner from the possibility of keen personal suffering.

At the present moment Mrs Gifford did, however, look really perturbed, for, after shutting her eyes to a disagreeable fact, and keeping them shut with much resolution

The Independence of Claire

and—it must be added—ease, for many years past, she was now driven to face the truth, and to break it to her daughter into the bargain.

"But I don't understand!" Claire repeated blankly. "How *can* the money be gone? We have spent no more this year than for years past. I should think we have spent less. I haven't been extravagant a bit. You offered me a new hat only last week, and I said I could do without—"

"Yes, yes, of course. It's quite true, *chérie*, you have been most good. But, you see, ours has not been a case of an income that goes on year after year—it never was, even from the beginning. There was not enough. And you *did* have a good education, didn't you? I spared nothing on it. It's folly to stint on a girl's education.—It was one of the best schools in Paris."

"It was, mother; but we are not talking about schools. Do let us get to the bottom of this horrid muddle! If it isn't a case of 'income,' what can it be? I'm ignorant about money, for you have always managed business matters, but I can't see what else we can have been living upon?"

Mrs Gifford crinkled her delicate brows, and adopted an air of plaintive self-defence.

"I'm sure it's as great a shock to me as it is to you; but, under the circumstances, I do think I managed very well. It was only nine thousand pounds at the beginning, and I've made it last over thirteen years, *with* your education! And since we've been here, for the last three years, I've given you a good time, and taken you to everything that was going on. Naturally it all costs. Naturally money can't last for ever..."

The blood flooded the girl's face. Now at last she *did* understand, and the knowledge filled her with awe.

"Mother! Do you mean that we have been living all this time on *capital*?"

Mrs Gifford shrugged her shoulders, and extended her hands in an attitude typically French.

"What would you, *ma chère*? Interest is so ridiculously low. They offered me three per cent. Four was considered high. How could we have lived on less than three hundred a year? Your school bills came to nearly as much, and I had to live, too, and keep you in the holidays. I did what I thought was the best. We should both have been miserable in cheap pensions, stinting ourselves of everything we liked. The money has made us happy for thirteen years."

Claire rose from her seat and walked over to the window. The road into which she looked was wide and handsome, lined with a double row of trees. The sun shone on the high white houses with the green *jalousies*, which stood *vis-à-vis* with the Pension. Along the cobble-stoned path a dog was dragging a milk-cart, the gleaming brass cans clanking from side to side; through the open window came the faint indescribable scent which distinguishes a continental from a British city. Claire stared with unseeing eyes, her heart beating with heavy thuds. She conjured up the image of a man's face—a strong kindly face—a face which might well make the sunshine of some woman's life, but which made no appeal to her own heart. She set her lips, and two bright spots of colour showed suddenly in her cheeks. So smooth and uneventful had been her life that this was the first time that she had found herself face to face with serious difficulty, and, after the first shock of realisation, her spirit rose to meet it. She straightened her shoulders as if throwing off a weight, and her heart cried valiantly, "It's my own life, and I will *not* be forced! There must be some other way. It's for me to find it!"

Suddenly she whirled round, and walked back to her mother.

"Mother, if you knew how little money was left, why wouldn't you let me accept Miss Farnborough's offer at Christmas!"

The Independence of Claire

For a moment Mrs Gifford's face expressed nothing but bewilderment. Then comprehension dawned.

"You mean the school-mistress from London? What was it she suggested? That you should go to her as a teacher? It was only a suggestion, so far as I remember. She made no definite offer."

"Oh, yes, she did. She said that she had everlasting difficulty with her French mistresses, and that I was the very person for whom she'd been looking. Virtually French, yet really English in temperament. She made me a definite offer of a hundred and ten pounds a year."

Mrs Gifford laughed, and shrugged her graceful shoulders. She appeared to find the proposal supremely ridiculous, yet when people were without money, the only sane course seemed to be to take what one could get. Claire felt that she had not yet mastered the situation. There must be something behind which she had still to grasp.

"Well, never mind the school for a moment, mother dear. Tell me what *you* thought of doing. You must have had some plan in your head all these years while the money was dwindling away. Tell me your scheme, then we can compare the two and see which is better."

Mrs Gifford bent her head over the table, and scribbled aimlessly with a pen in which there was no ink. She made no answer in words, yet as she waited the blood flamed suddenly over Claire's face, for it seemed to her that she divined what was in her mother's mind. "I expected that you would marry. I have done my best to educate you and give you a happy youth. I expected that you would accept your first good offer, and look after *me*!"

That was what a French mother would naturally say to her daughter; that was what Claire Gifford believed that her own mother was saying to her at that moment, and the accusation brought little of the revolt which an English girl would have experienced. Claire had been educated at a Parisian boarding school, and during the last three years had associated almost entirely with French-speaking Andrées and Maries and Celestes, who took for granted that their husbands should be chosen for them by their parents. Claire had assisted at betrothal feasts, and played *demoiselle d'honneur* at subsequent weddings, and had witnessed an astonishing degree of happiness as an outcome of these business-like unions. At this moment she felt no anger against her own mother for having tried to follow a similar course. Her prevailing sensation was annoyance with herself for having been so difficult to lead.

"It must be my English blood. Somehow, when it came to the point, I never *could*. But Mr Judge is different from most men. He is so good and generous and unmercenary. He'd be kind to mother, and let her live with us, and make no fuss. He is as charming to her as he is to me. Oh, dear, I *am* selfish! I *am* a wretch! It isn't as if I were in love with anyone else. I'm not. Perhaps I never shall be. I'll never have the chance if I live in lodgings and spend my life teaching irregular verbs. Why can't I be sensible and French, and marry him and live happily ever after? *Pauvre petite mère*! Why can't I think of *her*?"

Suddenly Claire swooped down upon her mother's drooping figure, wrapped her in loving arms, and swung her gently to and fro. She was a tall, strikingly graceful girl, with a face less regularly beautiful than her mother's, but infinitely more piquant and attractive. She was more plump and rounded than the modern English girl, and her complexion less pink and white, but she was very neat and dainty and smart, possessed deep-set, heavily-lashed grey eyes, red lips which curled mischievously upward at the corner, and a pair of dimples on her soft left cheek.

The dimples were in full play at this moment; the large one was just on the level with the upward curl of the lips, the smaller one nestled close to its side. In repose they were almost unnoticed, but at the slightest lighting of expression, at the first dawn of a smile, they danced into sight and became the most noticeable feature of her face. Claire without her dimples would have been another and far less fascinating personality.

"Mother darling, forgive me! Kiss me, *chérie*—don't look sad! I *have* had a good time, and we'll have a good time yet, if it is in my power to get it for you. Cheer up! Things won't be as bad as you fear. We won't allow them to be bad. ... How much does the horrid old bank say that we owe? Three hundred francs. I can pay it out of my own little savings. Does it mean literally that there is nothing more, nothing at all—not a single sou?"

"Oh no. I have some shares. They have been worthless for years, but just lately they have gone up. I was asking Mr Judge about them yesterday. He says I might get between two and three hundred pounds. They were worth a thousand, years ago."

Claire brightened with the quick relief of youth. Two or three hundred English pounds were a considerable improvement on a debit account. With two or three hundred pounds much might yet be done. Thousands of people had built up great fortunes on smaller foundations. In a vague, indefinite fashion she determined to devote these last pounds to settling herself in some business, which would ensure a speedy and generous return. School teaching was plainly out of the question, since two gentlewomen could not exist on a hundred and ten pounds a year. She must think of something quicker, more lucrative.

All through dinner that evening Claire debated her future vocation as she sat by her mother's side, halfway down the long dining-table which to English eyes appeared so bare and unattractive, but which was yet supplied with the most appetising of food. Claire's eyes were accustomed to the lack of pretty detail; she had quite an affection for the Pension which stood for home in her migratory life, and a real love for Madame Dupre, the cheery, kindly, most capable proprietor. Such of the *pensionnaires* as were not purely birds of passage she regarded as friends rather than acquaintances; the only person in the room to whom she felt any antagonism was Mr Judge himself, but unfortunately he was the one of all others whom she was expected to like best.

As she ate her salad and broke fragments of delicious crusty roll, Claire threw furtive glances across the table at the man who for the last weeks had exercised so disturbing an element in her life. Was it six weeks or two months, since she and her mother had first made his acquaintance at the tennis club at which they spent so many of their afternoons? Claire had noticed that a new man had been present on that occasion, had bestowed on him one critical glance, decided with youthful arrogance: "Oh, quite old!" and promptly forgotten his existence, until an hour later, when, as she was sitting in the pavilion enjoying the luxury of a real English tea, the strange man and her mother had entered side by side. Claire summoned in imagination the picture of her mother as she had looked at that moment, slim and graceful in the simplest of white dresses, an untrimmed linen hat shading her charming face. She looked about twenty-five, and Claire was convinced that she knew as much, and that it was a mischievous curiosity to see her companion's surprise which prompted her to lead the way across the floor, and formally introduce "My daughter!"

Mr Judge exhibited all the expected signs of bewilderment, but he made himself exceedingly amiable to the daughter, and it was not until a week later that it was discovered that he had concluded that the relationship must surely be "step," when fresh explanations were made, and all the bewilderment came over again.

Since then, oh, since then, Claire told herself, there had been no getting away from the man! He was, it appeared, an Indian merchant spending a few months on the Continent, at the conclusion of a year's leave. He had come to Brussels because of the presence of

The Independence of Claire

an old school friend—the same friend who was responsible for the introduction at the tennis club—but week after week passed by, and he showed no disposition to move on.

Now Brussels is a very gay and interesting little city, but when Paris looms ahead, and Berlin, Vienna, to say nothing of the beauties of Switzerland and the Tyrol, and the artistic treasures of Italy—well! it *did* seem out of proportion to waste six whole weeks in that one spot!

At the end of the last fortnight, too, Mr Judge declared that he was sick to death of hotels and lonely evenings in smoking rooms, and approached Madame Dupre with a view to joining the party at Villa Beau Séjour. Madame was delighted to receive him, but Claire Gifford told her mother resentfully that she considered Mr Judge's behaviour "very cool." How did he know that it would be pleasant for them to have him poking about morning, noon, and night?

"It isn't *our* Pension, darling, and he is very nice to you," Mrs Gifford had said in return, and as it was impossible to contradict either statement, Claire had tossed her head, and relapsed into silence.

For the first weeks of her acquaintance with Mr Judge, Claire had thoroughly enjoyed his attentions. It was agreeable to know a man who had a habit of noting your wishes, and then setting to work to bring them about forthwith, and who was also delightfully extravagant as regards flowers, and seemed to grow chocolates in his coat pockets. It was only when he spoke of moving to the Pension, and her girl friends at the tennis club began to tease, roll meaning eyes, and ask when she was to be congratulated, that she took fright.

Did people really think that she was going to *marry* Mr Judge?

Lately things had moved on apace, and as a result of the unwelcome revelations of the morning's post, Claire was to-day asking herself a different question. She was no longer occupied with other people; she was thinking of herself... "Am I going to marry Mr Judge? Oh, good gracious, is that *My Husband* sitting over there, and have I got to live with him every day, as long as we both shall live?"

She shuddered at the thought, but in truth there was nothing to shudder at in Robert Judge's appearance. He was a man of forty, bronzed, and wiry, with agreeable if not regular features. Round his eyes the skin was deeply furrowed, but the eyes themselves were bright and youthful, and the prevailing expression was one of sincerity and kindliness. He wore a loose grey tweed suit, with a soft-coloured shirt which showed a length of brown neck. The fingers of his right band were deeply stained with tobacco. During *déjeuner* he carried on a conversation with his right-hand companion, in exceedingly bad French, but ever and anon he glanced across the table as though his thoughts were not on his words. Once, on looking up suddenly, Claire found his eyes fixed upon herself, with a strained, anxious look, and her heart quickened as she looked, then sank down heavy as lead.

"It's coming!" she said to herself. "It's coming! There's no running away. I'll have to stay, and see it out. Oh, why can't I be French, and sensible? I ought to be thankful to marry such a kind, good man, and be able to give mother a comfortable home!"

But as a matter of fact she was neither glad nor thankful. Despite her French training, the English instinct survived and clamoured for liberty, for independence. "It's my own life. If I marry at all, I want to choose the man for no other reason than that I love him; not as a duty, and to please somebody else!" Then she glanced at her mother sitting by her side, slim, and graceful, with the little air of pathos and helplessness which even strangers found so appealing, and as she did so, a shiver passed through Claire's veins.

"But I'll have to do it!" she said to herself helplessly. "I'll have to do it!"

Chapter Two.

Too successful!

The next few days passed by slowly enough. It is a great trial for a young creature to realise that a change is inevitable and, at the same time, that one must be cautious about making it. The impulse is always to rush into action, and it is difficult to sit still and agree with the elderly precept in favour of consideration and delay. If matters had been left to Claire she would have started out forthwith to search for a cheap Pension, and would have also despatched a letter to Miss Farnborough by the first post, to inquire if the school post were still open, but her mother vetoed both proposals, and pleaded so urgently for delay, that there was nothing left but to agree, and compose herself as best she might.

The weather was too hot for tennis, and in truth Claire was not in the mood for games. With every hour she realised more keenly that she had come to the parting of the ways, and in the prospect of a new life old interests lost their savour. Her mother seemed to share her restlessness, but while Claire preferred to stay indoors, in the privacy of her own room, Mrs Gifford seemed to find relief in action, and was often out for hours at a time, without vouchsafing any explanation of her absence.

Claire was not curious. She was content to close the green shutters of her windows, slip into a muslin wrapper, and employ herself at some simple piece of needlework, which kept her hands busy while leaving her thoughts free.

Where would she be this time next year? It was a question which no mortal can answer with certainty, but many of us are happy in the probability that we shall be still living in the same dear home, surrounded by the people and the objects which we love, whereas Claire's one certainty was that she must move on to fresh scenes. Bombay or London—that seemed the choice ahead! Matrimony or teaching. On the one hand a luxurious home, carriages and horses, a staff of servants, and apparently as much society as one desired, with the incubus of a husband whom she did not love, and who was twenty years her senior. On the other hand, work and poverty, with the advantages of freedom and independence.

Claire's eyes brightened at the sound of those two words, for dear as liberty is to the heart of an Englishwoman, it was in prospect dearer still to this girl who had been educated in a country still enslaved by chaperonage, and had never known a taste of real freedom of action. Mrs Gifford had been as strict as or stricter than any Belgian mother, being rightly determined that no breath of scandal should touch her daughter's name; therefore wherever Claire went, some responsible female went with her. She was chaperoned to church, chaperoned on her morning constitutional, a chaperon sat on guard during the period of music and drawing lessons, and at their conclusion escorted her back to the Pension. What wonder that the thought of life as a bachelor girl in London seemed full of a thrilling excitement!

Suppose for one minute that she decided on London—what would become of mother? Again and again Claire asked herself this question, again and again she recalled the interview between herself and the headmistress, Miss Farnborough, when the subject of teaching had been discussed. It had happened one morning in the salon of the Pension, when Claire had been coaching an English visitor in preparation for a French interview which lay ahead, and Miss Farnborough, laying down her book, had listened with smiling interest. Then the Englishwoman left the room, and Miss Farnborough had said, "You did

The Independence of Claire

that very cleverly; very cleverly indeed! You have a very happy knack of putting things simply and forcibly. I've noticed it more than once. Have you ever done any teaching?"

"None professionally," Claire had replied with a laugh, "but a great deal by chance. I seem to drift into the position of coach to most of the English visitors here. It pleases them, and it interests me. And I used to help the French girls with their English at school."

Then Miss Farnborough had inquired with interest as to the details of Claire's education, the schools she had attended, the examinations she had passed, and finally had come the critical question, "Have you ever thought of taking up teaching as a profession?"

Claire had never thought of taking up work of any kind, but the suggestion roused a keen interest, as one of the temporary "tight" times was in process, so that the prospect of money-making seemed particularly agreeable. She discussed the subject carefully, and out of that discussion had arisen the final offer of a post.

The junior French mistress in the High School of which Miss Farnborough was head was leaving at midsummer. If Claire wished she could take her place, at a salary beginning at a hundred and ten pounds a year. In Trust Schools, of which Saint Cuthbert's was one, there was no fixed scale of advancement, but a successful teacher could reach a salary of, say, two hundred a year by the time she was thirty-eight or forty, as against the permanent sixty or seventy offered to mistresses in residential schools of a higher grade. Miss Farnborough's mistresses were women trained at the various universities; the school itself was situated in a fashionable neighbourhood, and its pupils were for the most part daughters of professional men, and gentlefolk of moderate incomes. There was no pension scheme, and mistresses had to live out, but with care and economy they could take out some insurance to provide for old age.

Claire took little interest in her own old age, which seemed too far away to count, but she was intensely interested in the immediate future, and had been hurt and annoyed when her mother had waved aside the proposal as unworthy of serious consideration. And now, only three months after Miss Farnborough's departure, the crisis had arisen, and that hundred and ten pounds assumed a vastly increased value. Supposing that the post was accepted, and mother and daughter started life in London with a capital of between two and three hundred pounds, and a salary of one hundred and ten, as regular income—how long would the nest-egg last out?

Judging from the experience of past years, a very short time indeed, and what would happen after that? Claire had read gruesome tales of the struggles of women in like positions, overtaken by illness, losing the salaries which represented their all, brought face to face with actual starvation, and in the midst of the midsummer heat, little shivers of fear trickled up and down her spine as she realised how easily she and her mother might drift into a like position.

Then, on the other hand, Bombay! Indian houses were large; mother could have her own rooms. In the hot weather they would go together to the hills, leaving Mr Judge behind. How long did the hot season last, four or five months? Nearly half the year, perhaps. It would be only half as bad as marrying a man for money in Europe, for you would get rid of him all that time! Claire shrugged her shoulders and laughed, and two minutes later whisked away a tear, dedicated to the memory of girlish dreams. Useless to dream any longer, she was awake now, and must face life in a sensible manner. Her duty was to marry Robert Judge, and to make a home for her mother.

Another girl might have cherished anger against the recklessness which had landed her in such a trap, but after the first shock of discovery there had been no resentment in Claire's heart. She implicitly believed her mother's assurance that according to her light she had acted for the best, and echoed with heartiness the assertion that the money had provided a good time for thirteen long years.

They had not been rich, but there had been a feeling of sufficiency. They had had comfortable quarters, pretty clothes, delightful holiday journeys, a reasonable amount of gaiety, and, over and beyond all, the advantages of an excellent education. Claire's happy nature remembered her benefits, and made short work of the rest. Poor, beautiful mother! who could expect her to be prudent and careful, like any ordinary, prosaic, middle-aged woman?

Even as the thought passed through the girl's mind the door of the bedroom opened, and Mrs Gifford appeared on the threshold. She wore a large shady hat, and in the dim light of the room her face was not clearly visible, but there was a tone in her voice which aroused Claire's instant curiosity. Mother was trying to speak in her ordinary voice, but she was nervous, she was agitated. She was not feeling ordinary at all.

"Claire, *chérie*, we are going to the forest to have tea. It is impossibly hot indoors, but it will be delightful under the trees. Mr Judge has sent for a *fiacre*, and Miss Benson has asked to come too. Put on your blue muslin and your big hat. Be quick, darling! I'll fasten you up."

"I'd rather not go, thank you, mother. I'm quite happy here. Don't trouble about me!"

Mrs Gifford was obviously discomposed. She hesitated, frowned, walked restlessly up and down, then spoke again with an added note of insistence—

"But I want you to come, Claire. I've not troubled you before, because I saw you wanted to be alone, but—it can't go on. Mr Judge wants you to come. He suggested the drive because he thought it would tempt you. If you refuse to-day, he will ask you again to-morrow. I think, dear, you ought to come."

Claire was silent. She felt sick and faint; all over her body little pulses seemed to be whizzing like so many alarm clocks, all crying in insistent voices, "Time's up! Time's up! No more lazing. Up with you, and do your duty!" Her forehead felt very damp and her throat felt very dry, and she heard a sharp disagreeable voice saying curtly—

"Oh, certainly, I will come. No need to make a fuss. I can dress myself, thank you. I'll come down when I'm ready!"

Mrs Gifford turned without a word and went out of the room, but Claire was too busy being sorry for herself to have sympathy to spare for anyone else. She threw off her wrapper and slipped into the cool muslin dress which was at once so simple, and so essentially French and up-to-date, and then, throwing open the door of a cupboard, stared at a long row of hats ranged on a top shelf, and deliberately selected the one which she considered the least becoming.

"I will *not* be decked up for the sacrifice!" she muttered rebelliously, then bent forward, so that her face approached close to the flushed, frowning reflection in the glass. "You are going to be proposed to, my dear!" she said scornfully. "You are going to be good and sensible, and say 'Yes, please!' When you see yourself next, you will be Engaged! It won't be dear little Claire Gifford any more, it will be the horrible future Mrs Robert Judge!"

She stuck hat-pins through the straw hat with savage energy; for once in her life noticed with distinct satisfaction that it was secured at an unbecoming angle, then, hearing through the *jalousies* the sound of approaching wheels, marched resolutely forth to meet her fate...

In the *fiacre* Mrs Gifford and Miss Benson took the seats of honour, leaving Claire and Mr Judge to sit side by side, and the one furtive glance which she cast in his direction showed him looking confident and unperturbed. Just like a French *prétendu*, already assured by Maman that Mademoiselle was meekly waiting to assent to his suit!

"He might at least pay me the compliment of *pretending*! It is dreadfully dull to be taken for granted," reflected Claire in disgust.

The next hour was a horrible experience. Everything happened exactly as Claire had known it would, from the moment the quartette set forth. Arrived at the forest, they took possession of one of the little tables beneath the trees, and made fitful conversation the while they consumed delicious cakes and execrable tea. Then the meal being finished, Mrs Gifford and her companion announced a wish to sit still and rest, while Mr Judge nervously invited Miss Claire to accompany him in a walk. She assented, of course; what was the use of putting it off? and as soon as they were well started, he spied another seat, and insisted upon sitting down once more.

"Now he'll begin," thought Claire desperately. "He'll talk about India, and being lonely, and say how happy he has felt since he's been here," and even as the thought passed through her mind, Mr Judge began to speak.

"Awfully jolly old forest this is—awfully nice place Brussels, altogether. Nicest place in the world. Never been so happy in my life as I've been the last month. Of course, naturally, you must realise that, when a fellow hangs on week after week, there—er, there must be some special attraction. Not that it isn't a rattling old city, and all that!" Mr Judge was growing a little mixed: his voice sounded flurried and nervous, but Claire was not in the least inclined to help him. She sat rigid as a poker, staring stolidly ahead. There was not the ghost of a dimple in her soft pink cheeks.

"I—er, your mother tells me that she has said nothing to you, but she is sure, all the same, that you suspect. I asked her to let me speak to you to-day. Naturally she feels the difficulty. She is devoted to you. You know that, of course. I have told her that I will make your happiness my special charge. There is nothing in the world I would not do to ensure it. You know that too, don't you, Claire?"

He stretched out his hand and touched her tentatively on the arm, but Claire drew herself back with a prickly dignity. If he wanted to propose at all, he must propose properly; she was not going to commit herself in response to an insinuation.

"You are very kind. I am quite happy as I am."

"Er—yes—yes, of course, but—but things don't go on, you know, can't go on always without a change!"

Mr Judge took off his straw hat, twirled it nervously to and fro, and laid it down on the bench by his side. Claire, casting a quick glance, noticed that his hair was growing noticeably thin on the temples, and felt an additional sinking of spirits.

"Claire!" cried the man desperately, "don't let us beat about the bush. I'm not used to this sort of thing—don't make it harder than you need! You *have* noticed, haven't you? You know what I want to tell you?"

Claire nodded dumbly. In the case of previous Belgian admirers affairs had been checked before they reached the extreme stage, and she found this, her first spoken proposal much less exciting than she had expected. As a friend pure and simple, she had thoroughly liked Mr Judge, and at the bottom of her heart there lived a lingering hope that perhaps if he loved her very much, and expressed his devotion in very eloquent words, her heart might soften in response. But so far he had not even mentioned love! She was silent for several minutes, and when she did speak it was to ask a side question.

"Is mother willing to go to India?"

She was looking at the man as she spoke, and the change which passed over his face, startled her by its intensity. His eyes shone, the rugged features were transfigured by a very radiance of joy. He looked young at that moment, young and handsome, and blissfully content. Claire stared at him in amazement, not unmingled with irritation. Even if mother *were* willing, her own consent had still to be obtained. It was tactless to make so sure!

Her own face looked decidedly sulky as she twitched round on her seat, and resumed her stolid staring into space. Again there was silence, till a hand stretched out to clasp her arm, and a voice spoke in deep appealing accents—

"Claire, dear child, you are young; you have never known loneliness or disappointment. We have! Happiness is fifty times more precious, when it comes to those who have suffered. You would not be cruel enough to damp our happiness! You *can* do it, you know, if you persist in an attitude of coldness and disapproval. I don't say you can destroy it. Thank God! it goes too deep for anyone to be able to do that. But you can rub off the bloom. Don't do it, Claire! Be generous. Be yourself. Wish us good luck!"

"Wish *who* good luck? What, oh, what are you talking about?" Claire was gasping now, quivering with a frenzy of excitement. Robert Judge stared in return, his face full of an honest bewilderment.

"Of our engagement, of course. Your mother's engagement to me. I have been talking about it all the time!"

Then Claire threw up both her hands, and burst into a wild peal of laughter. Peal after peal rang out into the air, she rocked to and fro on her seat, her eyes disappeared from view, her teeth shone, her little feet in their dainty French shoes danced upon the ground; she laughed till the tears poured down her cheeks, and her gloved hands pressed against her side where a "stitch" was uncomfortably making itself felt. Stout Belgian couples passing past the end of the avenue, looked on with indulgent smiles, a little shocked at so much demonstration in public, but relieved to perceive that *une Anglaise* could laugh with such *abandon*. Monsieur they observed looked not sympathetic. Monsieur had an air injured, annoyed, on his dignity. On his cheeks was a flush, as of wounded pride. When at length the paroxysm showed signs of lessening, he spoke in cold stilted tones.

"You appear to find it ridiculous. It seems to amuse you very much. I may say that to us it is a serious matter!"

"Oh no! You don't understand—you *don't* understand!" gasped Claire feebly. "I am not laughing at you. I'm laughing at myself. Oh, Mr Judge, you'll never guess, it's too screamingly funny for words. I thought all this time, from the very beginning I thought, it was *me*!"

"You thought it was—you thought I wanted—that I was talking of—that I meant to propose to—"

"Yes! Yes! Yes! Me! Me! Me! Of course I did. I've been thinking it for weeks. Everyone thought so. They've teased me to death. You were attentive to me, you know you were. You were always giving me things ..."

"Well, of course!" Poor Mr Judge defended himself with honest indignation. "What else could I do? I could not give them to *her*! And I wanted—naturally I wanted, to get you on my side. You were the difficulty. I knew that if she had only herself to consider I could win her round, but if you ranged yourself against me, it would be a hard fight. Naturally I tried to ingratiate myself. It appears that I have rather overdone the part, but I can't flatter myself," his eyes twinkled mischievously, "that I've been too successful! You don't appear exactly overcome with disappointment!"

They laughed together, but only for a moment. Then he was serious again, appealing to her in earnest tones.

"You won't range yourself against me, Claire? You won't dissuade her.—I love her very dearly, and I know I can make her happy. You won't make it hard for us?"

"Indeed, I won't! Why should I?" Claire cried heartily. "I'm only too thankful. Mother needs someone to look after her, and I'd sooner you did it than anyone else. I like you awfully—always did, until I began to be afraid—I didn't want to marry you myself, but if mother does, I think it's a splendid thing."

"Thank you, dear, thank you a thousand times. That's a *great* relief." Robert Judge stretched himself with a deep breath of satisfaction. Then he grew confidential, reviewing the past with true lover-like enjoyment.

"I fell in love with her that first afternoon at the tennis club. Thought Bridges introduced her as Miss Gifford, put her down at twenty-five, and hoped she wouldn't think me a hopeless old fogey. Never had such a surprise in my life as when she introduced you. Thought for a time I should have to give it up. Then she asked my advice on one or two business matters, and I discovered—" He hesitated, flushing uncomfortably, and Claire finished the sentence.

"That we are coming to the end of our resources?"

Mr Judge nodded.

"And so, of course," he continued simply, "that settled it. I couldn't go away and leave her to face a struggle. I was jolly thankful to feel that I had met her in time."

"I think you are a dear, good man. I think mother is very lucky. Thank you so much for being my step-papa!" cried Claire, her grey eyes softening with a charming friendliness as they dwelt on the man's honest face, and he took her hand in his, and squeezed it with affectionate ardour.

"Thank you, my dear. Thank *you*! I shall be jolly proud of having such a pretty daughter. I'm not a rich man, but I am comfortably well-off, and I'll do my best to give you a good time. Your mother feels sure she will enjoy the Indian life. Most girls think it great fun. And of course I have lots of friends."

Claire stared at him, a new seriousness dawning in her eyes. She looked very pretty and very young, and not a little pathetic into the bargain. For the first time since the realisation of her mistake the personal application of the situation burst upon her, and a chill crept through her veins. If she herself had married Robert Judge, her mother would have made her home with them as a matter of course; but it was by no means a matter of course that she should make her home with her mother. She stared into the honest face of the man before her—the man who was not rich, the man who was in love for the first time in his life, and a smile twisted the corner of her lips.

"Mr Judge, if I ask you a question, will you promise to give me an absolutely honest answer?"

"Yes, I will."

"Well, then, will you *like* having a third person living with you all the time?"

Up to the man's forehead rushed the treacherous blood. He frowned, he scowled, he opened his lips to protest; but that flush had answered for him, and Claire refused to listen. "No, no—don't! Of course you wouldn't. Who would, in your place? Poor darlings—I quite understand. You *are* middle-aged, you know, though you feel about nineteen, and mother is prettier and more charming than half the girl brides. And you will want to be just as young and foolish as you like, not to be *obliged* to be sensible because a grown-up daughter is there all the time, staring at you with big eyes? I should be in the way, and I should *feel* in the way, and—"

Mr Judge interrupted in an urgent voice:

"Look here, Claire, I don't think you ought to corner me like this. It's not fair. I've told you that I am prepared to do everything for your happiness. You ought surely to realise that I—"

"And *you* ought to realise that I—" Claire broke off suddenly, and held out her hand with a charming smile. "Oh, but there's plenty of time—we can arrange all that later on. Let's go and find mother and put her out of her misery. She will be longing to see us come back."

They walked down the avenue together, and, as they went, Claire turned her head from side to side, taking in the well-known scene with wistful intensity. How many times would she see it again? As she had said, many discussions would certainly take place as to her future destination, but she knew in her heart that the result was sure. Providence had decided or her. The future was London and work!

Chapter Three.

Mrs Gifford is married.

Claire lost no time in writing to Miss Farnborough to apply for the post of French mistress if it were still vacant, and by return of post received a cordial reply. Several applications had been received, but no appointment had been made, and the Head was pleased to confirm her previous offer of a commencing salary of a hundred and ten pounds, and would expect Miss Gifford to take up her duties at the beginning of the autumn term. She congratulated her on her decision, and felt sure she would never regret devoting her life to so interesting and valuable a work, instead of being content to waste it in the pursuit of idle pleasure.

Poor Claire looked a little dubious as she read those last words. The pursuit of pleasure does not as a rule begin to pall at twenty-one; and the old life looked very sweet and pleasant viewed from the new standpoint of change. She put on a bright face, however, and sternly repressed all signs of depression in discussing the matter with her mother and Mr Judge. Her determination evoked the expected opposition, but slowly and surely the opposition decreased, and her arguments were listened to with increasing respect. The lovers were sincerely desirous of securing the girl's happiness, but middle-aged though they were, they were deeply in love, and felt a natural desire to begin their married life without the presence of a third person, however dear that person might be.

Mr Judge applauded Claire's spirit, and prophesied her rapid success as a teacher. Mrs Gifford murmured sweetly, "And if you *don't* like it, dear, you can always come out by the next boat. Try it for a year. It will be quite an amusing experience to live the life of a bachelor girl. And, of course, in a year or two we'll be coming home. Then you must spend the whole leave with us. We'll see, won't we? We won't make any plans, but just be guided by circumstances. If you want somewhere to go in the holidays, there's my old Aunt Mary in Preston, but you'd be bored to sobs, darling. No doubt Miss Farnborough will introduce you to lots of nice people in London, and you will have all the fifteen other mistresses to take you about. I expect you'll be quite gay! ... Claire, darling, *would* you have gold tissue under this ninon, or just a handsome lace?"

For the next few weeks things moved quickly. In answer to inquiries about lodgings, Miss Farnborough wrote a second time to say that Miss Rhodes, the English mistress, had comfortable rooms which she was sharing with the present French teacher. She was willing to continue the arrangement, and, as a stranger in town, Claire would doubtless find it agreeable as well as economical. The letter was entirely business-like and formal, and, as such, a trifle chilling to Claire, for Miss Farnborough had been so warm in her spoken invitation that Claire had expected a more cordial welcome. Could it be that the shadow of officialdom was already making itself felt?

The next few weeks were given up to trousseau-hunting and farewell visits, and no girl could have shown a livelier interest in the selection of pretty things than did this bride of thirty-nine. Claire came in for a charming costume to wear at the wedding, and for the rest, what fitted her mother fitted herself, and as Mrs Gifford said sweetly, "It would be a sin to waste all my nice things, but they're quite unsuitable for India. Just use them out, darling, for a month or two, and then get what you need," an arrangement which seemed sensible enough, if one could only be sure of money to supply that need when it arose!

The day before her marriage Mrs Gifford thrust an envelope into her daughter's hand, blushing the while with an expression of real distress.

"I'm so sorry, darling, that it's so little. I've tried to be careful, but the money has flown. Going out to India one needs so many clothes, and there were quite a number of bills. I'll send more by and by, and remember always to say if you run short. I want you to have plenty for all you need. With what you have, this will see you nicely through your first term, and after that you'll be quite rich."

Claire kissed her, and was careful not to look at the cheque until she was alone. She had counted on at least a hundred to put in the bank as a refuge against a rainy day. Surely at this parting of the ways mother would wish her to have this security; but when she looked at her cheque, it was to discover that it was made out for fifty pounds—only half that sum. Claire felt sore at that moment, and for the first time a chill of fear entered into her anticipations. Fifty pounds seemed a dreadfully small sum to stand between herself and want. A hundred might be only twice its value, but its three figures sounded so much more substantial. She struggled hard to allow no signs of resentment to be seen, and felt that virtue was rewarded, when late that evening Mr Judge presented her with yet another envelope, saying awkwardly—

"That's—er—that's the bridesmaid's present. Thought you'd like to choose for yourself. Something to do, you know, some fine half-holiday, to go out and look in the shops. I've no views—don't get jewellery unless you wish. Just—er—'blew it' your own way!"

Claire kissed him, and remarked that he was a sweet old dear; and this time the opening of the envelope brought a surprise of an agreeable nature, for this cheque also was for fifty pounds, so that the desired hundred was really in her possession. No jewellery for her! Into the bank the money should go—every penny of it, and her bridesmaid present should be represented by peace of mind, which, after the financial shock of the last month, seemed more precious than many rubies.

Mr and Mrs Judge were married at the Embassy, and afterwards at an English church, the bride looking her most charming self in a costume of diaphanous chiffon and lace and the most fascinating of French hats, and the bridegroom his worst in his stiff conventional garments. They were a very radiant couple, however, and the *déjeuner* held after the ceremony at the "Hotel Britannique" was a cheerful occasion, despite the parting which lay ahead.

The gathering was quite a large one, for Mr Judge had insisted upon inviting all the friends who had been kind to his *fiancée* and her daughter during their three years' sojourn in the city, while the *pensionnaires* at "Villa Beau Séjour" came *en masse*, headed by Madame herself, in a new black silk costume, her white transformation elaborately waved and curled for the occasion.

There were speeches, and there were toasts. There were kindly words of farewell and cheerful anticipations of future meetings, there were good wishes for the bride and bridegroom, and more good wishes for the bridesmaid, and many protestations that it was "her turn next."

Then the bride retired to change her dress. Claire went with her, and tried valiantly not to cry as she fastened buttons and hooks, and realised how long it might be before she next waited on her mother. Mrs Judge was tearful, too, and the two knew a bitter moment as they clung together for the real farewell before rejoining the guests.

"I've been careless; I've made a mess of things. I've not been half as thoughtful as I should have been," sobbed the bride, "but I *have* loved you, Claire, and this will make no difference! I shall love you just the same."

Claire flushed and nodded, but could not trust herself to speak. The love of a mother in far-off India could never be the same as the love of the dear companion of every day. But she was too generous to add to her mother's distress by refusing to be comforted, and the bride nervously powdered her eyes, and re-arranged her veil before descending to the hall, anxious as ever to shelve a painful subject, and turn her face to the sun.

Five minutes later Mr and Mrs Judge drove away from the door, and the girl who was left behind turned slowly to re-enter the hotel. It was very big, and fine, and spacious, but at that moment it was a type of desolation in Claire's eyes. With a sickening wave of loneliness she realised that she was motherless and alone!

Chapter Four.

A fellow traveller introduces herself.

The next afternoon Claire started on her journey to London. She had spent the night with friends, and been seen off at the station by quite a crowd of well-wishers. Little souvenirs had been showered upon her all the morning, and everyone had a kindly word, and a hopeful prophecy of the future. There were invitations also, and promises to look her up in her London home, and a perfect shower of violets thrown into the carriage as the train steamed out of the station, and Claire laughed and waved her hand, and looked so complacent and beaming that no one looking on could have guessed the real nature of her journey. She was not pretending to be cheerful, she *was* cheerful, for, the dreaded parting once over, her optimistic nature had asserted itself, and painted the life ahead in its old rosy colours. Mother was happy and secured from want; she herself was about to enjoy a longed-for taste for independence; then why grumble? asked Claire sensibly of herself, and anything less grumbling than her appearance at that moment it would be hard to imagine.

She was beautifully dressed, in the simplest but most becoming of travelling costumes, she was agreeably conscious that the onlookers to her send-off had been unanimously admiring in their regard, and, as she stood arranging her bags on the rack overhead, she saw her own face in the strip of mirror and whole-heartedly agreed in their verdict.

"I'm glad I'm pretty! It's a comfort to be pretty. I should grow so tired of being with myself if I were plain!" she reflected complacently as she settled herself in her corner, and flicked a few grains of dust from the front of her skirt.

She had taken a through first-class ticket from sheer force of habit, for Mrs Gifford had always travelled first, and the ways of economy take some time to acquire. In the opposite corner of the carriage sat an elderly woman, obviously English, obviously also of the *grande dame* species, with aquiline features, white hair dressed pompadour fashion, and an expression compounded of indifference and quizzical good humour. The good humour was in the ascendant as she watched the kindly Belgians crowd round her fellow-passenger, envelop her in their arms, murmur tearful farewells, and kiss her soundly on either cheek. The finely marked eyebrows lifted themselves as if in commiseration for the victim, and as the door closed on the last farewell she heaved an involuntary sigh of relief. It was evident that the scene appealed to her entirely from the one standpoint; she saw nothing touching about it, nothing pathetic; she was simply amused, and carelessly scornful of eccentricities in manner or appearance.

On the seat beside this imposing personage sat a young woman in black, bearing the hall mark of lady's maid written all over her in capital letters. She sat stiffly in her seat, one gloved hand on her knee, the other clasped tightly round the handle of a crocodile dressing-bag.

Claire felt a passing interest in the pair; reflected that if it were her lot in life to be a maid, she would choose to live on the Continent, where an affectionate intimacy takes the place of this frigid separation, and then, being young and self-engrossed, promptly forgot all about them, and fell to building castles in the air, in which she herself lived in every circumstance of affluence and plenty, beloved and admired of all. There was naturally a prince in the story, a veritable Prince Charming, who was all that the most exacting mind could desire, but the image was vague. Claire's heart had not yet been touched. She was still in ignorance as to what manner of man she desired.

Engaged in these pleasant day-dreams Antwerp was reached before Claire realised that half the distance was covered. On the quay the wind blew chill; on the boat itself it blew chillier still. Claire became aware that she was in for a stormy crossing, but was little perturbed by the fact, since she knew herself to be an unusually good sailor. She tipped the stewardess to fill a hot bottle, put on a cosy dressing-jacket, and lay down in her berth, quite ready for sleep after the fatigue and excitement of the past week.

In five minutes the ship and all that was in it was lost in dreams, and, so far as Claire was concerned, it might have been but another five minutes before the stewardess aroused her to announce the arrival at Parkeston Pier. The first glance around proved, however, that the other passengers had found the time all too long. The signs of a bad crossing were written large on the faces of her companions, and there was a trace of resentment in the manner in which they surveyed her active movements. An old lady in a bunk immediately opposite her own seemed especially injured, and did not hesitate to put her feelings into words, "*You* have had a good enough night! I believe you slept right through... Are you aware that the rest of us have been more ill than we've ever been in our lives?" she asked in accusing tones. And Claire laughed her happy, gurgling little laugh, and said—

"I'm *so* sorry, but it's all over, isn't it? And people always say that they feel better afterwards!"

The old lady grunted. She certainly looked thoroughly ill and wretched at the moment, her face drawn and yellow beneath her scanty locks, and her whole appearance expressive of an extremity of fatigue. It seemed to her that it was years since she had left the quay at Antwerp, and here was this young thing as blooming as though she had spent the night in her own bed! She hitched a shawl more closely over her shoulders, and called aloud in a high imperious tone—

"Mason! Mason! You must really rouse yourself and attend to me. We shall have to land in a few minutes. Get up at once and bring me my things!"

The covering of another bunk stirred feebly, and two feet encased in black merino stockings descended slowly to the floor. A moment later a ghastly figure was tottering across the floor, lifting from a box a beautifully waved white wig, and dropping it carefully over the head of the aggrieved old lady of the straggly locks.

It was all that Claire could do to keep from exclaiming aloud, as it burst upon her astonished senses that this poor, huddled creature was none other than the *grande dame* of the railway carriage, the haughtily indifferent, cynically amused personage who had seemed so supremely superior to the agitations of the common ruck! Strange what changes a few hours' conflict with the forces of Nature could bring about!

Ill as the mistress was, the maid was even worse, and it was pitiful to see the poor creature's efforts to obey the exigent demands of her employer. In the end faintness overcame her, and if Claire had not rushed to the rescue, she would have fallen on the floor.

"It's no use struggling against it! You must keep still until the boat stops. You'll feel better at once when we land, and you get into the air." Claire laid the poor soul in her bunk, and turned back to the old lady who was momentarily growing younger and more formidable, as she continued the stages of her toilette.

"Can I help you?" she asked smilingly, and the offer was accepted with gracious composure.

"Please do. I should be grateful. Thank you. That hook fastens over here, and the band crosses to this side. The brooch is in my bag—a gold band with some diamonds—and the hat-pins, and a clean handkerchief. Can you manage? ... The clasp slides back."

Claire opened the bag and gazed with admiration at a brown *moiré* antique lining, and fittings of tortoiseshell, bearing raised monograms in gold. "I shall have one exactly to match, when I marry my duke!" was the mental reflection, as she selected the articles mentioned and put the final touches to the good lady's costume.

Later on there was Mason to be dressed; later on still, Claire found herself carrying the precious dressing-bag in one hand, and supporting one invalid with the other, while Mason tottered in the wake, unable for the moment to support any other burden than that of her own body.

Mrs Fanshawe—Claire had discovered the name on a printed card let into the lining of the bag—had no sympathy to spare for poor Mason. She plainly considered it the height of bad manners for a maid to dare to be sea-sick; but being unused to do anything for herself, gratefully allowed Claire to lead the way, reply to the queries of custom-house officials, secure a corner of a first-class compartment of the waiting train, and bid an attendant bring a cup of tea before the ordinary breakfast began.

Mason refused any refreshment, but Mrs Fanshawe momentarily regained her vigour, and was all that was gracious in her acknowledgment of Claire's help. The quizzical eyes roved over the girl's face and figure, and evidently approved what they saw, and Claire, smiling back, was conscious of an answering attraction. Thoughtless and domineering as was her behaviour to her inferior, there was yet something in the old lady's personality which struck an answering chord in the girl's heart. She was enough of a physiognomist to divine the presence of humour and generosity, combined with a persistent cheerfulness of outlook. The signs of physical age were unmistakable, but the spirit within was young, young as her own!

The mutual scrutiny ended in a mutual laugh, which was the last breaking of the ice.

"My dear," cried Mrs Fanshawe, "you must excuse my bad manners! You are so refreshing to look at after all those horrors on the boat that I can't help staring. And you've been so kind! Positively I don't know how I should have survived without you. Will you tell me your name? I should like to know to whom I am indebted for so much help."

"My name is Claire Gifford."

"Er—yes?" Plainly Mrs Fanshawe felt the information insufficient. "Gifford! I knew some Giffords. Do you belong to the Worcestershire branch?"

Claire hitched her shoulders in the true French shrug.

"*Sais pas*! I have no English relations nearer than second cousins, and we have lived abroad so much that we are practically strangers. My father died when I was a child. I went to school in Paris, and for the last few years my mother and I have made our headquarters in Brussels. She married again, only yesterday, and is going to live in Bombay."

Mrs Fanshawe arched surprised brows.

"And you are staying behind?"

"Yes. They asked me to go. Mr Judge is very kind. He is my—er—stepfather!" Claire shrugged again at the strangeness of that word. "He gave me the warmest of invitations, but I refused. I preferred to be left."

Mrs Fanshawe hitched herself into her corner, planted her feet more firmly on the provisionary footstool, and folded her hands on her knee. She had the air of a person settling down to the enjoyment of a favourite amusement, and indeed her curiosity was a quality well-known to all her acquaintances.

"Why?" she asked boldly, and such was the force of her personality that Claire never dreamt for a moment of refusing to reply.

"Because I want to be independent."

Mrs Fanshawe rolled her eyes to the hat-rail.

"My dear, nonsense! You're far too pretty. Leave that to the poor creatures who have no chance of finding other people to work for them. You should change your mind, you know, you really should. India's quite an agreeable place to put in a few years. The English girl is a trifle overdone, but with your complexion you would be bound to have a success. Think it over! Don't be in a hurry to let the chance slip!"

"It *has* slipped. They sail from Marseilles a week from to-day, and besides I don't want to change. I like the prospect of independence better even than being admired."

"Though you like that, too?"

"Of course. Who doesn't? I'm hoping—with good luck—to be admired in England instead!"

"Then you mustn't be independent!" Mrs Fanshawe said, laughing. "It was the rage a year or two ago; girls had a craze for joining Settlements, and running about in the slums, but it's quite out of date. Hobble skirts killed it. It's impossible to be utilitarian in a hobble skirt... And how do you propose to show your independence, may I ask?"

"I am going to be French mistress in a High School," Claire said sturdily, and hated herself because she winced before the eloquent change of expression which passed over her companion's face.

Mrs Fanshawe said, "Oh, really! How *very* interesting!" and looked about as uninterested the while as a human creature could be. In the pause which followed it was obvious that she was readjusting the first impression of a young gentlewoman belonging to her own leisured class, and preparing herself to cross-question an entirely different person—an ordinary teacher in a High School! There was a touch of patronage in her manner, but it was still quite agreeable Mrs Fanshawe was always agreeable for choice: she found it the best policy, and her indolent nature shrank from disagreeables of every kind. This pretty girl had made herself quite useful, and a chat with her would enliven a dull hour in the train. Curiosity shifted its point, but remained actively in force.

"Tell me all about it!" she said suavely. "I know nothing about teachers. Shocking, isn't it? They alarm me too much. I have a horror of clever women. You don't look at all clever. I mean that as a compliment—far too pretty and smart, but I suppose you are dreadfully learned, all the same. What are you going to teach?"

"French. I am almost as good as a Frenchwoman, for I've talked little else for sixteen years. Mother and I spoke English together, or I should have forgotten my own language. It seems, from a scholastic point of view, that it's a useful blend to possess—perfect French and an English temperament. 'Mademoiselle' is not always a model of patience!"

"And you think you will be? I prophesy differently. You'll throw the whole thing up in six months, and fly off to mamma in India. You haven't the least idea what you are in for, but you'll find out, you'll find out! Where is this precious school? In town, did you say? Shall you live in the house or with friends?"

"I have no friends in London except Miss Farnborough, the head mistress, but there are fifteen other mistresses besides myself. That will be fifteen friends ready-made. I am going to share lodgings with one of them, and be a bachelor girl on my own account. I'm so excited about it. After living in countries where a girl can't go to the pillar-box alone, it will be thrilling to be free to do just as I like. Please don't pity me! I'm going to have great fun."

Mrs Fanshawe hitched herself still further into her corner and smiled a lazy, quizzical smile.

"Oh, I don't pity you—not one bit! All young people nowadays think they are so much wiser than their parents; it's a wholesome lesson to learn their mistake. You're a silly, blind, ridiculous little girl, and if I'd been your mother, I should have insisted upon taking you with me, whether you liked it or not. I always wanted a daughter like you—sons are so dull; but perhaps it's just as well that she never appeared. She might have wanted to be independent, too, in which case we should have quarrelled.—So those fifteen school-mistresses make up your whole social circle, do they? I wouldn't mind prophesying that you'll never want to speak a word to them out of school hours! I have a friend living in town, quite a nice woman, with a daughter about your age. Shall I ask her to send you a card? It would be somewhere for you to go on free afternoons, and she entertains a good deal, and has a craze for the feminist movement, and for girls who work for themselves. You might come in for some fun."

Claire's flush of gratification made her look prettier than ever, and Mrs Fanshawe felt an agreeable glow of self-satisfaction. Nothing she liked better than to play the part of Lady Bountiful, especially when any effort involved was shifted onto the shoulders of another, and in her careless fashion she was really anxious to do this nice girl a good turn. She made a note of Claire's address in a dainty gold-edged pocket-book, expressed pleasure in the belief that through her friend she would hear reports of the girl's progress, and presently shut her eyes, and dozed peacefully for the rest of the ride.

Round London a fine rain was falling, and the terminus looked bleak and cheerless as the train slowed down the long platform. Mason, still haggard, roused herself to step to the platform and look around as if expecting to see a familiar face, and in the midst of collecting her own impedimenta Claire was conscious that Mrs Fanshawe was distinctly ruffled, when the familiar figure failed to appear. Once more she found herself coming to the rescue, marshalling the combined baggage to the screened portion of the platform where the custom-house officials went through the formalities incidental to the occasion, while the tired passengers stood shiveringly on guard, looking bleached and grey after their night's journey. The bright-haired, bright-faced girl stood out in pleasant contrast to the rest, trim and smart and dainty as though such a thing as fatigue did not exist. Mrs

Fanshawe, looking at her, stopped short in the middle of a mental grumble, and turned it round, so that it ended in being a thanksgiving instead.

"Most neglectful of Erskine to fail me after promising he would come... Perhaps, after all, it's just as well he did not."

And at that moment, with the usual contrariety of fate, Erskine appeared! He came striding along the platform, a big, loosely-built man, with a clean-shaven face, glancing to right and left over the upstanding collar of a tweed coat. He looked at once plain and distinguished, and in the quizzical eyes and beetling eyebrows there was an unmistakable likeness to the *grande dame* standing by Claire's side. Just for a moment he paused, as he came in sight of the group of passengers, and Claire, meeting his glance, knew who he was, even before he came forward and made his greeting.

"Holla, Mater! Sorry to be late. Not my fault this time. I was ready all right, but the car did not come round. Had a good crossing?"

"My dear, appalling! Don't talk of it. I was prostrate all night, and Mason too ill to do anything but moan. She's been no use."

"Poor beggar! She looks pretty green. But— er—" The plain face lighted with an expectant smile as he turned towards the girl who stood by his mother's side, still holding the precious bag. "You seem to have met a friend..."

"Oh—er—yes!" With a gesture of regal graciousness Mrs Fanshawe turned towards the girl, and held out her gloved hand. "Thank you *so* much, Miss Gifford! You've been quite too kind. I'm really horribly in your debt. I hope you will find everything as you like, and have a very good time. Thank you again. *Good-bye*. I'm really dropping with fatigue. What a relief it will be to get to bed!" She turned aside, and laid her hand on her son's arm. "Erskine, where *is* the car?"

Mother and son turned away, and made their way down the platform, leaving Claire with crimson cheeks and fast-beating heart. The little scene which had just happened had been all too easy to understand. The nice son had wished for an introduction to the nice girl who a moment before had seemed on such intimate terms with his mother: the mother had been quite determined that such an introduction should not take place. Claire knew enough of the world to realise how different would have been the proceedings if she had announced herself as a member of the "idle rich," bound for a course of visits to well-known houses in the country. "May I introduce my son, Miss Gifford? Miss Gifford has been an angel of goodness to me, Erskine. Positively I don't know what I should have done without her! Do look after her now, and see her into a taxi. Such a mercy to have a man to help!" That was what would have happened to the Claire Gifford of a week before, but now for the first time Claire experienced a taste of the disagreeables attendant on her changed circumstances, and it was bitter to her mouth. All very well to remind herself that work was honourable, that anyone who looked down on her for choosing to be independent was not worth a moment's thought, the fact remained that for the first, the very first time in her life she had been made to feel that there was a barrier between herself and a member of her own class, and that, however willing Mrs Fanshawe might be to introduce her to a casual friend, she was unwilling to make her known to her own son!

Claire stood stiff and poker-like at her post, determined to make no movement until Mrs Fanshawe and her attendants had taken their departure. The storm of indignation and wounded pride which was surging through her veins distracted her mind from her surroundings; she was dimly conscious that one after another, her fellow-passengers had taken their departure, preceded by a porter trundling a truck of luggage; conscious that where there had been a crowd, there was now a space, until eventually with a shock of surprise she discovered that she was standing alone, by her own little pile of boxes. At

The Independence of Claire

that she shook herself impatiently, beckoned to a porter and was about to walk ahead, when an uneasy suspicion made itself felt. The luggage! Something was wrong. The pile looked smaller than it had done ten minutes before. She made a rapid circuit, and made a horrible discovery. A box was missing! The dress-box containing the skirts of all her best frocks, spread at full length and carefully padded with tissue paper. It had been there ten minutes ago; the custom-house officer had given it a special rap. She distinctly remembered noticing a new scratch on the leather. Where in the name of everything that was inexplicable could it have disappeared? Appealed to for information the porter was not illuminating. "If it had been there before, why wasn't it there now? Was the lady *sure* she had seen it? Might have been left behind at Antwerp or Parkeston. Better telegraph and see! If it had been there before, why wasn't it there now? Mistakes did happen. Boxes were much alike. P'raps it was left in the van. If it was there ten minutes before, why wasn't it—"

Claire stopped him with an imperious hand.

"That's enough! It *was* there: I saw it. I counted the pieces before the custom-house officer came along. I noticed it especially. Someone must have taken it by mistake."

The porter shook his head darkly.

"On purpose, more like! Funny people crosses by this route. Funny thing that you didn't notice—"

Claire found nothing funny in the reflection. She was furious with herself for her carelessness, and still more furious with Mrs Fanshawe as the cause thereof. Down the platform she stalked, a picture of vivid impetuous youth, head thrown back, cheeks aflame, grey eyes sending out flashes of indignation. Every porter who came in her way was stopped and imperiously questioned as to his late load, every porter was in his turn waved impatiently away. Claire was growing seriously alarmed. Suppose the box was lost! It would be as bad as losing *two* boxes, for of what use were bodices minus skirts to match? Never again would she be guilty of the folly of packing bits of the same costumes in different boxes. How awful—how awful beyond words to arrive in London without a decent dress to wear!

Whirling suddenly round to pursue yet another porter, Claire became aware of a figure in a long tweed coat standing on the space beside the taxi-stand, intently watching her movements. She recognised him in a moment as none other than "Erskine" himself, who, having seen his mother into her car, was presumably bound for another destination. But why was he standing there? Why had he been so long in moving away? Claire hastily averted her eyes, but as she cross-questioned porter number four, she was aware that the tall figure was drawing nearer, and presently he was standing by her side, taking off his hat, and saying in the most courteous and deferential of tones—

"Excuse me—I'm afraid something is wrong! Can I be of any assistance?"

Claire's glance was frigid in its coldness; but it was difficult to remain frigid in face of the man's obvious sincerity and kindliness.

"Thank you," she said quietly. "Please don't trouble. I can manage quite well. It's only a trunk..."

"Is it lost? I say—what a fag! Do let me help. I know this station by heart! If it is to be found, I am sure I can get it for you."

This time there was a distinct air of appeal in his deep voice. Claire divined that the nice man was anxious to atone for his mother's cavalier behaviour, and her heart softened towards him. After all, why should she punish herself by refusing? Five minutes more or less on the station platform could make no difference one way or another, for at the end they would wish each other a polite adieu, and part never to meet again. And she *did* want that box!

She smiled, and sighed, and looked delightfully pretty and appealing, as she said frankly—

"Thank you, I *should* be grateful for suggestions. It's the most extraordinary and provoking thing—"

They walked slowly down the platform while she explained the situation, and reiterated the fact that she had seen the box ten minutes before. Erskine Fanshawe did not dispute the statement as each porter had done before him; he contented himself with asking if there was any distinctive feature in the appearance of the box itself.

Claire shook her head.

"The ordinary brown leather, with strappings and C.G. on one side. Just like a thousand other boxes, but it had a label, beside the initials. I don't see how anyone can have taken it by mistake." She set her teeth, and her head took a defiant tilt. "There's one comfort; if it *is* stolen, whoever has taken it will not get much for her pains! There's nothing in it but skirts. Skirts won't be much good without the bodices to match!"

The man looked down at her, his expression comically compounded of sympathy and humour. At that moment, despite the irregularity of his features, he looked wonderfully like his handsome mother.

"Er—just so! Unfortunately, however, from the opposite point of view, you find yourself in the same position! Bodices, I presume, without skirts—"

Claire groaned, and held up a protesting hand.

"Don't! I can't bear it. It's really devastating. My whole outfit at one fell sweep!"

"Isn't it—excuse my suggesting it—rather a mistake to—er—divide pieces of the same garment, *so* that if one trunk should be lost, the loss practically extends to two?"

"No, it isn't. It's the only sensible thing to do," Claire said obstinately. "Skirts must be packed at full length, and a dress-box is made for that very purpose. All the same, I shall never do it again. It's no use being sensible if you have to contend with—*thieves*!"

"I don't think we need leap to that conclusion just yet. You have only spoken to two or three porters. We'd better wait about a few minutes longer until the other men come back. Very likely the box was put on a truck by accident, and if the mistake was discovered before it was put on the taxi, it would be sent back to see if its owner were waiting here. If it doesn't turn up at once, you mustn't be discouraged. The odds are ten to one that it's only a mistake, and in that case when the taxi is unloaded, the box will be sent back to the lost luggage office, or forwarded to your address. Was the full address on the box, by the way?"

Claire nodded assent.

"Oh, yes; I have that poor satisfaction at least. I was most methodical and prudent, but I don't know that that's going to be much consolation if I lose my nice frocks, and am too poor to buy any more."

The last phrase was prompted by a proud determination to sail under no false colours in the eyes of Mrs Fanshawe's son; but the picture evoked thereby was sufficiently tragic to bring a cloud over her face. The memory of each separate gown rose before her, looking distractingly dainty and becoming; she saw a vision of herself as she might have been, and faced a future bounded by eternal blue serge. All the tragedy of the thought was in her air, and her companion cried quickly—

"You won't need to buy them! They'll turn up all right, I am quite sure of that. The worst that can happen is a day or two's delay. After all, you know, there are thousands of honest folk to a single thief, and even a thief would probably prefer a small money reward to useless halves of dresses! If you hear nothing by to-morrow, you might offer a reward."

The Independence of Claire

"Oh, I will!" Claire said gratefully. "Thank you for thinking of it."

No more porters having for the moment appeared in sight, they now turned, and slowly retraced their steps. Claire, covertly regarding her companion, wondered why she felt convinced that he was a soldier; Erskine Fanshawe in his turn covertly regarded Claire, and wondered why it was that she seemed different from any girl he had seen before. Then tentatively he put a personal question.

"Do you know London well, Miss Gifford? My mother told me you were—er—coming to settle—"

"Not at all well, as a whole. I know the little bit around Regent Street, and the Park, and the places one sees in a week's visit, but that's all. We never stayed long in town when we came to England. I shall enjoy exploring on half holidays when I am free from work. I am a school-mistress!" said Claire with an air, and gathered from her companion's face that he knew as much already, and considered it a subject for commiseration. He looked at her with sympathetic eyes, and asked deeply—

"Hate it very much?"

"Not at all. Quite the contrary. I adore it. At least, that's to say, I haven't begun yet, but I feel sure I *shall!*" Claire cried ardently; and at that they both laughed with a delightful sense of understanding and *camaraderie*. At that moment Claire felt a distinct pang at the thought that never again would she have the opportunity of speaking and laughing with this attractive, eminently companionable man; then her attention was distracted by the appearance of two more porters, who had each to be interviewed in his turn.

They had no good news to give, however, so the searchers left the platform in disgust, and repaired to the office for lost luggage, where the story of the missing box was recounted to an unsympathetic clerk. When a man spends his whole life listening to complaints of missing property, he can hardly be expected to show a vehement distress at the loss of yet another passenger, but to Claire at this moment there was something quite brutal in his callous indifference. The one suggestion which he had to make was that she could leave her name, and the manner in which it was given was a death-blow to hope.

At this very moment, however, just as Claire was bending forward to dictate the desired information she felt a touch on her arm, and looking in the direction of Mr Fanshawe's outstretched hand, beheld a porter approaching the office, trundling before him a truck on which reposed in solitary splendour, a long brown dress-box, and oh, joy of joys! even at the present distance the white letters C.G. could be plainly distinguished on the nearer side! Claire's dignity went to the winds at that sight, and she dashed forward to meet her property with the joyous impetuosity of a child.

The explanation was simple to a degree, and precisely agreed with Mr Fanshawe's surmise as to what had really happened. During Claire's trance of forgetfulness, the box had been wheeled away, with a large consignment of luggage, and the mistake discovered only when the various items were in process of being packed into a company's omnibus, when, there being no one at hand to claim it, it had been conveyed—by very leisurely stages—to the lost luggage office.

All's well that ends well! Claire gleefully collected her possessions, feeling a glow of delight in the safety which an hour before she would have taken as a matter of course, and stood at attention while each separate item was placed on the roof of the taxi. The little addresses of which she had boasted were duly inserted in leather framings on each box, the delicate writing too small to be deciphered, except near at hand. Claire saw her companion's eyes contract in an evident effort to distinguish the words, and immediately moved her position so as to frustrate his purpose. She did not intend Mr Fanshawe to know her address! When she was seated in the taxi, however, there came an awkward moment, for her companion waved the chauffeur to his seat, and stood by the window looking in at her, with a face which seemed unduly serious and earnest, considering the extremely slight nature of their acquaintance.

"Well! I am thankful the box turned up. I shall think of you enjoying your re-united frocks... Sure you've got everything all right? Where shall I tell the man to drive?"

For the fraction of a second Claire's eyes flickered, then she spoke in decided tones.

"'The Grand Hotel.'"

Mr Fanshawe's eyes flickered too, and turned involuntarily towards the boxes on the roof. What exactly were the words on the labels he could not see, but at least it was certain that they were not "The Grand Hotel!" He turned from the inspection to confront a flushed, obstinate face.

"Do you wish me to give the man that address?"

"I do."

Very deliberately and quietly Mr Fanshawe stepped back a pace, opened his long coat, and fumbled in an inner pocket for a leather pocket-book; very quietly and deliberately he drew from one bulging division a visiting card, and held it towards her. Claire caught the word "Captain" and saw that an address was printed in the corner, but she covered it hastily with her hand, refusing a second glance. Captain Fanshawe leant his arm on the window sash and said hesitatingly—

"Will you allow me to give you my card! As you are a stranger in town and your people away, there may possibly be—er—occasions, when it would be convenient to know some man whom you could make of use. Please remember me if they do come along! It would be a privilege to repay your kindness to my mother... Send me a wire at any time, and I am at your service. I hope you *will* send. Good morning!"

"Good-bye!" said Claire. Red as a rose was she at that moment, but very dignified and stately, bending towards him in a sweeping bow, as the taxi rolled away. The last glimpse of Captain Fanshawe showed him standing with uplifted hat, the keen eyes staring after her, with not a glint of humour in their grey depths. Quite evidently he meant what he said. Quite evidently he was as keen to pursue her acquaintance as his mother had been to drop it.

Claire Gifford sat bolt upright on her seat, the slip of cardboard clasped within her palms, and as she sat she thought many thoughts. A physiognomist would have been interested to trace the progress of those thoughts on the eloquent young face. There was surprise written there, and obvious gratification, and a demure, very feminine content; later on came pride, and a general stiffening of determination. The spoiled child of liberty and the High School-Mistress of the future had fought a heated battle, and the High School-Mistress had won.

Deliberately turning aside her eyes, so that no word of that printed address should obtrude itself on her notice, Claire tore the card sharply across and across, and threw the fragments out of the window.

A moment later she whistled through the tube, and instructed the chauffeur as to her change of address.

Adieu to the Fanshawes, and all such luxuries of the past. Heigh-ho for hard work, and lodgings at fifteen shillings a week!

Chapter Five.

Miss Rhodes, Poisoner.

It is a somewhat dreary feeling to arrive even at a friend's house before seven o'clock in the morning, and be received by sleepy-looking people who have obviously been torn unwillingly from their beds in deference to the precepts of hospitality, but it is infinitely worse to arrive at a lodging-house at the same hour, ring several times at the bell before a dingy servant can be induced to appear, and to realise a moment later that in a tireless parlour you perceive your journey's goal!

Claire Gifford felt a creep of the blood at the sight of that parlour, though if her first introduction had been at night, when the curtains were drawn and the lamps lit, she would have found it cosy enough. There was no sign of her room-mate; perhaps it was too much to expect her to get up at so early an hour to welcome a stranger, but Claire *had* expected it, felt perfectly sure that—had positions been reversed—she herself would have taken pains to deck both herself and her room in honour of the occasion, and so felt correspondingly downcast.

Presently she found herself following the dingy maid up three separate nights of stairs, and arriving at a tiny box of a bedroom on the top floor. There was a bed, a washstand, a chest of drawers doing service as a dressing-table, two chairs and a sloping roof. Claire would have been quite disappointed if that last item had been missing, for whoever heard of a girl who set out to make her own living who had not slept in a room with a sloping roof? On the whole, despite its tiny proportions, the little room made a pleasant impression. It was clean, it was bright, walls and furniture were alike of a plain unrelieved white, and through the open casement window could be seen a distant slope of green overtopping the intervening chimney tops. Claire's eyes roved here and there with the instinct of a born home-maker, saw what was lacking here, what was superfluous there, grasped neglected possibilities, and mentally re-arranged and decorated the premises before a slower person would have crossed the floor.

Then she took up her stand before the small mirror, and devoted a whole minute to studying her own reflection from the point of view of Captain Erskine Fanshawe of unknown address. By her own deliberate choice she had cut herself off from future chance of meeting this acquaintance of an hour; nevertheless it was distinctly reviving to discern that her hat was set at precisely the right angle, and that for an all-night voyager her whole appearance was remarkably fresh and dainty.

Claire first smiled, and then sighed, and pulled out the hat-pins with impatient tugs. To be prudent and self-denying is not always an exhilarating process for sweet and twenty.

Presently the maid came staggering upstairs with the smaller boxes, and Claire busied herself in her room until the clock had struck eight, when she again descended to the joint sitting-room. This time the fire was lighted, and the table laid for breakfast, and behind the tea-tray sat Miss Rhodes, the English mistress, already halfway through her meal. She rose, half smiling, half frowning, and held out a thin hand in welcome.

"Morning. Hope you've had a good crossing. Didn't know when you'd be down. Do you take coffee?"

"Please!" Claire felt that a cup of coffee would be just what she needed, but missed the familiar fragrant scent. She seated herself at the table, and while Miss Rhodes went on with her preparation, studied her with curious eyes.

She saw a woman of thirty-two or three, with well-cut features, dark eyes, and abundant dark hair—a woman who ought to have been distinctly good-looking but who succeeded in being plain and commonplace. She was badly-dressed, in a utility blouse of grey flannel, her expression was tired and listless, and her hair, though neat, showed obvious lack of care, having none of the silky sheen which rewards regular systematic brushing. So far bad, but, in spite of all drawbacks, it was an interesting face, and Claire felt attracted, despite the preliminary disappointment.

"There's some bacon in that dish. It will be cold, I'm afraid. You can ring, if you like, and ask them to warm it up, but they'll keep you waiting a quarter of an hour out of spite. I've given it up myself."

"Oh, I'm accustomed to French breakfasts. I really want nothing but some bread and coffee." Claire sipped at her cup as she finished speaking, and the sudden grimace of astonishment which followed roused her companion to laughter.

"You don't like it? It isn't equal to your French coffee."

"It isn't coffee at all. It's undrinkable!" Claire pushed away her cup in disgust. "Is it always as bad as that?"

"Worse!" said Miss Rhodes composedly. "They put in more this morning because of you. Sometimes it's barely coloured, and it's always chicory." She shrugged resignedly. "No English landlady can make coffee. It's no use worrying. Have to make the best of what comes."

"Indeed I shan't. Why should I? I shan't try. There's no virtue in drinking such stuff. We provide the coffee—what's to hinder us making it for ourselves?"

"No fire, as a rule. Can't afford one when you are going out immediately after breakfast."

Claire stared in dismay. It had never occurred to her that she might have to be economical to this extent.

"But when it's very cold? What do you do then?"

"Put on a jersey, and nurse the hot-water jug!"

Claire grimaced, then nodded with an air of determination.

"I'll buy a machine! There can be no objection to that. You would prefer good coffee, wouldn't you, if you could get it without any more trouble?"

"Oh, certainly. I'll enjoy it—while it lasts!"

"Why shouldn't it last?"

Miss Rhodes stared across at the eager young face. She looked tired, and a trifle impatient.

"Oh, my dear girl, you're *New*. We are all the same at first—bubbling over with energy, and determined to arrange everything exactly as we like. It's a phase which we all live through. Afterwards you don't care. You are too tired to worry. All your energy goes on your day's work, and you are too thankful for peace and quietness to bother about details. You take what comes, and are thankful it's not worse."

Claire's smile showed an elaborate forbearance.

"Rather a poor-spirited attitude, don't you think?"

"Wait and see!" said the English mistress.

She rose and threw herself in a chair by the window, and Claire left the despised coffee and followed her example. Through the half-opened panes she looked out on a row of brick houses depressingly dingy, depressingly alike. About every second house showed a small black card on which the word "Apartments" was printed in gilt letters. Down the middle of the street came a fruiterer's cart, piled high with wicker baskets. The cry of "Bananas, cheap bananas," floated raucously on the air. Claire swiftly averted her eyes and turned back to her companion.

"It is very good of you to let me share your *appartement*. Miss Farnborough said she had arranged it with you, but it must be horrid taking in a stranger. I will try not to be too great a bore!"

The Independence of Claire

But Miss Rhodes refused to be thanked.

"I'm bound to have somebody," said she ungraciously. "Couldn't afford them alone. You know the terms? Thirty-five shillings a week for the three rooms. That's cheap in this neighbourhood. We only get them at that price because we are out all day, and need so little catering." She looked round the room with her tired, mocking smile. "Hope you admire the scheme of decoration! I've been in dozens of lodgings, but I don't think I've ever struck an uglier room; but the people are clean and honest, and one has to put that before beauty, in our circumstances."

"There's a great *deal* of pattern about. It hasn't what one could call a restful effect!" said Claire, looking across at an ochre wall bespattered with golden scrawls, a red satin mantel-border painted with lustre roses, a suite of furniture covered in green stamped plush, a collection of inartistic pictures, and unornamental ornaments. Even her spirit quailed before the hopelessness of beautifying a room in which all the essentials were so hopelessly wrong. She gave it up in despair, and returned to the question of finance.

"Then my share will be seventeen and six! That seems very cheap. I am to begin at a hundred and ten pounds. How much extra must I allow for food?"

"That depends upon your requirements. We have dinner at school; quite a good meal for ninepence, including a penny for coffee afterwards."

"The same sort of coffee we have had this morning?"

"Practically. A trifle better perhaps. Not much."

"Hurrah!" cried Claire gaily. "That's a penny to the good! Eightpence for me—a clear saving of fivepence a week!"

Miss Rhodes resolutely refused to smile. She had the air of thinking it ribald to be cheerful on the serious question of pounds, shillings and pence.

"Even so, it's three-and-four, and you can't do breakfast and supper and full board on Saturday and Sunday under seven shillings. It's tight enough to manage on that. Altogether it often mounts up to twelve."

"Seventeen and twelve." Claire pondered deeply before she arrived at a solution. "Twenty-nine. Call it thirty, to make it even, and I am to begin at a hundred and ten. Over two pounds a week. I ought to do it comfortably, and have quite a lot over."

Miss Rhodes laughed darkly.

"What about extras?" she demanded. "What about laundry, and fires, and stationery and stamps? What about boot-mending, and Tubes on wet days, and soap and candles, and dentist and medicines, and subs, at school, and collections in church, and travelling expenses on Saturdays and Sundays, when you invariably want to go to the very other side of the city? London is not like a provincial town. You can't stir out of the house under fourpence or sixpence at the very least. What about illness, and amusement, and holidays? What about—"

Claire thrust her fingers in her ears with an air of desperation.

"Stop! Stop! For pity's sake don't swamp me any more. I feel in the bankruptcy court already, and I had imagined that I was rich! A hundred and ten pounds seemed quite a big salary. Everybody was surprised at my getting so much, and I suppose you have even more?"

"A hundred and fifty. Yes! You must remember that we don't belong to the ordinary rut of worker—we are experts. Our education has been a long costly business. No untrained worker could take our place; we are entitled to expert's pay. Oh, yes, they are quite good salaries if you happen to have a home behind you, and people who are ready to help over rough times, instead of needing to be helped themselves. The pity of it is that most High School-mistresses come from families who are *not* rich. The parents have made a big effort to pay for the girls' education, and when they are fairly launched, they expect to be helped in return. Some girls have been educated by relations, or have practically paid for themselves by scholarships. Three out of four of us have people who are more in need of help than able to give it. I give my own mother thirty pounds a year, so we are practically on the same salary. Have *you* a home where you can spend your holiday? Holidays run away terribly with your money. They come to nearly four months in the year."

For the first time those prolonged holidays appeared to Claire as a privilege which had its reverse side. Friends in Brussels might possibly house her for two or three weeks; she could not expect, she would not wish them to do more; and at the end there would still remain over three months! It was a new and disagreeable experience to look forward to holidays with *dread*! For a whole two minutes she looked thoroughly depressed, then her invincible optimism came to the top, and she cried triumphantly—

"I'll take a holiday engagement!"

The English mistress shook her head.

"That's fatal! I tried it myself one summer. Went with a family to the seaside, and was expected to play games with the children all day long, and coach them in the evening. I began the term tired out, and nearly collapsed before the end. Teaching is nerve-racking work, and if you don't get a good spell off, it's as bad for the pupils as yourself. You snap their heads off for the smallest trifle. Besides, it's folly to wear oneself out any sooner than one need. It's bad enough to think of the time when one has to retire. That's the nightmare which haunts us more and more every year."

"Don't you think when the time comes you will be *glad* to rest?" asked innocent Claire, whereupon Miss Rhodes glared at her with indignant eyes.

"We should be glad to rest, no doubt, but we don't exactly appreciate the prospect of resting in the workhouse, and it's difficult to see where else some of us are to go! There is no pension for High School-mistresses, and we are bound to retire at fifty-five—if we can manage to stick it out so long. Fifty-five seems a long way off to you—not quite so long to me; when you reach forty it becomes to feel quite near. Women are horribly long-lived, so the probability is that we'll live on to eighty or more. Twenty-five years after leaving off work, and—*where is the money to come from to keep us*? That's the question which haunts us all when we look into our bank-books and find that, with all our pains, we have only been able to save at the utmost two or three hundred pounds."

Claire looked scared, but she recovered her composure with a swiftness which her companion had no difficulty in understanding. She pounced upon her with lightning swiftness.

"Ah, you think you'll get married, and escape that way! We all do when we're new, and pretty, and ignorant of the life. But it's fifty to one, my dear, that you *won't*? You won't meet many men, for one thing; and if you do, they don't like school-mistresses."

"Doesn't that depend a good deal on the kind of school-mistress?"

"Absolutely; but after a few years we are all more or less alike. We don't *begin* by being dowdy and angular, and dogmatic and prudish; we begin by being pretty and cheerful like you. I used to change my blouse every evening, and put on silk stockings."

"Don't you now?"

"I do *not*! Why should I, to sit over a lodging-house table correcting exercises till ten o'clock? It's not worth the trouble. Besides, I'm too tired, and it wears out another blouse."

Claire's attention was diverted from clothes by the shock of the reference to evening work. She had looked forward to coming home to read an interesting book, or be lazy in whatever fashion appealed to her most, and the corrections of exercises seemed of all things the most dull.

"Shall I have evening work, too?" she inquired blankly, and Miss Rhodes laughed with brutal enjoyment.

"Rather! French compositions on the attributes of a true woman, or, 'How did you spend your summer holiday?' with all the tenses wrong, and the idioms translated word for word. And every essay a practical repetition of the one before. It's not once in a blue moon that one comes across a girl with any originality of thought. Oh, yes! that's the way we shall spend five evenings a week. You will sit at that side of the table, I will sit at this, and we'll correct and yawn, and yawn and correct, and drink a cup of cocoa and go to bed at ten. Lively, isn't it?"

"Awful! I never thought of homework. But if Saturday is a whole holiday there will still be one night off. I shall make a point of doing something exciting every Saturday evening."

"Exciting things cost money, and, as a rule, when you have paid up the various extras, there's no money to spare. I stay in bed till ten o'clock on Saturday, and then get up and wash blouses, and do my mending, and have a nap after lunch, and if it's summer, go and sit on a penny chair in the park, or take a walk over Hampstead Heath. In the evening I read a novel and have a hot bath. Once in a blue moon I have an extravagant bout, and lunch in a restaurant, and go to an entertainment—but I'm sorry afterwards when I count the cost. On Sunday I go to church, and wish some one would ask me to tea. They don't, you know. They may do once or twice, when you first come up, but you can never ask them back, and your clothes get shabby, and you know nothing about their interests, so they think you a bore, and quietly let you drop."

A smothered exclamation burst from Claire's lips; with a sudden, swirling movement she leapt up, and fell on her knees before Miss Rhodes's chair, her hands clasping its arms, her flushed face upturned with a desperate eagerness.

"Miss Rhodes! we are going to live together here, we are going to share the same room, and the same meals. Would you—if any one offered you a million pounds, would you agree to poison me slowly, day by day, dropping little drops of poison into everything I ate and everything I drank, while you sat by and watched me grow weaker and weaker till I *died*?"

"Good heavens, girl—are you mad! What in the world are you raving about?"

Miss Rhodes had grown quite red. She was indignant; she was also more than a little scared. The girl's sudden change of mood was startling in itself, and she looked so tense, so overwhelmingly in earnest. What could she mean? Was it possible that she was a little—*touched*?

"I suppose you don't realise it, but it's insulting even to put such a question."

"But you *are* doing it! It's just exactly what you are beginning already. Ever since I arrived you've been poisoning me drop by drop. Poisoning my *mind*! I am at the beginning of my work, and you've been discouraging me, frightening me, painting it all black. Every word that you've said has been a drop of poison to kill hope and courage and confidence—and oh, don't do it! don't go on! I may be young and foolish, and full of ridiculous ideas, but let me keep them as long as I can! If all that you say is true, they will be knocked out of me soon enough, and I—I've never had to work before, or been alone, and—and it's only two days since my mother left me to go to India—all that long way—and left me behind! It's hard enough to go on being alone, and believing it's all going to be *couleur de rose*, but it will be fifty times harder if I don't. Please—please don't make it any worse!"

The Independence of Claire

With the last words tears came with a rush, the tears that had been resolutely restrained throughout the strain of the last week. Claire dropped her head on the nearest resting-place she could find, which happened to be Miss Rhodes's blue serge lap, and felt the quick pressure of a hand over the glossy coils.

"Poor little girl!" said the English mistress softly. "Poor little girl! I'm sorry! I'm a beast! Take no notice of me. I'm a sour, disagreeable old thing. It was more than half jealousy, dear, because you looked so pretty and spry, so like what I used to look myself. The life's all right, if you keep well, and don't worry too much ahead. There, don't cry! I loathe tears! You will yourself, when you have to deal with silly, hysterical girls. Come, I'll promise I won't poison you any more—at least, I'll do my best; but I've a grumbling nature, and you'd better realise it, once for all, and take no notice. We'll get on all right. I like you. I'm glad you came. My good girl, if you don't stop, I'll shake you till you do!"

Claire sat back on her heels, mopped her eyes, and gave a strangled laugh.

"I hate crying myself, but I'll begin again on the faintest provocation. It's always like that with me. I hardly ever cry, but when I once begin—"

Miss Rhodes rose with an air of determination.

"We'd better go out. I am free till lunch-time. I'll take you round and show you the neighbourhood, and the usual places of call. It will save time another day. Anything you want to buy?"

Claire mopped away another tear.

"C–certainly," she said feebly. "A c–offee machine."

Chapter Six.

The Invitation.

The next morning Claire was introduced to the scene of her new labours, and was agreeably impressed with its outside appearance. Saint Cuthbert's High School was situated in a handsome thoroughfare, and had originally been a large private house, to which long wings had been added to right and left. On each side and across the road were handsome private houses standing in their own grounds, owned by tenants who regarded the High School with lively detestation, and would have borne up with equanimity had an earthquake swallowed it root and branch.

Viewed from inside, the building was less attractive, passages and class-rooms alike having the air of bleak austerity which seems inseparable from such buildings; but when nine o'clock struck, and the flood of young life went trooping up the stairways and flowed into the separate rooms, the sense of bareness was replaced by one of tingling vitality.

As is usual on an opening day, every girl was at her best and brightest, decked in a new blouse, with pigtails fastened by crisp new ribbons, and good resolutions wound up to fever point. To find a new French mistress in the shape of a pretty well-dressed girl, who was English at one moment, and at the next even Frenchier than Mademoiselle, was an unexpected joy, and Claire found the battery of admiring young eyes an embarrassing if stimulating experience.

Following Miss Farnborough's advice, she spent the first day's lessons in questioning the different classes as to their past work, and so turned the hour into an impromptu conversation class. The ugly English accents made her wince, and she winced a second time as she realised the unpleasant fact that just as her pupils would have to prepare for her, so would she be obliged to prepare for them! Forgotten rules of grammar must be looked up and memorised, for French was so much her mother tongue that she would find it difficult to explain distinctions which came as a matter of course. That meant more work at night, more infringement of holiday hours.

The girls themselves were for the most part agreeable and well-mannered. The majority were the daughters of professional men, and of gentle-folks of limited means; but there was also a sprinkling of the daughters of better-class artisans, who paid High School fees at a cost of much self-denial in order to train their girls for teachers' posts in the future. Here and there an awkward, badly-dressed child was plainly of a still lower class. These were the free "places"—clever children who had obtained scholarships from primary schools, and were undergoing the ordeal of being snubbed by their new school-mates as a consequence of their success.

From the teacher's point of view these clever children were a welcome stimulus, but class feeling is still too strong in England to make them acceptable to their companions.

At lunch-time the fifteen mistresses assembled in the Staff-Room, a dull apartment far too small for the purpose, a common fault in High Schools, where the different governing bodies are apt to spare no expense in providing for the comfort of the scholar, but grudge the slightest expenditure for the benefit of those who teach.

Fifteen mistresses sat round the table eating roast lamb and boiled cabbage, followed by rhubarb pie and rice pudding, and Claire, looking from one to the other, acknowledged the truth of Miss Rhodes's assertion that they were all of a type. She herself was the only one of the number who had any pretensions to roundness of outline, all the rest were thin to angularity, half the number wore pince-nez or spectacles, and all had the same strained pucker round the eyes. Each one wore a blue serge skirt and a white blouse, and carried herself with an air of dogmatic assurance, as who should say: "I know better than any one else, and when I speak let no dog bark!" The German mistress was the veteran of the party and was probably a good forty-five. Miss Bryce, the Froebel mistress, paired with Claire herself for the place of junior. Miss Blake, the Gym. mistress, was a graceful girl with an air of delicacy which did not seem in accord with her profession. Miss Rose, the Art mistress, was plain with a squat, awkward figure.

Rising from the table, Claire caught a glimpse of her own reflection in the strip of mirror over the chimney-piece, and at the sight a little thrill, half-painful, half-pleasant, passed through her veins. The soft bloom of her complexion, the dainty finish of her dress, differentiated her almost painfully from her companions, and she felt a pang of dread lest that difference should ever grow less. While she affected to read one of the magazines which lay on a side table, she was really occupied making a number of vehement resolutions: Never to slack in her care of her personal appearance; never to give up brushing her hair at night; never to wear a flannel blouse; never to give up manicuring her hands; never, no, never to allow herself to grow short-sighted, and be obliged to submit to specs!

The different mistresses seemed to be on friendly terms, but there was an absence of the camaraderie which comes from living under the same roof. School was a common possession, but home hours were spent apart, except when, as in Claire's own case, two mistresses shared the same rooms, and it followed as a matter of course that personal interests were divided. To-day the conversation was less scholastic than usual, the intervening holidays forming a topic of interest. The Art mistress had been on a bicycle sketching tour with a friend; the German mistress had taken a cheap trip home; Miss Blake announced that all her money had gone on "hateful massage," and the faces of her listeners sobered as they listened, for Sophy Blake, who led the exercises with such verve and go, had of late complained of rheumatic pains, and her companions heard of her symptoms with dread. What would become of Sophy if those pains increased? One after

The Independence of Claire

another the mistresses drifted over to where Claire sat turning the pages of her magazine, and exchanged a few fragments of conversation, and then the great bell clanged again, and afternoon school began.

The first half-hour of afternoon school proved the most trying of the day. Claire was tired after the exertions of the morning, and a very passion for sleep consumed her being. She fought against it with all her might, but the yawns would come; she fought against the yawns, and the tears flowed. To her horror the infection spread, and the girls began to yawn in their turn, with long, uncontrolled gapes. It was a junior class, and the new mistress shrewdly suspected that the infection was welcomed as an agreeable interlude. It was obvious that she could not afford to reject that cup of coffee. Good or bad it must be drunk! Rich or poor that penny must be dedicated to the task of vitalising that first hour of sleepiness.

At the end of six weeks Claire felt as though she had been a High School-mistress all her life. The regular methodical days, in which every hour was mapped out, had a deadening effect on one who had been used to constant variety, and except for a difference in the arrangement of classes there seemed no distinction between one and the other. She was a machine wound up to work steadily from Monday morning until Friday night, and absurdly ready to run down when the time was over.

Every morning after breakfast she started forth with Miss Rhodes, by foot if the weather were fine, by Tube if wet; every mid-day she dined in the Staff-Room with the fifteen other mistresses, and gulped down a cup of chicory coffee. At four o'clock the mistresses met once more for tea, a free meal this time, supplemented by an occasional cake which one of the fifteen provided for the general good. At five she and her table companion returned to their rooms, and rested an hour before taking the evening meal.

Claire was sufficiently French to be intolerant of badly cooked food, and instead of resigning herself to eat and grumble, after the usual habit of lodging-house dwellers, resolutely set to work to improve the situation. The coffee machine had now a chafing-dish as companion, and it was a delightful change of work to set the two machines to work to provide a dainty meal.

"High Tea" consisted as a rule of coffee and some light dish, the materials for which were purchased on the way home. On hungry days, when work had been unusually trying, the butcher supplied cutlets, which were grilled with tomatoes, or an occasional quarter of a pound of mushrooms: on economical days the humble kipper—legendary food of all spinsters in lodgings!—was transformed into quite a smart and restaurant-ey dish, separated from its bones, pounded with butter and flavouring, and served in neat little mounds on the top of hot buttered toast. Moreover, Claire was a proficient in the making of omelettes, and it was astonishing how large and tempting a dish could be compounded of two eggs, and the minutest scrap of ham left over from the morning's breakfast!

"Every luxury of the season, with the smell thrown in! In *nice* cooking the smell is almost the best part. All the cedars in Lebanon wouldn't smell as good at this moment as this nice ham-ey coffee-y frizzle," Claire declared one Friday evening as she served the meal on red-hot plates, and glowed with delight at her own sleight of hand. "Don't you admire eggs for looking so small, when they possess such powers of expansion? All the result of beating. Might make a simile out of that, mightn't you?"

"Might, but won't," the English teacher replied, sipping luxuriously at her coffee. "I'm not a teacher any more at this moment. I'm a gourmand, pure and simple, and I'll stay a gourmand straight on till this omelette is finished. When all trades fail, you might go out as a missioner to women living in diggings, and teach them how to prepare their meals, and sell chafing-dishes by instalment payments at the door, as the touts sell sewing machines to the maids. It would be a noble vocation!"

Claire smirked complacently. "I flatter myself I *have* made a difference to your material comfort! Poor we may be, but we do have nice, dainty little meals, and there's no reason why every able-bodied woman shouldn't have them at the same cost. I've just remembered another nice dish. We'll have it to-morrow night." She paused, and a wistful look came into her eyes, for the next day was Saturday, and it was on holiday afternoons that the feeling of loneliness grew most acute. School life was monotonous, but it was never lonely; from morning to night one lived in a crowd, and already each class had furnished youthful adorers eager to sit at the feet of the pretty new mistress, and bring her offerings of chocolates and flowers; for five long days there was always a crowd, always a hum and babble of voices, but at the end of the week came a dead calm.

On the first Saturday of the term Miss Farnborough had invited the new French mistress to tea, and had been all that was friendly and encouraging; but since that time no word had passed between them that was not strictly concerned with the work in hand, and Claire realised that as one out of sixteen mistresses she could not hope for frequent invitations.

On one Sunday the Gym. mistress had offered her company for a walk, and there the list of hospitalities ceased. No invitations came from that friend of Mrs Fanshawe's who was so fond of girls who were working for themselves. Claire had hardly expected it, but she was disappointed all the same. A longing was growing within her to sit again in a pretty, daintily-appointed room, and talk about something else than time-tables, and irregular verbs, and the Association of Assistant Mistresses which, amalgamated with the Association of Assistant Masters and the Teachers' Guild, were labouring to obtain a settled scale of salaries, and that great safeguard, desired above all others, a pension on retirement!

On this particular Friday evening the longing was so strong that she had deliberately gone out of her way to try to gain an invitation by walking home with a certain Flora Ross in the sixth form, who was the most ardent of her admirers. Flora lived in a cheerful-looking house about a quarter of a mile from the school, and every morning hung over the gate waiting for the chance occasions when her beloved Miss Gifford approached alone, and she could have the felicity of accompanying her for the rest of the way. On these occasions she invariably turned to wave her hand to a plump, smiling mother who stood at a bay window waving in return. An upper window was barred with brass rods, against which two little flaxen heads bobbed up and down. Both the house and its inmates had a cheerful wholesome air, which made a strong appeal to the heart of the lonely girl, and this Friday afternoon, meeting Flora waiting in the corridor, she had accepted her companionship on the way home with a lurking hope that when the green gate was reached, she would be invited to come inside.

Alas! no such thought seemed to enter Flora's brain. She gazed adoringly into Claire's face and hung breathlessly on her words, but for all her adoration there was a gulf between. Claire was the sweetest and duckiest of mistresses, but she *was* a mistress, a being shut off from the ordinary interests of life. When Flora said, "Isn't it jolly, we are going to have a musical party to-morrow! We have such lovely parties, and mother always lets me sit up!" she might have been speaking to a creature without ears, for all the consciousness she exhibited that Claire might possibly wish to take part in the fray. When the green gate was reached, the plump mamma was seen standing outside the drawing-room window and recognising the identity of her daughter's companion, she bent her head in a courteous bow, but she made no attempt to approach the gate.

"See you on Monday!" cried Flora fondly, then the gate clicked, and Claire walked along the road with her head held high, and two red spots burning on either cheek. That evening for the first time she felt a disinclination to change into the pretty summer frock which she had chosen as a compromise for evening dress; that evening for the first time the inner voice whispered to her as it had done to so many before her: "What's the good? Nobody sees you! Nobody cares."

Miss Rhodes finished her share of the omelette, turned on to bread and jam, and cast a glance of inquiry at her companion, who had relapsed into unusual silence.

"Anything wrong?"

"Yes, I think so. Usual symptoms, I suppose. I want to wear all my best clothes and go out to do something gay and exciting, Cecil!" The English teacher's name being Rhodes, it was obvious that she should be addressed as Cecil, especially as her parents had been misguided enough to give her the unsuitably gentle name of Mary. "Cecil, do none of the parents *ever* ask us out?"

"Why should they?"

"Why shouldn't they? If we are good enough to teach their children, we are good enough for them. If they are interested in their children's welfare, they ought to make a point of knowing us to see what kind of influence we use."

"Quite so."

"Well?"

"Well, my dear, there's only one thing to be said—they *don't*! As I told you before, there's a prejudice against mistresses. They give us credit for being clever, and cultivated, and hard-working; but they never grasp the fact that we are human girls, who would very much enjoy being frivolous for a change. I *have* been asked out to tea at rare intervals, and the mothers have apologised for the ordinary conversation, and laboriously switched it on to books. I didn't want to talk books. I wanted to discuss hats and dresses, and fashionable intelligence, and sing comic songs, and play puss-in-the-corner, and be generally giddy and riotous; but my presence cast a wet blanket over the whole party, and we discussed Science and Art. Now I'm old and resigned, but it's hard on the new hands. I think it was rather brutal of your mother to let you come to London without taking the trouble of getting *some* introductions. Don't mind me saying so, do you?"

Claire smiled feebly.

"You have said it, anyhow! I know it must seem unkind to anyone who does not know mother. She's really the kindest person in the world, but she's very easy-going, and apt to believe that everything will happen just as she wishes. She felt quite sure that Miss Farnborough and the staff would supply me with a whirl of gaiety. There *was* one lady, who said she would write to a friend—"

Cecil groaned deeply.

"I know that friend. She comes from Sheffield. A dear kind friend who would love to have you out on holidays. A friend who takes a special interest in school-mistresses. A friend who gives such nice inter-est-ing parties, and would certainly send you a card if she knew your address. Was that it, my dear—was that the kind of friend?"

Cecil chuckled with triumph at the sight of Claire's lengthening jaw. In truth there seemed something uncanny in so accurate a reproduction of Mrs Fanshawe's description. Was there, indeed, no such person? Did she exist purely as a dummy figure, to be dangled before the eyes of credulous beginners? Claire sighed, and buried her last lingering hope; and at that very moment the postman's rap sounded at the door, and a square white envelope was handed in, addressed in feminine handwriting to Miss Claire Gifford.

Claire tore it open, pulled forth a white card, gasped and flushed, and tossed it across the table with a whoop of triumph.

"Raven, look at that! What do you think now of your melancholy croaks?"

Cecil picked up the card, inscribed with the orthodox printed lines, beneath which a few words had been written.

Mrs Willoughby,

At Home

May 26th, 9 p.m.

Music.

"Have just received your address from Mrs Fanshawe. Shall hope to see you to-morrow.—E.B.W."

Cecil screwed up her face in disparagement.

"Nine o'clock. Mayfair. That means a taxi both ways. Can't arrive at a house like that in a mackintosh, with your shoes in a bag. Much wiser to refuse. It will only unsettle you, and make you unfit for work. She's done the polite thing for once, because she was asked, but she'll never do it again. I've been through it myself, and I know the ropes. A woman like that has hundreds of friends; why should she bother about you? You'll never be asked again."

But at that Claire laughed, and beat her hand on the table.

"But I say I shall! I say I'll be asked *often*! I don't care if you've had a hundred experiences, mine shall be different. She has asked me once; now, as the Yankees say, 'it's up to me' to do the rest. I'll make up my mind to make her *want* to ask me!"

Chapter Seven.

Transformation of Cecil.

In the days to come when Claire looked back and reviewed the course of events which followed, she realised that Mrs Willoughby's invitation had been a starting-point from which to date happenings to others as well as herself. It was, for instance, on the morning after its arrival that Cecil's chronic discontent reached an acute stage. She appeared at breakfast with a clouded face, grumbled incessantly throughout the meal, and snapped at everything Claire said, until the latter was provoked into snapping in return. In the old days of idleness Claire had been noted for the sunny sweetness of her disposition, but she was already discovering that teaching lays a severe strain on the nerves, and at the end of a week's work endurance seemed at its lowest ebb. So, when her soft answers met rebuff after rebuff, she began to grumble in her turn, and to give back as good as she got.

"Really, Cecil, I am exceedingly sorry that your form is so stupid, and your work so hard, but I am neither a pupil nor a chief, so I fail to see where my responsibility comes in. Wouldn't it be better if you interviewed Miss Farnborough instead of me?"

It was the first time that Claire had answered sharply, and for the moment surprise held Cecil dumb. Then the colour flamed into her cheeks, and her eyes sparkled with anger. Though forbearance had failed to soothe her, opposition evidently added fuel to the fire.

"Miss Farnborough!" she repeated jeeringly. "What does Miss Farnborough care for the welfare of her mistresses, so long as they grind through their daily tasks? It is the pupils she thinks about, not us. The pupils who are to be pampered and considered, and studied, and amused in school and out. They have to have games in summer, and a

The Independence of Claire

mistress has to give up her spare time to watch the pretty dears to see that they don't get into trouble; and they must have parties, and concerts, and silly entertainments in winter, with some poor wretch of a mistress to do all the work so that they may enjoy the fun. Miss Farnborough is an exemplary Head so far as her scholars are concerned, but what does she do for her mistresses? I ask you, does she do anything at all?"

Claire considered, and was silent. Her first term was nearly over, and she could not truthfully say that the Head had taken any concern for her as an individual who might be expected to feel some interest in life beyond the school door. It is true that almost every day brought the two in contact for the exchange of a few words which, if strictly on business, were always pleasant and kindly, but except for the one invitation to tea on the day before work began, they had never met out of school hours. Claire was a stranger in London, yet the Head had never inquired as to her leisure hours, never invited her to her house, or offered, her an introduction to friends, never even engaged the sympathies of other mistresses on her behalf. Claire had expected a very different treatment, and had struggled against a sense of injury, but she would not acknowledge as much in words.

"I suppose Miss Farnborough is even more tired than we are. She has a tremendous amount of responsibility. And she has a brother and sister at home. Perhaps they object to an incursion of school in free hours."

"Then she ought to leave them, and live where she can do her duty without interference. After all mistresses are girls, too, not very much older than some of the pupils when we begin work; it's inhuman to take *no* interest in our welfare. It wouldn't kill a Head to give up a night a month to ask us to meet possible friends, or to write a few letters of introduction. You agree with me in your heart, so it's no use pretending. It's a moral obligation, if it isn't legal, and I say part of the responsibility is hers if things go wrong. It's inhuman to leave a young girl alone in lodgings without even troubling to inquire if she has anywhere to go in her leisure hours. But it's the same tale all round. Nobody thinks. Nobody cares. I've gone to the same church for three years, and not a soul has spoken to me all that time. I've no time to give to Church work, and the seats are free, so there's no way of getting into touch. I don't suppose any one has ever noticed the shabby school-mistress in her shabby blue serge."

Suddenly Mary Rhodes thrust back her chair, and rising impetuously began to storm up and down the room.

"Oh, I'm tired, I'm tired of this second-hand life. Living in other people's houses, teaching other people's children, obeying other people's orders. I'm sick of it. I can't stand it a moment longer. I'd rather take any risk to be out of it. After all, what could be worse? Any sort of life lived on one's own must be better than this. Nearly twelve years of it—and if I have twenty more, what's the end? What is there to look forward to? Slow starvation in a bed-sitting-room, for perhaps thirty years. I won't do it, I won't! I've had enough. Now I shall choose for myself!"

Like a whirlwind she dashed out of the room, and Claire put her elbow on the table and leant her head on her hands, feeling shaken, and discouraged, and oppressed. For the first time a doubt entered her mind as to whether she could continue to live with Mary Rhodes. In her brighter modes there was much that was attractive in her personality, but to live with a chronic grumbler sapped one's own powers of resistance. Claire felt that for the sake of her own happiness and efficiency it would be wiser to make a change, but her heart sank at the thought of making a fresh start, of perhaps having to live alone with no one to speak to in the long evenings. The life of a bachelor girl made little appeal at that moment. Liberty seemed dearly bought at the price of companionship.

Claire spent the morning writing to her mother and reading over the series of happy letters which had reached her week after week. Mrs Judge was in radiant spirits, delighted with the conditions of her new life, full of praise of her husband and the many friends to whom she had been introduced. Three-fourths of the letter were taken up with descriptions of her own gay doings, the remaining fourth with optimistic remarks on her daughter's life. How delightful to share rooms with another girl! What a nice break to have every Saturday and Sunday free! What economical rooms! Claire must feel quite rich. What fun to have the girls so devoted!

Claire made an expressive grimace as she read that "quite rich." This last week she had been obliged to buy new gloves, and to have her boots mended. A new umbrella had been torn by the carelessness with which another teacher had thrust her own into the crowded stand, and one night she had been seized with a longing for a dainty well-cooked meal, and had recklessly stood treat at a restaurant. She did not feel at all "rich" as she made up the week's account, and reflected that next week the expense of driving to Mrs Willoughby's "At Home" would again swell up the total of these exasperating "extras" which made such havoc of advance calculations.

Cecil did not appear until lunch was on the table, when she flung the door wide open and marched in with an air of bravado, as if wanting her companion to stare at once and get over it. It would have been impossible not to stare, for the change in her appearance was positively startling to behold. Her dark hair was waved and fashionably coiffed. Her best coat and skirt had been embellished with frills of lace at neck and sleeves, a pretty little waistcoat had been manufactured out of a length of blue ribbon and a few paste buttons, while a blue feather necklet had been promoted a step higher, and encircled an old straw hat. The ribbon bow at the end of the boa exactly matched the shade of the waistcoat, and was cocked up at a daring angle, while a becoming new veil and a pair of immaculate new gloves added still further to the effect.

Claire had always suspected that Cecil could be pretty if she chose to take the trouble, and now she knew it for a fact. It was difficult to realise that this well-groomed-looking girl, with the bright eyes and softly-flushed cheeks, could really be the same person as the frumpy-looking individual who every morning hurried along the street.

Involuntarily Claire threw up her hands; involuntarily she cried aloud in delight "Cheers! Cheers! How do you do, Cecil? Welcome home, Cecil!—the real Cecil! How pretty you are, Cecil! How well that blue suits you! Don't dare to go back to your dull navy and black. I shall insist that you always wear blue. I feel quite proud of having such a fine lady to lunch. You are going to have lunch, aren't you? Why those gloves and veil?"

"Oh, well—I'm not hungry. I'll have some coffee. I may have lunch in town." Cecil was plainly embarrassed under her companion's scrutiny. She pushed up her veil, so that it rested in a little ridge across her nose, craned forward her head, sipping her coffee with exaggerated care, so that no drop should fall on her lacy frills.

Claire longed to ask a dozen questions, but something in Cecil's manner held her at bay, and she contented herself with one inquiry—

"What time will you be home?"

Cecil shrugged her shoulders.

"Don't know. Perhaps not till late." She was silent for a moment, then added with sudden bitterness, "You are not the *only* person who has invitations. If I chose, I could go out every Saturday."

"Then why on earth are you always grumbling about your loneliness?" thought Claire swiftly, but she did not put the thought into words. After the warmth of her own welcome, a kinder response was surely her due; she was angry, and would not condescend to reply.

The meal was finished in silence, but when Cecil rose to depart, the usual compunction seized her in its grip. She stood arranging her veil before the mirror over the mantelpiece, uttering the usual interjectory expressions of regret.

"Sorry, Claire. I'm a wretch. You must hate me. I ought to be shot. Nice Saturday morning I've given you! What are you going to do this afternoon?"

Claire's eyes turned towards the window with an expression sad to see on so young a face—an imprisoned look. Her voice seemed to lose all its timbre as she replied in one flat dreary word—

"Nothing!"

A spasm of irresolution passed across Cecil's face. For a moment she looked as if she were about to throw aside her own project and cast in her lot with her friend's. Then her face hardened, and she turned towards the door.

"Why not call for Sophie Blake, and see if she will go a walk? She asked you once before."

With that she was gone, and Claire was left to consider the proposition. Sophie Blake, the Games mistress, was the single member of the staff who had shown any disposition towards real friendship, though the intimacy was so far confined to one afternoon's walk, and an occasional chat in the dinner hour, but this afternoon the thought of her merry smile acted as an irresistible magnet. Claire ran upstairs to get ready, in a panic lest she might arrive at Sophie's lodgings to find she had already gone out for the afternoon. Cecil had hinted that she might not return until late, and suddenly it seemed unbearable to spend the rest of the day in solitude. Restlessness was in the air, first the pleasurable restlessness caused by the receipt of Mrs Willoughby's invitation, then the disagreeable restlessness caused by Cecil's erratic behaviour. As she hurried through the streets towards Sophie Blake's lodgings, Claire pondered over the mystery of this sudden development on Cecil's part. Where was she going? Whom was she going to see? Why declare with one breath that she was without a friend, and with the next that if she chose she might accept invitations every week? What special reason had to-day inspired such unusual care in her appearance?

Sophie was at home. Lonely Claire felt quite a throb of relief as she heard the welcome words. She entered the oil-clothed passage and was shown into a small, very warm, very untidy front parlour wherein stood Sophie herself, staring with widened eyes at the opening door.

"Oh, it's *you*!" she cried. "What a fright you gave me! I couldn't think *who* it could be. Come in! Sit down! Can you find a free chair? Saturday is my work day. I've been darning stockings, and trimming a hat, and ironing a blouse, and washing lace, and writing letters all in a rush. I love a muddle on Saturdays. It's such a change after routine all the week. What do you think of the hat? Seven and sixpence, all told. I flatter myself it looks worth every penny of ten. Don't pull down that cloth. The iron's underneath. Be careful of that table! The ink-pot's somewhere about. How sweet of you to call! I'll clear this muddle away and then we can talk ... Oh, my arm!"

"What's the matter with the arm?"

Sophie shrugged carelessly.

"Rheumatism, my dear. Cheerful, isn't it, for a gym. mistress? It's been giving me fits all the week."

"The east winds, I suppose. I know they make rheumatism worse."

"They do. So does damp. So does snow. So does fog. So does cold. So does heat. If you could tell me of anything that makes it *better*, I'd be obliged. Bother rheumatism! Don't let's talk of it... It's Saturday, my dear. I never think of disagreeables on Saturday. Where's Miss Rhodes this afternoon?"

"I don't know. She made herself look very nice and smart—she can be very nice-looking when she likes!—and went out for the day."

"Humph!" Sophie pursed her lips and contracted her brows as if in consideration of a knotty point. "She was awfully pretty when I came to the school ten years ago. And quite jolly and bright. You wouldn't know her for the same girl. She's a worrier, of course, but it's more than that. Something happened about six years ago, which took the starch out of her once for all. A love affair, I expect. Perhaps she's told you... I'm not fishing, and it's not my business, but I'm sorry for the poor thing, and I was sorry for you when I heard you were going to share her room. She can't be the most cheerful companion in the world!"

"Oh, she's quite lively at times," Claire said loyally, "and very appreciative. I'm fond of her, you know, but I wish she didn't grumble quite so much." She looked round the parlour, which was at once bigger and better furnished than the joint apartment in Laburnum Crescent, and seized upon an opportunity of changing the subject. "You have a very nice room."

Sophie Blake looked round with an air half proud, half guilty.

"Y–es. Too nice. I've no business to spend so much, but I simply can't stand those dreadful cheap houses. People are always fussing and telling one to save up for old age. I think it matters far more to have things nice in one's youth. I get a hundred and thirty a year, and have to keep myself all the year round and help to educate a young sister. We are orphans, and the grown-ups have to keep her between us. I couldn't save if I wanted to, so what's the use of worrying? I don't care very much what happens after fifty-five. Perhaps I shall be married. Perhaps I shall be dead. Perhaps some nice kind millionaire will have taken a fancy to me, and left me a fortune. If the worst comes to the worst, I'll go into a home for decayed gentlewomen and knit stockings—no, not stockings, I should never be able to turn the heels—long armlet things, like mittens, without the thumbs. Look here. Where shall we go? Isn't it a shame that all the nice shops close early on Saturday? We might have had such sport walking along Knightsbridge, choosing what we'd like best from every window. Have you ever done that? It's ripping fun. What about Museums? Do you like Museums? Rather cold for the feet, don't you think? What can we do that's warm and interesting, and exciting, and doesn't cost more than eighteenpence?"

Claire laughed gleefully, not at the thought of the eighteenpenny restriction, but from pure joy at finding a companion who could face life with a smile, and find enjoyment from such simple means as imaginary purchases from shop windows. Oh, the blessed effect of a cheerful spirit! How inspiring it was after the constant douche of discouragement from which she had suffered for the last nine weeks!

"Oh, bother eighteenpence! This is my treat, and we are going to enjoy ourselves, or know the reason why. I've got a lot of money in the bank, and I'm just in the mood to spend. We'll go to the Queen's Hall, and then on to have tea in a restaurant. You would like to hear some music?"

"So long as it is not a chorus of female voices—I *should*! I'm a trifle fed up with female voices," cried Sophie gaily. She picked up her newly-trimmed hat from the table and caressed it fondly. "Come along, darling. You're going to make your *début*!"

Chapter Eight.

The Reception.

It was almost worth while leading a life of all work and no play for six weeks on end, for the sheer delight of being frivolous once more; of dressing oneself in one's prettiest frock, drawing on filmy silk stockings and golden shoes, clasping a pearl necklace round a white throat and cocking a feathery aigrette at just the right angle among coppery swathes of hair. No single detail was wanting to complete the whole, for in the old careless days Claire's garments had been purchased with a lavish hand, the only anxiety being to secure the most becoming specimen of its kind. There were long crinkly gloves, and a lace handkerchief, and a fan composed of curling feathers and mother-of-pearl sticks, and a dainty bag hanging by golden cords, and a cloak of the newest shape, composed of layers of different-tinted chiffons, which looked more like a cloud at sunset than a garment manufactured by human hands and supposed to be of use!

Claire tilted her little mirror to an acute angle, gave a little skip of delight as she surveyed the completed whole, and then whirled down the narrow staircase, a flying mist of draperies, through which the little gold-clad feet gleamed in and out. She whirled into the sitting-room, where the solitary lamp stood on the table, and Cecil lay on the humpy green plush sofa reading a novel from the Free Library. She put down the book and stared with wide eyes as Claire gave an extra whirl for her benefit, and cried jubilantly—

"Admire me! Admire me! I'm dying to be admired! Don't I look fine, and smart, and unsuitable! Will any one in the world mistake me for a High School-mistress!"

Cecil rose from the sofa, and made a solemn tour of inspection. Obviously she was impressed, obviously she admired, obviously also she found something startling in her inspection. There was pure feminine interest in the manner in which she fingered each delicate fabric in turn, there was pure feminine kindness in the little pat on the arm which announced the close of the inspection.

"My dear, it's ripping! Rich and rare isn't in it. You look a dream. Poor kiddie! If this is the sort of thing you've been used to, it's been harder for you than I thought! Yes, horribly unsuitable, and when it's worn-out, you'll never be able to have another like it. White pongé will be your next effort."

"Bless your heart, I've three others just as fine, and these skimpy skirts last for an age. No chance of any one planting a great foot on the folds and tearing them to ribbons as in the old days. There *are* no folds to tread on."

But Cecil as usual was ready with her croak.

"Next year," she said darkly, "there will be flounces. Before you have a chance of wearing your four dresses, everybody will be fussy and frilly, and they'll be hopelessly out of date."

"Then I'll cut up two and turn them into flounces to fuss out the others!" cried Claire, the optimist, and gave another caper from sheer lightness of heart. "How do you like my feet?"

"I suppose you mean shoes. A pretty price you paid for those. I'm sure they're too tight!"

"Boats, my dear, boats! I've had to put in a sole. Didn't you know my feet were so small? How do you like my cloak? It's meant to look like a cloud. Layers of blue, pink and grey, 'superimposed,' as the fashion papers have it. Or should you say it was more like an opal?"

"No, I should not. Neither one nor the other. Considered as a cloak for a foggy November evening, I should call it a delusion and a fraud. You'll get a chill. I've a Shetland shawl. I'll lend it to you to wrap round your shoulders."

"No, you won't!" Claire cried defiantly. "Shetland shawl indeed! Who ever heard of a girl of twenty-one in a Shetland shawl? I'm going to a party, my dear. The joy of that thought would keep me warm through a dozen fogs."

"You'll have to come back from the party, however, and you mayn't feel so jubilant then. It's not too exciting when you don't know a soul, and sit on one seat all evening. I knew a girl who went to a big crush and didn't even get a cup of coffee. Nobody asked her to go down."

Claire swept her cloak to one side, and sat down on a chair facing the sofa, her white gloves clasped on her knee, the embroidered bag hanging by its golden cords to the tip of the golden slippers. She fixed her eyes steadily on her companion, and there was in them a spark of anger, before which Cecil had the grace to flush.

"Sorry! Really I am sorry—"

"'Repentance is to *leave*

The sins we loved before,

And show that we in earnest grieve

By doing so No More!'"

quoted Claire sternly. "Really, Cecil, you are the champion wet blanket of your age. It is too bad. I have to do all the perking up, and you can't even let me go to a party without damping my ardour. I was thinking it over the other night, and I've hit on a promising plan. I'm going to allow you a grumble day a week—but only one. On that day you can grumble as much as ever you like, from the moment you get up till the moment you go to bed. You'll be within your rights, and I shall not complain. I'll have my own day, too, when you can find out what it feels like to listen, but won't be allowed to say a word in return. For the rest of the week you'll just have to grin and bear it. You won't be allowed a single growl."

Cecil knitted her brows, and looked ashamed and uncomfortable, as she invariably did when taxed with her besetting sin. Claire's charge on mental poisoning had struck home, and she had honestly determined to turn over a new leaf; but the habit had been indulged too long to be easily abandoned. Unconsciously, as it were, disparaging remarks flowed from her lips, combined with a steady string of objections, adverse criticisms, and presentiments of darkness and gloom. At the present moment she felt a little startled to realise how firmly the habit was established, and the proposal of a licenced grumble day held out some promise of a cure.

"Then I'll have Monday!" she cried briskly. "I am always in a bad temper on Mondays, so I shall be able to make the most of my chance." She was silent for a moment considering the prospect, then was struck with a sudden thought. "But now and then I *do* have a nice week-end, and then I shouldn't want to grumble at all. I suppose I could change the day?"

There was a ring of triumph in Claire's laugh.

"Not you! My dear girl, that's just what I am counting upon! Sometimes the sun will shine, sometimes you'll get a nice letter, sometimes the girls will be intelligent and interesting, and then, my dear, you'll forget, and the day will skip past, and before you know where you are it will be Tuesday morning and your chance will have gone. Cecil, fancy it! A whole fortnight without a grumble. It seems almost too good to be true!"

"It does!" said the English mistress eloquently. She sat upright on the green plush sofa, her shabby slippers well in evidence beneath the edge of her shabby skirt, staring with curious eyes at the radiant figure of the girl in the opposite chair. "I don't think you need a day at all!"

"Because I'm going to a solitary party? Only two minutes ago, my love, you were sympathising with my hard lot! I shall have Fridays. I'm tired on Fridays, and it's getting near the time for making up accounts. I can be quite a creditable grumbler on Fridays."

"Well, just as you like! You *are* going to the party, I suppose? Haven't changed your mind by any chance, and determined to spend the evening hectoring me! If you are going, you'd better go. I'll sit up for you and keep some cocoa—"

Claire rose with a smile.

"I appreciate the inference! Starved and disillusioned, I am to creep home and weep on your bosom. Well, we'll see! Good-bye for the present. I'll tell you all about it when I get back..."

A minute's whistling at the front door produced a taxi, in which Claire seated herself and was whirled westward through brightly lighted streets. In the less fashionable neighbourhoods the usual Saturday crowd thronged round the shops and booths, making their purchases at an hour when perishable goods could be obtained at bargain prices. Claire and Cecil had themselves made such expeditions before now, coming home triumphant with some savoury morsel for supper, and with quite a lavish supply of flowers to deck the little room. At the time the expeditions had been pleasant enough, and there had seemed nothing in the least *infra dig* in taking advantage of the opportunity; but to-night the girl in the cloudy cloak looked through the windows of her chariot with an ineffable condescension, and found it difficult to believe that she herself had ever made one of so insignificant a throng!

"How I do love luxury! It's the breath of my nostrils," she said to herself with a little sigh of content, as she straightened herself in her seat, and smiled back at her own reflection in the strip of mirror opposite. Her hair had "gone" just right. What a comfort that was! Sometimes it took a stupid turn and could not be induced to obey. She opened the cloak at the top and peeped at the dainty whiteness within, with the daring, thoroughly French touch of vivid emerald green which gave a *cachet* to the whole. Yes, it was quite as pretty as she had believed. Every whit as becoming. "I don't look a bit like a school-mistress!" smiled Claire, and snoodled back again against the cushions with a deep breath of content.

She was not in the least shy. Many a girl about to make her *entrée* into a strange house would have been suffering qualms of misgiving by this time, but Claire had spent her life more or less in public, and was accustomed to meet strangers as a matter of course, so there was no dread to take the edge off her enjoyment.

Even when the taxi slowed down to take its place in the stream of vehicles which were drawn up before Mrs Willoughby's house, she knew only a heightened enjoyment in the realisation that it was not a party at all, but a real big fashionable At Home.

The usual crowd of onlookers stood on either side of the door, and as Claire descended from the taxi, the sight of her golden slippers and floating clouds of gauze evoked a gratifying murmur of admiration. She passed on with her head in the air, looking neither to right nor left, but close against the rails stood a couple of working girls whose wistful eyes drew her own as with a magnet. In their expression was a whole world of awe, of admiration; they looked at her as at a denizen of another sphere, hardly presuming even to be envious, so infinitely was she removed from their grey-hued life. As Claire met their eyes, an impulse seized her to stop and tell them that she was just a working girl like themselves, but convention being too strong to allow of such familiarities, she smiled instead, with such a frank and friendly acknowledgment of their admiration as brought a flash of pleasure to their faces.

"She's a real laidy, she is!" said Gladys to Maud; and Maud sniffed in assent, and answered strongly, "You bet your life!"

The inside of the house seemed out of all proportion with the outside appearance. This is a special peculiarity of the West End, which has puzzled many a visitor besides Claire Gifford. What *is* the magic which transforms narrow slips of buildings into spacious halls and imposing flights of stairways? Viewed from the street, the town houses of well-known personages seem quite inadequate for their purpose; viewed from within, they are all that is stately and appropriate. Those of us who live in less favoured neighbourhoods would fain solve the riddle.

Mrs Willoughby stood at the top of her own staircase, shaking hands with the stream of ascending guests, and motioning them forward to the suite of entertaining rooms from which came a steady murmur of voices. She was a stout woman, with a vast expanse of white shoulders which seemed to join right on to her head without any preliminary in the shape of a neck. Her hair was dark, and a plain face was lightened by a pair of exceedingly pleasant, exceedingly alert brown eyes. As soon as she met those eyes Claire felt assured that the kindness of which she had heard was a real thing, and that this woman could be counted upon as a friend. There was, it is true, a slight vagueness in the manner in which she made her greeting, but a murmur of "Mrs Fanshawe" instantly revived recollections.

"Of course—of course!" she cried heartily. "So glad you could come, my dear. I must see you later on. Reginald!"—she beckoned to a lad in an Eton suit—"I want you to take charge of Miss Gifford. Take her to have some coffee, and introduce her to some one nice."

A nod and a smile, and Mrs Willoughby had turned back to welcome the next guest in order, while the Eton boy offered his arm with the air of a prince of the blood, and led the way to a refreshment buffet around which the guests were swarming with an eagerness astonishing to behold when one realised how lately they must have risen from the dinner-table. Claire found her young cavalier very efficient in his attentions. He settled her in a comfortable corner, brought her a cup of coffee heaped with foaming cream, and gave it as his opinion that it was going to be "a beastly crush." Claire wondered if it would be tactful to inquire how he happened to be at home in the middle of a term; but while she hesitated he supplied the information himself.

"I'm home on leave. Appendicitis. Left the nursing home three weeks ago. Been at the sea, and came back yesterday in time for this show. Getting a bit tired of slacking!"

"You must be. Dear me! I *am* sorry. Too bad to begin so soon," murmured Claire pitifully; but Master Reginald disdained sympathy.

"Oh, I dunno," he said calmly. "It's quite the correct thing, don't you know? Everybody's doing it. Just as well to get it through. It might"—he opened his pale eyes with a startled look—"it might have come on in the hols! Pretty fool I should have looked if I'd been done out of winter sports."

"There's that way of looking at it!" Claire said demurely. For a moment she debated whether she should break the fact that she herself was a school-mistress, but decided that it would be wiser to refrain since the boy would certainly feel more at ease with her in her private capacity. So for the next half-hour they sat happily together in their corner, while the boy discoursed on the subjects nearest his heart, and the girl deftly switched him back to the subjects more congenial.

"Yes, I love cricket. At least I'm sure I should do, if I understood it better... *Do* tell me who is the big old lady with the eyeglass and the diamond tiara?"

"Couldn't tell you to save my life. Rather an out-size, isn't she? Towers over the men. I say! you ought to go to Lord's Will you turn up at Lord's next year to see our match? We might meet somewhere and I'd give you tea. Harrow won't have a chance. We've got a bowler who—"

"Can he really? How nice! Oh, that *is* a curious-looking man with the long hair! I'm sure he is something, or does something different from other people. Is he a musician, do you think? Do you ever have music on these evenings?"

"Rather! Sometimes the mater hires a big swell, sometimes she lets loose the amateurs. She knows lots of amateurs, y'know. People who are trying to be big-wigs, and want the chance to show off. The mater encourages them. Great mistake if you ask me, but you needn't listen if you don't want. She has one of these crushes once a month. Beastly dull, I call them. Can't think why the people come. But she gives them a rattling good feed. Supper comes on at twelve, in the dining-room downstairs."

But Claire was not interested in supper. All her attention was taken up in watching the stream of people passing by, and for a time the youth of her companion had seemed an advantage, since it made it easy to indulge her curiosity concerning her fellow-guests by a succession of questions which might have been boring to an adult. As time passed on, however, and she became conscious that more than one pair of masculine eyes turned in her direction, she wished frankly Master Reginald would remember his mother's instructions and proceed without further delay to introduce her to "someone nice." To return home and confess to Cecil that she had spent the evening in company with a schoolboy would be almost as humiliating as sitting alone in a corner.

It was at this point that Claire became aware of the presence of a very small, very wizened old woman sitting alone at the opposite side of the room, her mittened hands clawing each other restlessly in her lap, her sunken eyes glancing to right and left with a glance distinctly hostile. The passing of guests frequently hid her from view, but when a gap came again, there she sat, still alone, still twisting her mittened hands, still coldly staring around. Claire thought she looked a very disagreeable old lady, but she was sorry for her all the same. Horrid to be old and cross, and to be alone in a crowd! She put yet another question to the boy by her side.

"That," said Master Willoughby seriously, "is Great-aunt Jane. Great-aunt Jane is the skeleton in our cupboard. The mater says so, and she ought to know. Every time the mater has a show, the moment the door is opened, in comes Great-aunt Jane, and sits it out until every one has gone. If any one dares speak to her she snaps his head off, and if they let her alone, she's furious, and gives it to the mater after they're gone. Most of the crowd know her by now, and pretend they don't see, ... and she gets waxier and waxier. Would you like to be introduced?"

"Yes, please!" said Claire unexpectedly. She was tired of sitting in one corner, and wanted to move her position, but she was also quite genuinely anxious to try her hand at cheering poor cross Great-aunt Jane. The old lady *pensionnaires* in the "Villa Beau Séjour" had made a point of petting and flattering the pretty English girl, and Claire was complacently assured that this old lady would follow their example. But she was mistaken.

"Aunt Jane, Miss Gifford asks to be introduced to you. Miss Gifford—Lady Jane Willoughby."

Reginald beat a hurried retreat, and Claire seated herself at the end of the sofa and smilingly awaited her companion's lead. It did not come. After one automatic nod of the head, Lady Jane resumed her former position, taking no more notice of the new-comer than if she had remained at the far end of the room. Claire felt her cheeks begin to burn. Her complacence had suffered a shock, but pride came to her rescue, and she made a determined effort at conversation.

"That nice boy has been telling me that he has had appendicitis."

Lady Jane favoured her with a frosty glance.

"Yes, he has. Perhaps you will excuse me from talking about it. I object to the discussion of diseases at social gatherings."

Claire's cheeks grew hotter still. A quick retort came to her lips.

"I wasn't going to discuss it! I only mentioned it for—for something to say. I couldn't think how else to begin!"

The droop of Lady Jane's eyelids inferred that it was really quite superfluous to begin at all. Claire waited a whole two minutes by the clock, and then made another effort.

"I hear we are to have some music later on."

"Sorry to hear it," said Great-aunt Jane.

"Really! I was so glad. Aren't you fond of music, then?"

"I am very fond of music," said Aunt Jane, and there was a world of insinuation in her voice. Without a definite word being spoken, the hearer was informed that good music, real music, music worthy the name, was a thing that no sane person would expect to hear at Mrs Willoughby's "At Homes." She was really the most terrifying and disconcerting of old ladies, and Claire heartily repented the impulse which had brought her to her side. A pretty thing it would be if she were left alone on this sofa for the rest of the evening!

But fortune was kind, and from across the room came a good angel who was so exactly a reproduction of Mrs Willoughby herself, minus half her age, that it must obviously be her daughter. Janet Willoughby was not a pretty girl, but she looked gay, and bright, and beaming with good humour, and at this moment with a spice of mischief into the bargain. The manner in which she held out her hand to Claire was as friendly as though the two girls had been friends for years.

"Miss Gifford? I was sure it must be you. Mother told me to look for you. Aunt Jane, will you excuse my running away with Miss Gifford? Several people are asking to be introduced. Will you come with me, Miss Gifford? I want to take you into the music room."

Claire rose with a very leap of eagerness, and as soon as they had gained a safe distance, Miss Willoughby turned to her with twinkling eyes.

"I am afraid you were having a bad time! I caught sight of you across the room and was so sorry. Who took you over there? Was it that naughty Reginald?"

"He did, but I asked him. I thought she looked lonely. I thought perhaps she would be pleased."

Janet Willoughby's smile showed a quick approval.

"That was kind! Thanks for the good intention, but I can't let you be victimised any more. I want to talk to you myself, and half-a-dozen men have been asking for introductions to the girl with the green sash. You know Mrs Fanshawe, don't you? Isn't she charming? She and I are the greatest of chums. I always say she has never succeeded in growing older than seventeen. She is so delightfully irresponsible and impulsive. She wrote mother a charming letter about you. It made us quite anxious to meet you, but you know what town life is—a continual rush! Everything gets put off."

"It was awfully good of you to ask me at all, and very kind of Mrs Fanshawe to write. I only know her in the most casual way. We crossed over from Antwerp together, and her maid was ill, and I was able to be of some use, and when she heard that I was coming to work in London and that I knew nobody here—she—"

Jane Willoughby stared in frank amazement.

"Do you really mean that that was all? You met her only that one time? You know nothing of her home or her people?"

"Only that time. I hope—I hope you don't think—"

Claire suffered an anxious moment before she realised that for some unexplained reason Miss Willoughby was more pleased than annoyed by the intelligence. An air of something extraordinarily like relief passed over her features. She laughed gaily and said—

"I don't think anything at all except that it is delightfully like Mrs Fanshawe. She wrote as if she had known you for ages. As a matter of fact she probably *does* know you quite well. She is so extraordinarily quick and clever, that she crowds as much life into an hour as an ordinary person does into a week. She told us that you had chosen to come to London to work, rather than go to India and have a good time. How plucky of you! And you teach at one of the big High Schools... You don't look in the least like a school-mistress."

"Ah! I'm off duty to-night! You should see me in the morning, in my working clothes. You should see me at night, correcting exercises on the dining-table in a lodging-house parlour, and cooking sausages in a chafing-dish for our evening meal. I 'dig' with the English mistress, and do most of our cooking myself, as the landlady's tastes and ours don't agree. I'm getting to be quite an expert at manufacturing sixpenny dainties."

Janet Willoughby breathed a deep sigh; the diamond star on her neck sent out vivid gleams of light.

"What fun!" she sighed enviously. "What fun!" and as she spoke there flashed suddenly before the eyes of her listener a picture of the English mistress lying on the green plush sofa, her shabby slippers showing beneath the hem of her shabby skirt, spending the holiday Saturday evening at home because she had no invitations to go out, and no money to spare for an entertainment. "Oh, I *do* envy you!" sighed Janet deeply. "It's one of my greatest ambitions to share rooms with a nice girl, and live the simple life, and be free to do whatever one liked. Mother loves independence in other girls, but her principles don't extend to me. She says an only daughter's place is at home. But you are an only daughter, too."

"I am; but other circumstances were different. It was a case of being dependent on a stepfather or of working for myself—so I chose to work, and—"

"And I'm sure you never regret it!"

Claire extended her hands in the expressive French shrug.

"Ah, but I do! Horribly, at times. Even now, after three months' work I have a conviction that I shall regret it more and more as time goes on; but if I had to decide again, I'd do just the same. It's a question of principle versus so many things—laziness and self-indulgence, and wanting to have a good time, and the habits of a lifetime, and irritation with stupid girls who won't work."

Janet Willoughby gave a soft murmur of understanding.

"Yes, of course. Stupid of me to say that! Of course, you must get tired when you've never taught before. Does it bore you very much?"

"Teaching? Oh, no. As a rule I love it, and take a pride in inventing new ways to help the girls. It's the all work and no play that gets on one's nerves, and the feeling of being cut off from the world by an impassable barrier of something that really doesn't exist. People have a prejudice against school-mistresses. They think they are dull, and proper, and pedantic. If they want to be complimentary they say, 'You don't look like a school-mistress.' You did yourself, not two minutes ago. But really and truly they are just natural, everyday girls, wanting to have a good time in their leisure hours like other girls. You can't think how happy I was to come here to-night and have the chance of putting on pretty things again."

The Independence of Claire

Janet Willoughby put her hand on Claire's arm and piloted her deftly through the crowd.

"Now," she said firmly, "you just stay here, and I'll bring up all the nicest men in the room, and introduce them in turns. You *shall* have a good time, and you are wearing the very prettiest things in the room—if it's any comfort to you to hear it. We won't talk about school any more. To-night is for fun!"

The next hour passed on flying feet, while Claire sat the queen of a little court, and Janet Willoughby flitted to and fro, bringing up fresh arrivals to be introduced, and drafting off the last batch to other parts of the crowded rooms. All the men were agreeable and amusing, and showed a flattering appreciation of their position. Claire felt no more interest in one than in another, but she liked them all, and felt a distinct pleasure in talking to men again after the convent-like existence of the last months. She was pleased to welcome a new-comer, smiled unconcerned at a farewell.

From time to time the buzz of voices was temporarily broken by the crash of the piano, but always before the end of each performance it rose again, and steadily swelled in volume. In truth, the excellence of the performance was no great inducement to listen, and Mrs Willoughby's forehead showed a pucker of anxiety. She drifted across to Claire's corner, and spoke a few kindly words of welcome, which ended in a half apology.

"I am sorry the music is so poor. It varies so much on different nights. Sometimes we have quite a number of good singers, but to-night there are none. I am afraid so much piano grows a little boring."

She looked in the girl's face with a quick inquiry.

"Do *you* sing?"

"No-o." The word seemed final, yet there was an unmistakable hesitation in Claire's voice. Mrs Willoughby's glance sharpened.

"But you do something? Play? Recite? What is it? My dear, I should be so grateful!"

"I—whistle!" confessed Claire with a blush, and a little babble of delight greeted the words. Every one who heard hailed the chance of a variety in the monotonous programme. Mrs Willoughby beamed with all the relief of a hostess unexpectedly relieved of anxiety.

"Delightful! Charming! My dear, it will be such a help! You would like an accompaniment? I'll introduce you to Mr Helder. He can play anything you like. Will you come now! I am sure every one will be charmed."

There was no time for a second thought. The next moment the long-haired Mr Helder was bowing over Claire's hand, and professing his delight. The little group in the corner were pressing forward to obtain a point of vantage, and throughout the company in general was passing a wordless hum of excitement. Mr Helder was seating himself at the piano, a girl in a white dress had ascended the impromptu platform and now stood by his side, a pretty girl, a very pretty girl, a girl who acknowledged the scattered applause with a smile which showed two dimples on one cheek, a girl who looked neither shy nor conceited, but simply as if she were enjoying herself very much, and expected everybody to do the same. She was going to sing. It would be a relief to listen to singing after the continued performances upon the piano. They hoped sincerely that she could sing well. Why didn't the accompaniment begin?

Then suddenly a white-gloved hand gave a signal, Mr Helder's hands descended on the keys, and at the same instant from between Claire's pursed-up lips there flowed a stream of high, flute-like notes, repeating the air with a bird-like fluency and ease. She had chosen the old-world ballad, "Cherry Ripe," the quaint turns and trills of which lent themselves peculiarly well to this method of interpretation, and the swing and gaiety of the measure carried the audience by storm. Looking down from her platform Claire could see the indifferent faces suddenly lighten into interest, into smiles, into positive beams of approval. At the second verse heads began to wag; unconsciously to their owners lips began to purse. It was inspiring to watch those faces, to know that it was she herself who had wrought the magic change.

Those moments for Claire were pure undiluted joy. Whistling had come to her as a natural gift, compensating to some extent for the lack of a singing voice; later on she had taken lessons, and practised seriously to perfect her facility. At school in Paris, later on in attending social gatherings with her mother, she had had abundant opportunities of overcoming the initial shyness; but indeed shyness was never a serious trouble with Claire Gifford, who was gifted with that very agreeable combination of qualities,—an amiable desire to please other people, and a comfortable assurance of her own powers.

At the end of the third verse the applause burst out with a roar. "Bravos" sounded from every side, and "Encores" persisted so strenuously that Claire was not permitted even to descend from her platform. Mrs Willoughby rustled forward full of gratitude and thanks. Mr Helder rubbed his hands, and beamingly awaited further commands... What would Cecil have to say to a success like this?

Claire's second choice was one of Mendelssohn's "Songs without Words," a quieter measure this time, sweet and flowing, and giving opportunity for a world of delicate phrasing. It was one of the pieces which she had practised with a master, and with which she felt most completely at home; and if the audience found it agreeable to hear, they also, to judge from their faces, found it equally agreeable to watch. Claire's cheeks were flushed to a soft rose-pink, her head moved to and fro, unconsciously keeping time with the air; one little golden shoe softly tapped the floor. Her unconsciousness of self added to the charm of the performance. But once the audience noticed, with sympathetic amusement, her composure was seriously threatened, so that the bird-like notes quavered ominously, and the twin dimples deepened into veritable holes. Claire had caught sight of Great-aunt Jane standing in solitary state at the rear of the throng of listeners, her mittened fingers still plucking, her eyes frosty with disapproval.

After that Claire safeguarded her composure by looking steadily downward at the points of her shoes until the end of the song approached, when it seemed courteous, once more, to face her audience. She raised her eyes, and as she did so her heart leapt within her with a startling force. She was thankful that it *was* the end, that the long final note was already on her lips, for there, standing in the doorway, his face upraised to hers, stood her knight of the railway station, the rescuer of the lost box—Erskine Fanshawe himself!

Chapter Nine.

The supper.

Claire stepped down from the platform to be surrounded by a throng of guests all eager to express their admiration of her interesting performance, to marvel how she could "do it," and to congratulate her upon so unusual an accomplishment; and she smiled and bowed, declared that it was quite easy, and perjured herself by maintaining that anyone could do as well, acutely conscious all the time that Captain Fanshawe was drawing nearer with determined steps, edging his way towards the front of the crowd. The next moment her hand was in his, and he was greeting her with the assurance of a lifelong friend.

"Good evening, Miss Gifford. Hadn't we better make straight for supper now? I am sure you must need it."

It was practically the ordinary invitation. There was nothing to find fault with in the words themselves, yet the impression of a previous arrangement was obviously left with the hearers, who fell back, giving way as to a superior right. As for Claire, she laid her hand on the extended arm, with all the good will in the world, and made a triumphant passage through the crowd, which smiled upon her as though agreeing that it was now her turn to be amused.

"This table, I think!" Captain Fanshawe said, leading the way to the furthest corner of the dining-room, and Claire found herself sipping a hot cup of soup, and realising that the world was an agreeable place, and that it was folly ever to allow oneself to be downhearted, since such delightful surprises awaited round corners ready to transform the grey into gold!

Captain Fanshawe looked exactly as memory had pictured him—plain of feature, distinguished in bearing, grave, self-contained, yet with that lurking light in his eyes which showed that humour lay beneath. Claire smiled at him across the table, and asked an obvious question—

"Rather a different meeting-place from our last! Did you know me at once?"

"I did," he said, and added deliberately, "Just as you knew me."

"Oh, well!" Claire tried to look unconcerned. "Men are always pretty much the same. Evening dress does not make the same difference to them."

She knew a momentary fear lest he should believe she was fishing for a compliment, and give the ordinary banal reply; but he looked at her with a grave scrutiny, and asked quietly—

"Was that one of the frocks which went astray?"

"Yes! All of it. It wasn't even divided in half."

"It was a good thing the box turned up!" he said; and there, after all, was the compliment, but so delicately inferred that the most fastidious taste could not object.

With the finishing of the soup came the first reference to Claire's work, for the Captain's casual "Do you care for anything solid, or would you prefer a sweet?" evoked a round-eyed stare of dismay.

"Oh, *please*!" cried Claire deeply. "I want to go straight through. I've been living on mutton and cabbage for over two months, and cooking suppers on a chafing-dish. I looked forward to supper as part of the treat!"

The plain face lightened into a delightful smile.

"That's all right!" he cried. "Now we know where we are. I hadn't much dinner myself, so I'm quite game. Let us study the book of the words."

A *ménu* lay on the table, a square white card emblazoned with many golden words. Captain Fanshawe drew his chair nearer, and ran his finger down the list, while Claire bent forward to signify a yea or nay. Every delicacy in season and out of season seemed to find its place on that list, which certainly justified Master Reginald's eulogy of his mother's "good feeds." Claire found it quite a serious matter to decide between so many good things, and even with various curtailments, made rather out of pride than inclination, the meal threatened to last some considerable time.

Well! there was obvious satisfaction in the manner in which Captain Fanshawe delivered his orders, and for herself, she had been dignified and self-denying; she had

The Independence of Claire

resolutely shut the door between this man and herself, and devoted herself to work, and now, since fate had thrown him in her way for a chance hour, she could enjoy herself with a light mind. It was good to talk to a man again, to hear a deep masculine voice, to look at a broad strong frame. Putting aside all question of love and marriage, the convent life is no more satisfying than the monastic. Each sex was designed by God to be the complement of the other. Each must suffer from lack of the other's companionship.

"I arrived just as you began your performance," Captain Fanshawe informed her. "It was a great 'draw.' Everybody had crowded forward to listen. It was only towards the end of your second—er—how exactly should one express it?—*morceau*, that I managed to get into seeing line. It was a surprise! Have you known the Willoughbys long?"

Claire looked at him blankly.

"I never saw them before to-night. Your mother wrote to ask them if they would send me a card."

"Oh!" Captain Fanshawe was certainly surprised, and Claire mentally snubbed herself because at the bottom of her heart there had lain a suspicion that perhaps—just perhaps—he had come to-night in the hope of meeting his acquaintance of the railway station. This was not the case; no thought of her had been in his mind. Probably until the moment of meeting he had forgotten her existence. Never mind! They *had* met, and he was agreeable and friendly. Now for a delightful half-hour...

"That was a good thought of the *mater's*. You will like them. They are delightful people. Just the people you ought to know as a stranger in town. How goes the school teaching, by the way? As well as you expected?"

Claire deliberated, with pursed lips.

"No. I expected so much; I always do. But much better than other people expected for me. Theoretically it's a fine life. There are times when it seems that nothing could be finer. But—"

"But what?"

"I don't think it's quite satisfying, as a *whole* life!"

"Does anyone suppose it is?"

"They try to. They have to. For most teachers there is so little else."

The waiter handed plates of lobster mayonnaise, and Captain Fanshawe said quietly—

"Tell me about the times when the work seems fine."

"Ah—many times! It depends on one's own mood and health, because, of course, the circumstances are always the same. There are mornings when one looks round a big class-room and sees all the girls' faces looking upwards, and it gives one quite a thrilling sense of power and opportunity. That is what the heaven-born teacher must feel every time.—'Here is the fresh virgin soil, and mine is the joy of planting the right seed! Here are the women of the future, the mothers of the race. For this hour they are mine. What I say, they must hear. They will listen with an attention which even their parents cannot gain. The words which I speak this morning may bear fruit in many lives.' That's the ideal attitude, but the ordinary human woman has other mornings when all she feels is—'Oh, dear me, six hours of this! And what's the use? Everything I batter in to-day will be forgotten by to-morrow. What's the ideal anyway in teaching French verbs? I want to go to bed.'"

They laughed together, but Captain Fanshawe sobered quickly, and his brow showed furrows of distress. Claire looked at him and said quickly—

"Do you mind if we don't talk school? I am Cinderella to-night, wearing fine clothes and supping in state. I'd so much rather talk Cinderella to match."

52

"Certainly, certainly. Just as you wish." Lolling back in his chair, Captain Fanshawe adopted an air of *blasé* indifference, and drawled slowly, "Quite a good winter, isn't it? Lots going on. Have you been to the Opera lately?"

"Oh dear!" thought Claire with a gush, "how refreshing to meet a grown-up man who can pretend like a child!" She simpered, and replied artificially, "Oh, yes—quite often. The dear Duchess is *so* kind; her box is open to me whenever I choose to go. Wonderful scene, isn't it? All those tiers rising one above another. Do you ever look up at the galleries? Such funny people sit there—men in tweed suits; girls in white blouses. Who *are* they, should you think? Clerks and typists and school-mistresses, and people of that persuasion?"

"Possibly, I dare say. One never knows. They look quite respectable and quiet, don't you know!"

The twinkle was alight in Captain Fanshawe's eyes. It shone more brightly still as he added, "Everybody turns up sooner or later in the Duchess's box. Have you happened to meet—the Prince!"

For a moment Claire groped for the connection, then dimpled merrily.

"Not yet. No! but I am hoping—"

The waiter approached with plates of chicken in aspic, and more rolls of crisp browned bread. Claire sent a thought to Cecil finishing a box of sardines, with her book propped up against the cocoa jug. The Cinderella *rôle* was forgotten while her eyes roved around, studying the silver dishes on the various tables.

"When you were a small boy, Captain Fanshawe, did you go out to parties?"

Captain Fanshawe knitted his brows. This charming girl was a little difficult to follow conversationally; she leapt from one subject to another with disconcerting agility.

"Er—pardon me! Is that question put to me in my—er—private, or imaginary capacity?"

"Private, of course. But naturally you did. Did you have pockets?"

"To the best of my remembrance I was disguised as a midshipmite, with white duck trousers of a prodigious width. They used to crackle, I remember. There was room for a dozen pockets."

Claire laid her arms on the table, so that her face drew nearer his own. Her voice fell to a stage whisper—

"Did you—ever—take—something—home?"

The Captain threw back his head with a peal of laughter.

"Miss Gifford, what a question! I was an ordinary human boy. *Of course* I did. And sat on my spoils in the carriage going back, and was scolded for spoiling my clothes. I had a small brother at home."

"Well—I have a small friend! She has letters after her name, and is very learned and clever, but she has a *very* sweet tooth. Do you think, perhaps—in this bag—"

"Leave it to me!" he said firmly, and when the waiter next appeared, he received an order to bring more bon-bons—plenty of bon-bons—a selection of all the small dainties in silver dishes.

"He thinks I *am* having a feast!" Claire said demurely, as she watched the progress of selection; then she met Erskine Fanshawe's eyes, and nodded in response to an unspoken question, "And I *am*! I'm having a lovely time!"

"I wish it were possible that you could oftener—"

"Well, who knows? A week ago I had made up my mind that nothing exciting would ever happen again, and then this invitation arrived. What a perfect dear Miss Willoughby seems to be!"

"Janet? She *is*!" he said warmly. "She is a girl who has had everything the world can give her, and yet has come through unspoiled. It's not often one can say that. Many society girls are selfish and vain, but Janet never seems to think of herself. You'd find her an ideal friend."

Claire's brain leapt swiftly to several conclusions. Janet Willoughby was devoted to Mrs Fanshawe; Mrs Fanshawe returned her devotion. Janet Willoughby was rich, and of good birth. Mrs Fanshawe had mentally adopted her as a daughter-in-law. Given the non-appearance of a rival on the scene, her desire would probably be fulfilled, since such sincere liking could easily ripen into love. Just for a moment Claire felt a stab of that lone and lorn feeling which comes to solitary females at the realisation of another's happiness; then she rallied herself and said regretfully—

"I'm afraid I shan't have the chance! Our lives lie too far apart, and my time is not my own. It is only an occasional Saturday-night that I can play Cinderella."

"What do you do on Sundays?"

"Go to church in the morning, and sleep in the afternoon. Sounds elderly, doesn't it? But I do enjoy that sleep. The hour after lunch is the most trying of the school day. It's all I can do sometimes to smother my yawns, and not upset the whole class. It's part of the Sunday rest to be able to let go, lie down hugging a hot bottle, and sleep steadily till it's time for tea."

"Where do you go to church?"

"Oh!" Claire waved an airy hand, "it depends! I've not settled down. I am still trying which I like best."

Across the table the two pairs of eyes met. The man's questioning, protesting, the girl's steadily defiant. "Why won't you tell me?" came the unspoken question. "Why won't you give me a chance?"

"I am too proud," came the unspoken answer. "Your mother did not think me good enough. I will accept no acquaintance by stealth."

Interruption came in the shape of the waiter bearing a tray of little silver dishes filled with dainties, which he proceeded to arrange in rows on the table. Claire relapsed into giggles at the sight, and Captain Fanshawe took refuge, man-like, in preternatural solemnity; but he made no comment, and the moment that the man had disappeared, both heads craned eagerly to examine the spoils.

"Chocolates, *marrons glacis*, crystallised peaches, French bon-bons, plums. I don't recognise them by head mark. These are too sticky... These look uncommonly good!" The big fingers hovered over each dish in turn, lifting sample specimens, and placing them on Claire's plate, whence they were swiftly conveyed to her bag. Not a single sweetmeat touched her own lips. The unconventionality of the action seemed to receive some justification from the fact that she was confiscating only her own share. When the waiter returned with ices, the little bag bulged suspiciously, and the silver dishes were no longer required. The waiter was ordered to carry them away, and plainly considered that some people did not know what they wanted.

"The only thing lacking is a cracker. I invariably purloined a cracker, and doubled up the ends. I suppose we are hardly near enough to Christmas. By the by, what are you doing for Christmas? You will have holidays, of course," Captain Fanshawe said, with an elaborate unconsciousness, and Claire kept her eyes on her plate.

"I may go to Belgium. I haven't decided."

The Independence of Claire

"There seem to be a good many things you cannot—decide. Miss Gifford, you haven't forgotten what I asked you?"

"What did you ask?"

"That if ever I could help—if you ever needed help—"

"I shall want help badly during the next few weeks, when the examinations come on, and I have all the papers to set and correct."

Captain Fanshawe refused to smile.

"The kind of help that a man can give—"

"Yes, I remember. You were very kind, and I am still so much under the influence of the old life that I do feel you might be a comfort; but no doubt, after some more months of school-mistressing, I shall resent the idea that a man could do any more than I could myself. So it's a case of soon or never. You will hardly be cruel enough to wish to hasten my extremity!"

"I'm not so sure about that, if I could have the satisfaction of putting things to rights!"

It was while she was smiling her acknowledgment of this pretty speech that Claire became conscious of Janet Willoughby's eyes bent searchingly upon her. She had entered the room on the arm of her supper partner, and came to a pause not a yard away from the table where a very animated, apparently very intimate conversation was taking place between the son of her old friend and the girl to whom she had believed him to be unknown. As she met Claire's glance, Janet smiled automatically, but the friendliness was gone from her glance. The next moment Captain Fanshawe, had turned, seen her, and sprung to his feet.

"Janet! Are you waiting for a table? We have nearly finished. Won't you sit down and talk to Miss Gifford?"

"Oh, please don't hurry... We'll find another place. You have met before, then? I didn't know."

"I saw Miss Gifford when she was befriending my mother at Liverpool Street Station, and recognised her upstairs just now. Do sit down, Janet. You look tired."

Janet Willoughby took the offered chair and exchanged a few words with Claire as she gathered together her possessions, but the subtle change persisted. Claire felt vaguely disturbed, but the next half-hour passed so pleasantly that she had no time to puzzle over the explanation. Captain Fanshawe never left her side; they sat together on the same sofa which Great-aunt Jane had monopolised for the earlier part of the evening, and talked of many things, and discussed many problems, and sometimes agreed, and oftener disagreed, and when they disagreed most widely, looked into each other's eyes and smiled, as who should say, "What do words matter? We understand!"

At one o'clock Claire rose to depart, and said her adieu to her hostess and her daughter, who were standing side by side.

"My dear, it is too bad. I have had *no* time with you, and I am so grateful for the charming way in which you came to the rescue! We shall hope to see you often again. Shan't we, Janet? You girls must arrange a day which suits you both."

"Oh, yes, we must!" Janet said, as she shook hands, but she made no attempt to make the arrangement there and then, as her mother obviously expected, and Claire realised, with a sinking of the heart, that a promised friendship had received a check.

When she descended to the hall wrapped in her filmy cloak it was to find Captain Fanshawe waiting at the foot of the stairs. He looked worried and grave, and the front door was reached before he made the first remark. Then, lingering tentatively on the threshold, he looked down at her with a searching glance.

"Is—er—is your address still the Grand Hotel?"

Claire's face set into firm lines.

"Still the Grand Hotel!"

For a moment he looked her steadily in the eyes, then said quietly—

"And my address is still the Carlton Club!" He bowed, and turned into the house.

The footman banged the door of the taxi, and stood awaiting instructions.

"T–wenty-two, Laburnum Crescent," said Claire weakly. Halfway through the words a sudden obstacle arose in her throat. It was all she could do to struggle through. She hoped to goodness the footman did not notice.

"There now! what did I tell you? You look fagged to death, and as cross as two sticks. Five shillings wasted on taxis, and nothing for it but getting thoroughly upset. Next time I hope you will take my advice!" said Cecil, and took up her candle to grope her way up the dark stairway to bed.

Chapter Ten.

Nowhere to go.

Cecil's observance of her day of licenced grumbling was somewhat obstructed by the fact that for several weeks after Mrs Willoughby's At Home, Monday mornings found her in a condition of excitement and gaiety. It was a restless gaiety, which seemed to spring rather from the head than the heart, and Claire looking on with puzzled eyes had an instinct that her companion was assiduously whipping up her own spirits, playing the part of happiness with all her force, with the object of convincing the most critical of all audiences—her own heart! Life was a lonely thing to Claire in these days, for Cecil went out regularly every Saturday and Sunday, returning so late that the two girls did not meet from lunch one day until breakfast the next. She vouchsafed no explanation of her sudden plunge into society, neither beforehand when she sat stitching at pathetic little pieces of finery, nor afterwards when letting herself in with her latch-key she crept slowly to bed, never deigning to enter Claire's room for one of those "tell-all-about-it" *séances* dear to a girl's heart.

It was the sight of those pathetic little pieces of finery which first suggested the idea of a man to Claire's mind. However dear and intimate a woman friend may be, the prospect of meeting her does not inspire a fellow-woman with sufficient energy to sit up until after midnight to cover a shabby lace blouse with ninon, or to put a new silk collar and cuffs on a half-worn coat. It is only the prospect of meeting the eyes of some male creature, who in all probability will remain supremely unconscious of the result, which stimulates such effort, and Claire, noting Cecil's restless excitement, cast anxious thoughts towards the particular man in this case.

Was Sophie Blake correct in her deduction as to a previous unhappy romance? Claire had no tangible grounds to lead her to a conclusion, but instinct induced her to agree. Something beyond the troubles of her professional life had gone towards warping a nature that was naturally generous and warm. In imagination Claire lived over the pitiful romance. Poor Cecil had been badly treated. Some selfish man had made love to her, amusing his idle hours with the society of a pretty, clever woman; he had never seriously intended marriage, but Cecil had believed in his sincerity, had given him her whole heart, had dreamt dreams which had turned the grey of life to gold.

And then had come the end. How had the end come? Some day when they were walking together, had he suddenly announced: "I am sailing to India next month!" or, "We have been such capital friends, you and I. I should like you to be the first to hear my news. I am engaged to be married to the dearest girl in the world!" Then, because convention decrees that when her heart is wounded a woman may make no moan, had Cecil twisted her lips into a smile, and cried, "I am so glad to hear it. I hope you will be very happy," while the solid earth rocked around her? At such thoughts as these Claire flared with righteous anger. "If that should ever happen to me, I wouldn't pretend! I wouldn't spare him. I should look him straight in the face, and say, 'And all this time you have been pretending to love me.—I thank God that it *was* pretence. I thank God that He has preserved me from being the wife of man who could act a double part!'"

But perhaps there had been no real ending. Perhaps the man had simply grown tired, and ceased to call, ceased to write. Oh, surely that would be the greatest tragedy of all! Claire's quick brain summoned pictures of Cecil creeping down the oil-clothed stairs in her dressing-gown at the sound of the postman's earliest knock, and creeping back with no letter in her hand; of Cecil entering the little parlour on her return from work with a swift hungry look at the table on which the day's letters were displayed; seeing no letter lying there; never, never the letter for which she watched! And the days would pass, and the weeks, and the months, and the old routine of life would go on just the same. Whatever might be her private sufferings, the English mistress must be at her post each morning at nine o'clock; she must wrestle all day with the minds of dull girls, listless girls, clever girls, girls who were eager to learn, and girls whose energies seemed condensed in the effort to avoid learning at all. However sore might be the English mistress's heart, it was her duty to be bright and alert; however exhausted her own stock of patience, she must still be a female Job in her treatment of her many pupils. A schoolmistress must banish her individuality as a woman on the threshold of the form-room; while on duty she must banish every outside interest from her mind. No lying in bed, with her face to the pillow; no weeping far into the night. Headache and swollen eyelids are not for her. If her love-story goes wrong, she must lock her sorrow in her own heart. What wonder if, as a result, her mind grows bitter and her tongue grows sharp!

"That's a lesson for me! I must never, never allow myself to fall in love!" sighed Claire to herself. It was a depressing necessity, but vaguely she allowed herself to dream of a distant Someday, when the ban should be removed. Something might happen to set her free. Something most certainly *would* happen! Optimistic one-and-twenty is ready enough to face a short term of renunciation, but it resolutely refuses to believe in its continuance.

A shadow fell over Claire's happy face as the practical application of this resolve came into her mind. Erskine Fanshawe! At the moment he was the one masculine figure on her horizon, but she did not disguise from herself that of all the men she had met, he attracted her the most. What a mercy that she had had the resolution to put a stop to a friendship which might have ended in unfitting her for the work in hand! It had been hard to refuse the desired information, but the fact that the second refusal had been twice as hard as the first was in itself a proof of the wisdom of her decision. And then, in illogical girlish fashion, Claire fell to wondering if perchance Captain Fanshawe would discover her address for himself? It would be the easiest of tasks, since he had nothing to do but to put the question to Mrs Willoughby. At one moment Claire openly hoped that he would; at the next she recalled the expression on Janet Willoughby's face as she stood staring across the supper room, and then she was not so sure. What if the continuance of the friendship brought trouble on Janet as well as herself?

Laboriously Claire thrust the thought of Erskine Fanshawe from her mind, but just because inclination would have led her to so blithely meet him, she felt a keener sympathy with her companion's preparations for similar meetings.

The time of examinations had come, and night after night the dining-table of the little parlour was littered with the sheets of foolscap which were to test the progress of the pupils throughout the term. Cecil's older forms had been studying *The Merchant of Venice, Richard the Second*, and the *Essays of Elia*; the younger forms, *Tanglewood Tales* and Kingsley's *Heroes*. She had set the questions not only as a test of memory, but with a view of drawing out original thought. But, to judge from her groans and lamentations, the result was poor.

"Of all the dull, stupid, unimaginative—*sheep*! Not an original idea between them. Every answer exactly like the last—a hash-up of my own remarks in class. If there's a creature on earth I despise more than another, it's an English flapper. Silly, vain, egotistical—"

Then the French mistress would scowl across the table, and say, "Now you've put me out! I was just counting up my marks. Oh, do be quiet!"

"Sorry!" Cecil would say shortly, and taking up her pencil slash scathing comments at the side of the foolscap sheets. Anon she would smile, and smile again, and forgetting Claire's request, would interrupt once more.

"Can you remember the name of Florence Mason?"

"If I strain my intellect to its utmost, I believe I can."

"Well, remember, then! It will be worth while. She'll do something—that girl. When you are an insignificant old woman, you may be proud to boast that you used to sit at the very table on which her first English essays were corrected."

"So they are not all dull, stupid, unimaginative?"

"The exception proves the rule!" cried Cecil, and swept the papers together with a sigh of relief. "Done at last. Now for my blouse."

Claire cast a glance at the clock.

"Half-past ten. And you are so tired. Surely you won't begin to sew at this hour?"

"I must. I want it for Saturday. I tried it on last night, and it wasn't a bit nice at the neck. I've got to alter it somehow."

"I have some trimming upstairs. Just be quiet for five minutes, while I finish my list, and then I'll bring down my scrap-box, and we'll see what we can find."

That scrap-box was in constant request during the next weeks. It was filled with the dainty oddments which a woman of means and taste collects in the course of years; trimmings and laces, and scraps of fine brocades; belts and buckles, and buttons of silver and paste; glittering ends of tinsel, ends of silk and ribbons that were really too pretty to throw away, and cunning little motifs which had the magic quality of disguising deficiencies and making both ends meet. Claire gave with a lavish hand, and Cecil's gratitude was pathetic in its intensity. More and more as the weeks passed on did she become obsessed with the craze for decking herself in fine garments; new gloves, shoes, and veils were purchased to supplement the home-made garments, and one memorable night there arrived a large dress-box containing an evening dress and cloak.

"I have been out so little these last years. I have no clothes to wear," Cecil said in explanation. "It's not fair to—er—people, when they take you about, to look as if you had come out of the Ark... And these ready-made things are *so* cheap!"

She spoke with an air of excusing herself, and with a flush of embarrassment on her cheeks, and Claire hastened to sympathise and agree. She wondered if the embarrassment arose from the fact that for the last two weeks Cecil had not paid her share of the joint expenses! The omission had happened naturally enough, for on each occasion when the landlady appeared with the bill, Cecil had been absent on one of her now frequent excursions, when it had seemed the simplest thing to settle in full, and await repayment next day.

Repayment, however, had not come. Half a dozen times over Cecil had exclaimed, "Oh, dear, there's that money. I *must* remember!" but apparently she never had remembered at a moment when her purse was at hand.

Claire was honestly indifferent. The hundred pounds which she had deposited in a bank was considerably diminished, since it had been drawn on for all her needs, but the term's salary would be paid in a short time, and the thought of that, added to the remainder, gave her a pleasant feeling of ease. It was only when for the third Saturday Cecil hurried off with an air of fluster and embarrassment, that an unpleasant suspicion arose. The weekly bill was again due, and Cecil had not forgotten, she was only elaborately pretending to forget! Claire was not angry, she was perfectly willing to play the part of banker until the end of the term, but she hated the thought that Cecil was acting a part, and deliberately trying to deceive. What if she had been extravagant in her expenditure on clothes and had run herself short for necessary expenses, there was nothing criminal in that! Foolish it might be, but a fellow-girl would understand that, after being staid and sensible for a long, long time, it was a blessed relief to the feminine mind to have a little spell of recklessness for a change. Cecil had only to say, "I've run myself horribly short. Can you pay up till I get my screw?" and the whole matter would have been settled in a trice. But to pretend to forget was so *mean*!

The next morning after breakfast the vexed question of the Christmas holidays came up for discussion for the twentieth time. Cecil had previously stated that she always spent the time with her mother, but it now appeared that to a certain extent she had changed her plans.

"I shall have to go down over Christmas Day and the New Year, I suppose. Old people make such a fuss over those stupid anniversaries, but I shall come up again on the second. I prefer to be in town. We have to pay for the rooms in any case, so we may as well use them."

Claire's face lengthened.

"*Pay* for them! Even if we go away?"

"Of course. What did you expect? The landlady isn't let off her own rent, because we choose to take a holiday. There's no saving except for the light and coal. By the way, I owe you for a third week now. I *must* remember! Have you decided what you are going to do?"

Claire shook her head. It was a forlorn feeling that Christmas was coming, and she had nowhere to go. Until now she had gone on in faith, feeling sure that before the time arrived, some one would remember her loneliness, and invite her if only for the day itself. Possibly Cecil in virtue of three months' daily companionship would ask her mother's permission to invite her friend, if only for a couple of days. Or bright, friendly Sophie Blake, who had sympathised with her loneliness, might have some proposition to make, or Mrs Willoughby, who was so interested in girls who were working for themselves, or Miss Farnborough, who knew that it was the French mistress's first Christmas without her mother; but no such suggestion had been made. No one seemed to care.

"I must say it's *strange* that no one has invited you!" said Cecil sharply. "I don't think much of your grand friends if they can't look after you on Christmas Day. What about the people in Brussels? Did no one send you an invitation? If you lived there for three years, surely you must know some one intimately enough to offer to go, even if they don't suggest it."

"It is not necessary, thank you," said Claire with an air. "I have an open invitation to several houses, but I am saving up Brussels for Easter, when the weather will be better, and it will be more of a change. And I have an old grand-aunt in the North, but she is an invalid, confined to her room. I should be an extra trouble in the house. I shall manage to amuse myself somehow. It will be an opportunity for exploring London."

"Oh well," Cecil said vaguely, "when I come back!" but she spoke no word of Christmas Day.

The next week brought the various festivities with which Saint Cuthbert's celebrated the end of the Christmas term. There was a school dance in the big class-room, a Christmas-tree party, given to the children in an East End parish, and last and most important of all the breaking-up ceremony in the local Town Hall, when an old girl, now developed into a celebrated authoress, presented the prizes, and gave an amusing account of her own schooldays, which evoked storms of applause from the audience, even Miss Farnborough smiling benignly at the recital of misdoings which would have evoked her sternest displeasure on the part of present-day pupils! Then the singing-class girls sang a short cantata, and the eldest girls gave a scene from Shakespeare, very dull and exceedingly correct, and the youngest girls acted a little French play, while the French mistress stood in the wings, ready to prompt, her face very hot, and her feet very cold, and her heart beating at express speed.

This moment was a public test of her work during the term, and she had a horror that the children would forget their parts and disgrace their leader as well as themselves. She need not have feared, however, for the publicity which she dreaded was just the stimulus needed to spur the juvenile actors to do their very best, and they shrugged, they gesticulated, they rolled their r's, they reproduced Claire's own little mannerisms with an *aplomb* which brought down the house. Claire's lack of teaching experience might make her less sound on rules and routine, but it was obvious that she had succeeded in one important point; she had lifted "French" from the level of a task, and converted it into a living tongue.

Miss Farnborough was very gracious in her parting words to her new mistress.

"I have not come to my present position without learning to trust my perceptions," said she. "I recognised at once that you possessed the true teaching instinct, and to-day you have justified my choice. I have had many congratulations on your pupils' performance." Then she held out her hand with a charming smile. "I hope you will have very pleasant holidays!"

She made no inquiries as to the way in which this young girl was to spend her leisure. She herself was worn-out with the strain of the long term, and when the morrow came she intended to pack her bag, and start off for a sunny Swiss height, where for the next few weeks it would be her chief aim to forget that she had ever seen a school. But the new French mistress turned away with a heavy heart. It seemed at that moment as if nobody cared.

That year Christmas fell on a Monday. On the Saturday morning Cecil packed up her bag, and departed, grumbling, for her week at home. Before she left, Claire presented her with a Christmas gift in the shape of a charming embroidered scarf, and Cecil kissed her, and flushed, and looked at the same time pleased and oppressed, and hastily pulling out her purse extracted two sovereigns and laid them down on the table.

"I keep forgetting that money! Three weeks, wasn't it? There's two pounds; let me know the rest when I come back and I'll settle up. Christmas is an awful time. The money simply melts."

Claire had an uncomfortable and wholly unreasonable feeling of being paid for her present as she put the two sovereigns in her purse. Cecil had given her no gift, and the

The Independence of Claire

lack of the kindly attention increased the feeling of desolation with which she returned to her empty room. Even the tiniest offering to show that she had been thought of, would have been a comfort!

The landlady came into the room to remove the luncheon tray, her lips pursed into an expression which her lodger recognised as the preliminary to "a bit of my mind." When the outlying cruets and dishes had been crowded together in a perilous pile, the bit of her mind came out.

"I was going to say, miss, that of course you will arrange to dine out on Christmas Day. I never take ladies as a rule, but Miss Rhodes, she said, being teachers, you would be away all holiday time. I never had a lodger before who stayed in the house over Christmas, and of course you must understand that we go over to Highgate to my mother's for the day and the girl goes out, and I couldn't possibly think of cooking—"

"Don't be afraid, Mrs Mason. I am going out for the day."

Mrs Mason lifted the tray and carried it out of the room, shutting the door behind her by the skilful insertion of a large foot encased in a cashmere boot, and Claire stood staring at her, wondering if it were really her own voice which had spoken those last words, and from what source had sprung the confidence which had suddenly flooded her heart. At this last blow of all, when even the little saffron-coloured parlour closed the door against her, the logical course would have been to collapse into utter despair, instead of which the moment had brought the first gleam of hope.

"Now," said the voice in her heart, "everyone has failed me. I am helpless, I am alone. This is God's moment. I will worry no more, but leave it to Him. Something will open for me when the time arrives!"

She went upstairs, put on her hat, and sallied out into the busy streets. All the world was abroad, men and women and small eager children all bent on the same task, thronging the shops to the doors, waiting in rows for the favour of being served, emerging triumphant with arms laden with spoils. On every side fragments of the same conversation floated to the ears. "What can I get for Kate?"

"I can't think what in the world to buy for John."

"Do try to give me an idea what Rose would like!..."

Claire mingled with the throng, pushed her way towards the crowded counters, waited a preposterous time for her change, and then hurried off to another department to go through the same struggle once more. Deliberately she threw herself into the Christmas feeling, turning her thoughts from herself, considering only how she could add to the general happiness. She bought presents for everybody, for the cross landlady, for the untidy servant girl, for Sophie Blake, and Flora Ross, for the maid at Saint Cuthbert's who waited upon the Staff-Room, with a selection of dainty oddments for girl friends at Brussels, and when the presents themselves had been secured she bought prettily tinted paper, and fancy ribbons, and decorated name cards for the adornment of the parcels.

The saffron parlour looked quite Christmas-like that evening, and Claire knew a happy hour as she made up her gifts in their dainty wrappings. They looked so gay and seasonable that she decided to defer putting them into the sober outer covering of brown paper as long as possible. They were all the Christmas decoration she would have!

On Sunday morning the feeling of loneliness took an acute turn. Claire longed for a church which long association had made into a home; for a clergyman who was also a friend; for a congregation of people who knew her, and cared for her well-being, instead of the long rows of strange faces. She remembered how Cecil had declared that in London a girl might attend the same church for years on end, and never hear a word of welcome, and hope died low in her breast. The moment of exaltation had passed, and she told herself drearily that on Christmas afternoon she must take a book and sit by the fire in the waiting-room of some great station, dine at a restaurant, and perhaps go to a concert at night.

For weeks past Claire had been intending to go to a West End church to hear one of the finest of modern preachers. She decided to go this morning, since the length of journey now seemed rather an advantage than a drawback, as helping to fill up another of the long, dragging hours.

She dressed herself with the care and nicety which was the result of her French training, and which had of late become almost a religious duty, for the study of the fifteen women who daily assembled round the table in the Staff-Room was as a danger signal to warn new-comers of the perils ahead. With the one exception of Sophie Blake, not one of the number seemed to make any effort to preserve their feminine charm. They dressed their hair in the quickest and easiest fashion without considering the question of appearance; they wore dun-coloured garments with collars of the same material; though severely neat, all their skirts seemed to suffer from the same depressing tendency to drop at the back; their bony wrists emerged from tightly-buttoned sleeves. The point of view adopted was that appearance did not matter, that it was waste of time to consider the adornment of the outer woman. Brain was the all-important factor; every possible moment must be devoted to the cultivation of brain; but an outsider could not fail to note that, with this destroying of a natural instinct, something which went deeper than the surface was also lost; with the grace of the body certain feminine graces of soul died also, and the world was poorer for their loss.

The untidy servant maid peered out of the window to watch Claire as she left the house that morning, and evolved a whole feuilleton to account for the inconsistency of her appearance with her position as a first floor front. "You'd take her for a lady to look at her! P'raps she *is* a lady in disguise!" and from, this point the making of the feuilleton began.

The service that morning was food to Claire's hungering soul, for the words of the preacher might have been designed to meet her own need. As she listened she realised that the bitterness of loneliness was impossible to one who believed and trusted in the great, all-compassing love. Sad one might still be, so long as the human heart demanded a human companionship, but the sting of feeling uncared for, could never touch a child of God. She took the comfort home to her heart, and stored it there to help her through the difficult time ahead, and on her knees at the end of the service she sent up her own little petition for help.

"There are so many homes in this great city! Is there no home for me on Christmas Day?" With the words the tears sprang, and Claire mopped her eyes with her handkerchief, thankful that she was surrounded by strangers by whom her reddened eyes would pass unnoticed. Then rising to her feet, she turned to lift the furs which hung on the back of the pew, and met the brown eyes of a girl who had been sitting behind her the whole of the service.

The girl was Janet Willoughby.

Chapter Eleven.

Enter Major Carew.

In the street outside the church door the two girls shook hands and exchanged greetings. Janet wore a long fur coat, and a toque of dark Russian sable, with a sweeping feather at one side. The price of these two garments alone would equal the whole of

The Independence of Claire

Claire's yearly salary, but it had the effect of making the wearer look clumsy and middle-aged compared with the graceful simplicity of the other's French-cut costume. Janet Willoughby was not thinking of clothes at that moment, however; she was looking at reddened eyelids, and remembering the moment when she had seen a kneeling figure suddenly shaken with emotion. The sight of those tears had wiped away the rankling grudge which had lain at her heart since the evening of her mother's At Home, and revived the warm liking which at first sight she had taken to this pretty attractive girl.

"Which way are you going? May I walk with you? It's just the morning for a walk. I hope it will keep cold and bright over Christmas. It's so inappropriate when it's muggy. Last year we were in Switzerland, but mother is old-fashioned, and likes to have the day at home, so this time we don't start till the new year. You are not going sporting by any chance?"

"I'm not!" said Claire, and, for all her determination, could not resist a grimace, so far from sporting seemed the prospect ahead. Janet caught the grimace, and smiled in sympathy, but the next moment her face sobered.

"But I hope you *are* going to have jolly holidays?"

"Oh, I hope so. Oh, yes, I mean to enjoy them very much," Claire said valiantly, and swiftly turned the subject. "Where do you go in Switzerland?"

"Saint Moritz. We've gone there for years—a large party of friends. It has become quite a yearly reunion. It's so comfy to have one's own party, and be independent of the other hoteliers. They may be quite nice, of course, but then, again, they may not. I feel rather mean sometimes when I see a new arrival looking with big eyes at our merry table. Theoretically, I think one *ought* to be nice to new-comers in an hotel. It's such a pelican-in-the-wilderness feeling. I'd hate it myself, but practically I'm afraid I'm not particularly friendly. We are so complete that we don't want outsiders. They'd spoil the fun. Don't you think one is justified in being a little bit selfish at Christmas-time?"

Claire laughed, her old, happy, gurgling laugh. It warmed her heart to have Janet Willoughby's companionship once more.

"It isn't exactly the orthodox attitude, is it? Perhaps you will be more justified this year, after you have got through your Christmas duties at home."

"Yes! That's a good idea. I *shall*, for it was pure unselfishness which prevented me running away last week with the rest of the party. Mother would have given in if I'd persisted, and I wanted to so dreadfully badly." She sighed, and looked quite dejected, but Claire remained unmoved.

"I don't pity you one bit. You have only a week to wait. That's not a great trial of patience!"

"Oh, yes, it is.—Sometimes!" said Janet with an emphasis which gave the words an added eloquence.

Claire divined at once that Switzerland had an attraction apart from winter sports—an attraction centred in some individual member of the merry party. Could it by any chance be Erskine Fanshawe? She longed to ask the question. Not for a hundred pounds would she have asked the question. She hoped it was Captain Fanshawe. She hoped Janet would have a lovely time. Some girls had everything. Some had nothing. It was unfair—it was cruel. Oh, dear, what was the use of going to church, and coming out to have such mean, grudging thoughts? Janet Willoughby too! Such a dear! She deserved to be happy. Claire forced a smile, and said bravely—

"It will be all the nicer for waiting."

"It couldn't be nicer," Janet replied.

Then she looked in the other girl's face, and it struck her that the pretty eyelids had taken an additional shade of red, and her warm heart felt a throb of compunction. "Grumbling about my own little bothers, when she had so much to bear—hateful of me! I've been mean not to ask her again; mother wanted to; but she's so pretty. I admired her so much that I was afraid—other people might too! But she was crying; I saw her cry. Perhaps she is lonely, and it's my fault—"

"What do you generally do on Sundays?" she asked aloud. "There are lots of other mistresses at your school, aren't there? I suppose you go about together, and have tea at each other's rooms in the afternoon, and sit over the fire at night and talk, and brew cocoa, as the girls do in novels. It all sounds so interesting. The girls are generally rather plain and very learned; but there is always one among them who is like you. I don't mean that you are not learned—I'm sure you are—but—er—pretty, you know, and attractive, and fond of things! And all the others adore her, and are jealous if she is nicer to one than to the others..."

Claire grimaced again, more unrestrainedly than before.

"That's not my part. I wish it were. I could play it quite well. The other mistresses are quite civil and pleasant, but they don't hanker after me one bit. With two exceptions, the girl I live with, and one other, I have not spoken to one of them out of school hours. I don't even know where most of them live."

Janet's face lengthened. Suddenly she turned and asked a sharp direct question:

"Where are you going on Christmas Day?"

Pride and weakness struggled together in Claire's heart, and pride won. She would *not* pose as an object of pity!

"Oh, I'm going—out!" said she with an air, but Janet Willoughby was not to be put off so easily as that. Her brown eyes sent out a flash of light. She demanded sternly:

"Where?"

"Really—" Claire tossed her head with the air of a duchess who was so overburdened with invitations that she found it impossible to make a choice between them. "Really, don't you know, I haven't quite decided—"

"Claire Gifford, you mean, horrid girl, don't dare to quibble! You are going nowhere, and you know it. Nobody has invited you for Christmas Day; that's why you were crying just now—because you had nowhere to go. And you would have gone away this morning, and said nothing, and sat alone in your rooms... I call it *mean*! Talk of the spirit of Christmas! It's an insult to me and to mother. How do you suppose we should have felt if we'd found out *afterwards*?"

"W—what else could I do? How could I tell you?" stammered Claire, blushing. "It would have seemed such a barefaced *hint*, and I detest hints. And really why should you have felt bad? I'm a stranger. You've only seen me once. There could be no blame on you. There's no blame on anyone. It just happens that it doesn't quite fit in to visit friends at a distance, and in town—well! I'm a stranger, you see. I *have* no friends!"

Janet set her lips.

"Just as a matter of curiosity I should like to know exactly what you *were* going to do? You said, I believe, that you were going out. And now you say you had nowhere to go. Both statements can't be true—"

"Oh, yes, they can. I have nowhere to go, but I had to find somewhere, because my good landlady is going to her mother's at Highgate, and disapproves of lodgers who stay in on Christmas Day. She gave me notice that I must go out as the house would be locked up."

"But where—what—where *could* you go?"

"I thought of a restaurant and a concert, and a station waiting-room to fill in the gaps. Quite comfortable, you know. They have lovely fires, and with a nice book—"

"If you don't stop this minute I shall begin to cry—here, in the open street!" cried Janet hotly. "Oh, you poor dear, you poor dear! A station waiting-room. I never heard of anything so piteous. Oh, how thankful I am that I met you! Tell me honestly, was it about that that you were crying?"

"Y–yes, it was. I was saying a little prayer and trying not to feel lonesome, and then I looked round and saw—you."

"End of volume one!" cried Janet briskly. "No more waiting-rooms, my dear. You must come to us for the whole of Christmas Day. I wish I could ask you to stay, but we are chock-a-block with cousins and aunts. I'll come round in my car in time to take you to church, and send you back at night after the Highgate revels are over. We can't offer you anything very exciting, I'm afraid—just an old-fashioned homey gathering."

"It's just what I want. I am thirsty for a home; but your mother—what will she say? Will she care for a stranger—"

"Mother says what I say," Janet declared with the assurance of an only daughter. "And she'll say in addition, 'What a blessing! She'll whistle for us, and amuse Aunt Jane.' Did you realise that Aunt Jane was coming? She's generally *very* cross all day, and makes a point of giving away her presents to other members of the party under the very noses of the givers, to let them see what she thinks of their choice. The great idea is to sit down by her quickly when you see her begin to fumble with something you would like to have. I got quite a nice bag that way last Christmas!"

Presents! That was another idea. Claire went home mentally reviewing her own treasures with a view to selecting some trifle which Janet in the midst of her plenty might still be glad to receive. She decided on a silver clasp of quaint Breton manufacture, which had the merit that in the whole of London it would be impossible to purchase another to match.

Claire returned to her room in a frame of mind vastly different from that in which she had started forth. Her buoyant spirits soared upwards at the prospect of a Christmas spent in the midst of a happy family party, and all the difficulties of life seemed to dissolve into thin air, since, after the providential meeting just vouchsafed, it seemed faithless to doubt that future difficulties would be solved in the same way.

She intended to devote the afternoon to writing a long letter to her mother, which had been delayed owing to her recent depression of spirits, for it seemed cruel to write in a pessimistic strain to the happy bride, who now, more than ever, saw everything *couleur de rose*. Mrs Judge's present had arrived the week before, in the shape of a richly embroidered Indian table-cloth, for which her daughter had as much use as she herself would have found for a fur rug. To use it in the saffron parlour was a sheer impossibility, for every separate article of furniture shrieked at it, and it shrieked at them in return; so Claire folded it away at the bottom of her box, reflecting, between a sigh and a smile, that the choice was "just like mother." It was not agreeable to the bride to picture her daughter living in an ugly lodging-house parlour, so she had mentally covered the ugliness beneath the gorgeous embroidery of that cloth, and happily dismissed the subject from her mind. At the time of the opening of the parcel, Claire had felt a sense of sharp disappointment, amounting even to irritation, but this morning she could see the humour of the situation, and she chuckled softly to herself as she walked homeward, rehearsing words of thanks that would be at once cordial and truthful. "Just what I wanted," was plainly out of the question; "So useful" was also ruled out, but she could honestly admire the workmanship of the cloth, and enlarge on the care with which it should be preserved! It was an easy

The Independence of Claire

task to satisfy a correspondent who was eager to interpret words into the meaning most agreeable to herself!

Claire entered the house prepared to devote herself to writing letters to absent friends, but the excitements of the day were not yet over, for the little maid met her on the threshold with the exciting intelligence that a gentleman was in the parlour waiting to see her.

The feuilleton made an exciting leap forward, as Lizzie watched the blood rush into the "first floor's" cheeks, and ebb away suddenly, leaving her white and tense. "Struck all of a heap, like! I shouldn't have thought meself as she'd look at him! Queer thing, love!" soliloquised Lizzie, as she clumped down the kitchen stairs, and returned to her superintendence of Sunday's "jint."

The "first floor" meanwhile stood motionless in the oil-clothed hall, struggling to regain self-possession before turning the handle of the door. A gentleman waiting to see her! Who could the gentleman be? But at the bottom of her heart Claire believed the question to be superfluous, for there was only one "gentleman" who could possibly come. Captain Fanshawe had found out her address, and it was Christmas-time, when a visitor was justified in counting on a hospitable reception. At Christmas-time it would be churlish for a hostess to deny a welcome. Every pulse in Claire's body was throbbing with anticipation as she flung open that door.

The visitor was standing with his back towards her, bending low to examine a photograph on the mantelpiece. At the sound of her entrance he straightened himself and wheeled round, and at the sight of his face Claire's heart dropped heavy as lead. They stood for a moment staring in a mutual surprise, the girl's face blank with disappointment, the man's brightening with interest.

He was a tall, thickly-set man, trim and smart in his attire, yet with a coarseness of feature which aroused Claire's instant antagonism. Compared with the face she had expected to see, the florid good looks which confronted her were positively repugnant. Before the obvious admiration of the black eyes she stiffened in displeasure.

"You wished to see me?"

"Miss Gifford, I believe! I called about a little matter of a parcel for Miss Rhodes. To be sent on. I wanted to ask if you—"

"Oh, certainly! I shall be delighted."

Claire thawed at the prospect of a present for Cecil, but could it be possible that it was this man with the flushed cheeks, and harsh, uncultivated voice, who had so revolutionised Cecil's life! Could it be for the delectation of those bold eyes that she had worked far into the night, contriving her pitiful fineries? Claire's instinctive dislike was so strong that she would not seat herself and so give an opportunity for prolonging the interview; she crossed the room to a bureau that stood in the corner, and took a slip of paper from one of the pigeon-holes.

"Perhaps it would be simpler if I gave you the address?"

The man laughed complacently.

"No need, thank you, I've got it all right, but it's safer not to write. The old lady, you know! Parcel coming in for her daughter addressed in a man's writing—no end of fuss and questioning. You know what old ladies are! Never satisfied till they've ferreted to the bottom of everything that comes along. It's not good enough, that sort of thing, but she'll expect a present. It's all stamped and made up, if you'll be good enough just to address it, and slip it into the post to-morrow."

He put his hand in his pocket as he spoke and drew out a little package some two inches square, the sort of package which might contain an article of jewellery, such as a brooch or ring. Could it by any chance be an engagement ring? Claire's blood shuddered as she took the little packet and dropped it quietly on the bureau.

"Certainly I will post it. Do you wish it registered?"

He looked at her sharply as though suspicious of an under-meaning to the inquiry, then, meeting the glance of her clear eyes, had the grace to look ashamed.

"N–no. No! It is not worth while. A trifle, just a trifle—Christmas, you know—must do the proper thing!" He mumbled vaguely the while he collected his hat and gloves, the aloofness in Claire's attitude making it impossible to prolong the interview; but as he held out his hand in farewell, his self-possession returned. He laughed meaningly, and said—

"Odd, you know; I imagined that you were quite old! Miss Rhodes gave me that impression. Nothing definite, you know; no false statements; just the way she spoke. Clever of her, what?—very clever! Knew better than to spoil her own game!"

If looks could have slain, the saffron parlour would have seen a dead man at that moment. Claire withdrew her hand, and surreptitiously rubbed it against her skirt. She would not condescend to notice that last remark.

"I'll post the parcel to-morrow. Perhaps you will tell me your name, as I shall have to explain."

He drew out a pocket-book and extracted a card. Claire dropped it unread upon the table, and bowed stiffly in farewell. The next moment he was gone, and she could satisfy her curiosity unseen. Then came surprise number two, for the card bore the inscription, "Major J.F. Carew," and in the corner two well-remembered words, "Carlton Club." An officer in the Army—who would have thought it! He was emphatically not a gentleman; he was rough, coarse, mannerless, yet he was in a position which would bring him into intimate association with gentle people; by a strange coincidence, he might know, he almost certainly would know, the man whom she had expected to see in his stead—Erskine Fanshawe himself! They could never be friends, but they would meet, they would sit in the same rooms, they would exchange occasional remarks. Claire's mood of intolerable disgust changed suddenly into something strangely approaching envy of this big rough man! Christmas morning brought Janet bright and early, to find Claire standing at the window ready to rush out the moment the car stopped at the door. It felt delightfully luxurious to seat herself on the springy cushions, draw the fur rug over her knees, and feel the warmth of a hot tin beneath her feet.

"*Wasn't* it lacerating?" Janet cried. "Just as I was starting the parcel post arrived, and there were about half-a-dozen parcels for me from Saint Moritz! There was no time to open them, and I simply die to know what's inside. I care about those presents more than anything else. We had our family presents this morning. Mother gave me this." She opened her coat to show a glittering crescent. "Quite pretty, isn't it, but I'd rather have had pearls. That's the worst of Christmas presents, you so seldom get what you want. Half the time you feel more disappointed than pleased. People cling to the idea that they ought to give you a surprise, and you *are* surprised, but not in the way they expect. I have given mother thousands of hints about pearls. Ah, well!" She hooked the coat with an air of resignation. "We must take the will for the deed. Have you had nice things?"

"My mother sent me a very handsome present," Claire said demurely. She had no personal agitations about the day's post; but she did feel interested in the thought of those parcels from Switzerland which lay awaiting Janet Willoughby's return. Half eager, half shrinking, she looked forward to seeing their contents.

It was in Janet's dainty boudoir that the unpacking took place. The two girls went straight upstairs on their return from church, and there, on a gate-legged table, lay the pile of parcels which had arrived by the morning's delivery. Janet pounced upon the Swiss packets, and cut the fastenings with eager haste. From across the room Claire watched her eager face as she read the inscriptions one by one. As she neared the end of the pile, the eagerness became tinged with anxiety; she picked up the last parcel of all, and the light died out of her face.

Claire turned aside and affected to be absorbed in examining the contents of an old cabinet, and Janet moved to the nearer side of the table so that her face was hidden from view; after a few minutes of silence, she broke the silence in a voice of forced lightness.

"Won't you come and look at my trophies? Switzerland is not a very happy hunting-ground, for there is so little variety to be had. That's my fifth carved chalet, and about the seventeenth bear. Rather a dear, though, isn't he? Such a nice man sent it—one of the nicest of men. That's his photograph on the mantelpiece."

Claire looked, met a straight keen glance which lived in her memory, and felt a tingle of blood in her cheeks. Janet's eyes followed hers, and she said quickly—

"Not that; that's Erskine Fanshawe. He is a casual person, and doesn't go in for presents. He hasn't even troubled to send a card. I meant the man in the leather frame. He always remembers. I do like that, in a man! They are all good enough in an emergency, but so few of them think of the nice *little* things!" Janet sighed, and dropped the carved wooden bear on to the table. However much she might appreciate the donor's thoughtfulness, it had not had a cheering effect. The light had died out of her eyes, and she turned over the various trophies without a trace of the enthusiasm with which she had torn open the parcel. Claire standing beside her felt torn between sympathy and a guilty sense of relief. She was sorry for Janet's obvious disappointment, but she was also (it was a dog-in-the-manger feeling, for how could it possibly affect herself?) *relieved* that Captain Fanshawe was not the donor of the bear!

As the two girls stood together turning over the little collection of carved toys, Claire slipped her hand through Janet's arm with an affectionate pressure, which was an outward apology for the inward disloyalty, and Janet stretched out her own hand to clasp it with unexpected fervour.

"Oh, I am glad you are here! I'm glad to have another girl! Girls understand. I wish I hadn't opened those horrid old parcels. It's just as I said—presents are disappointing. Now I feel thoroughly humped and dumpy! It's so stupid, too, for I know quite well that I've every sane reason to be pleased. How exasperating it is that one's head and one's heart so seldom agree!"

Claire gave the plump arm another squeeze, but made no further answer. She was afraid to show how well she understood. Janet would forget her hasty words, and believe that her secret was locked within her own breast; but the other girl realised the position as clearly as if she had been told in so many words—"I am in love with one man, and another man is in love with me. I am throwing away the substance for the shadow!"

"Ah, well, such is life!" continued Janet, sighing. "Now I'm supposed to go downstairs and be the life of the party! How I do dislike family parties! Mother says it's the ideal thing for relations to gather together for Christmas Day, but I've been gathered together for so *many* years!"

"You are too well-off, my dear, that's what's the matter! I have never met a girl before who had so much to make her happy, and yet you are not satisfied. How would you like to be a High School-mistress living in poky lodgings, not able to have a holiday because she can't afford two rents, and getting only one present all told?"

Janet looked at her quickly.

"Have you had only one?"

The Independence of Claire

"I said *a* High School-mistress, not any special mistress, but I will be definite if you like. How would you like to be *Me*?"

Janet turned suddenly, laid her free hand on Claire's shoulder, and stared deeply into her face.

"I—don't—know!" she said slowly. "Sometimes I think it's just what I should like. I have a great deal, but you have more. Look at our two faces in that glass!"

She drew Claire round so that they stood in front of the Chippendale mirror over the mantelpiece, from whence a row of pictured faces stared back, as though stolidly sitting in judgment. The clear tints of Claire's skin made Janet look sallow and faded, the dark curve of her eyebrows under the sweep of gold brown hair, the red lips and deeply cleft chin, made Janet's indeterminate features look insignificant, the brown eyes seemed the only definite feature in her face, and they were clouded with depression.

"Look at yourself," she said deeply, "and look at me!"

It was an awkward moment, and Claire shrugged uncomfortably.

"But my face is—it has to be—my fortune!"

"Oh, beauty! I wasn't thinking of beauty," Janet cried unexpectedly. "You are very pretty, of course, but heaps of girls are pretty. It's something more—I suppose it is what is called Charm. When people see you once, they remember you; they want to see you again. You make a place for yourself. I am one in a crowd. People like me well enough when they are with me, but—they forget!"

"And I never meet anyone to remember. We're two love-lorn damsels, and this is Merrie Christmas. Would you have thought it?" cried Claire, and that wrought the desired effect, for Janet awoke with a shock to her responsibilities as hostess, and led the way downstairs to join the rest of the house-party.

The rest of the day was spent in conventional English fashion in a praiseworthy effort to sustain spirits at concert pitch, and keep up a continuous flow of gaiety, a mountainous task when guests are brought together by claims of birth, without consideration as to suitability! Mrs Willoughby's party consisted of four distinct elements; there were Great-aunt Jane, and second cousin William, two octogenarians, who for health's sake dined early all the year round, and sipped a cup of Benger at eight, but who dauntlessly tackled sausages and plum pudding on Christmas Day, and suffered for it for a week to come. There were Mr and Mrs Willoughby, and two cousin husbands and their wives, and a spinster aunt to represent the next generation, then came sweet and twenty as represented by Janet and Claire, followed by Reginald of Eton, on whom they looked down as a mere boy, the while he in his turn disdained to notice the advances of two curly-headed cousins of nine and ten! Claire enjoyed herself because it was in her nature to enjoy, and it felt good to be once more in a beautiful, well-appointed home, among friends; but driving home in the taxi she yawned persistently from one door to the other. It was dreadfully tiring work being pleasant at the same time to the whole five ages of man!

With the opening of the door of the saffron parlour came an end of sleepiness, for on the table lay a square parcel, and the parcel bore the same stamp, the same markings which she had seen duplicated in Janet Willoughby's boudoir! Red as a rose was Claire as she stared at the bold masculine writing of the address, tore open the wrappings of the box, and drew forth a carved cuckoo clock with the well-known chalet roof and long pendulum and chains. It was an exquisite specimen of its kind, the best that could be obtained, but for the moment Claire had no attention to spare for the gift itself; she was absorbed in hunting among the paper and straw for a card which should settle the identity of the donor. Not a line was to be found. Pink deepened to crimson on Claire's cheeks.

The Independence of Claire

"Who in the world could have sent it? Who *could* it be?" She played at bewilderment, but in spite of herself the dimples dipped. "Now how in the world has he found out my address?" asked Claire of herself.

For the next week Claire experienced the sensation of being "alone in London." From the evening of Christmas Day until Cecil returned on January 2nd, not one friendly word did she hear; she walked abroad among a crowd of unknown faces, she returned to a solitary room.

Miss Farnborough was spending the Christmas abroad; the other mistresses were either visiting or entertaining relations, the ladies of the committee were presumably making merry each in her own sphere. It was no one's business to look after the new member of the staff out of term time, and no one troubled to make it her business.

The only friendly sound which reached Claire's ears during those days was the striking of the cuckoo clock, as a minute before every hour a sliding door flew open, and a little brown bird popped out and piped the due number of cuckoos in a clear, sweet note. Claire loved that little bird; the sight of him brought a warmth to her heart, which was as sunshine lighting up the grey winter days. Someone had remembered! Someone had cared! In the midst of a merry holiday, time and thought had been spared for her benefit.

The presence of the cuckoo clock preserved Claire from personal suffering, but during that silent week there was borne in upon her a realisation of the loneliness of the great city which was never obliterated. A girl like herself, coming to London without introductions, might lead this desert life, not for a week alone, but for *years*! Her youth might fade, might pass away, she might grow middle-aged and old, and still pass to and fro through crowded street, unnoted, uncared for, unknown beyond the boundaries of the schoolroom or the office walls. A working-woman was as a rule too tired and too poor to join societies, or take part in social work which would lead to the making of friends; she was dependent on the thoughtfulness of her leisured sisters, and the leisured sisters were too apt to forget. They invited their own well-off friends, exhausted themselves in organising entertainments which were often regarded as bores pure and simple, and cast no thought to the lonely women sitting night after night in lodging-house parlours. "If I am ever rich—if I ever have a home, I'll remember!" Claire vowed to herself. "I'll take a little trouble, and *find out*! I couldn't do a hundredth or a thousandth part of what ought to be done, but I'd do my share!" Cecil announced her return for the evening of January 2nd, and remindful of the depressing influence of her own arrival, Claire exerted herself to make the room look as homelike as possible, and arranged a dainty little meal on a table spread with a clean cloth and decorated with a bowl of holly and Christmas roses. At the first sound of Cecil's voice she ran out into the hall, hugged her warmly, and relieved her of a bundle of packages of all sorts and sizes.

"You look a real Mother Christmas hidden behind parcels. What are they all? Trophies? You *have* come off well! It is lovely to see you back. If you'd stayed away the whole time I think I should have grown dumb. My tongue would have withered from sheer lack of use. I never realised before how much I love to talk. I do hope you feel sociable. I want to talk and talk for hours at a time, and to hear *you* talk, too."

"Even to grumble?"

Claire grinned eloquently.

"Oh, well—if you *must*, but it would be rather mean, wouldn't it, after a holiday, and when I've got everything so nice? I am driven to praise myself, because *you* take no notice."

"You have given me no time. You chatter so that no one else can get in a word." Cecil took off hat and gloves, and threw them down on the sofa. "I must say your looks don't pity you. You look as if you had been enjoying yourself all right. That kettle's boiling!

I'm dying for a cup of tea! Let's have it at once, and talk comfortably." She seated herself by the table, and helped herself to a buttered scone. "What did you do on Christmas Day?"

"The Willoughbys asked me. I went to church with them, and stayed until eleven."

"Anything going on, or just the ordinary family frumps?"

Claire laughed.

"Nobody but relations and my fascinating self; but you needn't be so blighting. I enjoyed every moment, and they were angelically kind. Janet was like an old friend."

"Did she give you a present?"

"Yes, she did. Half a dozen pairs of gloves."

"The wrong size, of course! They always are!"

"No, my pessimist, they were not! She had diagnosed me as a six and a half, and six and a half I am, so all was peace and joy. I put on a new pair the next day when I went out for a constitutional. It was quite a tonic. Gloves are much cheaper abroad, and I never wore a shabby pair in my life until this winter. It's been one of the things I've hated most."

"Six pairs will soon go," said Cecil; "I prefer to have things that last. Oh, by the way, you addressed a parcel. How did it come? Was it left at the door?"

Instinctively Claire busied herself over the tea-tray. She had a feeling that Cecil would rather be unobserved; she was also afraid that her own expression might betray too much.

"Oh no, he called. When I came in after morning church on Sunday, Lizzie said that a gentleman was waiting. It was Major Carew. He asked me if I would address the parcel and send it on."

Silence. Claire bent over the tea-tray, but she knew without looking that Cecil's face had fallen into the cold set lines which she had seen times and again, when things had gone wrong; she knew that when she spoke again the coldness would be in her voice, but her own conscience was clear. She had done nothing to offend.

"Really! That's curious. *Waiting*, you say? You didn't ask him in? What did he say?"

"He said, 'Miss Gifford, I presume. I have called to ask if you will be kind enough to address a small parcel for Miss Rhodes.' I said, 'Wouldn't it be better if I gave you her address?' He said, 'I should prefer if you wrote it yourself.' I said, 'I will do so with pleasure. Good morning.' He said, 'Good morning.' He then took up his hat and departed. He showed himself out, and shut the door after him. I went upstairs and took off my things."

"He didn't stay long then?"

"About three minutes, I should say, perhaps four; I can't tell you to a second, unfortunately. I didn't look at the clock."

Cecil laughed, half apologetic, half relieved.

"Oh, well, you needn't be sarcastic. Naturally I wanted to know. I couldn't make it out when I saw your writing, for you had given me the scarf—I'm going to buy your present at the sales, by the way—but, of course, when I took off the paper, there was a message inside. I was expecting that present."

"I hope it was very nice?"

"Oh, yes—yes! A brooch," Cecil said carelessly. Claire hoped it was not the insignificant little golden bar which she was wearing at the moment, but she had never seen it before, and Cecil's jewellery was of the most limited description. She determined to ask no more questions on the subject, since evidently none were desired. Cecil helped herself to a second scone, and asked suddenly—

"Why didn't he sit down?"

"It wasn't necessary, was it? He gave his message, and then there was nothing to say. I wasn't going to make conversation."

"You didn't like him!" cried Cecil, but she laughed as she spoke, and her face relaxed; it was evident that she was more pleased than disconcerted at her friend's lack of approval. "You're no good at hiding your feelings, Claire; your voice gives you away as well as your face. *Why* didn't you like Major Carew? I suppose you don't deny that he is a handsome man?"

"I don't think I care about handsome men," said Claire, seeing before her a clean-shaven face which could lay no claims to beauty, but in comparison with which the Major's coarse good looks were abhorrent in her eyes.

"Prefer men plain, I suppose? Well, I don't; I shouldn't like Frank half so much, if he didn't look so big and imposing. And other people admire him, too. People stare at him as we pass. I suppose you have guessed that it is with him that I've been going out? There didn't seem any need to speak of it before, but during the rest of the holidays you might expect me to go about with you, and sometimes—often, I hope, I'll be engaged, so it's just as well to explain. We can do things together in the morning, but naturally—"

"Yes, of course; I quite understand. Don't worry about me, Cecil. I'd love you to have a good time. Are you—are you engaged to him, dear?"

There was in her voice that soft, almost awed note with which an unengaged girl regards a companion who has actually plighted her troth. Cecil softened at the sound.

"Well—I suppose we are. Between ourselves. It's not public yet, but I think it soon will be. Half a dozen years ago I should have been sure, but I know better now. You can never be sure! Men are such brutes. They think of nothing but themselves, and their own amusement."

"Some men!"

"Most men! Of course, every girl who falls in love thinks her own particular man is the exception, and believes in him blindly until she gets her heart broken for her pains. I believed in a man, too, years ago, when I was not much older than you are now."

She paused, as though waiting for comment, but Claire sat silent, listening with grave, tender eyes.

Cecil sent her a flickering smile.

"You are a nice child, Claire; you have some sense! I'll tell you, because you never pried or asked questions. You would never have got anything out of me that way, but sometimes I feel as if it would be a relief to talk. I was twenty-three, and very pretty; not as pretty as you are, perhaps, but very nearly, and he was twenty-eight, a lawyer—brother of one of the girls. He came to one of the prize-givings, and we were introduced. After that he made his people invite me once or twice, and he found out where I was going in the summer holidays, and came down to the same inn. He stayed a fortnight." Cecil sighed, and stared dreamily at her cup. "Even now, Claire, after all that has happened, I can never quite make up my mind to be sorry that he came. It made things harder when the parting came, but I *had had it*. For two whole weeks I had been as perfectly, blissfully happy as a human creature can be! I had wakened every morning to feel that life was too good to be true, I had gone to bed every night grudging the time for sleep. A fortnight is not very long, but it's not every woman who gets even as much as that. I shall never feel that happiness again, but I'm glad that I know what it is like."

"But, Cecil dear, if—if Major Carew—"

Cecil shook her head.

"No! Never again. One may be happy enough, but it's never the same. I can't feel now as I did then. The power has gone. I cared so much, you see; I would have given my life for him a dozen times over. I thought of him night and day for over a year; I lived for the times when we could meet. It wasn't very often, for his people had taken fright, and would not ask me to the house. They were rich people, and didn't want him to marry a poor girl who was working for herself. It's a great mistake, Claire, to be friends with a man when his relations ignore you. If I'd had any pride I would have realised that, but I hadn't, and I didn't care; I didn't care for anything but just to see him, and do what he wished. And then, my dear, after a year he began to change. He didn't write to me for weeks, and I had to go to school every day, and try to think of the work, and be patient with the girls, and seem bright and interested, as if I had nothing on my mind. It was near Christmas-time, and we were rehearsing a play. I used to feel as if I should go mad, staying behind after four o'clock to go over those wretched scenes, when I was panting to run home to see if a letter had come! But each time that we met again I forgot everything; I was so happy that I had no time to grumble. That surprises you, doesn't it? You can hardly believe that of me, but I was different then. I was quite nice. You would have liked me, if you had known me then!"

"Dear old Cecil! I like you now. You know I do!"

"Oh, you put up with me! We get along well enough, but we are not *friends*. If we had not been thrown together, you would never have singled me out. Don't apologise, my dear; there's no need. I'm a grumbling old thing, and you've been very patient. Well, that's how it happened. I went out to meet him one night, and he told me quite calmly that he was going to be married. She was the sweetest girl in the world, and he was the happiest of men. Wanted me to know, because we had been such *good* friends, and he was sure I should be pleased!"

Claire drew her breath with a sharp, sibilant sound.

"And *you*? Oh, Cecil! What did you say?"

Mary Rhodes compressed her lips; the set look was in her face.

"I said what I thought! Quite plainly, and simply, and very much to the point. I suppose it would have been dignified to congratulate him, and pretend to be delighted; but I couldn't do it. He had broken my heart for his own amusement, and he knew it as well as I did, so why should I pretend? Something inside me seemed to go snap at that moment, and I've been sour and bitter ever since; but I've learnt *one* lesson, and that is, that it is folly to go on waiting for perfection in this world. Much better take what comes along, and make the best of it!"

Claire was silent, applauding the sentiment in the abstract, but shrinking from its application to the swarthy Major Carew. She stretched her hand across the table, and laid it caressingly on Cecil's arm.

"*Pauvre*! Dear old girl! It's no use saying he wasn't worth having—that's no comfort. When you have loved a man, it must be the worst blow of all to be obliged to despise him; but men are not all like that, Cecil; you mustn't condemn them all because of one bad specimen. I've a great admiration for men. As a whole they are *bigger* than women— I mean mentally bigger—freer from mean little faults. As a rule they have a stricter sense of honour. That's an old-fashioned attitude, I suppose, but I don't care; it's been my experience, and I can only speak what I know. The average man *is* honourable, *is* faithful!"

"Ah, you are speaking of your experience as a leisured girl—a girl living at home with her mother behind her. It's a different story when you are on your own. A man finds it pleasant enough to be friends with a bachelor girl, to take her about, give her little presents, and play the fairy prince generally. The dear little soul is so grateful"—Cecil's voice took a bitter note—"so appreciative of his condescension! He can enjoy her society without being bothered with chaperons and conventions. It is really an uncommonly jolly way of passing the time. But, when it comes to *marrying*, does he want to *marry* the bachelor girl?"

Claire pushed her chair from the table, her face looked suddenly white and tired, there was a suspicious quiver in her voice.

"Oh, Cecil, don't, don't! You are poisoning me again. Leave me *some* faith! If I can't believe in my fellow-creatures, I'd rather die at once, and be done with it. It stifles me to breathe the atmosphere of distrust and suspicion. And it isn't true. There *are* good men, who would be all the more chivalrous because a girl was alone. I know it! I'm sure of it! I refuse to believe that every man is a blackguard because you have had an unfortunate experience."

Mary Rhodes stared, abashed. Since the night when Claire had implored her not to poison her mind, she had never seen her merry, easy-going companion so aroused; but for the moment regret was swamped in curiosity. Ostensibly Claire was arguing in the plural, but in reality she was defending a definite man; Cecil was sure of it; saw her suspicion confirmed in the paling cheeks and distended eyes; heard it confirmed in the shaking voice. But who could the man be? Claire was the most candid, the most open of colleagues; she loved to talk and describe any experiences which came her way; every time she returned from an afternoon in town she had a dozen amusing incidents to recount, which in themselves constituted a guide to her doings. Cecil felt satisfied that Claire had had no masculine escort on any of these occasions, and with the one exception of Mrs Willoughby's "At Home" she had paid no social visits. Yet there did exist a man on whose honour she was prepared to pin her faith; of that Cecil was convinced. Probably it was someone in Brussels whom she was still hoping to meet again?

"Well, don't get excited," she said coolly. "If you choose to look upon life as a fairy tale, it's not my business to wake you up. The Sleeping Beauty position is very soothing while it lasts. Don't say I didn't warn you, that's all! I don't call it exactly 'poisonous' to try to prevent another girl from suffering as badly as one has suffered oneself."

"Perhaps not—certainly not, but it was the way you did it. Sorry, Cecil, if I was cross! I hope *this* time, dear, all will go well, and that you'll be very, very happy. Do tell me anything you can. I won't ask questions, but I'd love to hear."

Cecil's laugh had rather a hard intonation.

"Oh, well! once bitten, twice shy. I'm older this time, and it's a different thing. Perhaps I shall be all the happier because I don't expect too much. He's very devoted, and he'll be rich some day, but his father gives him no allowance, which makes things tight just now. He is an erratic old man, almost a miser, but there are pots of money in the family. Frank showed me the name in *Landed Gentry*; there's quite a paragraph about them, and I've seen a picture of the house, too. A beautiful place; and he's the eldest son. It's in Surrey—quite near town."

"He hasn't taken you down to see it?"

"Not yet. No. It's a private engagement. His father doesn't know. He is waiting for a chance to tell him."

"Wouldn't the father be glad for his heir to marry?"

"He wouldn't be glad for him to marry *me*! But the estate is entailed, so Frank can do as he likes. But the old man is ill, always having asthma and heart attacks, so it wouldn't do to upset him, and of course till he knows, Frank can't tell any other members of the family."

Claire, standing by the fireplace, gave a vague assent, and was glad that her face was hidden from view. For Cecil's sake she intensely wanted to believe in Major Carew and his account of his own position, but instinctively she doubted, instinctively she feared. She remembered the look of the man's face as he had stood facing her across the little room, and her distrust deepened. He did not look straight; he did not look true. Probably the old father had a good reason for keeping him short of money. If he were really in love with Cecil, and determined to marry her, that was so much to his credit; but Claire hated the idea of that secrecy, marvelled that Cecil could submit a second time to so humiliating a position. Poor Cecil! how *awful* it would be if she were again deceived! A protective impulse stirred in Claire's heart. "She shan't be, if I can help it!" cried the inner voice. At that moment she vowed herself to the service of Mary Rhodes.

"A big country house in Surrey! That's the ideal residence of the heroine of fiction. It does sound romantic, Cecil! I should love to think of you as the mistress of a house like that. Come and sit by the fire, and let us talk. It's so exciting to talk of love affairs instead of exercises and exams... Let's pretend we are just two happy, ordinary girls, with no form-rooms looming ahead, and that one of us is just engaged, and telling the other 'all about it.' Now begin! Begin at the beginning. How did you meet him first?"

But there a difficulty arose, for Cecil grew suddenly red, and stumbled over her words.

"Oh—well—I— We *met*! It was an accident—quite an accident—rather a romantic accident. I was coming home one Sunday evening a year ago. I had been to church in my best clothes, and when I was halfway here the skies opened, and the rain *descended*. Such rain! A deluge! Dancing up from the pavement, streaming along the gutters. I hadn't an umbrella, of course—just my luck!—and I'd had my hat done up that very week. I tore it off, and wrapped it in the tails of my coat, and just as that critical moment Frank passed, saw me doing it, and stopped. Then he asked if I would allow him to shelter me home beneath his umbrella. Well! I'm *not* the girl to allow men to speak to me in the street, but at that moment, in that deluge, when he'd just seen me take off my hat, *could* a gentleman do less than offer to shelter me? Would it have been sane to refuse?"

"No; I don't think it would. I should certainly have said yes, too. That's the sort of thing that would have been called chivalry in olden times. It's chivalry *now*. He was quite right to offer. It would have been horrible if he had passed by and left you to be drenched."

Cecil brightened with relief.

"That's what *I* thought! So I said 'Yes'; and, of course, while we walked we talked, and the wind blew my hair into loose ends, and the damp made them curl, and the excitement gave me a colour; and it was so nice to talk to a man again, Claire, after everlasting women! I *did* look pretty when I saw myself in the glass when I came in, almost as I used to look years before. And he looked handsome, too, big and strong, and so delightfully like a man, and unlike a member of staff! We liked each other very much, and when we got to this door—"

Silence. Mary Rhodes waited wistfully for a helping word. Claire stared into the fire, her brows knitted in suspense.

"Well, naturally, we were sorry to part! He asked if I usually went to Saint C— for the evening service. I didn't, but I said 'Yes.' I knew he meant to meet me again, and I *wanted* to be met."

Claire sent her thoughts back and recalled a certain Sunday evening when she had offered to accompany Cecil to church, and had been bluntly informed that her company was not desired. She had taken the hint, and had not offered it again. She was silent, waiting for the revelations which were still to come.

"So after that it became a regular thing. He met me outside the church door, and saw me home. He often asked me to go out with him during the week, but I always refused, until suddenly this term I was so tired, so hungry for a change that I gave in, and promised that I would. I suppose that shocks you into fits!"

"It does rather. You see," explained Claire laboriously, "I've been brought up on the Continent, where such a thing would be impossible. It would be an insult to suggest it. Even here in England it doesn't seem right. Do you think a really nice man who was attracted by a girl wouldn't find some other way—get an introduction *somehow*?"

"How? It's easy to talk, but *how* is he to do it? We live in different worlds. I am a High School teacher, living in rooms in London, without a relation or a house open to me where I am intimate enough to take a friend. He is an officer in a crack regiment, visiting at fashionable houses. Can't you imagine how his hostesses would stare if he asked them to call upon me here, in this poky room! And if he loves me, if I interest him more than the butterflies of Society, if he wants to know me better, what is he to do? Tell me that, my dear, before you blame me for taking a little bit of fun when I get the chance!"

But Claire had no suggestion to make. She herself had been strong enough to refuse a friendship on similar lines, but she had been living a working life for a bare four months, while Cecil had been teaching for twelve years. Twelve years of a second-hand life, living in other women's houses, teaching other women's children, obeying other women's rules; with the one keen personal experience of a slighted love!

The tale of close on four thousand nights represented a dreary parlour and a pile of exercise books. For twelve long years this woman had worked away, losing her youth, losing her bloom, cut off from all that nature intended her to enjoy; and then at the end behold a change in the monotony, the sudden appearance of a man who sought her, admired her, craved her society as a boon!

The tears came to Claire's eyes as she put herself in such a woman's place, and realised all that this happening would mean. Renewal of youth, renewal of hope, renewal of interest and zest...

"I don't know! I don't know!" she said brokenly. "It's all wrong, somehow. You ought not to be forced into such a position, but I don't blame you, Cecil. It's the *other* women who deserve the blame, the women who are better off, and could have opened their houses. You have been so drearily dull all these long years that you would have been more than human to refuse. But now, dear, now that you are engaged, surely he has some friends to whom he could introduce you?"

Mary Rhodes shook her head.

"Not till his people know. It might come round to their ears, and that would make things more difficult still; but I am hoping it won't be long. Now, Claire, I've told *you*, because you are such a kind understanding little soul, and it's a comfort to talk things out; but I'll kill you if you dare to breathe a word to another soul—Sophie Blake, or Mrs Willoughby, or even your mother when you write to her. You can never tell how these things are repeated, and Frank would never forgive me if it came out through me. Promise faithfully that you'll never mention his name in connection with me."

"Of course I will. What do you take me for? I shouldn't dream of doing such a thing!"

"Of course, at the Willoughbys', for instance, if anyone *did* mention his name—they might, quite well, for I should think they were in much the same set—there would be no harm in saying that you'd heard of him. I should rather like to hear what they said."

Cecil's face looked wistful as she spoke these last words, but the next moment her expression changed to one of pure amazement as the whirr of the cuckoo clock made itself heard, and the little brown bird hopped out of its niche, and sounded five clear notes.

"Gracious, what's that? Where did that come from?"

"It was a Christmas present to me from abroad."

Claire added the last words in the fond hope that they would save further criticism, and Cecil rose from her seat, and stood in front of the hanging clock examining it with critical eyes.

"It's a good one. Most of them are so gimcrack. From abroad? One of your Belgian friends, I suppose? Does it make that awful row every hour? I can't stand it here, you know, if it does."

"Don't trouble yourself. I'll take it upstairs. I *like* the 'awful row.' I put it here because I thought it would be a pleasure to you as well as to myself. I'm sorry."

"What a tantrum! Evidently the clock is a tender point. Better leave it here and stop the gong. It will keep you awake all night."

"I won't stop the gong! I—I like to be waked!" declared Claire obstinately. She lifted the clock from its nail, and stalked out of the room, head in air.

Cecil whistled softly between pursed lips.

Chapter Twelve.

An unpleasant tea-party.

In the inevitable fatigue which had marked Claire's first experience of regular work, she had looked forward with joy to the coming of the holidays when she would be able to take her ease, and for a month on end laze through the hours at her own sweet will. A teacher scores above other workers in the length of holidays she enjoys. Several months in the year contrasts strongly with the fortnight or three weeks enjoyed by a female clerk or typist; in no other profession is so large a proportion of the year given to rest.

Claire had condemned the staff at Saint Cuthbert's for want of appreciation of this privilege; but, before the four weeks of the Christmas holidays were over, her eyes were opened to the other side of the picture. Holidays were horribly expensive! Living "at home" meant an added bill for fire and light to add to the necessary expenses abroad; that the last items were necessary could hardly be denied, for a girl who had been shut up in a schoolroom through three months of term, naturally wished to amuse herself abroad during holiday time, and in London even the most carefully planned amusement has a habit of costing money.

Even that mild dissipation of shop-gazing, enjoyed by Sophie Blake, plus the additional excitement of choosing an imaginary present from every window, could only be enjoyed at the price of two Tube or omnibus fares. Boots wore out, too, and gloves grew shabby, and the January sales furnished a very fire of temptation. Claire had never before seen such bargains as confronted her down the length of Oxford and Regent Streets, and, though she might be firm as adamant on Monday or Tuesday, Wednesday was bound to bring about a weak moment which carried her over the threshold of a shop, and once inside, with sensational sacrifices dangling within reach, resistance melted like wax.

"Where do you suppose you are going to wear that concoction?" Mary Rhodes asked blightingly as Claire opened a cardboard box which had arrived by the morning delivery, and displayed a blue muslin dress inset with lace. "Lords, I suppose, or Ascot, or Ranelagh, or Hurlingham, or Henley... They come on in June and July, just as poor High School-mistresses are in the thick of cramming for the Matric. But *no* doubt you are the exception to the rule! ... You must think you are, at least, to have bought a frock like that!"

"Cecil, it was wickedly cheap—it was, indeed! It was one of a few summer dresses which were positively given away, and it's made in the simple, picturesque style which I love, and which does not go out of date. I hadn't the least intention of buying anything, until I saw it hanging there, at that price, and it looked at me so longingly, as if it *wanted* to come!"

"It's well to be rich! It might have longed at me as much as it liked, I couldn't have bought it, if it had been two-and-six! I need all my money for necessities," Mary Rhodes said, sighing; and Claire felt a pang of reproach, for, since her return, Cecil had indeed seemed painfully short of loose cash. The debt still outstanding had been increased by various small borrowings, insignificant in themselves, yet important as showing how the wind blew. Claire wondered if perchance the poor soul had crippled herself by presenting her lover with a Christmas gift which was beyond her means.

The third week of the holidays arrived; in another week school would begin. Claire succumbed to temptation once more, purchased two good tickets for an afternoon concert at the Queen's Hall, and invited Cecil to be her guest. Cecil hesitated, evidently torn between two attractions, asked permission to defer her answer until the next day, but finally decided to accept. From remarks dropped from time to time Claire had gathered that Major Carew was not fond of indoor entertainments, and somewhat disappointed his *fiancée* by his unwillingness to indulge her wishes in that respect. In this instance she had evidently balanced the concert against an afternoon in the Major's society, and the concert had won. Claire found herself cordially in agreement.

When the afternoon arrived the two girls arrayed themselves in their best clothes, and set off in high spirits for their afternoon's amusement. Their seats were in a good position, and the concert was one of the best of the season. All went as happily as it could possibly go, until the last strains of "God save the King" had been played, and the audience filed out of the hall on to the crowded pavement, and then, with a throb of disgust, Claire recognised the figure of a man who was standing directly beneath a lamp-post, his black eyes curiously scanning the passing stream—Major Carew! He had evidently been told of the girls' destination, and had come with the express purpose of meeting them coming out. For the moment, however, they were unrecognised, and Claire gave a quick swerve to the right, hurrying out of the patch of light into the dimness beyond. The street was so full that, given a minute's start, it would surely be easy to escape. She slid her hand through Cecil's arm, drawing her forward.

"Come along! Come along! Let's hurry to Fuller's before all the tables are taken!"

"Fuller's? Tea? How scrumptious! Just what I longed for. Listening to classical music *is* thirsty work!" Cecil replied, laughing. She was so lively, so natural and unconcerted that Claire absolved her on the moment from any arrangement as to a *rendez-vous*. In her anxiety to secure the longed-for cup of tea she broke into a half-run, but it was too late; the sharp black eyes had spied them out, the tall figure loomed by their side, the large face, with its florid colouring, smiled a broad smile of welcome.

"Hulloa, Mary! Thought it was you. I was just passing along. Good afternoon, Miss Gifford. It *is* Miss Gifford, isn't it? Had a good concert, I hope—a pleasant afternoon?"

"Very good, thank you," said Claire shortly.

Mary cried, "Oh, Frank! *You!* How did you come? I didn't expect—" And the tone of her voice showed that the surprise was hardly more agreeable to her than to her companion. However welcome her lover might be on other occasions, it was obvious that she had not wished to see him at this particular moment.

"Well, well, we must move on; we mustn't block up the pavement," the Major said hastily. He took his place by the kerb, which placed him next to Claire, and bent over with an assiduous air. "You must let me escort you! Where were you bound for next?"

Claire hesitated. She wished with all her heart that she had not mentioned Fuller's, so that she could reply that they were bound for the Tube. Oxford Circus was only a step away; in five minutes they could have been seated in the train; but Cecil had declared that she was longing for tea, so it would be ungracious to withdraw the invitation.

"We were going to Fuller's."

"Right!" The Major's tone was complacent. "Good idea! How shall we go? Taxi? Tube? Which do you prefer?"

Claire stared at him in surprise.

"But it's here! Quite close. We're nearly there."

He looked disconcerted, unnecessarily disconcerted, Claire thought; for it was surely no disgrace for a man to be ignorant of the locality of a confectioner's shop! From the other side came Cecil's voice, cool and constrained—

"If you were going anywhere, Frank, you needn't stay with us. We can look after each other. We are accustomed to going about alone."

"Please allow me the pleasure. There's plenty of time. I should enjoy some tea immensely. Always take it when I get the chance!"

The block on the pavement made consecutive conversation impossible, and the three edged their way in and out in silence until Fuller's was reached, and one of the last tables secured. The room looked very bright and dainty, the Christmas garlands still festooning the walls and framing the mirrors, the hanging lights covered by rose-coloured shades. The soft pink light was very kind to the complexions of the visitors, nevertheless Claire felt a guilty pang as she looked into the nearest mirror and beheld the reflection of herself and her friend as they sat side by side. As a rule, it was pure pleasure to realise her own fair looks; but for the moment they were of no importance, whereas poor dear Cecil had a lover to please, and there was no denying Cecil was not looking her best! Her expression was frowning and dissatisfied. She had taken off her veil in the hall and her hair was disarranged; compared with the fashionable groups round the other tables, she looked suddenly shabby and insignificant, her little attempts at decoration pitifully betraying the amateur hand.

"Oh, dear me, why *won't* she smile? She looks quite pretty when she smiles. I'll hold her before a mirror some day and show her the difference it makes. Ten years disappear in a flash! Now what in the world had I better be—agreeable and chatty, or cold and stand-off? I'll do anything to please her, but it *is* hard lines having our afternoon spoiled, and being sulked at into the bargain. Cakes, please—lots of sweet, sugary cakes! Won't that do, Cecil? We can have bread-and-butter at home!"

"Cecil! Cecil! Her name is Mary. Why do you call her Cecil?" cried the Major quickly, looking from one girl to another. Claire fancied there was a touch of suspicion in his voice, and wondered that he should show so much interest in a mere nickname.

"Because she is 'Rhodes,' of course."

For a moment his stare showed no understanding, then, "Oh! that fellow!" he said slowly. "I see! It's a pretty name anyway. Beats Mary to fits. Mary is so dull and prosaic. Too many of them about. One gets sick of the sound."

"Is that intended for me by any chance?" asked Cecil in her most acid tones, whereupon the Major cried, "Oh! Put my foot in it that time, didn't I?" and burst into a long guffaw of laughter, which brought on him the eyes of the surrounders.

Claire's interest had already been aroused by a little party of two men and two women who were sitting at a table in the corner of the room, and who were, to her thinking, by far the most attractive personalities present. The men were tall, well set up, not especially handsome in any way, but possessing an unmistakable look of breeding. One of the women was old, the other young, and it would have been hard to say which was the more attractive of the two. They were quietly but very elegantly dressed, handsome furs being thrown back, to show pretty bodices of ninon and lace.

When Major Carew gave that loud unrestrained laugh, the four members of this attractive party turned to see whence the sound arose; but whereas three faces remained blankly indifferent, the fourth was in the moment transformed into an expression of the liveliest surprise. He stared, narrowing his eyes as if doubting that they were really seeing aright, twisted his head to get a fuller view, and, obtaining it, twisted back into his original position, his lips twitching with laughter. Then he spoke a few words, his companions leant forward to listen, and to two faces out of the three, the laughter spread on hearing what he had to say.

Only the elder of the two ladies retained her gravity. Her sweet glance rested on Claire's face, and her brow contracted in distress. In the Major and Cecil she showed no interest, but Claire's appearance evidently aroused curiosity and pity. "What is *she* doing in that *galère*?" The question was written on every line of the sweet high-bred face, and Claire read its significance and flinched with distaste.

"How they stare!" cried Mary Rhodes. "The man looked as if he knew you, Frank. Do you know who he is?"

"He's a member of the Club. His name is Vavasour. We know each other by sight." Major Carew's florid colour had grown a shade deeper, he was evidently disconcerted by the encounter; but he made a strong effort to regain his composure, smiled at the two girls in turn, and cried lightly, "Envies me, I suppose, seeing me with two such charmers!"

"He didn't look exactly envious!" Cecil said drily. She also had noticed that reflection in the mirror, and it had not helped to soothe her spirits. She felt an unreasoning anger against Claire for appearing more attractive than herself, but it did not occur to her that she was heightening the contrast by her own dour, ungracious manner. Altogether that tea-party was a difficult occasion, and as it proceeded, Claire's spirits sank ever lower and lower. She had spent more than she had any right to afford on those two expensive tickets, hoping thereby to give pleasure, and now Cecil was in a bad temper, and would snap for days to come.—It was not a cheerful outlook, and for the second time a feeling of restiveness overtook her, a longing for a companion who would help the gaiety of life—such a companion as pretty, lively, happy-go-lucky Sophie Blake, for example. How refreshing it would be to live with Sophie! Just for a moment Claire dwelt wistfully on the possibility, then banished it with a loyal "She doesn't need me, and Cecil does. She's fond of me in her funny way. She must be, for she has confided in me already, more than in any of the others whom she's known for years, and perhaps I may be able to help..."

The Major passed his cup for a second supply; a waitress brought a plate of hot cakes; the occupants of the corner table stood up, fastening furs and coats, and passed out of the door. With their going Major Carew regained his vivacity, chaffed the girls on their silence, recounted the latest funny stories, and to Claire's relief addressed himself primarily to his *fiancée*, thus putting her in the place of honour.

Nevertheless Claire was conscious that from time to time keen glances were cast in her own direction. She had a feeling that no detail of her attire escaped scrutiny, that the black eyes noted one and all, wondered, and speculated, and appraised. She saw them dwell on the handsome fur stole and muff which Mrs Judge bequeathed to her daughter on sailing for India, on the old diamond ring and brooch which had been handed over to her on her twenty-first birthday; she had an instinctive feeling that she rose in the man's estimation because of her air of prosperity. He made tentative efforts to arrange a further meeting. "Where do *you* go on Sundays, Miss Gifford? I say, we must arrange another tea like this. Lots of good tea places in town. We must sample them together. What do you say, Miss Gifford?"

Claire's answers were politely evasive, and presently he began to grow restless, and finally pulled out his watch, and jumped to his feet.

"How time flies! I had no idea it was so late. I must run. So sorry to leave you like this."

Mary Rhodes stared in surprise.

"Leave! Frank! But you said—I thought we were going—"

"Yes, I know, I know. I'm sorry, I thought I was free—but—a regimental engagement! Can't get out of it. I'll fix up another night. I'll write."

There was no doubt that he was genuinely disconcerted at the lateness of the hour, and his leave-taking was of the most hasty description, though he found time to give a lingering pressure to Claire's hand; then he was gone, and the waitress came across the room and presented the bill.

Cecil flushed uncomfortably.

"I must pay this. Frank has forgotten. He rushed off in such a hurry."

She pulled out her shabby purse, and Claire made no protest. In a similar position she herself would have wished to pay, but it was inconceivable that she should ever be in such a position. However hurried a man might be— She rubbed her hand on her knee with a little shudder of distaste. "Wretch! He would make love to me, too, if I would allow it! How can Cecil possibly care for such a man?"

And then she forgot Cecil's feelings to ponder on a more perplexing problem.

Why had the man called Vavasour looked so amused, and why had the sweet-faced woman looked so distressed?

Chapter Thirteen.

A double invitation.

Janet Willoughby sent Claire a picture postcard, all white snow and strong shadow, and dazzling blue sky, and little black figures pirouetting on one leg with the other raised perilously in the rear. "This is me!" was written across the most agile of the number, while a scrawling line across the top ran, "Happy New Year! Returning on Tuesday. Hope to see you soon." Tuesday was the day on which school re-opened; but Janet's holiday was year long, not a short four weeks.

Cecil moaned loudly, but Claire was tired of aimless days, and welcomed the return to work. She determined to throw her whole heart into her task, and work as no junior French mistress had ever worked before; she determined never to lose patience, never to grow cross, never to indulge in a sarcastic word, always to be a model of tact and forbearance. She determined to wield such an ennobling influence over the girls in her form-room that they should take fire from her example, and go forth into the world perfect, high-souled women who should leaven the race. She determined also to be the life and soul of the staff-room—the general peace-maker, confidante, and consoler, beloved by one and all. She determined to seize tactfully upon every occasion of serving

The Independence of Claire

the Head, and acting as a buffer between her and disagreeables of every kind. She arranged a touching scene wherein Miss Farnborough, retiring from work and being asked by the Committee to name a worthy successor, pronounced unhesitatingly, "Claire Gifford; she is but young, but her wisdom and diplomacy are beyond all praise." She saw herself Head of Saint Cuthbert's, raised to the highest step of her scholastic ladder, but somehow the climax was not so exhilarating as the climb itself. To be head mistress was, no doubt, a fine achievement, but it left her cold.

Inside Saint Cuthbert's all was life and bustle. Girls streaming along the corridors, in and out of every room; girls of all ages and sizes and shapes, but all to-day bearing an appearance of happiness and animation. Bright-coloured blouses shone forth in their first splendour; hair-ribbons stood out stiff and straight; many of the girls carried bunches of flowers to present to the special mistress for whom they cherished the fashionable "G.P." (grand passion) so characteristic of school life.

Flora had a bunch of early daffodils for Claire. Another girl presented a pot of Roman hyacinths for the decoration of the form-room, a third a tiny bottle of scent; three separate donors supplied buttonholes of violets. The atmosphere was full of kindness and affection. Girls encountering each other would fall into each other's arms with exclamations of ecstatic affection. "Oh, you precious lamb!"

"My angel child!"

"You dear, old, darling duck!" Claire heard a squat, ugly girl with spectacles and a turned-up nose addressed as "a princely pet" by an ardent adorer of fourteen. The mistresses came in for their own share of adulation—"Darling Miss Gifford, I *do* adore you!"

"Miss Gifford, darling, you are prettier than ever!"

"Oh, Miss *Gifford*, I was *dying* to see you!"

The morning flew past, and lunch-time brought the gathering of mistresses in staff-room. Mademoiselle's greetings were politely detached, Fräulein was kindly and discursive, Sophie's smile was as bright as ever, but she did not look well.

"Oh, I'm all right! It's nothing. Only this horrid old pain!" she said cheerfully. Into her glass of water she dropped three tabloids of aspirin. Every one had been away for a longer or shorter time, visiting relatives and friends; they compared experiences; some had enjoyed themselves, some had not; but they all agreed that they were refreshed by the change.

"And where have *you* been?" asked the drawing mistress of Claire, and exclaimed in surprise at hearing that she had remained in town. "Dear me, I wish I had known! I've been back a fortnight. We might have done something together. Weren't you *dull*?" asked the drawing mistress, staring with curious eyes.

"Very!" answered poor Claire, and for a moment struggled with a horrible inclination to cry.

After lunch Miss Bates took her cup of coffee to Claire's side, and made an obvious attempt to be pleasant.

"I feel quite remorseful to think of your holidays. It's astonishing how little we mistresses know of each other out of school hours. The first school I was in—a much smaller one by the sea,—we were so friendly and jolly, just like sisters, but in the big towns every one seems detached. It's hard on the new-comers. I don't know *what* I should have done if I hadn't a brother's house to go to on Sundays and holiday afternoons. Except through him, I haven't made a single friend. At the other place people used to ask us out, and we had quite a good time; but in town people are engrossed in their own affairs. They haven't time to go outside."

"I wonder you ever left that school! What made you want to change?"

"Oh, well! London was a lure. Most people want to come to London, and I had my brother. Do tell me, another time, if you are not going away. It worries me to think of you being alone. How did you come to get this post, if you have no connections in town?"

"Miss Farnborough came to stay in Brussels, in the *pension* which my mother and I had made headquarters for some time. She offered me the post."

Miss Bates stared with distended eyes. "How long had she known you?"

"About a fortnight, I think. I don't remember exactly."

"And you had never seen her before? She knew nothing about you?"

"She had never seen me before, but she *did* know something about me. Professionally speaking, she knew all there was to know."

"That accounts for it," said Miss Bates enigmatically. "I wondered— You are not a bit the usual type."

"I hope that doesn't mean that I can't teach?"

Miss Bates laughed, and shrugged her thin shoulders. "Oh, no. I should say, personally, that you teach very well. That play was extraordinarily good. It absolutely sounded like French. Can't think how you knocked the accent into them! English girls are so self-conscious; they are ashamed of letting themselves go. Mademoiselle thinks that your classes are too like play; but it doesn't matter what she thinks, so long as—" she paused a moment, lowered her voice, and added impressively, "Keep on the right side of Miss Farnborough. You are all right so long as you are in her good books. Better be careful."

"What do you mean?" Claire stared, puzzled and discomposed, decidedly on the offensive; but Miss Bates refused a definite answer.

"Nothing!" she said tersely. "Only—people who take sudden fancies, can take sudden dislikes, too. Ask no more questions, but don't say I didn't warn you, that's all!"

She lifted her coffee-cup, and strolled away, leaving Claire to reflect impatiently, "*More* poison! It's too bad. They won't *let* one be happy!"

Before the end of the week school work settled into its old routine, and the days passed by with little to mark their progress. The English climate was at its worst, and three times out of four the journey to school was accomplished in rain or sleet. The motor-'buses were crammed with passengers, and manifested an unpleasant tendency to skid; pale-faced strap-holders crowded the carriages of the Tube; for days together the sky remained a leaden grey. It takes a Mark Tapley himself to keep smiling under such conditions. As Claire recalled the days when she and her mother had sat luxuriously under the trees in the gardens of Riviera hotels, listening to exhilarating bands, and admiring the outline of the Esterels against the cloudless blue of the sky, the drab London streets assumed a dreariness which was almost insupportable. Also, though she would not acknowledge it to herself, she was achingly disappointed, because something which she had sub-consciously been expecting did not come to pass. She had expected something to happen, but nothing happened; all through February the weeks dragged on, unrelieved by any episode except the weekly mail from India.

The little brown bird still industriously piped the hour; but his appearance no longer brought the same warm thrill of happiness. And then one morning came a note from Janet Willoughby.

"Dear Miss Gifford,—

"I should really like to call you 'Claire,' but I must wait to be asked! I have been meaning to write ever since we returned from Saint Moritz; but you know how it is in town, such a continual rush, that one can never get through half the things that ought to be done! We should all like to see you again. Mother has another 'At Home' on Thursday evening next, and would be glad to see you then, if you cared to come; but what *I* should like is to have you to myself! On Saturday next I could call for you, as I did at Christmas, and keep you for the whole day. Then we could talk as we couldn't do at the 'At Homes,' which are really rather dull, duty occasions.

"Let me know which of these propositions suits you best. Looking forward to seeing you,—

"Your friend, (if you will have me!)

"Janet Willoughby."

Claire had opened the letter, aglow with expectation; she laid it down feeling dazed and blank. For the moment only one fact stood out to the exclusion of every other, and that was that Janet did not wish her to be present at the "At Home." Mrs Willoughby had sent the invitation, but Janet had supplemented it by another, which could not be refused. "I would rather have you to myself." How was it possible to refuse an invitation couched in such terms? How could one answer with any show of civility, "I should prefer to come with the crowd?"

Claire carried the letter up to her cold bedroom, and sat down to do a little honest thinking.

"It's very difficult to understand what one really wants! We deceive ourselves as much as we do other people... Why am I so hideously depressed? I liked going to the 'At Home,' I liked dressing up, and driving through the streets, and seeing the flowers and the dresses, and having the good supper; but, if that were all, I believe I'd prefer the whole day with Janet. I suppose, really, it's Captain Fanshawe that's at the bottom of it. I want to meet him, I thought I should meet him, and now it's over. I shan't be asked again when there's a chance of his coming. Janet doesn't want me. She's not jealous, of course—that's absurd—but she wants to keep him to herself, and she imagines somehow that I should interfere—"

Imagination pictured Janet staring with puzzled, uneasy eyes across the tables in the dining-room, of Janet drearily examining the piled-up presents in the boudoir, and then, like a flash of light, showed the picture of another face, now eager, animated, admiring, again grave and wistful. "Is your address still the Grand Hotel?—*My* address is still the Carlton Club."

"Ah, well, well!" acknowledged Claire to her heart, "we *did* like each other. We did love being together, and he remembered me; he sent me the clock when he was away. But it's all over now. That was our last chance, and it's gone. He'll go to the At Home, and Mrs Willoughby will tell him I was asked, but preferred to come when they were alone, and he'll think it was because I wanted to avoid him, and—and, oh, goodness, goodness, goodness! how *miserable* I shall feel sitting here all Thursday evening, imagining all that is going on! Oh, mother, mother, your poor little girl is *so* lonesome! Why did you go so far away?"

Claire put her head down on the dressing-table, and shed a few tears, a weakness bitterly regretted, for like all weaknesses the consequences wrought fresh trouble. Now her eyelids were red, and she was obliged

SHE CAUGHT SIGHT OF HER OWN REFLECTION IN THE OVER-MANTEL, AND EXCLAIMED, "WHAT A FRIGHT I LOOK!"

to hang shivering out of the window, until they had regained their natural colour, before she could face Cecil's sharp eyes.

Janet arrived soon after eleven o'clock on Saturday morning, and was shown into the saffron parlour where Claire sat over her week's mending. She wore a spring suit purchased in Paris, and a hat which was probably smart, but very certainly was unbecoming, slanting as it did at a violent angle over her plump, good-humoured face, and almost entirely blinding one eye. She caught sight of her own reflection in the overmantel and exclaimed, "What a fright I look!" as she seated herself by the table, and threw off her furs. "Don't hurry, please. Let me stay and watch. What are you doing? Mending a blouse? How clever of you to be able to use your fingers as well as your brains! I never sew, except stupid fancy-work for bazaars. So this is your room! You told me about the walls. Can you imagine any one in cold blood choosing such a paper? But it looks cosy all the same. I *do* like little rooms with everything carefully in reach. They are ever so much nicer than big ones, aren't they?"

"No."

Janet pealed with laughter.

"That's right, snub me! I deserve to be snubbed. Of course, I meant when you have big ones as well! Who is the pretty girl in the carved frame? Your mother! Do you mean it, really? What a ridiculous mamma! I'm afraid, Claire, I'm afraid she is even prettier than you!"

"Oh, she is; I know it. But I have more charm," returned Claire demurely, whereat they laughed again—a peal of happy girlish laughter, which reached Lizzie's ears as she polished the oilcloth in the hall, and roused an envious sigh.

"It's well to be some folks!" thought poor Lizzie. "Motor-cars, and fine dresses, and nothing to do of a Saturday morning but sit still and laugh. I could laugh myself if I was in her shoes!"

Claire folded away her blouse, and took up a bundle of gloves.

"These are your gloves. They have been such a comfort to me. There's a button missing somewhere. Tell me all about your holiday! Did you have a good time? Was it as nice as you expected?"

"Yes. No. It *was* a good time, but—do you think anything ever *quite* comes up to one's expectation? I had looked forward to that month for the whole year, and had built so many fairy castles. You have stayed in Switzerland? You know how the scene changes when the sun sinks, how those beautiful alluring rose-coloured peaks become in a minute awesome and gloomy. Well, it was rather like that with me. I don't mean that it was gloomy; that's exaggerating, but it was prose, and I had pictured it poetry. Heigho! It's a weary world."

Claire's glance was not entirely sympathetic.

"There are different kinds of prose. You will forgive my saying that your especial sort is an *Edition de luxe*."

"I know! I know! You can't be harder on me than I am on myself. My dear, I have a most sensible head. I'm about as practical and long-headed as any woman of forty. It's my silly old heart which handicaps me. It *won't* fall into line... Have you finished your mending? May I come upstairs and see your room while you dress?"

For just the fraction of a moment Claire hesitated. Janet saw the doubt, and attributed it to disinclination to exhibit a shabby room; but in reality Claire was proud of her attic, which a little ingenuity had made into a very charming abode. Turkey red curtains draped the window, a low basket-chair was covered in the same material, a red silk eiderdown covered the little bed. On the white walls were a profusion of photographs and prints, framed with a simple binding of leather around the glass. The toilet table showed an array of well-polished silver, while a second table was arranged for writing, and held a number of pretty accessories. A wide board had been placed over the narrow mantel, on which stood a few good pieces of china and antique silver. There was nothing gimcrack to be seen, no one-and-elevenpenny ornaments, no imitations of any kind; despite its sloping roof and its whitewashed walls, it was self-evidently a lady's room, and Janet's admiration was unfeigned.

"My dear, it's a lamb! I love your touches of scarlet. Dear me, you've quite a view! I shall have sloping walls when I change my room. They are *ever* so picturesque. It's a perfect duck, and everything looks so bright. They *do* keep it well!"

"*I* keep it well!" Claire corrected. "Lizzie 'does' it every morning, but it's not a doing which satisfies me, so I put in a little manual labour every afternoon as a change from using my brain. I do all the polishing. You can't expect lodging-house servants to clean silver and brass."

"Can't you? No; I suppose you can't." Janet's voice of a sudden sounded flat and absent. There was a moment's pause, then she added tentatively, "You have a cuckoo clock?"

Claire was thankful that her face was screened from view as she was in the process of tying on her veil. A muffled, "Yes," was her only reply.

Janet stood in front of the clock, staring at it with curious eyes.

"It's—it's like—there were some just like this in a shop at Saint Moritz."

"They are all much alike, don't you think?"

"I suppose they are. Yes—in a way. Some are much better than others. This is one of the best—"

"Yes, it is. It keeps beautiful time. I had it in the sitting-room, but Miss Rhodes objected to the noise."

"Was it in Saint Moritz that you bought it?"

"I didn't buy it. It was a present."

That finished the cross-questioning, since politeness forbade that Janet should go a step further and ask the name of the friend, which was what she was obviously longing to do. She stood a moment longer, staring blankly at the clock, then gave a little sigh, and moved on to examine the ornaments on the mantelpiece. Five minutes later the two girls descended the staircase, and drove away from the door.

The next few hours passed pleasantly enough, but Claire wondered if it were her own imagination which made her think that Janet's manner was not quite so frank and bright as it had been before she had caught sight of the cuckoo clock. She never again said, "Claire"; but her brown eyes studied Claire's face with a wistful scrutiny, and from time to time a sharp little sigh punctuated her sentences.

"But what could I tell her?" Claire asked unhappily of her sub-conscience. "I don't *know*—I only think; and even if he *did* send it, it doesn't necessarily affect his feelings towards her. He was going to see her in a few days; and she is rich and has everything she wants, while I am poor and alone. It was just kindness, nothing more." But though her head was satisfied with such reasoning, her heart, like Janet's, refused to fall into line.

At tea-time several callers arrived, foremost among them a tall man whom Claire at once recognised as the original of a portrait which stood opposite to that of Captain Fanshawe on the mantelpiece of Janet's boudoir. This was "the kind man, the thoughtful man," the man who remembered "little things," and in truth he bore the mark of it in every line of his good-humoured face. Apart from his expression, his appearance was ordinary enough; but he was self-evidently a man to trust, and Claire found something pathetic in the wistful admiration which shone in his eyes as they followed Janet Willoughby about the room. To ordinary observers she was just a pleasant girl with no pretensions to beauty; to him she was obviously the most lovely of her sex. He had no attention to spare for Claire or the other ladies present; he was absorbed in watching Janet, waiting for opportunities to serve Janet, listening eagerly to Janet's words. It is not often that an unengaged lover is so transparent in his devotion, but Malcolm Heward was supremely indifferent to the fact that he betrayed his feelings.

At ten o'clock Claire rose to take leave, and Mrs Willoughby made a request.

"I am going to ask you to do me a favour, dear. A friend is having a Sale of Work at her house for a charity in which we are both interested, and she has asked me to help. It is on a Saturday afternoon and evening, and I wondered if I might ask you to take part in the little concerts. Whistling is always popular, and you do it so charmingly. I would send the car for you, and take you home, of course, and be so very much indebted. You don't mind my asking?"

"No, indeed; I should be delighted. Please let me help you whenever you can."

In the bedroom upstairs Janet deliberately introduced Malcolm Heward's name.

"That was the man I told you about at Christmas. He was one of the party at Saint Moritz. What did you think of him?"

"I liked him immensely. He looks all that you said he was. He has a fine face."

"He wants to marry me."

Claire laughed softly.

"That's obvious! I never saw a man give himself away so openly."

"Do you think I ought to accept him?"

"Oh, how can I say? It's not for me to advise. I hope, whoever you marry, you'll be very, very happy!"

Suddenly Janet came forward and laid her hands on Claire's arm.

"Oh, Claire, I do like you! I do want to be friends, but sometimes I have the strangest thoughts." Before Claire had time to answer, she had drawn back again, and was saying with a little apologetic laugh, "I am silly! Take no notice of what I say. Here's your fur; here's your muff. Are you quite sure you have all your possessions?"

Chapter Fourteen.

A Question of Money.

The next week was memorable to Claire as marking the beginning of serious anxiety with regard to Sophie. She had looked ill since the beginning of the term, and the bottle of aspirin tabloids had become quite an accustomed feature on the luncheon table; but when questioned she had always a smile and an easy excuse.

"What can you expect in this weather? No one but a fish could help aching in these floods. I'm perfectly all right!"

But one morning this week, meeting her on an upper landing, Claire discovered Sophie apparently dragging herself along with her hands, and punctuating each step with a gasp of pain. She stood still and stared, whereupon Sophie instantly straightened herself, and ascended the remaining steps in a normal manner.

"Sophie," cried Claire sternly, "don't pretend! I heard you; I saw you! My dear girl, is the rheumatism so bad?"

Sophie twisted her head this way and that, her lips pursed in warning.

"S–sh! Be careful! You never know who is about. I *am* rather stiff to-day. This raw fog has been the last straw. I shall be all right when we get through this month. I hate March! It finds out all the weak spots. Please, Claire, don't take any notice. A Gym. mistress has no business to have rheumatism. It's really very good for me to be obliged to keep going. It is always worse at the beginning of the day."

Claire went away with a pain in her heart, and the pain grew steadily as she watched Sophie throughout the week. The pretty face was often drawn with pain, she rose and sat down with an obvious effort; and still the rain poured, and the dark fog enveloped the

The Independence of Claire

city, and Sophie struggled to and from her work in a thin blue serge suit which had already seen three winters' wear.

One day the subject came up for discussion in the staff-room, and Claire was shocked and surprised at the attitude of the other teachers. They were sorry for Sophie, they sympathised, to a certain extent they were even anxious on her account, but the prevailing sentiment seemed to be that the kindest thing was to take no notice of her sufferings. No use pitying her; that would only make her more sorry for herself. No use suggesting cures; cures take time, not to speak of money. The Easter holidays would soon be here; perhaps she might try something then. In the meantime—*tant pis*! she must get along as best she could. There was simply no time to be ill.

"I've a churchyard cough myself," declared the Arts mistress. "I stayed in bed all Saturday and Sunday, and it was really a little better, but it was as bad as ever after a day in this big draughty hole."

"And I am racked with neuralgia," chimed in Miss Bates. The subject of Sophie was lost in a general lamentation.

Friday evening came, and after the girls had departed Claire went in search of Sophie, hoping tactfully to be able to suggest remedial methods over the week-end. She peeped into several rooms before at last, in one of the smallest and most out-of-the-way, she caught sight of a figure crouched with buried head at the far end of the table. It was Sophie, and she was crying, and catching her breath in a weak exhausted fashion, pitiful to hear. Claire shut the door tightly, and put her arms round the shaking form.

"Miss Blake—Sophie! You poor, dear girl! You are tired out. You have been struggling all the week, but it's Friday night, dear, remember that! You can go home and just tumble into bed. Don't give way when you've been so brave."

But for the moment Sophie's bravery had deserted her.

"It's raining! It's raining! It *always* rains. I can't face it. The pain's all over me, and the omnibuses *won't* stop! They expect you to jump in, and I can't jump! I don't know how to get home."

"Well, I do!" Claire cried briskly. "There's no difficulty about that. I'm sick of wet walks myself. I'll whistle for a taxi, and we'll drive home in state. I'll take you home first, and then go on myself; or, if you like, I'll come in with you and help you to bed."

"P–please. Oh, yes, please, do come! I don't want to be alone," faltered Sophie weakly; but she wiped her eyes, and in characteristic fashion began to cheer up at the thought of the drive home.

There was a cheerful fire burning in Sophie's sitting-room, and the table was laid for tea in quite an appetising fashion. The landlady came in at the sound of footsteps, and showed a sympathetic interest at the sight of Sophie's tear-stained face.

"I *told* you you weren't fit to go out!" she said sagely. "Now just sit yourself down before the fire, and I'll take your things upstairs and bring you down a warm shawl. Then you shall have your teas. I'll bring in a little table, so you can have it where you are." She left the room, and Sophie looked after her with grateful eyes.

"That's what I pay for!" she said eloquently. "She's so kind! I love that woman for all her niceness to me. I told you I had no right to pay so much rent. I came in just for a few weeks until I could find something else, and I haven't had the *heart* to move. I've been in such holes, and had such awful landladies. They seem divided into two big classes, kind and dirty, or clean and *mad*! When you get one who is kind *and* clean, you feel so grateful that you'd pay your last penny rather than move away. Oh, how lovely! how lovely! how lovely! It's Friday night, and I can be ill comfortably all the time till Monday

The Independence of Claire

morning! Aren't we jolly well-off to have our Saturdays to ourselves? How thankful the poor clerks and typists would be to be in our place!"

She was smiling again, enjoying the warmth of the fire, the ease of the cushioned chair. When Mrs Rogers entered she snoodled into the folds of a knitted shawl, and lay back placidly while the kind creature took off her wet shoes and stockings and replaced them by a long pair of fleecy woollen bed-socks, reaching knee high. The landlady knelt to her task, and Sophie laid a hand on the top of starched lace and magenta velvet, and cried, "Rise, Lady Susan Rogers! One of the truest ladies that ever breathed..."

"How you do talk!" said the landlady, but her eyes shone. As she expounded to her husband in the kitchen, "Miss Blake had such a way with her. When ladies were like that you didn't care what you did, but there was them as treated you like Kaffirs."

Tea was quite a cheerful and sociable little meal, during which no reference was made to Sophie's ailments, but when the cups had been replaced on the central table, Claire seated herself and said with an air of decision—

"Now we're going to have a disagreeable conversation! I don't approve of the way you have been going on this last month, and it's time it came to an end. You are ill, and it's your business to take steps to get better!"

"Oh!"

"Yes; and you are going to take them, too!"

"What am I going to do?"

"You are going to see a specialist next week."

"You surprise me!" Sophie smiled with exaggerated lightness. "What funny things one does hear!"

"Why shouldn't you see a specialist? I defy you to give me one sensible reason?"

"I'll do better than that. I'll give you two."

"So do, then! What are they?"

"Guineas!" said Sophie.

For a moment Claire stared blankly, then she laughed.

"Oh, I see! Yes. It is rather a haul. But it's better to harden your heart once for all, and pay it down."

"The two guineas is only the beginning."

"The beginning of what?"

"Trouble!" said Sophie grimly. "Baths, at a guinea apiece. Massage, half-a-guinea a time. Medicine, liniments, change of air. My dear, it's no use. What's the use of paying two guineas to hear a man tell you to do a dozen things which are hopelessly impossible? It's paying good money only to be aggravated and depressed. If it comes to that, I can prescribe for myself without paying a sou... Knock off all work for a year. Go to Egypt, or some perfectly dry climate, and build up your strength. Always get out of London for the winter months. Live in the fresh air, and avoid fatigue... How's that? Doesn't that strike you as admirable advice?"

She put her head on one side with a gallant attempt at a smile, but her lips twitched, and the flare of the incandescent light showed her face lined and drawn with pain. Claire was silent, her heart cramping with pain. The clock ticked on for several minutes, before she asked softly—

"Have you no savings, Sophie? No money to keep you if you *did* take a rest?"

"Not a sou. It's all I can do to struggle along. I told you I had to help a young sister, and things run up so quickly, that it doesn't seem possible to save. I suppose many people would say one ought to be able to do it on a hundred a year; that's all I have left for

The Independence of Claire

myself! Hundreds of women manage on less, but as a rule they come from a different class, and can put up with a style of living which would be intolerable to us. I don't complain of the pay. I don't think it is bad as things go: it's only when illness comes that one looks ahead and feels—frightened! Suppose I broke down now, suppose I broke down in ten years' time! I should be over forty, and after working hard for twenty years I should be left without a penny piece; thrown on the scrap heap, as a worn-out thing that was no more use. But I might still live on, years upon years. Oh, dear! why did you make me think of it? It does no good; only gives one the hump. There *is* no Pension scheme, so I simply can't afford to be ill. That's the end of it."

"Don't you think if you went to Miss Farnborough, and explained to her—"

Sophie turned a flushed, protesting face.

"Never! Not for the world, and you mustn't either. Promise me faithfully that you will never give so much as a hint. Miss Farnborough is a capital head, but her great consideration is for the pupils; we only count in so far as we are valuable to them. She'd be sorry for me, of course, and would give me quite a lot of advice, but she'd think at once, 'If she's rheumatic, she won't be so capable as a Gym. mistress; I must get some one else!' No, no, my dear, I must go on, I must fight it out. You'd be surprised to see how I *can* fight when Miss Farnborough comes on the scene!"

"Very well. You have had your say, now I'm going to have mine! If you go on as you have been doing the last month, growing stiffer week by week, you won't be *able* to hide it! The other mistresses talk about it already. They were discussing you in staff-room last week. If you go on trusting to chance, you are simply courting disaster. Now I'll tell you what I am going to do. I'm going to find out the address of a good specialist, and make an appointment for next Saturday morning. You shan't have any trouble about it, and I'll call in a taxi, and take you myself, and bring you safely back. And it will be the wisest and the cheapest two guineas you ever spent in your life. Now! What have you got to say to that?"

"Oh, I don't know, I don't know! You are very kind. I suppose I ought to be grateful. I suppose you are right. Oh, I'll go, I suppose, I must go. *Bother!*" cried Sophie ungraciously, whereupon Claire hastily changed the conversation, and made no further reference to health during the rest of her visit.

Mrs Willoughby supplied the name of a specialist; the specialist granted an appointment for the following Saturday at noon, when the two girls duly appeared in his consulting-room; and Sophie underwent the usual examination, during which the great doctor's face assumed a serious air. Finally he returned to the round-backed chair which stood against the desk, and faced his patient across the room. Sophie was looking flushed and pretty, she was wearing her best clothes, and she wore them with an air which might well delude a masculine eye into believing them much better than they really were. Claire had her usual smart, well-turned-out appearance. They seemed to the doctor's eyes two prosperous members of Society.

"I fear," he said gravely, "I fear that there is no doubt that your rheumatism is the sort most difficult to treat. It is a clear case of rheumatoid arthritis, but you are young, and the disease is in an early stage, so that we must hope for the best. In olden times it was supposed to be an incurable complaint, but of late years we have had occasional cures, quite remarkable cures, which have mitigated that decision. You must realise, however, that it is a difficult fight, and that you will need much patience and perseverance."

"How soon do you think you can cure me?"

The doctor looked into Sophie's face, and his eyes were pitiful.

"I wish I could say, but I fear that's impossible. Different people are affected by different cures. You must go on experimenting until you find one that will suit your case;

meanwhile there are certain definite instructions which you would do well to observe. In what part of London do you live?" He pursed-up his lips at the reply. "Clay! Heavy clay. The worst thing you could have. That must be altered at once. It is essential that you live on light, gravelly soil, and even then you should not be in England in winter. You should go abroad for four or five months."

Sophie cast a lightning glance at her companion. "It's impossible!" she said shortly. "I can't move. I can't go abroad. I am a High School-mistress. I am obliged to stay at my work. I am dependent on my salary. I knew it was stupid to come. I knew what you would say. I told my friend. It was her doing. She made me come—"

"I am very much indebted to your friend," the doctor said genially. "She was quite right to insist that you should have advice, and now that I know the circumstances, I'll try not to be unreasonable. I know how aggravating it must be to be ordered to do things which are clearly impossible; but you are young, and you are threatened with a disease which may cripple your life. I want to do all that is in my power to help you. Let's talk it over quietly, and see what can be done."

"I'm in school every day until half-past four, except on Saturdays, and I can't afford to wait. I *must* get better, and I must be quick about it, or I shall lose my post. If I leave this school through rheumatism, it will go down in my testimonial, and I should never get another opening. I'm the Gym. mistress."

"Poor girl!" said the doctor kindly. "Well," he added, "I can say one thing for your encouragement; you could not help yourself more than by preserving your present attitude of mind. To determine to get better, and to get better quickly, is a very valuable aid to material means. And now I will tell you what I propose."

He bent forward in his chair, talking earnestly and rapidly. There was no time to be lost, since the disease was apt to take sudden leaps forward; at this stage every day was of value; the enemy must be attacked before he had made good his hold. There was a new treatment which, within his own experience, had had excellent results. It was not a certainty; it was very far from a certainty, but it was a chance, and it had this merit, that a month or six weeks would prove its efficacy in any special case. If this failed, something else must be tried, but most cures were very long, very costly. He would propose in the first instance giving two injections a week; later on three or even four. There might be a certain amount of reaction.

"What do you mean by reaction?" Sophie asked.

"Fever, headache. Possibly sickness, but not lasting for more than twenty-four hours."

Sophie set her lips.

"I have no time to be ill!"

The doctor looked at her with deliberate sternness.

"You will have all your life to be ill, if you do not take care now! I will do what I can to help you; we will arrange the times most convenient to you. You might come to me at first direct from school on Wednesdays and Saturdays. Later on the system will accustom itself, and you will probably feel no bad effects. I should like to undertake your case myself. My charge to you will be a quarter of my ordinary fee."

"Thank you very much," stammered Sophie, "but—"

Claire jumped up, and hastily interposed.

"Thank you so very much! We are most grateful, but it's—it's been rather a shock, and we have not had time to think. Will you allow us to write and tell you our decision?"

"Certainly. Certainly. But be quick about it. I am anxious to help, but every week's delay will make the case more difficult. Try to arrange for Wednesday next."

As he spoke he led the way towards the door. He had been all that was kind and considerate, but there were other patients waiting; all day long a procession of sufferers were filing into that room. He had no more time to give to Sophie Blake. The two girls went out into the street, got into a taxi and were driven swiftly away. Neither spoke. They drew up before the door of Sophie's lodgings, entered the cosy sitting-room and sat down by the fire.

"Well!" Sophie's face was flushed, her eyes were dry and feverishly bright. "I hope you are satisfied, my dear. I've been to a specialist to please you, and a most depressing entertainment it has been. Arthritis! That's the thing people have who go about in Bath chairs, and have horrible twisted fingers. It was supposed to be incurable, but now they have 'an occasional cure,' so I must hope for the best! I do think doctors are the stupidest things! They have no tact. He could tell me that in one breath, and in the other that it was most important that I should have hope. Well! I *have* hope. I *have* faith, but it's not because of his stupid injections. I believe in God, and God knows that I need my health, and that other people need it too. My little sister! What would happen to her if I crocked now? I don't believe He will *let* me grow worse!"

"That's all right, Sophie dear, but oughtn't you to use the means? I don't call it trusting in the right sense if you set yourself against the help that comes along. God doesn't work miracles as He did in the old way; the world has progressed since those old times, and now He works through men. It is a miracle just the same, though it shows itself in a more natural fashion. Don't you call it a miracle that a busy doctor should offer to treat you himself, at the hours most convenient to you, and to do it at a quarter of his usual fees?"

"His fee for to-day was two guineas. They always charge that, I suppose—these specialist people. A quarter of that would mean half-a-guinea a visit. Two half-guineas equal one guinea. Later on, three or four half-guineas a week would equal one-and-a-half to two guineas. Two guineas equal my whole income. Very kind, no doubt—very kind indeed. And just about as feasible as if he'd said a thousand pounds."

Claire was busy calculating, her fingers playing upon her knee. Ten guineas ought to pay for the six weeks which would test the efficacy of the vaccine. Surely there could not be any serious difficulty about ten guineas?

"Wouldn't your brother?"

Sophie shook her head.

"I wouldn't ask him. He has four small children, and he does so much for Emily. More than he can afford. He works too hard, poor fellow. If it were a certainty, perhaps it might be managed somehow; but it's only a chance, and six weeks won't see the end."

"But the end will be quicker if you begin at once. The doctor said that every day was of importance. Sophie, listen! I've got the money. I've got it lying in the bank. I'll lend it to you. I'd love to lend it. If you'll let me, I'll send you a cheque to-night; that will pay for the first six weeks—"

Sophie stretched out her hand, and gave a momentary clasp to Claire's fingers.

"You *are* a good soul! Fancy offering that to a stranger like me! It's noble of you, my dear. Perfectly sweet! I'm awfully grateful, but it's absolutely impossible that I could accept. When could I pay you back? I've never been able to save, but I *have* kept out of debt, and it would worry me to death to have ten pounds hanging round my neck. Besides, we shouldn't be any further. At the end of the six weeks I should either be better, in which case he would certainly want me to go on; or worse, when I should have to try something else! You don't propose that I should go on borrowing from you at the rate of one or two guineas a week?"

"I—I'm afraid I haven't got it to give."

"Very well, then—there you are! What's the good of beginning at all?"

Claire put her hands over her face and thought with that intense and selfless thought which is as a prayer for help. The future seemed dark indeed, and the feeling of helplessness was hard to bear. Two lonely girls, with no one to help, and so much help that was needed! Here was indeed the time for prayer.

"Sophie, it's horribly difficult; we can't see ahead. We can only 'do the next thing.' It is your duty to take this cure *now*, and the way has opened for that. When we've come to the end of the six weeks, it may open again. You said you have trust in God. It's no use talking generalities, if you are not prepared to put your faith into practice. The question for to-day is, *Can you trust Him for the beginning of May?*"

Sophie smiled.

"I like that! That's a nice way of putting it. Yes, I can; but, Claire (I must call you Claire, you are such a dear!), I wish it didn't mean borrowing other people's money! It will be years before I can pay you back. It may be that I can never do it."

"I would have said 'give,' but I was afraid it would hurt your pride. My stepfather gave me some money to buy jewellery for a wedding present, and as a pure matter of selfishness I'd get more pleasure out of helping you than out of a stupid brooch. And listen, Sophie, listen! I'm going to explain.—I chose to take up teaching because I wanted to be independent, and I knew my mother would be happier without me during the first years of her marriage; but she is devoted to me, and I know in time she will crave to have me back. She isn't strong, and she finds the Indian climate trying, so very likely she may *need* my help. I shall never be sorry that I came to London, for work is a splendid experience, and I am glad to have it; but I have never the feeling that it is going to *last*. Mother comes first, and my stepfather is quite well-off, and can afford to keep me; so if I were *needed*, I should not feel that I was sacrificing my independence in letting him do it. So you see I am not quite in the same position as the other mistresses, and money is not of the same importance. If you were in my place, Sophie, would you hesitate to lend me a ten-pound note?"

"Guineas, please!" cried Sophie, laughing to hide her tears. "All right, my dear, all right! I give in. I lie down. You've beaten me. I've nothing more to say. I'll take the horrid old injections, and pay for them with your money, and—and—I think I'll go to bed now, please! I've had about as much as I can bear for one short day!"

"And I'll go home and have a rest myself. I am to help at a bazaar this afternoon, and I don't feel at all in my full beauty. Good-bye, Sophie. Cheer up! There's a good time coming!"

"There's a good time coming for *you!*" predicted Sophie confidently.

Chapter Fifteen.

"Lend me five pounds!"

The contrasts of life seemed painfully strong to Claire Gifford that Saturday afternoon as she seated herself in the luxurious car by Mrs Willoughby's side, and thought of Sophie Blake obliged to borrow ten pounds to pay for a chance of health, and the contrast deepened during the next few hours, as she watched beautifully gowned women squandering money on useless trifles which decked the various "stalls." Embroidered cushions, painted sachets, veil cases, shaving cases, night-dress cases, bridge bags, fan bags, handkerchief bags, work bags; bags of every size, of every shape, of every conceivable material; bead necklaces, mats—a wilderness of mats—a very pyramid of drawn-thread work. Claire found a seat near the principal stall, where she caught the remarks of the buyers as they turned away. "...I detest painted satin! Can't think why I bought that ridiculous sachet. It will have to go on to the next bazaar."

"...That makes my twenty-third bag! Rather a sweet, though, isn't he? It will go with my grey dress."

"This is awful! I'm not getting on at all. I can't decently spend less than five pounds. For goodness' sake tell me what to buy!"

"Can't think why people give bazaars! Such an upset in the house. For some charity, I believe—I forget what. She asked me to come..."

So on and so on; scores of women surging to and fro, swinging bags of gold and silver chain, buying baubles for which they had no use; occasionally—very occasionally, for love of the cause; often—very often because Lady — had sent a personal invitation, and Lady — was a useful friend, and gave such charming balls!

At the two concerts Claire had a pleasant success, which she enjoyed with all her heart. Her whistling performance seemed to act as a general introduction, for every listener seemed to be anxious to talk to her, and to ask an infinitude of questions. Was it difficult? How long did it take to learn? Was she nervous? Wasn't it difficult not to laugh? How did she manage not to look a fright? Did she do it often? Did she *mind*? This last question usually led up to a tentative mention of some entertainment in which the speaker was interested, but after the first refusal Claire was on guard, and regretted that her time was filled up. She was eager to help Mrs Willoughby, but had no desire to be turned into an unpaid public performer!

Janet did not appear at the bazaar, so the drive home was once more a *tête-à-tête*, during which Mrs Willoughby questioned Claire as to the coming holidays, and expressed pleasure to hear that they were to be spent in Brussels. She was so kind and motherly in her manner that Claire was emboldened to bespeak her interest on Sophie's behalf.

"I suppose," she said tentatively, "you don't know of any family going abroad to a dry climate—it must be a very dry climate—who would like to take a girl with them to—er—to be a sort of help! She's a pretty girl, and very gay and amusing, and she's had the highest possible training in health exercises. She would be splendid if there was a delicate child who needed physical development, and, of course, she is quite well educated all round. She could teach up to a certain point. She is the Gym. mistress in my school, and is very popular with the girls."

"And why does she want to leave?"

"She's not well. It's rheumatism—a bad kind of rheumatism. It is just beginning, and the doctor says it ought to be tackled at once, and that to live on clay soil is the worst thing for her. If she stays at Saint Cuthbert's she's practically bound to live on clay. And he says she ought to get out of England for the next few winters. She has not a penny beyond her salary, but if she could find a post—"

"Well, why not?" Mrs Willoughby's voice was full of a cheerful optimism. "I don't know of anything at present, but I'll make inquiries among my friends. There ought not to be any difficulty. So many people winter abroad; and there is quite a craze for these physical exercises. Oh, yes, my dear, I am sure I can help. Poor thing! poor girl! it's so important to keep her health. I must find some one who will be considerate, and not work her too hard."

She spoke as if the post were a settled thing; as if there were several posts from which to choose. Probably there were. Among her large circle of wealthy friends this popular and influential woman, given a little trouble, could almost certainly find a chance for

The Independence of Claire

Sophie Blake. *Given a little trouble*! That was the rub! Five out of six of the women who had thronged Lady —'s rooms that afternoon would have dismissed Sophie's case with an easy sympathy, "Poor creature! Quite too sad, but really, you know, my dear, it's a shocking mistake to recommend any one to a friend. If anything goes wrong, you get blamed yourself. Isn't there a Home?" Mrs Willoughby was the exception to the rule; she helped in deed, as well as in word. Claire looked at the large plain face with a very passion of admiration.

"Oh, I wish all women were like you! I'm so glad you are rich. I hope you will go on growing richer and richer. You are the right person to have money, because you help, you *want* to help, you remember other women who are poor."

"My dear," said Mrs Willoughby softly, "I have been poor myself. My father lost his money, and for years we had a hard struggle. Then I married—for love, my dear, not money, but there was money, too,—more money than I could spend. It was an intoxicating experience, and I found it difficult not to be carried away. My dear husband had settled a large income on me, for my own use, so I determined, as a safeguard, to divide it in two, and use half for myself and half for gentlewomen like your friend, who need a helping hand. I have done that now for twenty-five years, but I give out of my abundance, my dear; it is easy for me to give money; I deserve no credit for that."

"You give time, too, and sympathy, and kindness. It's no use, Mrs Willoughby. I've put you on the topmost pinnacle in my mind, and nothing that you can say can pull you down. I think you are the best woman in London!"

"Dear, dear, you will turn my head! I'm not accustomed to such wholesale flattery," cried Mrs Willoughby, laughing; then the car stopped, and Claire made her adieux, and sprang lightly to the ground.

The chauffeur had stopped before the wrong house, but he did not discover his mistake as Claire purposely stood still until he had turned the car and started to retrace his way westward. The evening was fine though chill, and the air was refreshing after the crowded heat of Lady —'s rooms. Claire had only the length of a block to walk, and she went slowly, drawing deep breaths to fill her tired lungs.

The afternoon had passed pleasantly enough, but it had left her feeling flat and depressed. She questioned herself as to the cause of her depression. Was she jealous of those other girls who lived lives of luxury and idleness? Honestly she was not. She was not in the position of a girl who had known nothing but poverty, and who therefore felt a girl's natural longing for pretty rooms, pretty clothes, and a taste of gaiety and excitement. Claire had known all these things, and could know them again; neither was she in the position of a working girl who has no one to help in the day of adversity, for a comfortable home was open to her at any moment. No! she was not jealous: she probed still deeper, and acknowledged that she was disappointed! Last time that she had whistled in public—

Claire shook her head with an impatient toss. This was feeble. This was ridiculous. A man whom she had met twice! A man whose mother had refused an introduction. A man whom Janet—

"I must get to work, and prepare my lesson for Monday. Nothing like good work to drive away these sentimental follies!"

But Fate was not kind, for right before her eyes were a couple of lovers strolling onward, the man's hand through the girl's arm, his head bent low over hers. Claire winced at the sight, but the next moment her interest quickened in a somewhat painful fashion, as the man straightened himself suddenly, and swung apart with a gesture of offence. The lovers were quarrelling! Now the width of the pavement was between them; they strode onward, ostentatiously detached. Claire smiled to herself at the childishness

The Independence of Claire

of the display. One moment embracing in the open street, the next flaunting their differences so boldly that every passer-by must realise the position! Surely a grown man or woman ought to have more self-control. Then suddenly the light of a lamp shone on the pair, and she recognised the familiar figures of Mary Rhodes and Major Carew. He wore a long light overcoat. Cecil had evidently slipped out of the house to meet him, for she was attired in her sports coat and knitted cap. Poor Cecil! The interview seemed to be ending in anything but a pleasant fashion.

Claire lingered behind until the couple had passed her own doorway, let herself in with her latch-key, and hastened to settle down to work. When Cecil came in, she would not wish to be observed. Claire carried her books to the bureau, so as to have her back to the fire, but before she had been five minutes writing, she heard the click of the lock, and Cecil herself came into the room.

"Halloa! I saw the light go up. I thought it must be you." She was silent for a couple of minutes, then spoke again in a sharp, summoning voice: "Claire!"

"Yes?"

Claire turned round, to behold Cecil standing at the end of the dining-table, her bare hands clasping its rim. She was so white that her lips looked of a startling redness; her eyes met Claire with a defiant hardness.

"I want you to lend me five pounds *now*!"

Claire's anxiety was swallowed in a rising of irritation which brought an edge of coldness into her voice.

"Five pounds! What for? Cecil, I have never spoken of it, I have never worried you, but I've already paid—"

"I know! I know! I'll pay you back. But I must have this to-night, and I've nowhere else to go. It's important. I would lend it to you, Claire, if it were in my power."

"Cecil, I hate to refuse, but really—I *need* my money! Just now I need it particularly. I can't afford to go on lending. I'm dreadfully sorry, but—"

"Claire, please! I implore you, just this one time! I'll pay you back... There's my insurance policy—I can raise something on that. For pity's sake, Claire, help me this time!"

Claire rose silently and went upstairs. It was not in her to refuse such a request while a five-pound note lay in her desk upstairs. She slipped the crackling paper into an envelope, and carried it down to the parlour. Cecil took it without a word, and went back into the night.

When she had gone, Claire gathered her papers together in a neat little heap, ranged them in a corner of the bureau, and seated herself on a stiff-backed chair at the end of the table. She looked as if she were mounted on a seat of justice, and the position suited her frame of mind. She felt angry and ill-used. Cecil had no right to borrow money from a fellow-worker! The money in the bank was dwindling rapidly; the ten guineas for Sophie would make another big hole. She did not grudge that—she was eager and ready to give it for so good a cause; but *what* was Cecil doing with these repeated loans? To judge from appearances, she was rather poorer than richer during the last few months, while bills for her new clothes came in again and again, and received no settlement. An obstinate look settled on Claire's face. She determined to have this thing out.

In ten minutes' time Cecil was back again, still white, still defiant, meeting Claire's glance with a shrug, seating herself at the opposite end of the table with an air of callous indifference to what should come next.

"Well?"

"Well?"

"You look as if you had something to say!"

"I have. Cecil, what are you doing with all this money?"

"That's my business, I suppose!"

"I don't see it, when the money is mine! I think I have the right to ask?"

"I've told you I'll pay you back!"

"That's not the question. I want to know what you are doing *now*! You are not paying your bills."

"I'll sell out some shares to-morrow, and—"

"You shall do no such thing. I can wait, and I will wait, but I can't go on lending; and if I did, it could do you no good. Where does the money go? It does *you* no good!"

"I am the best judge of that."

"Cecil, *are you lending money to that man?*"

The words leapt out, as on occasion such words will leap, without thought or premeditation on the speaker's part. She did not intend to speak them; if she had given herself one moment for reflection she dared not have spoken them; when their sound struck across the quiet room she was almost as much startled as Cecil herself; yet heart and brain approved their utterance; heart and brain pronounced that she had discovered the truth.

Cecil's face was a deep glowing red.

"Really, Claire, you go too far! Why in the world should you think—"

"I saw you with him now in the street. I could see that you were quarrelling; you took no pains to hide it. You left him to come in to me, and went back again. It seems pretty obvious."

"Well! and if I did?" Cecil had plainly decided that denial was useless. "I am responsible for the loan. What does it matter to you who uses it?"

But at that Claire's anger vanished, and she shrank back with a cry of pain and shame.

"And he *took* it from you? Money! Took it from a girl he professes to love—who is working for herself! Oh, Cecil, how *could* he? How could you allow him? How can you go on caring for such a man?"

"Don't get hysterical, Claire, please. There's nothing so extraordinary in a man being hard up. It's happened before now in the history of the world. Frank has a position to keep up, and his father—I've told you before how mean and difficult his father is, and it's so important that Frank should keep on good terms just now.—He dare not worry him for money. When he is going to make me a rich woman some day, why should I refuse to lend him a few trifling pounds when he runs short? He's in an expensive regiment; he belongs to an expensive Club; he is obliged to keep up with the other men. If I had twice as much I would lend it with pleasure."

Claire opened her lips to say that at least no more borrowed money should be supplied for Major Carew, but the words were never spoken. Pity engulfed her, a passion of pity for the poor woman who a second time had fallen under the spell of an unscrupulous man. Cecil's explanation had fallen on deaf ears, for Claire could accept no excuses for a man who borrowed from a woman to ensure comfort and luxury for himself. An officer in the King's army! The thing seemed incredible; so incredible that, for the first time, a rising of suspicion mingled with her dislike. Mentally, she rehearsed the facts of Major Carew's history as narrated by himself, and found herself doubting every one. The beautiful house in the country—did it really exist? The eccentric old father who refused to part with his gold—was he flesh and blood, or a fictitious figure invented as a convenient excuse? The fortune which was to enrich the future—*was* there such a fortune? Or, if there were, was Major Carew in truth the eldest son? Claire felt a devastating helplessness her life abroad had left her ignorant of many British institutions; she knew nothing of the books in which she might have traced the Carew history; she had nothing to guide her but her own feminine instinct, but if that instinct were right, what was to become of Mary Rhodes?

Her face looked so sad, so downcast, that Cecil's conscience was pricked.

"Poor old Claire!" she said gently, "how I do worry you, to be sure! Never mind, my dear, I'll make it up to you one day. You've been a brick to me, and I shan't forget it. And I'll go to my mother's for the whole of the Easter holidays, and save up my pennies to pay you back. The poor old soul felt defrauded because I stayed only a week at Christmas, so she'll be thankful to have me. You can go to Brussels with an easy mind, knowing that I'm out of temptation. That will be killing two birds with one stone. What do you say to having cocoa now, instead of waiting till nine o'clock? We've tired ourselves out with all this fuss?"

Chapter Sixteen.

The Meeting in Hyde Park.

It was the end of May. The weather was warm and sunny, the windows of the West End were gay with flowers; in the Park the great beds of rhododendrons blazed forth in a glow of beauty. It was the season, and a particularly gay and festive season at that. "Everybody" was in town, including a few million "nobodies." There were clerks toiling by their thousands in the City, chained all day long to their desks; there were clerks' wives at home in the suburbs, toiling all day too, and sometimes far into the night; there were typists, and shop assistants, and prosperous heads of households, who worked steadily for five and a half days a week, in order that their families might enjoy comfort and ease, condensing their own relaxation into short Saturday afternoons. And there were school-mistresses, too, who saw the sun through form-room windows, but felt its call all the same—the call of the whole glad spring—and grew restless, and nervous, and short in temper. It was not the leaders of society whom they envied; they read of Court balls, and garden parties, of preparations for Ascot and Henley with a serene detachment, just as they read with indifference in the fashion page of a daily newspaper that "Square watches are the vogue this season, and our *élégantes* are ordering several specimens of this dainty bauble to match the prevailing colours of their costumes," the while they suffered real pangs at the sight of an "alarming sacrifice" at twenty-nine and six. The one was almost within their grasp; the other floated in the nebulous atmosphere of a different sphere.

In the staff-room at lunch-time the staff grew restless and critical. The hot joints no longer appealed to their appetites, the watery vegetables and heavy puddings became things abhorred. They thought of cool salads and *compôtes* on ice, and hated the sight of the greasy brown gravy. They blamed the cook, they blamed the Committee, they said repeatedly, "Nobody thinks of *us*!" and exchanged anecdotes illustrative of the dulness, the stupidity of their pupils. As for the Matric. candidates, they would *all* fail! There wasn't a chance for a single one. The stupidest set of girls the school had ever possessed! Oh, certainly they would all fail!

"And then," said Mary Rhodes bitterly, "*we* shall be blamed."

The Arts mistress said with a sigh—

"Oh, wouldn't it be heavenly to run away from it all, and have a week-end in the country! The gorse will be out, and the hawthorn still in blossom. What's the very cheapest one could do it on for two days?"

Mademoiselle said—

"Absolutely, *ma chère*, there is no help for it. It is necessary that I have a distraction. I must buy a new hat."

Sophie Blake said defiantly to herself—

"Crippled? Ridiculous! I *refuse* to be crippled. I want to run, and run, and run, and run, and dance, and sing, and jump about! I feel pent! I feel caged! And all that precious money squandered on injections..."

The six weeks' course of treatment had been, from the doctor's point of view, a complete success; from Sophie's a big disappointment. She argued that she was still stiff, still in pain, that the improvement was but small; he pointed out that without the injections she would of a certainty have been worse, and since in arthritis even to remain stationary was a success, to have improved in the smallest degree in six weeks' time might be regarded as a triumph. He prescribed a restful holiday during the Easter vacation, and a second course of treatment on her return. Sophie resigned herself to do without new clothes for the summer, and sold her most treasured possession, a diamond ring which had belonged to her mother, so that the second ten pounds was secure. But how was she to pay back the original loan?

Meanwhile Mrs Willoughby was inquiring among her friends for a suitable post, and had played the good fairy by arranging to send Sophie for the Easter holidays to a country cottage on the Surrey heights, which she ran as a health resort for gentlewomen. Here on a fine dry soil, the air scented with the fragrant breath of the pines, with nothing to do, and plenty of appetising food to eat, the Gym. mistress's general health improved so rapidly that she came back to school with her thin cheeks quite filled out.

"Very satisfactory," said the doctor. "Now I shall be able to get on to stronger doses!"

"What's the good of getting better, only to be made worse?" cried Sophie in rebellion.

Cecil's loan remained unpaid. She had spent her holidays with her mother as arranged, but her finances did not appear to have profited thereby. Dunning for bills became so incessant that the landlady spoke severely of the "credit of the house." She went out constantly in the evening, and several times Claire heard Major Carew's voice at the door, but he never came into the house, and there was no talk of an open engagement.

As for Claire herself, she had had a happy time in Brussels, staying with both English and Belgian friends and re-visiting all the old haunts. She thoroughly enjoyed the change, but could not honestly say that she wished the old life to return. If she came back with a heavy heart, it was neither poverty nor work which she feared, but rather the want of that atmosphere of love and kindliness which make the very essence of home. At the best of times Mary Rhodes was a difficult companion and far from affectionate in manner, but since the giving of that last loan, there had arisen a mental barrier which it seemed impossible to surmount. It had become difficult to keep up a conversation apart from school topics, and both girls found themselves dreading the evening's *tête-à-tête*.

Claire felt like a caged bird beating against the bars. She wanted an outlet from the school life, and the call of the spring was insistent to one who until now had spent the summer in wandering about some of the loveliest scenes in Europe. She wearied of the everlasting streets, and discovered that by hurrying home after afternoon school, making a quick change of clothing, and catching a motor-'bus at the corner of the road, she could reach Hyde Park by half-past five, and spend a happy hour sitting on one of the green chairs, enjoying the beauty of the flowers, and watching the never-ending stream of pedestrians and vehicles. Sometimes she recognised Mrs Willoughby and Janet bowling

The Independence of Claire

past in their luxurious motor, but they never saw her, and she was not anxious that they should. What she wanted was to sit still and rest. Sometimes a smartly-dressed woman, obviously American, would seat herself on the next chair, and inquire as to the best chance of seeing the Queen, and the question being amiably answered, would proceed to unasked confidences. She thought England "sweet." She had just come over to this side. She was staying till the fall. Who was the lady in the elegant blue auto? The London fashions were just too cute! When they parted, the fair American invariably said, "Pleased to have met you!" and looked as though she meant it into the bargain, and Claire whole-heartedly echoed the sentiment. She liked these women with their keen, child-like enthusiasm, their friendly, gracious ways. In contrast to them the ordinary Englishwoman seemed cold and aloof.

One brilliant afternoon when the Park was unusually bright and gay, Claire was seated near the Achilles statue, carelessly scanning the passers-by, when, with a sudden leap of the heart, she saw Erskine Fanshawe some twenty yards ahead, strolling towards her, accompanied by two ladies. He was talking to his companions with every appearance of enjoyment, and had no attention to spare for the rows of spectators on the massed green chairs. Claire felt the blood rush to her face in the shock of surprise and agitation. She had never contemplated the possibility of such a meeting, for Captain Fanshawe had not appeared the type of man who would care to take part in a fashionable parade, and the sudden appearance of the familiar face among the crowd made her heart leap with a force that was physically painful. Then, the excitement over, she realised with a second pang, almost as painful as the first, that in another minute he would have passed by, unseeing, unknowing, to disappear into space for probably months to come. At the thought rebellion arose in her heart. She felt a wild impulse to leave her seat and advance towards him; she longed with a sudden desperation of longing to meet his eyes, to see his smile, but pride held her back. She sat motionless watching with strained eyes.

One of Captain Fanshawe's companions was old, the other young—a pretty, fashionably-dressed girl, who appeared abundantly content with her escort. All three were watching with amusement the movements of a stout elderly dame, who sauntered immediately ahead, leading by a leash a French poodle, fantastically shaved, and decorated with ribbon bows. The stout dame was evidently extravagantly devoted to her pet, and viewed with alarm the approach of a jaunty black and white terrier.

The terrier cocked his ears, and elevating his stump of a tail, yapped at the be-ribboned spaniel with all a terrier's contempt, as he advanced to the attack. The stout dame screamed, dropped the leash, and hit at the terrier with the handle of her parasol. The poodle evidently considering flight the best policy, doubled and fled in the direction of the green chairs, to come violently to anchor against Claire's knee. The crowd stared, the stout dame hurried forward. Claire, placing a soothing hand on the dog's head, lifted a flushed, smiling face, and in so doing caught the lift of a hat, met for the moment the glance of startled eyes.

The stout lady was not at all grateful. She spoke as sharply as though Claire, and Claire alone, had been the cause of her pet's upset. She strode majestically away, leaving Claire trembling, confused, living over again those short moments. She had seen him; he had seen her! He was alive and well, living within a few miles of herself, yet as far apart as in another continent. It was six months since they had last met. It might be six years before they met again. But he had seemed pleased to see her. Short as had been that passing glance, there was no mistaking its interest. He was surprised, but pleasure had overridden surprise. If he had been alone, he would have hurried forward with outstretched hand. In imagination she could see him coming, his grave face lightened with joy. Oh, if *only, only* he had been alone! But he was with friends; he had the air of being content and interested, and the girl was pretty, far prettier than Janet Willoughby.

101

"Good afternoon!"

She turned gasping; he was standing before her, holding out his hand. He had left his companions and come back to join her. His face looked flushed, as though he had rushed back at express speed. He had seemed interested and content, and the girl was pretty, yet he had come back to her! He seated himself on the chair by her side, and looked at her with eager eyes.

"I haven't seen you for six months!"

"I was just—" Claire began impulsively, drew herself up, and finished demurely—"I suppose it is."

"You haven't been at either of Mrs Willoughby's 'At Homes.'"

"No; but I've seen a good deal of them all the same. They have been so kind."

"Don't you care for the 'At Homes'? I asked Mrs Willoughby about you, and she seemed to imply that you preferred not to go."

"Oh, no! Oh, no! That was quite wrong. I *did* enjoy that evening. It was a—a misunderstanding, I think," said Claire, much exercised to find an explanation of what could not really be explained. Of the third "At Home" she had heard nothing until this moment, and a pang of retrospective disappointment mingled with her present content. "I have been to the house several times when they were alone," she continued eagerly. "They even asked me on Christmas Day."

"I know," he said shortly. "I was in Saint Moritz, skating in the sunshine, when I heard how you were spending *your* Christmas holidays." His face looked suddenly grim and set. "A man feels pretty helpless at a time like that. I didn't exactly enjoy myself for the rest of that afternoon."

"That was stupid of you, but—but very nice all the same," Claire said softly. "It wouldn't have made things easier for me if other people had been dull, and, after all, I came off better than I expected."

"You were all alone—in your Grand Hotel?"

"Only for a week." Claire resolutely ignored the hit. "Then my friend came back, and we made some little excursions together, and enjoyed being lazy, and getting up late, and reading lots of nice books. I had made all sorts of good resolutions about the work I was going to get through in the holidays, but I never did one thing."

"Do you often come to the Park?"

Claire felt a pang of regret. Was it possible that even this simple pleasure was to be denied her? She knew too well that if she said "yes," Captain Fanshawe would look out for her again, would come with the express intention of meeting her. To say "yes" would be virtually to consent to such meetings. It was a temptation which took all her strength to reject, but rejected it must be. She would not stoop to the making of a rendez-vous.

"I have been several times, but I shan't be able to come any more. We get busier towards the end of the term. Examinations—"

Captain Fanshawe straightened himself, and said in a very stiff voice—

"I also, unfortunately, am extremely busy, so I shall not be able to see the rhododendrons in their full beauty. I had hoped you might be more fortunate."

Claire stared at a passing motor, of which she saw nothing but a moving mass; when she turned back it was to find her companion's eyes fixed on her face, with an expression half guilty, half appealing, altogether ingratiating. At the sight her lips twitched, and suddenly they were laughing together with a delicious consciousness of understanding.

"Well!" he cried, "it's true! I mean it! There's no need to stay away because of me; but as I *am* here to-day, and it's my last chance, won't you let me give you tea? If we walk along to Victoria Gate—"

Claire thought with a spasm of longing of the little tables under the awning; of the pretty animated scene; but no, it might not be. Her acquaintance with this man was too casual to allow her to accept his hospitality in a public place.

"Thank you very much, but I think not. I would rather stay here."

"Well, at any rate," he said defiantly, "I've paid for my chair, and you can't turn me out. Of course, you can move yourself."

"But I don't want to move. I like being here. I'm very glad to see you. I should like very much to have tea, too. Oh, if you don't understand I can't explain!" cried poor Claire helplessly; and instantly the man's expression altered to one of sympathy and contrition.

"I do understand! Don't mind what I say. Naturally it's annoying, but you're right, I suppose—you're perfectly right. I am glad, at any rate, that you allow me to talk to you for a few minutes. You are looking very well!" His eyes took her in in one rapid comprehensive sweep, and Claire thanked Providence that she had put on her prettiest dress. "I am glad that you are keeping fit. Did you enjoy your holiday in Belgium?"

"How did you know I was in Belgium?"

He laughed easily, but ignored the question.

"You have good news of your mother, I hope?"

"Very good. She loves the life, and is very happy and interested, and my stepfather writes that his friends refuse to believe in the existence of a grown-up daughter. He is so proud of her youthful looks."

"How much did you tell her about your Christmas holidays?"

"All the nice bits! I don't approve of burdening other people!"

"Evidently not. Then there have been burdens? You've implied that! Nothing by any chance, in which a man—fairly intelligent, and, in this instance, keen after work—could possibly be of some use?"

The two pairs of eyes met, gazed, held one another steadily for a long eloquent moment.

"Yes," said Claire.

Captain Fanshawe bent forward quickly, holding his stick between his knees. The side of his neck had flushed a dull red colour. For several moments he did not speak. Claire had a curious feeling that he could not trust his voice.

"Good!" he said shortly at last. "Now may I hear?"

"I should like very much to ask you some questions about—about a man whom I think you may know."

The grey eyes came back to her face, keen and surprised.

"Yes! Who is he?"

"A Major Carew. His Christian name is Frank. He belongs to your Club."

"I know the fellow. Yes! What do you want to know about him?"

"Everything, I think; everything you can tell me!"

"You know him personally, then? You've met him somewhere?"

"Yes," Claire answered to the last question, "and I'm anxious—I'm interested to know more. Do you know his people, or anything about him?"

"I don't know them personally. I know Carew very slightly. Good family, I believe. Fine old place in Surrey."

The Elizabethan manor house was true, then! Claire felt relieved, but not yet satisfied. Her suspicion was so deep-rooted that it was not easily dispelled. She sat silent for a moment, considering her next question.

"Is he the eldest son?"

"I believe he is. I've always understood so."

The eldest son of a good family possessing a fine old place! Claire summoned before her the picture of the coarse florid-faced man who had tried to flirt with her in the presence of the woman to whom he was engaged; a man who stooped to borrow money from a girl who worked for her own living. *What* excuse could there be for such a man? She drew her brows together in puzzled fashion, and said slowly—

"Then surely, if he is the heir, he ought to be rich!"

"It doesn't necessarily follow. I should say Carew was not at all flush. Landed property is an expensive luxury in these days. I've heard, too, that the father is a bit of a miser. He may not be generous in the matter of allowance!"

Claire sat staring ahead, buried in thought, and Captain Fanshawe stared at her in his turn, and wondered once more why this particular girl was different from every other girl, and why in her presence he felt a fullness of happiness and content. She was very pretty; but pretty girls were no novelty in his life; he knew them by the score. It was not her beauty which attracted him, but a mysterious affinity which made her seem nearer to him than he had hitherto believed it possible for any human creature to be. He had recognised this mysterious quality at their first meeting; he had felt it more strongly at Mrs Willoughby's "At Home"; six months' absence had not diminished his interest. Just now, when he had caught sight of her flushed upturned face, his heart had leapt with a violence which startled him out of his ordinary calm. Something had happened to him. When he had time he must think the thing out and discover its meaning. But how did she come to be so uncommonly interested in Carew? He met Claire's eyes, and she asked falteringly—

"I wish you would tell me what you think of him personally! Do you think he is—nice?"

"Tell me first what you think yourself."

"Honestly? You won't mind?"

"Not one single little bit! I told you he is a mere acquaintance."

"Then," said Claire deliberately, "I think he is the most horrible, detestable, insufferable, altogether despicable creature I have ever met in the whole of my life!"

"What! What! I say, you *are* down on him!" Captain Fanshawe stared, beamed with an obvious relief, then hastened to defend an absent man. "You're wrong, you know; really you're wrong! I don't call Carew the most attractive fellow you can meet; rather rough manners, don't you know, but he's all right—Carew's all right. You mustn't judge by appearances, Miss Gifford. Some of the most decent fellows in the Club are in his set. Upon my word, I think he is quite a good sort." Captain Fanshawe waxed the more eloquent as Claire preserved her expression of incredulous dislike. He looked at her curiously, and said, "I suppose I mustn't ask—I suppose you couldn't tell me exactly why you are so interested in Carew?"

"I'm afraid not. No; I'm afraid I can't," Claire said regretfully. Then suddenly there flashed through her mind a remembrance of the many tangles and misunderstandings which take place in books for want of a little sensible out-speaking. She looked into Captain Fanshawe's face with her pretty dark-lashed eyes and said honestly, "I wanted to know about him for the sake of—another person? *Nothing* to do with myself! I have only met him twice. I hope I shall never meet him again!"

"Thank you," said the man simply, and at the time neither of the two realised the full significance of those quiet words. It was only on living over the interview on her return home that Claire remembered and understood!

For the next quarter of an hour they abandoned the personal note, and discussed the various topics of the hour. They did not always agree, and neither was of the type to be easily swayed from a preconceived opinion, but always they were interested, always they felt a sympathy for the other view, never once was there a fraction of a pause. They had so much to say that they could have talked for hours.

Gradually the Park began to empty, the string of motors grew less, the crowd on the footpath no longer lounged, but walked quickly with a definite purpose; the green chairs stood in rows without a single occupant. Claire looked round, realised her isolation, drew an involuntary sigh, and rose in her turn.

"It's getting late. I must be hurrying home. I go to the Marble Arch and take a motor-'bus. Please don't let me take you out of your way!"

He looked at her straightly but did not reply, and they paced together down the broad roadway, past the sunken beds of rhododendrons with the fountain playing in the centre, towards the archway which seemed to both so unnecessarily near! Claire thought of the six months which lay behind, saw before her a vision of months ahead unenlightened by another meeting, and felt suddenly tired and chill. Captain Fanshawe frowned and bit at his lower lip.

"I am going away to-morrow. We shall be in camp. In August I am taking part of my leave to run up to Scotland, but I can always come to town if I'm needed, or if there's a special inducement. I came up for both the Willoughbys' 'At Homes.'"

"Did you?" Claire said feebly, and fell a-thinking. The inference was too plain to be misunderstood. The "special inducement" in this instance had been the hope of meeting herself. Actually it would appear that he had travelled some distance to ensure this chance, but the chance had been deliberately denied. Kind Mrs Willoughby would have welcomed her with open arms; it was Janet who had laid the ban. Janet was friendly, almost affectionate. As spring progressed she had repeatedly called at Saint Cuthbert's after afternoon school and carried Claire off for refreshing country drives. Quite evidently she enjoyed Claire's society, quite evidently also she preferred to enjoy it when other visitors were not present. Claire was not offended, for she knew that there was no taint of snobbishness in this decision; she was just sorry, and, in a curious fashion, remorseful into the bargain. She did not argue out the point, but instinctively she felt that Janet, not herself, was the one to be pitied!

They reached the end of the footpath: in another minute they would be in the noise and bustle of Oxford Street. Erskine Fanshawe came to an abrupt halt, faced Claire and cried impulsively—

"Miss Gifford!"

"Yes?"

Claire shrank instinctively. She knew that she was about to be asked a question which it would be difficult to answer.

Erskine planted his stick on the ground, and stared straight into her eyes.

"Why are you so determined to give me no chance of meeting you again?"

"I—I'm *not* determined! I hope we *shall* meet. Perhaps next winter—at Mrs Willoughby's."

He laughed grimly.

"But if I were not content to wait for 'perhaps next winter—at Mrs Willoughby's.' ... What then?"

Claire looked at him gravely.

"What would you suggest? I have no home in London, and no relations, and your mother, Captain Fanshawe, would not introduce me to you when she had the chance!"

He made a gesture of impatience.

"Oh, my mother is the most charming of women—and the most indiscreet. She acts always on the impulse of the moment. She introduced you to Mrs Willoughby, or asked Mrs Willoughby to introduce herself, which comes to the same thing. Surely that proves that she—she—"

He broke off, finding a difficulty in expressing what he wanted to say; but Claire understood, and emphatically disagreed. To enlist a friend's sympathy was a very different thing from running the risk of entangling the affections of an only son! Obviously, however, she could not advance this argument, so they stood, the man and the girl, looking at one another, helpless, irresolute, while the clock opposite ticked remorselessly on. Then, with an abruptness which lent added weight to his words, Erskine said boldly—

"I want to meet you again! I am not content to wait upon chance."

Claire did not blush; on the contrary, the colour faded from her cheeks. Most certainly she also was not content, but she did not waver in her resolution.

"I'm afraid there's nothing else for it. It's one of the hardships of a working girl's life that she can't entertain or make plans. It seems more impossible to me, perhaps, from having lived abroad where conventions are so strict. English girls have had more freedom. I don't see what I can do. I'm sorry!"—she held out her hand in farewell. "I hope some day I *shall* see you again!"

Quite suddenly Captain Fanshawe's mood seemed to change. The set look left his face; he smiled—a bright confident smile.

"There's not much fear about that! I shall take very good care that we do!"

Chapter Seventeen.

God's opportunity.

After the meeting with Captain Fanshawe in the Park, Claire's relationship with Mary Rhodes sensibly improved. In the first place, her own happiness made her softer and more lenient in her judgment, for she *was* deeply, intensely happy, with a happiness which all her reasonings were powerless to destroy.

"My dear, what nonsense!" she preached to herself in elderly remonstrating fashion. "You met the man, and he was pleased to see you—he seemed quite anxious to meet you again. Perfectly natural! Pray don't imagine any special meaning in *that*! You looked quite an attractive little girl in your pretty blue dress, and men like to talk to attractive little girls. I dare say he says just the same to dozens of girls!" So spake the inner voice, but spoke in vain. The best things of life are beyond reasoning. As in religion reason leads us, as it were, to the very edge of the rock of proven fact, then faith takes wing, and soars above the things of earth into the great silence where the soul communes with God, so in love there comes to the heart a sweetness, a certainty, which no reasoning can shake. As Erskine's eyes had looked into hers in those moments of farewell, Claire had realised that between this man and herself there existed a bond which was stronger than spoken word.

So far as she could foresee, they were hopelessly divided by the circumstances of life, but in the first dawn of love no lover troubles himself about what the future may bring; the sweetness of the present is all-sufficient. Claire was happy, and longed for every one else to be as happy as herself. Moreover, her suspicions concerning Major Carew had been lulled to rest by Erskine's favourable pronouncement. Personally she did not like him, but this was, after all, a matter of taste; she could not approve his actions, but conceivably there might be explanations of which she was unaware. Her manner to Cecil regained its old spontaneous friendliness, and Cecil responded with almost pathetic readiness. In her ungracious way she had grown fond of her pretty, kindly companion, and had missed the atmosphere of home which her presence had given to the saffron parlour. As they sat over their simple supper, she would study Claire's face with a questioning glance, and one night the question found vent in words.

"You look mightily pleased with yourself, young woman! Your eyes are sparkling as if you were having a firework exhibition on your own account. I never saw a school-mistress look so perky at the end of the summer term! Look as if you'd come into a fortune!"

"Wish I had!" sighed Claire, thankful to switch the conversation on to a safe topic. "It would come in most usefully at the moment. What are you going to do for the summer hols, Cecil? Is there any possibility of—"

"No," Cecil said shortly. "And the regiment is going into camp, so he will be out of town. I'm not bothering my head about holidays—quite enough to do with this wretched Matric. The Head is keen to make a good show this year, for the Dulwich School beat us last year, and, as usual, all the responsibility and all the blame is put on the poor mistresses. You can't make girls work if they don't want, you can't cram their brains when they've no brains to cram; but those wretched examiners send a record of all the marks, so you can see exactly where they fall short. Woe betide the mistress who is responsible for that branch! I wouldn't mind prophesying that if the German doesn't come out better than last year, Fräulein will be packed off. I wouldn't be too sure of myself. I've done all right so far, but the Head is not as devoted to me as she might be. I don't think she'd be sorry to have an excuse for getting rid of me. That's one of the delightful aspects of our position—we are absolutely at the mercy of a woman who, from sheer force of circumstances, becomes more of an autocrat every year. The Committee listen to her, and accept every word she says; the staff know better than to dispute a single order. We'd stand on our head in rows if she made it a rule! The pupils scuttle like rabbits when they see her coming, and cheer themselves hoarse every time she speaks. No human woman can live in that atmosphere for years and keep a cool head!"

"She's rather a dear, though, all the same!" Claire said loyally. She had been hurt by the lack of personal interest which Miss Farnborough showed in the different members of her staff, but she was unwilling to brand her as a heartless tyrant. "Anyway," she added hastily, "you are not satisfied here. If you were going on teaching I should have thought you'd be glad of a change. It would be easy to get another school."

Mary Rhodes looked at her; a long eloquent glance.

"With a good testimonial—yes! Without a good testimonial—no! A testimonial for twelve years' work depends on one woman, remember—on her prejudice or good nature, on the mood in which she happens to be on one particular day. It might read quite differently because she happened to have a chill on her liver."

"My dear! there *is* a sense of justice! There is such a thing as honesty."

"My dear, I agree. Even so, would you dare to say that the wording of a testimonial would be unaffected by the writer's mood?"

"Surely twelve years in one school—"

"No, it wouldn't! Not necessarily. 'Miss Rhodes has been English Mistress at Saint Cuthbert's for twelve years. Of late has been erratic in temper. Health uncertain. Examination records less satisfactory.' Well! If you represented another school, would *you* engage Miss Rhodes?"

Claire was silent. For the first time she realised the danger of this single-handed power. It meant—what might it not mean? It might mean that the mistress who was unfortunate enough to incur the dislike of her chief, might *never* be able to procure another post! She might be efficient, she might be hard-working; given congenial surroundings she might develop into a treasure untold, yet just because of a depreciating phrase in the wording of a testimonial, no chance would be vouchsafed. No doubt the vast majority of head mistresses were women of judgment, possessing a keen sense of justice and responsibility, yet the fact remained that a hasty impulse, a little access of temper in penning those all-important lines, might mean the end of a career, might mean poverty, might mean ruin!

Claire shivered, looked across the table at the thin, fretted face and made a hesitating appeal—

"Cecil dear, I know you are a good teacher. I just love to hear you talking over your lessons, but you *are* irritable! One of my girls was crying the other day. You had given so much homework, and she didn't understand what was to be done, and said she daren't ask. You had been 'so cross!' I made a guess at what you wanted, and by good chance I was right; but if I'd been wrong, the poor thing would have been in disgrace, and honestly it wasn't her fault! She was willing enough."

"Oh, that imbecile Gladys Brown! I know what you mean. I'd explained it a hundred times. If she'd the brains of a cow she'd have understood. No wonder I was cross. I should have been a saint if I wasn't, and no one can be a saint in the summer term. Did—did any one else see her cry?"

"I think not. No, I managed to comfort her; but if Miss Farnborough had happened to come in just at that moment—"

Cecil shrugged and turned the subject, but she took the hint, to the benefit of her pupils during the next few weeks.

July came in, and with it a spell of unbearable heat. In country places and by the seashore there was space and air, and clean fragrant surroundings; but over London hung a misty pall, and not a branch of the dusty trees quivered to the movement of a passing breeze. It was a thunderous, unnatural heat which sapped every scrap of vitality, and made every movement a dread.

Claire was horrified at the effect of this heat wave on Sophie Blake. In superficial fashion she had always believed that rheumatism must be better in hot weather; but, according to the specialist, such heat as this was more trying than damp or cold, and Sophie's stiffness increased with alarming suddenness.

There came a day when by no effort of will could she get through her classes, when sheer necessity drove her to do the thing she had dreaded most of all—inform the Head that she could not go on with her work.

Miss Farnborough was seated in her private room, and listened with grave attention to what the Games mistress had to say. Her forehead puckered in surprise as she noted Sophie's halting gait, and the while she listened, her keen brain was diving back into the past, collecting impressions. She had seen less than usual of Miss Blake during the term;

The Independence of Claire

once or twice she had received the impression that Miss Blake avoided her approach; Miss Blake had been looking pale. She waited until Sophie had finished speaking, her hands folded on her knee, her penetrating eye fixed on the girl's face. Then she spoke—

"I am sorry to hear this, Miss Blake. Your work has been excellent hitherto, but rheumatism is a serious handicap. You say that this heat is responsible for the present attack? Am I to understand that it is a first attack—that you have had no threatening before?"

"I have been rheumatic all winter, more or less. Before the Easter holidays it was pretty bad. I began to feel stiff."

Miss Farnborough repeated the word gravely.

"Stiff! That was bad; that was very bad! How could you take your classes if you were feeling stiff?"

"I managed somehow!" Sophie said.

For a moment she had imagined that the Head Mistress's concern had been on her account; she believed it no longer when she saw the flash of indignation which lighted the grey eyes.

"Managed—*somehow*? And you went on in that fashion—you were content to go on!"

"No. I was not content. I was very far from content. I suffered horrible pain. I went to a specialist and paid him two guineas for his advice. Since then I have paid twenty pounds for treatment."

On Miss Farnborough's face the disapproval grew more and more pronounced.

"Miss Blake, I am afraid you have not been quite straightforward in this matter. It appears that you have been ill for months, with an illness which must necessarily have interfered with your work, and this is the first time I hear about it. I am Head Mistress of this school; if anything is wrong with a member of the staff, it is her first duty to come to me. You tell me now that you have been ill for three months, since before the last holidays, and acknowledge that you can go on no longer."

"In ten days we break up. I ask you to allow me ten extra days. The weather is so hot that the girls would be thankful to escape the exercises. By the end of the holidays I hope to be quite better."

"The Easter holidays do not seem to have done you much good," Miss Farnborough said cruelly. Then, seeing the girl flush, she added, "Of course you shall have your ten days. I can see that you are unfit for work, and we must manage without you till the end of the term. I am very sorry for you, Miss Blake; very sorry, indeed. It is very trying and upsetting and—and expensive into the bargain. Twenty pounds, did you say? That is surely a great deal! Have you tried the shilling bottles of gout and rheumatic pills? I have been told they are quite excellent. But I must repeat that you have been wrong in not coming to me sooner. As a pure matter of honesty, do you think that you were justified in continuing to take classes for which you were unfit?"

The tears started to Sophie's eyes; she lowered her lids to hide them from sight.

"The girls did not suffer," she said deeply. "I did the suffering!"

Miss Farnborough moved impatiently. She was intensely practical and matter-of-fact, and with all her heart hated any approach to sentiment.

"You suffered *because* you were unfit," she repeated coldly, "and your obvious duty was to come to me. You must have known that under the circumstances I should not have wished you to continue the classes!"

Sophie was silent for a moment, then she said very quietly, very deliberately—

"Yes, I did know; but I also knew that if I could nerve myself to bear the pain and the fatigue, I *could* train the girls as well as ever, and I knew, too, that if you sent me away in the middle of term you would be less likely to take me back. It means everything to me, you see. What would happen to me if I were permanently invalided—without a pension—at thirty-one?"

"You have been paid a good salary, Miss Blake—an exceptionally good salary—because it is realised that your work is especially wearing. You ought to have saved—"

"If I had had no home claims I might have been able to save one or two hundred pounds—not a very big life provision! As it happens, however, I have given thirty pounds a year towards the education of a young sister, and it has been impossible to save at all."

"But now, of course, your sister will help *you*," Miss Farnborough said, and turned briskly to another topic. "You said that you have been to a specialist? Will you give me his address? I should like to communicate with him direct. You understand, Miss Blake, that if this stiffness continues, it will be impossible for you to continue your duties here?"

"Quite impossible," faltered Sophie, in low tones.

Miss Farnborough pushed back her chair, and rose to her feet.

"But one hopes, of course, that all may go well. I have never had any complaint to make with respect to your work. You have been very successful, very popular with the girls. I should be sorry to lose you. Be sure to let me know how you go on. Perhaps I had better be guided by Dr Blank. I should try the pills, I think; they are worth trying. And avoid the sea; sea air is bad for rheumatism. Try some high inland place. We had better say good-bye, now, I suppose, as you will not come back after to-night. Good-bye, my dear. Let me hear soon. All good wishes for your recovery."

Sophie left the room, and made her way upstairs to the Staff-Room. She moved very slowly, partly because every movement was an effort, partly because the familiar objects on which her eyes rested became suddenly instinct with new interest. For ten long working years she had passed them daily with indifference, but this afternoon it was borne in upon her that she would never see them again, and the conviction brought with it a bitter pang. After all, they had been happy years, spent in a bustle of youthful life and energy, in an atmosphere of affection, too, for the girls were warm-hearted, and the "Gym. mistress" had been universally popular. Even as the thought passed through Sophie's mind, one of her special adorers appeared suddenly at the far end of the corridor and hurried forward to meet her.

"Miss Blake! Darling! You look so white. Are you faint? Take my arm; lean on me. Were you going to lie down?"

"I'm going to the Staff-Room. I can manage myself; but, Gladys, find Miss Gifford, and ask her to come to me as soon as she is free. Tell her I'm not well. You're a dear girl, Gladys. Thank you for being so kind to me all these years."

Gladys rolled adoring blue eyes, and sped on her mission. The next morning she realised that those thanks had been darling Miss Blake's farewell, and shed bitter tears; but for the moment she was filled with complaisance.

Claire appeared in due time, heard what had happened, and helped Sophie to collect her various small belongings. The other teachers had already dispersed, so the ordeal of leave-taking was avoided.

"You can explain when you meet them next term!" said Claire.

"I can write my good-byes," corrected Sophie. She blinked away a few tears and said piteously, "Not much chance for me if she consults Dr Blank! He's as much discouraged as I am myself. What do you suppose he will advise now? I suppose I'll have to see him to-morrow."

"And lie awake all to-night, wondering what he will say! We'll do better than that—we'll call this very afternoon. If he is in, I'm sure he will see us, and a day saved is a day gained. I'll get a taxi."

"Another taxi! I'm ruining you, Claire. How I do hate sponging on other people!"

"Wouldn't you do it for me, if things were reversed?"

"Of course I should, but it's so much more agreeable to help than to be helped. It's ignoble, I suppose, but I do hate to feel grateful!"

"Well! No one could by any possibility call you *gracious*, my dear. Is that any consolation?" cried Claire mischievously, and Sophie was surprised into the travesty of a smile.

Dr Blank was at home, and listened to what Sophie had to tell him with grave attention. He expressed satisfaction to hear that her holidays had begun, but when questioned as to his probable report to Miss Farnborough, had no consolation to offer.

"I am afraid I must tell you honestly that you are not fit for the work. Of course, it is quite possible that there may be a great improvement by September, but, even so, you would be retarding your recovery by going on with such exhausting work. You must try to find something lighter."

Sophie laughed, and her laugh was not good to hear.

Claire said firmly—

"She *shall* find it! I will find it for her. There's no need to worry about September. What we want to know is what she is to do *now*?—to-morrow—for the rest of the holidays?"

"I can't afford any more injections! They've done me no good, and they cost too much. I can't afford any more treatments. I can only take medicines. If you will give me some medicines—"

Dr Blank sat silent; tapping his desk with noiseless fingers; staring thoughtfully across the room. It was evident that he had a proposition to make; evident also that he doubted its reception.

"The best thing under the circumstances—the wisest thing," he said slowly at last, "would be for you to go into hospital as an ordinary patient. I could get you a bed in one of my own wards, where I could look after you myself, in consultation with the first men in town. You could have massage, electricity, radium, heat baths, every appliance that could possibly be of use, and you could stay on long enough to give them a chance. It would be an ordinary ward, remember, an ordinary bed in an ordinary ward, and your neighbours would not be up to Newnham standard! You would be awakened at five in the morning, and settled for the night at eight. You would have to obey rules, which would seem to you unnecessary and tiresome. You would be, I am afraid, profoundly bored. On the other hand, you would have every attention that skill and science can devise. You would not have to pay a penny, and you would have a better chance than a duchess in a ducal palace. Think it over, and let me know! If you decide to go, I'll manage the rest. Take a day—a couple of days."

"I won't take two minutes, thank you! I'll decide now. I'll go, of course, and thank you very much!"

Dr Blank beamed with satisfaction.

"Sensible girl! Sensible girl! That's right! That's right! That's very good! You are doing the right thing, and we'll all do our best for you, and your friend here will come to see you and help to make the time pass. Interesting study, you know; valuable opportunity of studying character if you look at it in that light! Why not turn it into literary capital? 'Sketches from a Hospital Bed,' 'My Neighbours in B Ward,' might make an uncommonly good series. Who knows? We may have you turning out quite a literary star!"

Sophie smiled faintly, being one of the people who would rather walk five miles than write the shortest letter. Many unexpected things happen in this world, but it was certain that her own rise to literary eminence would never swell the number! But she knew that Dr Blank was trying to cheer her, so she kept that certainty to herself.

The two girls made their way back to Sophie's lodgings, and discussed the situation over the ever-comforting tea.

"I shall have to give my landlady notice," Sophie said, looking wistfully round the little room which had been so truly a home. "If I'm to be in hospital for many weeks, it's folly to go on paying the rent; and in any case I can't afford so much now. One can't have doctor's bills, and other luxuries as well. What shall I have to take into hospital? Will they allow me to wear my own things? I don't think I *could* get better in a calico nightdress! Pretty frills and a blue ribbon bow are as good as a tonic, but will the authorities permit? Have you ever seen ribbon bows in a hospital bed?"

"I haven't had much experience, but I should think they would be encouraged, as a ward decoration! I hope so, I'm sure, for I mean to present you with a duck of a dressing-jacket!"

"Oh, nothing more, Claire; don't give me anything more. I shall never be able to pay you back," cried Sophie; then, in a voice of poignant suffering, she cried sharply, "Oh, Claire, my little sister! *What* is to become of my little sister? If I am not able to help, if I need to be helped myself, her education will be interrupted, for it will be impossible to go on paying. Oh, it's too hard—too dreadful! Everything seems so hopeless and black!"

"Yes, it does. The way seems blocked. One can't see a step ahead. *Man's extremity*, Sophie!" cried Claire deeply—"*Man's extremity*;" and at that a gleam of light came into Sophie's eyes.

"Yes, yes! That's just what it is. Thanks for reminding me. *God's opportunity*!" Sophie leant back in her chair, staring dreamily into space, till presently something of the old bright look came back to her face. "And that," she said softly, "that's the kind of help it is sweet to accept!"

Chapter Eighteen.

An Invitation.

With Sophie in hospital, pathetically anxious for visits, with the rent of the Laburnum Road lodgings to pay whether one lived in them or not, Claire nerved herself to spend August in town, with the prospect of a September holiday to cheer her spirits. Through one of the other mistresses she had heard of an ideal farmhouse near the sea where the kindly housewife "mothered" her guests with affectionate care, where food was abundant, and cream appeared upon the table at every meal—thick, yellow, country cream in which a spoon would stand upright. There was also a hammock swung between two apple-trees in the orchard, a balcony outside the bedroom window, and a shabby pony-cart, with a pony who could really go. What could one wish for more?

Claire planned a lazy month, lying in that hammock, reading stories about other people, and dreaming still more thrilling romances about herself; driving the pony along country lanes, going out on to the balcony in the early morning to breathe the scent of honeysuckle, and sweetbriar, and lemon thyme, and all the dear, old-world treasures to be found in the gardens of well-conducted farmhouses. She had a craving for flowers in these hot summer days; not the meagre sixpennyworth which adorned the saffron parlour, but a wealth of blossom, bought without consideration of cost. And one day, with the unexpectedness of a fairy gift, her wish was fulfilled.

It lay on the table when she returned from school—a long cardboard box bearing the name of a celebrated West End florist, the word "fragile" marked on the lid, and inside were roses, magnificent, half-opened roses with the dew still on their leaves, the fat green stalks nearly a yard in length—dozens of roses of every colour and shade, from the lustrous whiteness of Frau Carl to the purple blackness of Prince Camille. Claire gathered them in her arms, unconscious of the charming picture which she made, in her simple blue lawn dress, with her glowing face rising over the riot of colour, gathered them in a great handful, and ran swiftly upstairs.

There was no card inside the box, no message of any kind, but her heart knew no doubt as to the sender, and she dare not face the fire of Mary Rhodes' cross-examination. In the days of daffodils she had treated herself to a high green column of a vase, which was an ideal receptacle for the present treasures. When it was filled there were still nearly half the number waiting for a home, so these were plunged deep into the ewer until the morrow, when they would be taken to Sophie in hospital. The little room was filled with beauty and fragrance, and Claire knew moments of unclouded happiness as she looked around.

Presently she extracted two roses from the rest, ran downstairs to collect box, paper and string, and handed rubbish and roses together to Lizzie at the top of the kitchen stairs. Lizzie received her share of the treasures with dignity, cut off the giant stems, which she considered straggly and out of place, and crammed the two heads into a brown cream-jug, the which she deposited on a sunny window-ledge. Claire saw them as she next left the house and shrugged resignedly, for she was beginning to learn the lesson which many of us take a lifetime to master, the wisdom of allowing people to enjoy themselves in their own fashion!

The Willoughbys were leaving town in mid July, *en route* for Switzerland, and later on for a Scottish shooting-box. Claire received an invitation to tea on their last Saturday afternoon, and arrived to find the drawing-room full of visitors.

Malcolm Heward was assisting Janet at the tea-table, but with this exception she recognised no one in the room, and was thankful for the attentions of Master Reginald, who hailed her as an old acquaintance, and reproached her loudly for not turning up at "Lord's."

"I looked out for you, you know!" he said impressively, and Claire was the more gratified by his remembrance because Malcolm Heward had required a second introduction to awaken his recollection. It is no doubt gratifying to the object of his devotion when a man remains blind to every other member of her sex, but the other members may feel a natural objection to be so ignored! Claire was annoyed by the necessity of that second introduction, and as a consequence made herself so fascinating to the boy who *had* remembered, that he hugged the sweet delusion that she considered him a man, and was seriously smitten by his charms. He waited upon her with assiduity, gave her exclusive tips as to her choice of cakes, and recited the latest funny stories which were already stale in his own circles, but which came to her ears with agreeable freshness.

It was while the two were laughing together over an unexpected *dénouement* that the departure of two guests left a space across which Claire could see a far corner of the room, and perceived that a lady seated on a sofa had raised a tortoiseshell-bound *lorgnon*, to stare across at herself. She was an elderly lady, and at first sight her appearance awoke no recollection. She was just a grey-haired woman, attired in handsome black, in no way differentiated from one or two other visitors of the same age: even when the *lorgnon* dropped to her side, disclosing a pair of very bright, very quizzical grey eyes, it was a full moment before Claire realised that this was her acquaintance of that first eventful journey to London, none other than Mrs Fanshawe herself. There she sat, smiling, complacent, *grande dame* as ever, nodding with an air of mingled friendliness and patronage, laying one hand on the vacant place by her side, with an action which was obviously significant. Claire chose, however, to ignore the invitation, and after a grave bow of acknowledgment, turned back to Reginald, keeping her eyes resolutely averted from that far corner. It was Mrs Fanshawe herself who was finally compelled to cross the room to make her greetings.

"Miss Gifford! Surely it is Miss Gifford? Mrs Willoughby told me she expected you this afternoon. And how are you, my dear, after this long time?"

The tone was all that was cordial and friendly.

Claire stood up, tall and stately, and extended a perfectly gloved hand. It was not in human nature to be perfectly natural at that moment. Sub-consciously she was aware that, as the Americans would express it, she was "putting on frills"; sub-consciously she was amused at the artificiality of her own voice.

"Quite well, thank you. Exceedingly flourishing!"

"You look it," Mrs Fanshawe said, and seated herself ruthlessly in Reginald's chair. "Tell me all about it! You were going to work, weren't you? Some new-fangled idea of being independent. So ridiculous for a pretty girl! And you've had—how long—nearly a year? Haven't got tired of it yet, by any chance?"

"Oh, yes; quite often I feel very tired, but I should have felt the same about pleasuring, and work is more worth while. It has been very interesting. I have learnt a great deal."

"More than the pupils—hey?" chuckled Mrs Fanshawe shrewdly. "Don't try to pretend that you are a model school-mistress. I know better! I knew you were not the type when I saw you on that journey, and after a year's trial you are less the type than ever." She screwed up her eyes and looked Claire over with deliberate criticism up and down, down and up. "No, my dear! Nature did *not* intend you to be shut up in a girls' school!" Suddenly she swerved to another topic. "What a journey that was! I nearly expired. If it hadn't been for you, I should never have survived. I told my son you had saved my life. That was my son who met me on the platform!"

Was it fancy that an expression of watchfulness had come into the gay eyes? Claire imagined that she recognised such an expression, but, being prepared for some such reference, had herself well in command. Not a nicker of embarrassment passed over her face as she said quietly—

"Yes, I knew it was your son. I met Captain Fanshawe here one evening last winter, so I have been introduced."

Mrs Fanshawe waved her *lorgnon*, and murmured some vague words which might, or might not, have been intended as an apology.

"Oh, yes. So nice! Naturally, that morning I was worn-out. I did not know what I was doing. I crawled into bed. Erskine told me about meeting you, and of your pretty performance. Quite a professional *siffleuse*! More amusing than school teaching, I should say. *And* more profitable. You ought to think of it as a profession. Erskine was quite pleased. He comes here a great deal. Of course—"

Mrs Fanshawe's smile deepened in meaning fashion, then suddenly she sighed. "Very delightful for them, of course; but I see nothing of him. We mothers of modern children

The Independence of Claire

have a lonely time. I used to wish for a daughter, but perhaps, if I'd had one, *she* would have developed a fancy to fly off to India!"

That was a hit at Claire, but she received it in silence, being a little touched by the unaffected note of wistfulness in the other's voice as she regretted her lonely estate. It *was* hard to be a widow, and to see so little of an only child, especially if that only child happened to be so altogether charming and attractive!

Mrs Fanshawe glanced across at the tea-table where Janet and her cavalier were still busy ministering to the needs of fresh arrivals.

"I asked Janet Willoughby to take pity on me for a few weeks this summer, but she's too full up with her own plans. Says so, at least; but I dare say it would have been different if— Well, well! I have been young myself, and I dare say I shouldn't have been too keen to accept an invitation to stay in the country with only an old woman as companion. Enjoy yourself while you are young, my dear. It gets more and more difficult with every year you live."

Claire made a protesting grimace.

"Does it? That's discouraging. I've always flattered myself that it would grow easier. When one is young, everything is vague and unsettled, and naturally one feels anxious about what is to happen next. It is almost impossible to be philosophical about the unknown, but when your life has shaped itself, it ought to be easy to settle down and make the best of it, and cultivate an easy mind."

Mrs Fanshawe laughed.

"Well reasoned, my dear, well reasoned! Most logical and sound. And just as futile in practice as logical things usually are! You wouldn't believe me if I told you that it is the very uncertainty which makes the charm of youth, or that being certain is the bane of old age, but it's the truth, all the same, and when you are sixty you will have discovered it for yourself. Well! so my letter to Mrs Willoughby was of some use after all? She did send you a card!"

Claire looked across the room to where Mrs Willoughby sat. Hero-worship is an instinct in hearts which are still fired with youth's enthusiasm, and this stout, middle-aged woman was Claire's heroine *par excellence*. She was *kind*, and to be kind is in good truth the fulfilment of Christ's law. Among Claire's favourite books was Professor Drummond's "The Greatest Thing in the World," with its wonderful exposition of the thirteenth chapter of 1st Corinthians. When she read its pages, her thoughts flew instinctively to this rich woman of society, who was not puffed up, thought no evil, was not easily provoked, suffered long, *and was kind*.

The girl's eyes were eloquent with love and admiration as they rested on the plain, elderly face, and the woman who was watching felt a stab of envy at the sight. The old crave for the love of the young, and cherish it, when found, as one of their dearest possessions, and despite the natural gaiety of her disposition there were moments when Mrs Fanshawe felt the burden of loneliness press heavily upon her.

"She has done much more than send me a card!" Claire said deeply. "She has been a friend. She has taken away the terrible feeling of loneliness. If I were in trouble, or needed any help, I *know* that she would give it!"

"Oh, yes, yes, naturally she would. So would any one, my dear, who had the chance. But she's a good creature, of course; a dear creature. I'm devoted to her, and to Janet. Janet and I are the best of friends!"

Again the meaning look, the meaning tone, and again in Claire's heart the same sweet sense of certainty mingled with a tender compassion for Janet, who was less fortunate than herself. It was a help to look across at the tea-table, and to realise that consolation was waiting for Janet if she chose to take it.

Suddenly Mrs Fanshawe switched off on to yet another topic.

"And where are you going to spend your summer holidays, my dear?"

"In September I am probably going to a farmhouse near the sea."

"And in August?"

"In town, I think. I have an invalid friend—"

Mrs Fanshawe swept aside the suggestion with an imperious hand.

"Nonsense! Utter nonsense! *Nobody* stays in town in August, my good child. The thing's impossible. I've passed through once or twice, *en route* for country visits, and it's an unknown place. The wierdest people walking up and down! Where they come from I can't conceive; but you never saw anything more impossible. And the shops! I knew a poor girl who became engaged at the end of July, and had to get her trousseau at once, as they sailed in September. She was in despair. *Nothing* to be had. She was positively in tears."

"I shall get engaged in June," Claire said firmly, "and take advantage of the summer sales. I call it most thoughtless of him to have waited till the end of July."

But Mrs Fanshawe was not attending; her eyes had brightened with a sudden thought; she was saying to herself, "Why not? I should be alone. There would be no danger of complications, and the child would be a delightful companion, good to look at, plenty to say for herself, and a mind of her own. Quite useful in entertaining, too. I could play off some of my duty debts, and she could whistle to us after dinner. Quite a novelty in the country. It would be quite a draw... A capital idea! I'll say a week, and if it works she can stay on—"

"No, my dear, you cannot possibly endure town in August, at least not the entire month. Run down to me for a break. Quite a short journey; an hour and a half from Waterloo, and the air is delightfully fresh. I shall be alone, so I can't offer you any excitement, but if you are fond of motoring—"

The blood rushed into Claire's face. She was so intensely, overpoweringly surprised, that, for the moment, all other feelings were in abeyance. The last thing in the world which she had expected was that Erskine's mother should invite her to visit her home.

"I don't know if you care for gardening. I'm mad about it myself. My garden is a child to me. I stand no interference. The gardeners are paid to obey me, and carry out my instructions. If they get upsetting, off they go. You'd like my garden. It is not cut out to a regulation pattern; it has a personality of its own. I have all my meals on the verandah in summer. We could get you some tennis, too. You wouldn't be buried alive. Well? What do you say? Is it worth while?"

"It's exceedingly kind. It's awfully good of you. I—I am so completely taken by surprise that I hardly know—I shall have to think."

"Nonsense, my dear; what is there to think about? You have no other engagement, and you need a change. Incidentally also *I* want a companion. You would be doing me a good turn as well as yourself. I'm sure your mother would wish it!"

No doubt about that! Claire smiled to herself as she realised how Mrs Judge would rejoice over the visit; turning one swallow into a summer, and in imagination beholding her daughter plunged into a very vortex of gaiety. She was still smiling, still considering, when Janet came strolling across the room, and laid her hand affectionately on Mrs Fanshawe's shoulder.

"I haven't had a word with you all afternoon! Such a rush of people. You had tea comfortably, I hope: and you, too—Claire!" There was just a suspicion of hesitation before the Christian name.

"I have just been asking Miss Gifford to take pity on my loneliness for part of August. She is not knee-deep in engagements, as you are, my dear, and that precious son of mine; so we are going to amuse each other, and see how much entertainment we can squeeze out of the countryside!"

"But I haven't—I didn't—I'm not sure," stammered Claire, acutely conscious of the hardening of Janet's face, but once again Mrs Fanshawe waved aside her objections.

"But *I* am sure! It's all settled, my dear—all but the day. Put your address on this silly little tablet, and I'll write as soon as I've looked over my dates. Now, Janet, I'm ready for a chat. Take me out to the balcony, away from this crowd."

"And I must go, I think. I'll say good-bye." Claire held out her hand to the daughter of the house. "I hope you may have a delightful summer."

"Oh, thanks so much. Oh, yes, yes, I'm quite sure I will," Janet answered mechanically. She touched Claire's hand with her fingers, and turned hastily aside.

Chapter Nineteen.

Erskine Fanshawe's Home.

Claire dreaded Mary Rhodes' curiosity on the subject of her proposed visit, but in effect there was none forthcoming. Cecil was too much engrossed in her own affairs to feel anything but a passing interest.

"Some one you met at the Willoughbys'? Only the old lady? Rather you than me! Nice house though, I suppose; gardens, motors, that kind of thing. Dull, but luxurious. Perhaps you'll stay on permanently as her companion."

"That," Claire said emphatically, "will never happen! I was thinking of clothes... I am quite well-off for evenings, and I can manage for afternoons, but I do think I ought to indulge in one or two 'drastic bargains' for morning wear. I saw some particularly drastic specimens in Knightsbridge this week. Cecil ... could you—I hate asking, but *could* you pay me back?"

Cecil's stare of amazement was almost comical under the circumstances.

"My—good—girl! I was really pondering whether I dare, I'm horribly hard up, and that's the truth. I've had calls..."

"Not Major Carew again? I can't understand it, Cecil. You know I inquired about him, you told me to ask if I had a chance, and his father *is* rich. He might fly into a rage if he were asked for money, but he would give it in the end. Major Carew might have a bad half-hour, but what is that compared with borrowing from you! And from a man's point of view it's so little, such very small sums!" She caught a change of expression on the other's face, and leapt at its meaning. "Cecil! You have been giving more! Your savings!"

"And if I have, Claire Gifford, what business is it of yours? What was I saving for? To provide for my old age, wasn't it? and now that the need has gone, why shouldn't I lend it, if I chose? Frank happens to be hard up for a few months, and besides, there's a reason! ... We are getting tired of waiting... You must never, never breathe a word to a soul, but he wants me ... he thinks it might be better..."

Claire stared with wide eyes, Cecil frowned, and finished the sentence in reckless tones—

"We shall probably get married this autumn, and tell his father afterwards."

"Oh, Cecil, no! Don't do it! It's madness. It's folly. He ought not to ask you. It will make things fifty times more difficult."

"It would make things *sure*!" Mary Rhodes said.

The words were such an unconscious revelation of her inner attitude towards her lover, that Claire was smitten with a very passion of pity. She stretched out her hand, and cried ardently. "Cecil, I am thinking of your happiness: I long for you to be sure, but a private marriage is an insult to a girl. It puts her into a wrong position, and no man has the right to suggest it. Where is your pride?"

"Oh, my dear," interrupted Cecil wearily, "I'm past worrying about pride. I'm thirty-three, and look older, and feel sixty at the least. I'm tired out in body and soul. I'm sick of this empty life. I want a home. I want rest. I want some one to care for me, and take an interest in what I do. Frank isn't perfect, I don't pretend that he is. I wish to goodness he *would* own up, and face the racket once for all, but it's no use, he won't! Between ourselves I believe he thinks the old man won't live much longer, and there will be no need to worry him at all. Any way there it is, he won't tell at present, however much I may beg, but he will marry me; he wants to be married in September, and that proves that he *does* care! He is looking out for a flat, and picking up furniture. *We* are picking up furniture," Cecil corrected herself hastily. "I go in and ask the prices, and he sends his servants the next week to do the bargaining. And there will be my clothes, too... I'll pay you back in time, Claire, with ten per cent, interest into the bargain, and perhaps when I'm a rich woman the time may come when you will be glad to borrow from me!"

The prospect was not cheering, but the intention was good, and as such had to be suitably acknowledged. Claire adjourned upstairs to consult her cheque-book, and decided bravely that the drastic bargains could not be afforded. Then, being a very human, and feminine young woman she told herself that there could be no harm in going to look at the dresses once more, just to convince herself that they were not so very drastic after all, and lo! close inspection proved them even more drastic than she had believed, and by the evening's delivery a choice specimen was speeding by motor van to Laburnum Road.

On visiting days Claire went regularly to visit Sophie, who, by her own account, was being treated to seventeen different cures at the same time, and was too busy being rubbed, and boiled, and electrified, and dosed, and put to bed in the middle of the afternoon, and awakened in the middle of the night, to have any time to feel bored. She took a keen interest also in her fellow patients, and was the confidante of many tragic stories which made her own lot seem light in comparison. Altogether she was more cheerful and hopeful than for months back, but the nurses looked dubious, and could not be induced to speak of her recovery with any certitude.

On the tenth of August, Claire packed her boxes with the aid of a very mountain of tissue paper, and set forth on her journey. The train deposited her at Hazlemere station, outside which Mrs Fanshawe was waiting in a big cream car, smiling her gay, quizzical smile. She was one of the fortunate women who possess the happy knack of making a guest feel comfortable, and at home, and her welcome sent Claire's spirits racing upwards.

Many times during the last fortnight had she debated the wisdom of visiting Erskine Fanshawe's home, but the temptation was so strong that at every conflict prudence went to the wall. It was not in girl nature to resist the longing to see his home and renew her acquaintance with his mother; and as it had been repeatedly stated that he himself was to

The Independence of Claire

spend most of August in Scotland, she was absolved from any ulterior design. Janet Willoughby had obviously looked upon the visit with disfavour, but Claire was too level-headed to be willing to victimise herself for such a prejudice. Janet would have a fair field in Scotland. She could not hold the whole kingdom as a preserve!

"You are looking charming, my dear," Mrs Fanshawe said. "I always say it is one of the tests of a lady to know how to dress for a journey. A little pale, perhaps, but we shall soon change that. This high air is better than any tonic. I laze about during the heat of the day, and have a two hours' spin after tea; I never appear until eleven, and I rest in my own room between lunch and tea, so you won't have too much of my society, but I've a big box of new books from Mudie's for you to read, and there's a pony-cart at your disposal, so I dare say you can amuse yourself. I love companionship, but I couldn't talk to the cleverest woman in Europe for twelve hours at a stretch."

"Nor I!" agreed Claire, who to tell the truth was more elated at the prospect of so much time to herself than she felt it discreet to betray. She was enchanted with her first view of the beautiful Surrey landscape, and each turn of the road as they sped uphill seemed to open out more lovely vistas. They drove past spinneys of pine trees, past picturesque villages, consisting of an old inn, a few scattered cottages, a pond and a green, along high roads below which the great plain of thickly-treed country lay simmering in a misty haze. Then presently the road took a sudden air of cultivation, and Claire staring curiously discovered that the broad margin of grass below the hedge on either side, was mown and rolled to a lawn-like smoothness, the edges also being clipped in as accurate a line as within the most carefully tended garden. For several hundred yards the margin stretched ahead, smooth as the softest velvet, a sight so rare and refreshing to the eye that Claire could not restrain her delight.

"But how charming! How unexpected! I never saw a lane so swept and garnished. It has a wonderful effect, those two long lines of sward. It *is* sward! grass is too common a word. But what an amount of work! Twenty maids with twenty mops sweeping for half a year.—I think the whole neighbourhood ought to be grateful to the owner of this land."

Mrs Fanshawe beamed, complacently.

"I'm glad you think so. *I* am the owner! This is my property, mine for my lifetime, and my son's after me. It's one of my hobbies to keep the lane mown. I like to be tidy, outside as well as in. Erskine began by thinking it a ridiculous waste of work, but his friends are so enthusiastic about the result, that he is now complacently convinced that it was entirely his own idea. That's a man, my dear! Illogical, self-satisfied, the best of 'em, and you'll never change them till the end of time... What's your opinion of men?"

"I rather—like them!" replied Claire with a *naïveté* which kept her listener chuckling with amusement until the lodge gates were reached, and the car turned into the drive.

The house was less imposing than the grounds, just a large comfortable English country house, handsome and dignified, but not venerable in any way. The hall was good, running the entire length of the house, and opening by tall double doors on to the grounds at the rear. In summer these doors were kept open, and allowed a visitor a charming vista of rose pergolas and the blue-green foliage of an old cedar. All the walls of the house from top to bottom were painted a creamy white, and there was noticeable a prevailing touch of red in Turkey carpets, cushion-covers, and rose-flecked chintzes.

Tea was served on a verandah, and after it was over Mrs Fanshawe escorted her visitor round the flower gardens, and finally upstairs to her own bedroom, where she was left with the announcement that dinner would be served at eight o'clock. After dinner the ladies played patience, drank two glasses of hot-water, and retired to bed at ten o'clock. It was not exciting, but on the other hand it was certainly not dull, for Mrs Fanshawe's personality was so keen, so youthful in its appreciation, that it was impossible not to be infected, and share in her enjoyment.

The next week passed quickly and pleasantly. The weather was good, allowing long drives over the lovely country, a tennis party at home, and another at a neighbouring house introduced a little variety into the programme, and best of all Mrs Fanshawe grew daily more friendly, even affectionate in manner. She was a woman of little depth of character, whose main object in life was to amuse herself and avoid trouble, but she had humour and intelligence, and made an agreeable companion for a summer holiday. As her intimacy with her guest increased she spoke continually of her son, referring to his marriage with Janet Willoughby with an air of complacent certitude.

"Of course he will marry Janet. They've been attached for years, but the young men of to-day are so deliberate. They are not in a hurry to give up their freedom. Janet will be just the right wife for Erskine, good tempered and yielding. He is a dear person, but obstinate. When he once makes up his mind, nothing will move him. It would never do for him to have a high-spirited wife."

"I disapprove of pandering to men," snapped Claire in her most High School manner, whereupon the conversation branched off to a discussion on Women's Rights, which was just what she had intended and desired.

On the seventh afternoon of her visit, Claire was in her room writing a letter to Sophie when she heard a sudden tumult below, and felt her heart bound at the sound of a familiar voice. The pen dropped from her hand, and she sat transfixed, her cheeks burning with excitement. It could not be! It was preposterous, impossible. He was in Scotland. Only that morning there had been a letter.—It was impossible, impossible, and then again came the sound of that voice, that laugh, and she was on her feet, running across the floor, opening the door, listening with straining ears.

A voice rose clear and distinct from the hall beneath, the deep, strong voice about which there could be no mistake.

"A perfect flood! The last five days have been hopeless. I was tired of being soaked to the skin, and having to change my clothes every two hours, so I cut it, picked up Humphreys in town, and came along home. And how have you been getting on, mater? You look uncommonly fit!"

"I'm quite well. I am perfectly well. You need not have come home on my account," Mrs Fanshawe's voice had a decided edge. "I suppose this is just a flying visit. You will be going on to pay another visit. I have a friend with me—a Miss Gifford. You met her at the Willoughbys'."

"So I did! Yes. That's all right. I'm glad you had company. I suppose I *shall* be moving on one of these days. I say, mother, what about tea?"

Claire shut the door softly, and turned back into the room. Erskine's voice had sounded absolutely normal and unmoved: judging by it no one could have imagined that Miss Gifford's presence or absence afforded him the slightest interest, and yet, and yet, the mysterious inner voice was speaking again, declaring that it was not the wet weather which had driven him back ... that he had hurried home because he knew, he knew—

In ten minutes' time tea would be served. Claire did not change her dress or make any alteration in her simple attire, her energies during those few minutes were chiefly devoted to cooling her flushed cheeks, and when the gong sounded she ran downstairs, letters in hand, and evinced a politely impersonal surprise at the sight of Captain Erskine and his friend.

Mrs Fanshawe's eyes followed the girl's movements with a keen scrutiny. It seemed to her that Claire's indifference was a trifle overdone: Erskine also was unnaturally composed. Under ordinary circumstances such a meeting would have called forth a frank, natural pleasure. She set her lips, and determined to leave nothing to chance.

Chapter Twenty.

The Flowery Way.

Only a few hours before her son's unexpected arrival, Mrs Fanshawe had warmly pressed Claire to extend her visit to a fortnight at least, and Claire had happily agreed. Mrs Fanshawe recalled the incident as she poured out tea, and rated herself for her imprudence, but the deed was done; there was the girl, looking pretty enough to turn any young man's head, and there, alas! was Erskine, who should, by all the laws of what was right and proper, be even now making love to Janet Willoughby in Scotland! Janet was rich, Janet was well born, Janet was amiable and easily led, for years past Mrs Fanshawe had set her heart on Janet as a daughter-in-law, and she was not easily turned from her purpose. Throughout that first afternoon her thoughts were busily engaged planning ahead, striving to arrange the days to the hindrance of dangerous *tête-à-têtes*, Erskine appeared to have returned in ignorance of Miss Gifford's presence. Mrs Fanshawe had been careful to avoid all reference to the girl in her letters, and was unable to think how the information could have leaked out, nevertheless the choice of Major Humphreys as a companion filled her with suspicion. Never before had such an invitation been given on Erskine's initiative; on more than one occasion, indeed, he had confessed that he found the Major a bore, and had expressed surprise at his mother's liking for so dull a man.

Mrs Fanshawe had never found the Major dull, since he shared with enthusiasm her own passion for gardening, and was a most valuable adviser and assistant. Together they had planned the flagged path winding low between the high banks of the rock garden, together they had planted the feathery white arenaria calearica in the crevices of the steps leading upward to the pergola, together they had planned the effect of clusters of forget-me-not, and red tulips among the long grasses in the orchard. There was never any dearth of conversation between Major Humphreys and Mrs Fanshawe, and a stroll round the rose garden might easily prolong itself into a discussion lasting a couple of hours. Hence came the suspicion, or Erskine knew as much, and had deliberately invited this man before any one of his own friends. Despite all appearance to the contrary, Mrs Fanshawe felt convinced that "the bore" had been brought down to engage her own attention, and so leave her son free to follow his own devices. She set her lips, and determined on a counter move.

A *partie carrée* was dangerous under the circumstances; safety lay in a crowd. That evening when Mrs Fanshawe retired to dress for dinner, the telephone in her boudoir was used to ring up all the big houses in the neighbourhood, invitations were given galore for tennis, for dinner, for lunch; and return invitations were accepted without consultation with her son. At the end of half an hour she hung up the receiver, satisfied that Erskine's opportunities for *tête-à-têtes* would be few. Perhaps also time would suggest some excuse for shortening the girl's visit to the ten days originally planned. She must think it out, put her wits to work. Claire was a pretty creature and a delightful companion, but a nobody, and poor into the bargain. She could not be allowed to upset a cherished plan!

During dinner Mrs Fanshawe alluded casually to the coming gaieties, and mentally paid a tribute of admiration to the *aplomb* with which Claire listened, and smiled, betraying not a flicker of surprise at the sudden change of programme. The good lady was so pleased with the result of her own scheming, that when later on the Major proposed a game of patience, she accepted at once, and viewed with equanimity the sight of the two young people strolling down the garden path. It would be the last night when such an escape would be possible!

It was an exquisite moonlight night, clear enough to show the colour of the flowers in the beds and borders. Claire's white dress took on a ghostly hue against the deep background of the trees, her cheeks were pale, too, and the long line of eyelash showed dark against her cheeks. She felt very happy, very content, just the least little bit in the world, afraid! Captain Fanshawe was smoking a cigarette, and in the intervals drawing deep sighs of enjoyment.

"There's only one thing that worries me—why didn't I come back last week? To think of rain, and mist, and smoky fires, and then—This! I feel like a man who has been transported into fairyland!"

Claire felt as if she also was in fairyland, but she did not say so. There are things that a girl does not say. They paced up and down the winding paths, and came to the flight of steps leading to the pergola, "The Flowery Way" as Mrs Fanshawe loved to call it, where the arenaria calearica shone starry white in the moonlight. Erskine stopped short, and said urgently—

"Would you mind walking on alone for a few yards? I'll stand here ... while you go up the steps. Please!"

Claire stared in surprise, but there seemed no reason to deny so simple a request.

"And what am I to do when I get there?"

"Just stand still for a moment, and then walk on... I'll come after!"

Claire laughed, shrugged, and went slowly forward along the flagged path, up the flower-sprinkled stair, to pause beneath an arch of pink roses and look back with an inquiring smile. Erskine was standing where she had left him, but he did not smile in response, while one might have counted twenty, he remained motionless, his look grave and intent, then he came quickly forward, leapt up the shallow steps and stood by her side.

"Thank you!" he said tersely, but that was all. Neither then or later came any explanation of the strange request.

For a few moments there was silence, then Erskine harked back to his former subject.

"Scottish scenery is very fine, but for restful loveliness, Surrey is hard to beat. You haven't told me yet how you like our little place, Miss Gifford! It's on a very modest scale, but I'm fond of it. There's a homey feeling about it that one misses in bigger places, and the mater is a genius at gardening, and gets the maximum of effect out of the space. Are you fond of a garden?"

"I've never had one!" Claire said, and sighed at the thought. "That's one of the Joys that does *not* go with a roving life! I've never been able to have as many flowers as I wanted, or to choose the right foliage to go with them, or to pick them with the dew on their leaves." She paused, smitten with a sudden recollection. "One day this year, a close, smouldering oven-ey day, I came in from school and found—a box full of roses! There were *dewdrops* on the leaves, or what looked like dewdrops. They were as fresh as if they had been gathered an hour before. Dozens of roses, with great long stems. They made my room into a bower."

"Really! Did they? How very jolly," was Erskine's comment.

His voice sounded cool and unperturbed, and Claire did not venture to look at his face. She thought with a pang, that perhaps after all she had been mistaken. Perhaps Mrs Willoughby had been the real donor ... perhaps he had never thought... She hurried on terrified lest her thoughts might be suspected.

"Mrs Fanshawe has been so kind, allowing me to send boxes of fruit and flowers to a friend in hospital. One of our mistresses, who is being treated for rheumatism."

"Poor creature!" said the Captain with careless sympathy. "Dull work being in hospital in this weather. How have you been getting on with my mother, Miss Gifford? I'm awfully glad to find you down here, though I should have enjoyed showing you round myself. I'm a bit jealous of the mater there! She's a delightful companion, isn't she? So keen and alert. I don't know any woman of her age who is so young in spirit. It's a great gift, but—" he paused, drew another cigarette from his case, and stared at it reflectively, "it has its drawbacks!"

"Yes. I can understand that. It must be hard to feel young, to *be* young in heart and mind, and to be handicapped by a body that persists in growing old. I've often thought how trying it must be."

"I suppose so. Yes. I'm afraid I wasn't thinking about it in that light. I was not discussing the position from my mother's point of view, but from—her son's! It would be easier sometimes to deal with a placid old lady who was content with her knitting, and cherished an old-fashioned belief in the superiority of man! Well! let us say the equality. But the mater won't even grant that. By virtue of her superior years she is under the impression that she can still manage my affairs better than I can myself, which, of course, is a profound delusion!"

Looking at the firmly cut profile it seemed ridiculous to think of any one managing this man if it were not his will to be managed. Mother and son were alike in possessing an obstinate self-will. A conflict between them would be no light thing. Woman-like, Claire's sympathies leant to the woman's side.

"It must be very difficult for a mother to realise that her son is really past her control. And when she *does*, it must be a painful feeling. It isn't painful for the son; it's only annoying. The mother fares worst!"

Captain Fanshawe laughed, and looked down at the girl's face with admiring eyes.

"What a faculty you have of seeing the other side! Do you always take the part of the person who isn't here? If so, all the better for me this last week, when the mater has been spinning stories of my obstinacy, and pig-headedness, and general contradictiveness. I thought I had better hurry home at once, before you learnt to put me down as a hopeless bad lot!"

Claire stood still, staring with widened eyes.

"Hurry home—hurry home before—" She stopped short, furious with herself for having taken any notice of the slip, and Erskine gave a short embarrassed laugh, and cried hastily—

"Oh, I knew; of course I knew! The rain was only an excuse. The real reason was that as soon as I knew you were staying here, I hadn't patience to stay on. I stood it for exactly three hours, thinking of you in this garden, imagining walking about as we are walking now, and then—I bolted for the afternoon train!"

Claire felt her cheeks flame, and affected dignity to hide her deep, uncontrollable joy.

"If *I* had been your hostess—"

"But you weren't, you see... You weren't! For goodness' sake don't put yourself in her place next. Be Claire Gifford for once, and say you are glad to see me!" His eyes met hers and twinkled with humour as he added solemnly. "There's not a single solitary convention that could possibly be broken by being civil to a man in his own home! Even your ultra sensitive conscience—"

"Never mind my sensitive conscience. What I want to know is, how did you know? Who told you that I was here?"

It was significant that the possibility that Mrs Fanshawe had written of her guest never occurred to Claire's mind; that Erskine like herself discounted such a possibility. He replied with a matter-of-fact simplicity which left Claire marvelling at the obtuseness of mankind—

"Janet, of course. Janet Willoughby. We were staying in the same house. We were talking of you yesterday morning, and comparing notes generally. She said you were—oh! quite a number of agreeable things—and I agreed with her, with just one exception. She considered that you were responsive. I said I had never found any one less so. She said you were always so ready to meet her halfway. I complained that you refused to meet me at all. I ... er ... told her how I felt about it, and she said my chance was waiting if I choose to take it—that you were staying here keeping the mater company. So—"

Claire said nothing. She was thinking deeply. For how many days had Janet been staying in the same house with Erskine? Perhaps a week, certainly several days, yet it had been only yesterday morning that she had given the news. Yesterday morning; and in three hours he had flown! How was Janet faring now, while Claire was walking in fairyland?

"You are not angry? Why do you look so serious? Tell me you are not sorry that I came?" said a deep voice close to her ear, but before she had time to answer, footsteps approached, and Mrs Fanshawe's voice was heard calling in raised accents—

"Erskine! are you there? Give me your arm, dear; I am so tired. It's such a perfect night, that it seemed a shame to stay indoors. The Major has been admiring 'The Flowery Way.' It certainly looks its best to-night." She turned towards Major Humphreys with her light, cynical laugh. "My son declares that it is profanation to allow ordinary, commonplace mortals to walk up those steps! He always escorts my visitors round by another way. He is ungallant enough to say that he has never yet seen a girl whom he would care to watch walk up those steps in the moonlight. She would have to be quite ideal in every respect to fit into the picture. We'll go round by the lily garden, Erskine, and then I think Miss Gifford and I will be off to bed. You men will enjoy a smoke."

For the next ten minutes Mrs Fanshawe kept tight hold of her son's arm, and Claire talked assiduously to Major Humphreys. She knew now why Erskine had asked her to walk ahead up "The Flowery Way!"

Chapter Twenty One.

All in a garden fair.

The next afternoon a party of friends had been bidden for tennis. For the morning no plans had been made, but throughout its length Mrs Fanshawe fought a gallant fight against overwhelming odds, and was hopelessly beaten for her pains. It was her strong determination that her son should be prevented from holding another *tête-à-tête* with Claire Gifford. Erskine actively, and Claire passively, desired and intended to bring about just that very consummation, while Major Humphreys, shrewdly aware of the purpose for which he had been invited, aided and abetted their efforts by the development of a veritable frenzy of gardening enthusiasm. He questioned, he disputed, he meekly acknowledged his mistakes; he propounded schemes for fresh developments, the scenes of which lay invariably at the opposite end of the grounds from that in which the young people were ensconced.

Mrs Fanshawe struggled valiantly, but the Triple Entente won the day, and for a good two hours before lunch, Erskine and Claire remained happily lost to sight in the farthest recesses of the grounds. They had left behind the region of formal seats and benches, and sat on the grass at the foot of a great chestnut, whose dark green foliage made a haven of shade in the midst of the noonday glare. Claire wore her bargain frock, and felt thankful for the extravagant impulse of that January morn. Erskine was in flannels, cool and becoming as a man's *négligé* invariably is; both had discarded hats, and sat bareheaded in the blessed shade, and Erskine asked questions, dozens of questions, a very *viva voce* examination, the subject being the life, history, thoughts, hopes, ambitions, and dreams of the girl by his side.

"You were an only child. So was I. Were you a lonely little kiddie?"

"No, I don't think I was. My mother was a child with me. We were blissfully happy manufacturing a doll's house out of a packing chest, and furnishing it with beds made out of cardboard boxes, and sofas made out of pin-cushions. I used to feel other children a bore because they distracted her attention."

"That would be when you were—how old? Six or seven? And you are now—what is it? Twenty-two? I must have been a schoolboy of seventeen at that time, imagining myself a man. Ten years makes a lot of difference at that age. It doesn't count so much later on. At least I should think not. Do I appear to you very old?"

"Hoary!"

"No, but I say... Honestly!"

"Don't be conceited. You know perfectly well—"

"But I wanted to make sure! And then you went to school. Did you have a bad time at first among the other girls?"

"No. I'm afraid the other girls had a bad time with me. I was very uppish and British, and insisted on getting my own way. Did *you* have a bad time?"

"Yes, I did," he said simply. "Small boys have a pretty stiff time of it during their first term, and my time happened to be stiffer than most. I may be as miserable again. I hope I never may be! But I'm pretty sure it's impossible to be *more* miserable than I was at nine years old, bullied on every side, breaking my heart with home sickness, and too proud to show a sign."

"Poor little lad!" sighed Claire softly, and for a long minute the two pairs of eyes met, and exchanged a message. "But afterwards? It grew better after that?"

"Oh, yes. I learnt to stand up for myself, and moved up in the school, and began to bully on my own... Did you make many real friends in your school days?"

"No real lasting friends. They were French girls, you see, and there was the difference of race, and religion, to divide us as we grew up. And we were birds of passage, mother and I; always moving about."

"You felt the need of companionship?"

"No. I had mother, and we were like girls together." The twin dimples showed in a mischievous smile. "You seem very anxious to hear that I was lonely!"

"Well!" said Erskine, and hesitated as though he found it impossible to deny the accusation. "I wanted to feel that you could sympathise with me! I've been more or less lonely all my life, but I have always felt that a time would come when it would be all right—when I'd meet some one who'd understand. I was great chums with my father, but he died when I was twelve, and my school chum went off to China, and comes home for a few months every three years, when it has usually happened that I've been abroad. There are nice enough fellows in the regiment, but I suppose I'm not quick at making friends—"

Strive as she would Claire could not resist a twinkle of amusement, their eyes met, and both went off into a peal of laughter.

"Oh, well, there are exceptions! That's different. I felt that I knew you at once, without any preliminary stages. It must always be like that when people really fit." And then after a short pause he added in boyish, ingenuous tones, "Did you feel that you knew me?"

"I—I think I did!" Claire acknowledged. To both it seemed the most wonderful, the most absorbing of conversations. They were blissfully unconscious that it was old as the hills themselves, and had been repeated with ceaseless reiteration from prehistoric periods. Only once was there an interruption of the deep mutual happiness and that came without warning. Claire was smiling in blissful contentment, unconscious of a care, when suddenly a knife-like pain stabbed her heart. Imagination had wafted her back to Staff-Room. She saw the faces of the fifteen women seated around the table, women who were with but one exception past their youth, approaching nearer and nearer to dreaded age, and an inward voice whispered that to each in her turn had come this golden hour, the hour of dreams, of sweet, illuminative hope. The hour had come, and the hour had passed, leaving behind nothing but a memory and a regret. Why should she herself be more blessed than others? She looked forward and saw a vision of herself ten years hence still hurrying along the well-known street looking up at the clock in the church tower to assure herself that she was in time, still mounting the same bare staircase, still hanging up her hat on the same peg. The prose of it in contradistinction with the poetry of the present was terrifying to Claire's youthful mind, and her look was so white, so strained, that Erskine took instant alarm.

"What is it? What is it? Are you ill? Have I said anything to upset you? I say, what *is* the matter!"

"Nothing. Nothing! I had a—thought! Talk hard, please, and make me forget!"

The end of the two hours found the cross-questioning still in full force; the man and the girl alike still feeling that the half was not yet told. They resented the quick passage of time, resented the disturbance of the afternoon hours.

"What on earth do we want with a tennis party?" grumbled the Captain. "Wish to goodness we could be left alone. I suppose the mater wanted them to amuse you before I came back."

Claire murmured incoherently. She knew better, but she was not going to say so! They turned unwillingly towards the house.

In the afternoon the guests arrived. They came early, for the Fanshawe tennis courts were in fine condition, and the prospect of meeting a new man and a new girl, plus the son of the house, was a treat in itself in the quiet countryside where the members of the same set met regularly at every function of the year. One of the courts was reserved for men's fours, for Mrs Fanshawe believed in giving her guests what they liked, and there is no doubt that men as a rule are ungallant enough to prefer their own sex in outdoor games.

In the second court the younger girls took part in mixed fours, while others sat about, or took part in lengthy croquet contests on the furthest of the three lawns. Claire as a member of the house-party had a good deal of time on her hands, and helped Mrs Fanshawe with the entertainment of the older guests, who one and all eyed her with speculative interest.

One thin, faded woman had spent a few years in Bombay and was roused to interest by hearing that Claire's mother was now settled in that city. Yes! she had met a Mr Judge. Robert Judge, was it not? Her husband knew him quite well. He had dined at their house. Quite a dear man. She had heard of his marriage, "but"—here came a look of mystification—"to a *young* wife; very pretty, very charming—"

Claire laughed, and held out a little coloured photograph in a round glass frame which hung by a chain round her neck.

"That is my mother. She is thirty-nine, and looks thirty. And she is prettier than that."

The faded lady looked, and sighed. Mrs Fanshawe brightened into vivid interest. "You know Mr Judge, then? You have met him? That's quite interesting. That's very interesting!" Claire realised with some irritability that the fact that one of her own acquaintances knew and approved, instantaneously raised Mr Judge in her hostess's estimation. Hitherto he had been a name, a nobody; now he became a real man, "quite a dear man," a man one could know! The result was satisfactory enough, but Claire was irritated by the means. She was irritated also by the subtle but very real change in her hostess's manner to herself in the last twenty-four hours; irritated because the precious hours were passing, and Erskine was surrounded by his guests, playing endless sets on the hot lawn. He looked as though he were enjoying himself, too, and that added to her annoyance, for like many another girl she had not yet realised that a man can forget even his love in his whole-hearted enjoyment of sport!

At tea-time, however, there was a lull when Erskine carried a chair to Claire's side, and seated himself with an air of contentment. Once and again as the meal progressed she saw his eyes rove around, and then come back to dwell upon herself. She knew that he was comparing her with the other girls who were present, knew also by the deep glow of that returning glance, that in his eyes she was fairest and best. The former irritation dropped from her like a cloak.

Tea was over, the guests rose from their seats. Erskine stood by Claire's side looking down at her with a quizzical smile.

"Er—did you notice that man who came in just before tea, with the girl in the pink frock? He was sitting over there, on the right?"

"Yes, I noticed him. I could see him quite well. Why?"

"What did you think of him?"

"Quite nice. I liked his face. Good-natured and interesting."

Erskine laughed.

"Sure?"

"Quite sure. Why?"

"Don't recognise him at all? Doesn't remind you of any one you know?"

"Not in the least. Why should he?"

Erskine laughed again.

"I'm afraid your memory is defective. I must introduce you again!" He walked away, laid his hand on the arm of the new-comer, and led him back to Claire's side. "Miss Gifford," he said gravely, "allow me to introduce—Major Carew!"

Chapter Twenty Two.

Found out.

The man with the good-natured, interesting face bowed to Claire with the alacrity which the normal man shows at an introduction to a pretty girl; Claire stared blankly, recovered herself, and returned his bow in formal manner. Erskine looked from one to the other in undisguised surprise.

"I thought you had met... You told me you had met Carew in town!"

"Not *this* Major Carew!" Claire could not suppress a tone of regret. With all her heart she wished that the man before her had been Cecil's fiancé.

"It was the same name, but—"

"Not the same man? It's not an unusual name, I expect there are several of us knocking about," the present Major Carew said smilingly. "Do you happen to know his regiment?"

Claire knew it well, but as she pronounced the name, the hearer's face crinkled in confusion.

"But that is my own regiment! There *is* no other Carew! There's some mistake. You have mixed up the names."

"Oh no. I've heard it a hundred times. It is impossible to be mistaken. His Christian name is Frank."

"*My* name is Frank!" the strange man said, and stared at Claire in increasing perplexity. "There is certainly not another Frank Carew in the M—. There is something wrong about this. I don't understand!"

"He is a member of the — Club, and his people live in Surrey. He has an old father who is an invalid, and the name of the house is 'The Moat'—"

Major Carew's face turned a deep, apoplectic red, his light eyes seemed to protrude from his head, so violent was his anger and surprise.

"But—that's *me*! That's my club, my father, my home! Somebody has been taking my name, and passing himself off under false colours for some mysterious reason. I can't imagine what good it is going to do him."

He broke off in alarm, and cast an appealing look at Erskine as Claire suddenly collapsed on the nearest chair, her face as white as her gown.

"I say, this is a bad business I'm most awfully sorry. I'm afraid Miss Gifford is distressed—"

Erskine's lips were set in a fury of anger. He glanced at Claire and turned hurriedly away, as though he could not trust himself to look at her blanched face. To see the glint of his eye, the set of the firm jaw, was to realise that it would fare badly with the masquerader should he come within reach. There was a moment of tense, unhappy silence, then Erskine drew forward two more chairs, and motioned to the Major to be seated.

"I think we shall have to thresh this out! It is naturally a shock, but Miss Gifford's acquaintance with this person is very slight. She took a violent dislike to him at first sight, so you need not fear that she will feel any personal distress. That is so, isn't it? That's the real position?"

Claire nodded a quick assent.

"Yes, yes. I met him twice, and I hated him from the first; but my friend believes..." Her voice broke, and she struggled for composure, her chin quivering with pitiful, child-like distress. "He is engaged to be *married* to my friend!"

A deep murmur of anger came simultaneously from both hearers. The real Major Carew straightened himself with an air of determination.

"Engaged to her? Under my name? This is too strong! And in the name of wonder, what for? I'm nobody. I've nothing. I'm the most insignificant of fellows, and chronically hard up. What had he to gain by taking my name?"

"You are a gentleman, and he is not. Everything is comparative. He wanted to impress my friend, and he knew you so well that it was easy to pretend, and make up a good tale. He *said* he was hard up. He—he—borrowed money!"

"From the girl?" Again came that deep murmur of indignation. "What an unspeakable cur, and—excuse me, what a poor-spirited girl to have anything to do with him after that! Could you do nothing to prevent her making such a fool of herself?"

"Nothing. I tried. I tried hard, but—"

Erskine looked at her with his keen, level glance.

"And she borrowed from you to supply his needs? No, never mind, I won't ask any more questions, but I know! I know!" His eyes hardened again as he turned towards the other man. "Carew, this is pure swindling! We shall have to worry this out!"

"I believe you, my boy!" said the Major tersely. He turned to Claire and added more gently, "Tell us some more about this fellow, Miss Gifford! Describe him! Would you recognise him if you met again?"

"Oh, yes. At once. He is tall and dark, good-looking, I suppose, though I detest his type. Very dark eyes. Large features."

The Major ruminated, finding apparently no clue in the description.

"Tall. Dark. Large features! I know about a hundred men to whom that description might apply. Could you think of anything more definite?"

Claire ruminated in her turn; recalled the image of Cecil's lover, and tried to remember the details of his appearance.

"He has very thick hair, and brushes it straight across his forehead. His eyebrows are very short. He has a high colour, quite red cheeks."

Major Carew made a short, choking sound; lay back in his chair, and stared aghast. This time it was evident that the description awoke a definite remembrance, but he appeared to thrust it from him, to find it difficult to give credence to the idea.

"Impossible!" he murmured to himself. "Impossible! High colour, you say; short eyebrows. When you say 'short,' what exactly do you mean?"

"They begin by being very thick, then they stop abruptly. They don't follow the line of the eye, like most eyebrows. They look—unfinished!"

Major Carew bounced upon his chair.

"Erskine, I have an idea.—It seems almost incredible, but I'm bound to find if it is correct! There is a man who is in our camp now. I'll make an excuse, and send him over to-night, if you can arrange that Miss Gifford sees him when he comes. I'll give him a message for you."

"*Send*!" repeated Erskine sharply; then he glanced at Claire, and sent a frowning message towards the other man. "That can easily be arranged. We'll leave it till evening, then. We can't get any further now, and I must get back to my duties. The mater is scowling at me. Go and soothe her like a good fellow, but for your life—not a word of this to her!"

Major Carew rose obediently, perfectly aware that his company was not wanted, and Erskine bent towards Claire with a few earnest words.

"Don't worry! If this man is an impostor, the sooner it is found out, the better. He *is* an impostor, there's no getting away from that, and he is making a dupe of that poor girl for his own ends. If we had not made this discovery, he would have stuck to her until he had bled her of her last penny, and then would probably have disappeared into space. She knows nothing of his real name or position, so it would have been difficult to trace him, and probably nothing to be gained, if he *were* found. One reads of these scoundrels from time to time, but I've never had the misfortune to meet one in the flesh. I'd like to horsewhip the fellow for upsetting you like this!"

"Oh, what does it matter about me?" Claire cried impatiently. "It's Cecil I'm thinking about—my poor, poor friend! She's not young, and she is tired out after twelve years of teaching, and it's the *second* time! Years ago a man pretended to love her, it was only pretence, and it nearly broke her heart. She has never been the same since then. It made her bitter and distrustful."

"Poor creature! No wonder. But that was some time ago, and now she is engaged to this other fellow. Is she in love with him, do you suppose?"

Claire shrugged vaguely.

"I—don't—know! She is in love with the idea of a home."

"And he? You have seen them together. He is a cur, there's no getting away from that, but he might be attached to the girl all the same. Do you think he is?"

"Oh, how can I tell?" Claire cried impatiently. "She thinks he is, but she thought the same about the other man. It doesn't seem possible to tell! Men amuse themselves and pretend, and act a part, and then laugh at a girl if she is so foolish as to believe—"

Captain Fanshawe bent forward, his arm resting on his knees, his face upraised to hers; a very grave face, fixed and determined.

"Do you believe that, Claire? Do you believe what you are saying?"

The grey eyes looked deep into hers, compelling an answer.

"I—I think many of them—"

"Some of them!" the Captain corrected. "Just as some girls encourage a man to gratify their own vanity. They are the exceptions in both cases; but you speak in generalities, condemning the whole sex. Is it what you really think—that most men pretend?"

The grey eyes were on her face, keen, compelling eyes from which there was no escape. Claire flushed and hesitated.

"No! No, I don't. Not most. But there are some!"

"We are not concerned with 'some'!" he said quietly, and straightening himself, he cast a glance around.

The guests were standing about in little groups, aimless, irresolute, waiting to be broken up into twos and fours, and drafted off to the empty lawns; across the deserted tea-tables his mother's eyes met his, coldly reproachful. Erskine sighed, and rose to his feet.

"I must go. These people need looking after. Don't look so sad. It hurts me to see you sad."

Just those few, hastily-spoken words and he was gone, and Claire strolled off in an opposite direction, anxious to screen herself from observation among the crowd. She ached with pity for Cecil, but through all her distresses the old confidence lay warm at her heart. There was one man in the world who towered high above the possibility of deceit; and between that man and herself was a bond stronger than spoken word. The future seemed full of difficulties, but Claire did not trouble herself about the future. The present was all-absorbing, full of trouble; full of joy!

It was seven o'clock before the last of the guests had departed, and Mrs Fanshawe saw to it that her son was fully engaged until it was time to dress for dinner. Her keen eyes had noticed signs of agitation as the two young people sat together at tea. And what had Erskine been talking about with that tense expression on his face? And what had happened to the girl that she looked at one moment so radiant, and at the next so cast-down? Mrs Fanshawe's affections, like those of most selfish people, were largely influenced by personal considerations. A week before she had felt quite a warm affection for the agreeable companion who had rescued her from the boredom of lonely days, now hour by hour, she was conscious of a rising irritation against the girl who threatened to interfere with her own plans. The verdict of others confirmed her own suspicions as to

Erskine's danger, for during the afternoon half a dozen intimate friends referred to Claire with significant intonation. "Such a graceful creature. No wonder Erskine is *épris*!" ... "Miss Gifford is quite charming." ... "*So* interested to meet Miss Gifford!" Eyes and voice alike testified to the conviction that if an engagement were not already arranged, it was a certainty in the near future. Mrs Fanshawe set her lips, and determined by hook or crook to get Claire Gifford out of the house.

That evening at nine o'clock the parlour-maid announced that Major Carew's soldier servant wished to see Captain Fanshawe on a message from his master, and Erskine gave instructions that he should be sent round to the verandah, and stepped out of the window, leaving Claire wondering and discomfited. What had happened? Was the impostor not to be found? In her present tension of mind any delay, even of the shortest, seemed unbearable.

The murmur of voices sounded from without, then Erskine stepped back into the room, and addressed himself pointedly to Claire, but without using her name.

"Would you come out just for two minutes? It's some plan for to-morrow."

Claire crossed the room, acutely conscious of Mrs Fanshawe's displeasure, stepped into the cool light of the verandah and beheld standing before her, large and trim in his soldier's uniform, Cecil's lover, the man who had masqueraded under his master's name.

For one breathless moment the two stood face to face, staring, aghast, too petrified by surprise to be able to move or speak. Claire caught hold of the nearest chair, and clutched at its back; the florid colour died out of the man's cheeks, his eyes glazed with horror and dismay. Then with a rapid right-about-face, he leapt from the steps, and sped down the drive. Another moment and he had disappeared, and the two who were left, faced each other aghast.

"His servant! His *servant*! Oh, my poor Cecil!"

"The scoundrel! It was a clever ruse. No need to invent details: he had them all ready to his hand. The question is, what next? The game is up, and he knows it. What will be his next move?"

Claire shook her head. She was white and shaken. The reality was even worse than she had expected, and the thought of Cecil's bitterness of disillusion weighed on her like a nightmare. She tried to speak, but her lips trembled and Erskine drew near with a quick word of consolation—

"Claire!"

"What is this plan, Erskine? Am I not to be consulted? Remember that you are engaged to lunch with the Montgomerys to-morrow."

Mrs Fanshawe stood in the doorway, erect, haughty, obviously annoyed. Her keen eyes rested on Claire's face, demanding a reason for her embarrassment. Erskine made a virtue of necessity, and offered a short explanation.

"A disagreeable thing has happened, mother. Miss Gifford has discovered through Major Carew that a friend is in serious trouble. It has been rather a shock."

"Dear me. Yes! It would be. Perhaps you would like to go to your room, my dear. I'm tired myself, and shall be glad to get to bed. I am sure you must wish to be alone. Shall we go?"

Claire said good night to the two men and went wearily upstairs. At this moment even her own inward happiness failed to console. When contrasted with her own fate, Cecil's seemed so cruelly unfair!

Chapter Twenty Three.

"No!"

Sleep refused to come to Claire that night. She lay tossing on her bed while the old clock in the corridor without struck hour after hour.

Two, three, four, and still she tossed, and turned, and again and again asked herself the world-old question, "What shall I do? What shall I do?" and shuddered at the thought of the disillusionment which was coming to her poor friend.

What was her own duty in the matter? Obviously Cecil must be told the truth; obviously she was the one to tell it. Would it be possible to *write*? Inclination clamoured in favour of such a course. It would be so much easier: it would obviate the necessity for a lacerating interview. Would it not be easier for Cecil, also? Claire felt that if positions had been reversed, she would crave above all things to be alone, hidden from the eyes of even the most sympathising of friends; but Cecil's nature was of a different type. Having heard the one abhorrent fact, she would wish to probe further, to be told details, to ask a score of trifling questions. However full a letter might be, she would not be satisfied without an interview. "But I might write first, and see her afterwards!" poor Claire said to herself. "It would not be quite so bad, when she had got over the first shock. I could *not* bear to see her face..."

It was five o'clock before at last sleep came to drive away the haunting questions, and when she woke it was to find her early tea had grown cold on the table by her side, and to see on looking at her watch that it was nearly ten o'clock. She dressed hurriedly and went downstairs to find Mrs Fanshawe alone in the dining-room, reading the *Morning Post*. She waved aside Claire's apologies for her late appearance with easy good nature. No one was *expected* to be punctual at breakfast. It was sheer tyranny to decree that visitors should get up at a definite hour. If Claire had slept badly, why didn't she order breakfast in her room, and spend the morning in bed?

"You look a wreck!" she said frankly, and threw down the paper with an impatient gesture. "Such a nuisance about this bad news. Erskine seems disgusted with the whole affair. He has gone off with Major Carew to see what can be done, and is to go straight to the Willoughbys. So tiresome, for I particularly wanted him to be in good form this afternoon! What's it all about? As it has happened in my house, I think I am entitled to an explanation. Something to do with Major Carew's servant? How can your friend be associated with a servant? The man has bolted, it appears. The Major came over half an hour ago to say that he never returned last night. Thought flight the best policy, I suppose, but what I am waiting to be told, is—what has he *done*?"

Claire sat down on the nearest chair, feeling more of a wreck than ever.

"Deserted! A soldier! But if he is found? The punishment..."

"He has already been found out, it appears, so that it was a choice between certain punishment if he stayed, or the chance of getting safely away. I am waiting to hear what it's all about!"

"Oh, Mrs Fanshawe, it's so difficult. It's not my secret!" cried poor Claire desperately. "He, this man, has been masquerading under his master's name. My friend knew him as Major Carew. She, they, became very intimate."

"Engaged, I suppose! It doesn't say much for her discrimination. Her ideas of what constitute a gentleman must be somewhat vague!" Mrs Fanshawe said disagreeably. She felt disagreeable, and she never made any effort to conceal her feelings, kindly or the reverse. It was annoying that one of her own guests should be mixed up in an unsavoury scandal with a common soldier: annoying to have people going about with long faces,

The Independence of Claire

when she had planned a festive week. Really this Claire Gifford was becoming more and more of an incumbrance! Mrs Fanshawe paused with her hand on the coffee-pot, to ask a pointed question—

"Have *you* also known this man under his false name, may I ask?"

Claire flushed uncomfortably.

"I met him twice. Only twice. For a very short time."

Mrs Fanshawe did not speak, but she arched her eyebrows in a fashion which was more scorching than words. "So you, also, are ignorant of what constitutes a gentleman!" said those eyebrows. "You also have been including my friend's servant among your acquaintances!"

Claire felt the hopelessness of trying to justify herself, and relapsed into silence also, the while she made a pretence of eating one of the most miserable meals of her life. According to his mother, Erskine was "quite disgusted" with the whole affair! Claire's heart sank at the thought, but she acknowledged that such an attitude would be no more than was natural under the circumstances. A soldier himself, Captain Fanshawe would be a stern judge of a soldier's fraud, while his *amour propre* could not fail to be touched. Claire had too much faith to believe that his displeasure would be extended to herself, yet she was miserably aware that it was through her instrumentality that he had been brought in contact with the scandal.

In the midst of much confusion of mind only one thing seemed certain, and that was that it was impossible to face a tennis party that afternoon. Claire made her apologies to Mrs Fanshawe as she rose from the table, and they were accepted with disconcerting readiness.

"Of course! Of course! I never imagined that you would. Under the circumstances it would be most awkward. I expect by afternoon the story will be the talk of the place. Your friend, I understand, is still ignorant of the man's real station? What do you propose to do with regard to breaking the news?"

"In. I'm going to write. I thought I would sit in my room and compose a letter.—It will be difficult!"

"Difficult!" Mrs Fanshawe repeated the word with disagreeable emphasis. "Impossible, I should say, and, excuse me! cruel into the bargain. To open a letter from a friend, expecting to find the ordinary chit-chat, and to receive a blow that shatters one's life! My dear, it's unthinkable! You cannot seriously intend it."

"You think it would be better if I *told*, her?" Claire asked anxiously. "I wondered myself, but naturally I dreaded it, and I thought she might prefer to get over the first shock alone. I had decided to write first, and see her later on. But you think..."

"I think decidedly that you ought to break the news in person. You can lead up to it more naturally in words. Even the most carefully written letters are apt to read coldly; perhaps the more care we spend on them, the more coldly they read."

"Yes, that's true, that's quite true, but I thought it would be better not to wait. She is staying at home just now. I don't think he will visit her there, for he seemed to shrink from meeting her mother, but he may write and try—" Claire drew herself up on the point of betraying that borrowing of money which was the most shameful feature of the fraud, but Mrs Fanshawe was too much absorbed in her own schemes to notice the omission. She had seen a way of getting rid of an unwelcome guest, and was all keenness to turn it to account.

"He is sure to try to see her again while he is at large. He will probably urge her to marry him at once. You should certainly not defer your visit if it is to be of any use. How dreadful *it* would be if she were to marry him under an assumed name! You mustn't let us interfere with your arrangement, my dear. You only promised me ten days, so I can't grumble if you run away, and for the short time that Erskine is at home, there are so many friends to fit in... You understand, I am sure, that I am thinking of your own convenience!"

"I understand perfectly, thank you!" Claire replied, her head in the air, the indignant colour dying her cheeks with red. Mrs Fanshawe's arguments in favour of haste might be wise enough, but her personal desire was all too plainly betrayed. And she pointedly ignored the fact that the proposed interview need not have interrupted Claire's visit, since it and the journey involved could easily have been accomplished in the course of a day. "I understand perfectly, thank you. I will go upstairs and pack now. Perhaps there is a train I could catch before lunch?"

"The twelve-thirty. That will give you the afternoon in town. I'll order a fly from the inn. I'm *so* sorry for you, dear! Most nerve-racking to have to break bad news, but you'll feel happier when it's done. Perhaps you could take the poor thing with you to that sweet little farm!"

Not for the world would Claire have spent the next hour in Mrs Fanshawe's company. She hurried to her room, and placing her watch on the dressing-table, so timed her packing that it should not be completed a moment before the lumbering country "fly" drove up to the door. Then, fully dressed, she descended the staircase, and held out a gloved hand to her hostess, apparently unconscious of an offered kiss.

It was some slight consolation to note the change of bearing which had come over Mrs Fanshawe during the last hour, and to realise that the success of her scheme had not brought much satisfaction. She was nervous, she was more than nervous, she was afraid! The while Claire had been packing upstairs, she had had time to realise Erskine's return, and his reception of the news she would have to break. As she drove away from the door, Claire realised that her hostess would have paid a large sum down to have been able to undo that morning's work!

For her own part, Claire cared nothing either way: literally and truthfully at that moment even the thought of leaving Erskine had no power to wound. The quickly-following events of the last twenty-four hours had had a numbing effect on her brain. She was miserable, sore, and wounded; the whole fabric of life seemed tumbling to pieces. Love, for the moment, was in abeyance. As the fly passed the last yard of mown grass which marked the boundary of the Fanshawe property, she threw out her arms with one of the expressive gestures, which remained with her as a result of her foreign training.

"*Fini*!" she cried aloud. Mentally at that moment, she swept the Fanshawes, mother and son, from the stage of her life.

Where should she go next? Back to solitude, and the saffron parlour? London in August held no attraction, but the solitary prospect of being able to see Sophie, and at the moment Claire shrank from Sophie's sharp eyes. Should she telegraph to the farm, and ask how soon she could be received; and at the same time telegraph to Mary Rhodes asking for an immediate interview? A few minutes' reflection brought a decision in favour of this plan, and she drew a pocket-book from her dressing-bag, and busied herself in composing the messages. One to the farm, a second to Laburnum Crescent announcing her immediate return, then came a pause, to consider the difficult wording of the third. Would it be possible to drop a word of warning, intelligible to Cecil herself, but meaningless to anyone else who might by chance open the wire?

"Back in town. Have important news. Imperative to see you to-day, if possible. Appoint meeting. Delay dangerous."

It was not perfect, but in Claire's dazed condition it was the best she could concoct, and it left a tactful uncertainty as to whether the news affected herself or Cecil, which would make it the easier to explain. Claire counted the words and folded the three messages in her hand-bag, ready to be sent off the moment she reached the station.

The fly lumbered on; up a toilsome hill, down into the valley, up another hill on the farther side; then came a scattering of houses, a church, a narrow street lined with shops, and finally the station itself, the clock over the entrance showing a bare four minutes to spare.

The porter labelled the luggage, and trundled it down the platform. Claire hurried through her business in the telegraph office, and ran after him just as the train slowed down on the departure platform. One carriage showed two empty corner places on the nearest side, Claire opened the door, seated herself facing the engine, and spread her impedimenta on the cushions. But few passengers had been waiting, for this was one of the slowest trains in the day, but now at this last moment there came the sound of running footsteps, a man's footsteps, echoing in strong heavy beats. With a traveller's instinctive curiosity Claire leant forward to watch the movements of this late comer, and putting her head out of the window came face to face with Erskine Fanshawe himself.

At sight of her he stopped short, at sight of him she stood up, blocking the window from sight of the other occupants of the carriage; by a certain defiance of pose, appearing to defend it also against his own entrance. But he did not attempt to enter. Though he had been running, it was his pallor, not his heat, which struck Claire in that first moment. He was white, with the pallor of intense anger; the flash of his eyes was like cold steel. He rested his hands on the sill of the window, and looked up into her face.

"This is my mother's doing!"

It was a statement, not a question, and Claire made no reply. She stood stiff and silent, while down the length of the platform sounded the quick banging of doors.

"I got through sooner than I expected and went home to change. I did not waste time in talking... I could guess what had happened. She made it impossible for you to stay on?"

Still silence. The guard's whistle sounded shrilly. Erskine came a step nearer. His white tense face almost touched her own.

"Claire!" he whispered breathlessly, "will you marry me?"

"Stand back there! Stand back!" cried an authoritative voice. The wheels of the carriage rolled slowly forward. Claire bent forward, and gave her answer in one incisive word—

"No!"

The wheels rolled faster and faster: left the station, whirled out into the green, smiling plain.

Chapter Twenty Four.

A Rupture.

In after days Claire often looked back upon that journey to London, and tried to recall her own feelings, but invariably the effort ended in failure. She could remember nothing but a haze of general misery and confusion, which deepened with every fresh mile, and reached its acutest point at the moment of arriving "home."

The landlady was flustered at having to prepare for so hasty a return, and did not scruple to show her displeasure. She took for granted that Claire had had lunch, and the poor girl had not the courage to undeceive her. A telegram was lying on the dining-room table which announced Cecil's arrival at four o'clock. Claire ordered tea to be ready at that hour, and stretched herself on her bed in the room upstairs which looked so bare and cold, denuded of the beautifying personal touches. She felt incredibly tired, incredibly lonely; she longed with a very passion of longing for some one of her own, for the dear, beautiful mother, who if she did not always understand, was always ready to love. Oh, it was hard, unnatural work, this fighting the world alone! Did the girls who grew weary of the restraints of home, ever realise how their working sisters sickened with longing for some one who cared enough even to *interfere*!

Three o'clock, half-past three, a quarter to four. Claire was faint for want of food, and had enough sense to realise that this was a poor preparation for the ordeal ahead; she went downstairs, and threw herself upon Lizzie's mercy.

"Lizzie, I have had no lunch. I'm starving. Could you bring up the tea *now*, and make some fresh for Miss Rhodes when she arrives?"

"Why couldn't you say so before?" Lizzie asked with the freedom of the lodging-house slavey, but the question was spoken in sympathy rather than anger. "The kettle's boiling, and I've cut the bread and butter. You shall have it in two two's. I'll cut you a sanguidge," she cried as a supreme proof of goodwill, and clattered down the kitchen stairs at express speed.

She was as good as her word. In five minutes tea was ready, and Claire ate and drank, keeping her eyes turned resolutely from the clock. Before it had struck the hour, there came from the hall the sound of a well-known double knock, and she knew that the hour of her ordeal had arrived.

She did not rise from the table; the tea-things were clattering with the trembling of the hand that was resting upon the tray, she literally had not the strength to rise. She lay back in her chair and stared helplessly at the opening door.

Cecil came in. It came as a shock to see her looking so natural, so entirely the Cecil Claire was accustomed to see. She looked tired, and a trifle cross, but alas! these had been prevailing expressions even in the days when things were going comparatively well. Casual in her own manner, she saw nothing unusual in Claire's lack of welcome, she nodded an off-hand greeting, and drew up a chair to the table.

"Well! I've come. Give me a cup of tea as a start. I've had a rush for it. You said to-day, if possible, and I had nothing special on hand, so I thought I had better come. What's the news, and what's the danger? Which of us does it affect,—me or you?"

"Oh, it's—horrid, horrid, horrid! It's a long story. Finish your tea first, then I'll tell you. I'm *so* miserable!"

"Poor old girl!" Cecil said kindly, and helped herself to bread and butter. Claire had a miserable conviction that her reply had had a deceptive effect, and that the shock when it came, would be all the more severe. Nevertheless, she was thankful for the reprieve; thankful to see Cecil eat sandwiches with honest enjoyment, until the last one had disappeared from the plate.

"Well!" Cecil pushed aside her cup, and rested an arm on the table. "Let's get to business. I promised mother I'd catch the six o'clock train back. What's it all about? Some young squire wanting to marry you, and you want my advice? Take him, my dear! You won't always be young and beautiful!"

Claire shook her head.

"Nothing about me. I wouldn't have worried you in the holidays, if—if it hadn't been for your own sake..."

The red flowed into Cecil's cheeks, her face hardened, the tone of her voice was icy cold.

"*My* sake? I don't understand. I am not aware that you have any responsibility about my affairs!"

"Cecil, I have! I must have. We have lived together. I have loved you—"

Mary Rhodes waved aside the protestations with impatient scorn.

"Don't be sentimental, please! You are not one of the girls. If it's the money, and you are in a hurry to be repaid—"

"I'm not. I'm not! I don't care if you *never* pay..." Tears of distress rose in Claire's eyes, she caught her breath and cried in a choking sob. "Cecil, it's about—him! I've found out something. I've seen him... Only last night..."

"I thought you might meet as his camp was so near. Suppose you did! What was so terribly alarming in that?"

"You haven't heard? He hasn't been to see you, or written, or wired, to-day?"

"He has not. Why should he? Don't be hysterical, Claire. If you have anything to say, say it, and let me hear. What have you 'found out' about Major Carew?"

"He's—*not* Major Carew!" Claire cried desperately. "He has deceived you, Cecil, and pretended to be

CECIL ROSE FROM HER CHAIR AND WENT OVER TO THE
EMPTY FIREPLACE.

[See page 347.

... to be something quite different from what he really is. There *is* a real Major Carew, and his name is Frank, and he has a home in Surrey, and an invalid father—everything that he told you was true, only—he is not the man! Oh, Cecil, how shall I tell you? It's so dreadfully, dreadfully hard. He knew all about the real Major Carew, and could get hold of photographs to show you, because he—he is his servant, Cecil—his soldier servant... He was with him in camp!"

Cecil rose from her chair, and went over to the empty fireplace, standing with her back to her companion. She spoke no word, and Claire struggled on painfully with her explanations.

"He—the real Major Carew—came over to a tennis party at Mrs Fanshawe's yesterday. I thought, of course, that it was another man of the same name, but he said—he said there

The Independence of Claire

was no other in that regiment, and he asked me to tell him some more, and I did, and everything I said amazed him more and more, for it was true about *himself*! Then he asked me to describe—the man, and he made an excuse to send his servant over in the evening so that I should see him. He came. Oh, Cecil! He saw me, and he—ran away! He had not returned this morning. He has *deserted*!"

Still silence. It seemed to Claire of most pitiful import that Cecil made no disclaimer, that at the word of a stranger she accepted her lover's guilt. What a light on the past was cast by that stoney silence, unbroken by a solitary protest. Poor Mary Rhodes had known no doubts as to the man's identity, she had given him affection and help, but respect and trust could never have entered into the contract!

Claire had said her say: she leant her elbows on the table, and buried her head in her hands. The clock on the mantelpiece ticked steadily for an endless five minutes. Then Cecil spoke:—

"I suppose," she said harshly, "you expect me to be grateful for this!"

The sound of her voice was like a blow. Claire looked up, startled, protesting.

"Oh, Cecil, surely you would rather know?"

"Should I?" Cecil asked slowly. "Should I?" She turned back to the tireless grate, and her thoughts sped... With her eyes opened she would not, of course, consent to marry this man who had so meanly abused her trust, but—suppose she had not known! Suppose in ignorance the marriage had taken place? If he had been loving, if he had been kind, would she in after days have regretted the step? At the bottom of her weary woman's heart, Cecil answered that she would *not*. The fraud was unpardonable, yet she could have pardoned it, if it had been done for love of herself. No stately Surrey mansion would have been her home, but a cottage of three or four rooms, but it would have been her *own* cottage, her *own* home. She would have felt pride in keeping it clean and bright. There would have been some one to work for: some one to care: some one to whom she *mattered*. And suddenly there came the thought of another joy that might have been; she held to her breast a child that was no paid charge, but her very own, bone of her bone, flesh of her flesh...

"No! No!" she cried harshly, "I am not grateful. *Why* did you tell me? Why did you spoil it? What do I care who he was? He was my man; he wanted me. He told lies *because* he wanted me... I am getting old, and I'm tired and cross, but he cared.—He *did* care, and he looked up to me, and wanted to appear my equal... Oh, I'm not excusing him. I know all you would say. He deceived me—he borrowed money that he could never pay back, but he would have confessed some day, he would have had to confess, and I should have forgiven him. I'd have forgiven him anything, *because* he cared ... and after that—he would have cared more—I should have had him. I should have had my home..."

Claire hid her face, and groaned in misery of spirit. From her own point of view it seemed impossible that any woman should regret a man who had proved so unworthy, but once again she reminded herself that her own working life counted only one year, as against Cecil's twelve; once again she felt she had no right to judge. Presently she became aware that Cecil was moving about the room, opening the bureau, and taking papers out of a drawer. At the end of ten minutes she came back to the table, and began drawing on her gloves. Her face was set and tearless, but the lines had deepened into a new distinctness. Claire had a pitiful realisation that this was how Cecil would look when she was *old*.

"Well," she said curtly, "that's finished! I may as well go for my train. I'm sorry to appear ungracious, but you could hardly expect me to be pleased. You meant well, of course, but it's a pity to interfere. There's just one thing I'd like to make clear—you and I can hardly live together after this. I never was a very agreeable companion, and I shall be worse in the future. It would be better for your own sake to make a fresh start, and for myself—I'm sorry to appear brutal, but I could not stand another winter together. It would remind me too much..."

She broke off abruptly, and Claire burst into helpless tears.

"Oh, Cecil, Cecil ... don't hate me—don't blame me too much! It's been hard on me, too. Do you think I *liked* breaking such news? Of course I will take fresh rooms. I can understand that you'd rather have some one else, but let us still be friends! Don't turn against me altogether. I'm lonely, too... I've got my own trouble!"

"Poor little Claire!" Cecil melted at once, with the quick response which always rewarded an appeal to her better feelings. "Poor little Claire. You're a good child; you've done your best. It isn't *your* fault." She lifted her bag from the table, and took a step towards the door, then resolutely turned back, and held out her hand. "Good-bye. Don't cry. What's the good of crying? Good luck to you, my dear, and—take warning by me. I don't know what your trouble is, but as it isn't money, it's probably love.—If it is, don't play the fool. If the chance of happiness comes along, don't throw it away out of pride, or obstinacy, or foolish prejudice. You won't always be young. When you get past thirty, it's ... it's hard ... when there's nothing—"

She broke off again, and walked swiftly from the room.

The next moment the front door banged loudly. Cecil had gone.

Chapter Twenty Five.

A sudden resolve.

The next morning brought a letter from the farm bidding Claire welcome as soon as she chose to arrive, but there was no second letter on the table. Claire had not realised how confidently she had expected its presence, until her heart sank with a sick, heavy faintness as she lifted the one envelope, and looked in vain for a second.

Erskine had not written. Did that mean that he had taken her hasty answer as final, and would make no further appeal? She had read of men who had boasted haughtily that no girl should have an opportunity of refusing them *twice*; that the woman who did not know her own mind was no wife for them, but like every other lover she felt her own case to be unique. Driven to answer in a moment of intolerable irritation, what else could she have said?

But he had not written! What did that mean? At the moment of discovering her departure, Erskine had been consumed with anger, but afterwards, had his mother's counsels prevailed? Had he repented himself of his hasty impulse? Would the days pass on, and the months, and the years, and leave her like Cecil, solitary, apart?

Claire made a pretence at eating her breakfast, and then, too restless to stay indoors, put on her hat, and went out to roam the streets until it should be time to visit Sophie in her hospital.

Two hours later she returned and packed up not only her entire wardrobe, but the whole of her personal possessions. In the course of her walk there had come to her one of those curious contradictory impulses which are so characteristic of a woman's nature. Having poured out her heart in grief because Erskine had neither written nor followed her to town, she was now restlessly impatient to make communication impossible, and to bury herself where she could not be found. Before leaving the house she made Lizzie happy by a present of money, accompanied by quite a goodly bundle of clothing, after which she interviewed the landlady, gave notice that she no longer needed the rooms, and wrote out a cheque in payment of all claims. Then a taxi was summoned, the various boxes piled on top, and another chapter of life had come to an end.

Claire drove to the station, whence she proposed to take a late afternoon train to the farm, deposited her boxes in the left luggage office, and strolled listlessly towards the great bookstall under the clock. Another hour remained to be whiled away before she could start for the hospital; she would buy a book, sit in the waiting-room, and try to bury herself in its pages. She strolled slowly down the length of the stall, her eyes passing listlessly from one pile of books to another, finding little interest in them, and even less in the men and women who stood by her side. As Mrs Fanshawe would have said, "No one was in town"; even school-mistresses had flown from the region of bricks and mortar. If she had thought about it at all, Claire would have said that there was no one she *could* meet, but suddenly a hand grasped her arm, and brought her to a halt. She started violently, and for an instant her heart leapt with a wild glad hope. It was not Erskine Fanshawe who confronted her, however, but a girl clad in a tweed costume with a cloth cap to match, on the side of which a sprig of heather was fastened by a gold brooch fashioned in the shape of a thistle. In bewildered surprise Claire recognised the brown eyes and round freckled face of Janet Willoughby, whom she had believed to be hundreds of miles away, in the highlands of Scotland.

"Just come back," Janet explained. "The weather was impossible. Nothing but sheets of rain. I got tired, and came back to pay some visits in the south." She hesitated, then asked a sudden question. "Are you busy? Going anywhere at once? Could you spare half an hour? We might have lunch together in the refreshment room!"

"Yes. No. I'd like to. I've had no lunch." Claire faltered nervously, whereupon Janet turned to her maid, who was standing near, dressing-bag in hand, and gave a few quick instructions.

"Get a taxi, Ross, and take all the things home. The car can wait for me. I'll follow later."

The maid disappeared, and the two girls made their way across the open space. Both looked nervous and ill at ease, both dreaded the coming *tête-à-tête*, yet felt that it was a thing to be faced. Janet led the way to a table in the farthest corner of the room, and they talked trivialities until the ordered dishes were set on the table, and the waiter had taken his departure. Claire had ordered coffee, and drank eagerly, hoping that the physical refreshment would help to steady her nerves. Janet played with her knife and fork, and said, without looking up—

"You have left the Fanshawes, then! I heard that you were staying on."

"Yes. Yesterday I—came back."

The very lameness of the answer made it significant. Janet's freckled face turned noticeably pale.

"Erskine went straight home after he left Scotland?"

"Yes."

"And before he arrived, you had promised to stay on?"

"Mrs Fanshawe asked me, before he came, if I could stay for another week, and I was very glad to accept. I had no other engagement."

"And then?"

"Oh, then things were different. She didn't need company, and—and—things happened. My friend, Miss Rhodes—"

Janet waved aside "my friend, Miss Rhodes," with an impatient hand.

"And Erskine? What did *he* say to your leaving?"

The colour flamed in Claire's cheek; she stammered in hopeless confusion, and, in the midst of her stammering, Janet laid both hands on the table, and, leaning forward so that the two faces were only a few inches apart, spoke a few startling words—

"Has he—*proposed* to you? I must know! You must tell me!"

It was a command, rather than an appeal, and Claire automatically replied—

"He—he did! Yes, but—"

"And you?"

"I—couldn't. I said no!"

"You said no! Erskine asked you to be his wife, and you *refused*?" Janet stared in incredulous bewilderment. A spark of indignation shone in her brown eyes. "But why? You care for him. Any girl might be proud to marry Erskine Fanshawe. *Why*?"

"I can't tell you. It's so difficult. His mother—she didn't want me. She would have hated it. She almost turned me out."

"His *mother*! Mrs Fanshawe!" Janet's voice was full of an ineffable surprise. "You refused Erskine because of *her* prejudice? But she is always changing; she is the most undependable woman on the face of the earth! She is charming, and I'm fond of her, but I should not take her advice about a pair of gloves. Nothing that she could say would possibly have the slightest influence on my life. She's irresponsible; she sees entirely from her own standpoint. And Erskine—Erskine is a rock!" She paused, pressing her lips together to still their trembling, and Claire answered with a note of apology in her voice.

"Janet, I *know*! Don't think I don't appreciate him. Wait till you hear how it happened... He followed me to the station; it was the very last moment, just as the train was starting. There was time for only one word, and—I was sore and angry!"

Janet looked at her, a long, searching look.

"It's curious, but I always knew this would come. When I saw you sitting together at supper that first night, I knew then. All the time I knew it in my heart, but on the surface it seemed ridiculous, for you never met!"

"Never that you did not know, except one time in the park. There was nothing to tell you, Janet; nothing to hide."

"No. So he said. We talked of you in Scotland, you know, and it was just as I thought—a case of recognising each other at first sight. He said the moment he saw you you seemed different from everyone else, and he hoped and believed that you felt the same. That is how people ought to love; the right way, when both are attached, both feel the same... And it is so rare. Yet you *refused*!"

"Would you marry a man if his family disapproved?"

"Oh, yes! I should not be marrying the family. I'd be sorry, of course, but I'd make up my mind that in time I'd make them fall in love with me, too. What are you going to do now?"

"Going away. Into the country. I want to be quiet, and think."

Janet did not ask the address. She sat silent, staring into space, then asked a sudden irrelevant question:

"Did he send you the cuckoo clock?"

"I—think so! It had no name, but it came from Switzerland while he was there. He has never referred to it since."

"Ah!" Janet began pulling on her gloves. "I knew that, too. I *felt* that he had sent it. Well! I must go. It will all come right, of course, and you will be very happy. I've known Erskine so long, and his wife is sure to be happy." Janet forced an artificial little laugh.

"You will be engaged before me, after all, but I dare say I shall soon follow suit. It's nice to be loved. As one grows older, one appreciates it more. And Captain Humphreys is a good man."

"He is splendid! I loved his face. And he is so devoted to you. It was quite beautiful to watch him," cried Claire, thankful from her heart to be able to enthuse honestly.

A load was lifted from her heart by Janet's prophecy of her own future. For the moment it had no doubt been made more out of bravado than any real conviction, and inevitably there must be a period of suffering, but Janet was of a naturally buoyant nature, and her wounded spirit would gradually find consolation in the love which had waited so patiently for its reward. It needed no great gift of prophecy to see her in the future, a happy, contented wife.

Chapter Twenty Six.

Easier to die.

When Janet had taken her departure Claire looked at the clock and found that it was time to start for the hospital. She went out of the station, and, passing a shop for flowers and fruit went in, spent ten shillings in the filling of a reed basket, and, leaving the shop, seated herself in one of the taxis which were standing in readiness outside the great porch. Such carelessness of money was a natural reversion to habit, which came as a consequence of her absorbed mind.

The great hospital looked bare and grim, the smell of iodoform was more repellent than ever, after the sweet scents of the country. Claire knew her way by this time, and ascended by lift to the women's ward, where Sophie lay. Beside almost every bed one or two visitors were seated, but Sophie was alone. Down the length of the ward Claire caught a glimpse of a recumbent form, and felt a pang at the thought of the many visiting days when her friend had remained alone. With no relations in town, her brother's family too pressed for means to afford expeditions from the country, Sophie had no hope of seeing a familiar face, and her very attitude bespoke dejection.

Claire walked softly to the further side of the bed, and dangled the basket before the half-covered face, whereupon Sophie pushed back the clothes and sat up, her eyes lighting with joy.

"*Claire*! You! Oh, you dearly beloved, I thought you were still away! Oh, I am glad—I am glad! I was so dreadfully blue!"

She looked it. Even in the eagerness of welcome her face looked white and drawn, and the pretty pink jacket, Claire's own gift, seemed to accentuate her pallor. The hands with which she fondled the flowers were surely thinner than they had been ten days before.

"My dear, what munificence! Have you come into a fortune? And fruit underneath! I shall be able to treat the whole ward! When did you come back? Have you had a good time? Are you going on to the farm? It *is* good of you to come again. It's—it's hard being alone when you see the other patients with their own people. The nurses are dears, but they are so rushed, poor things, they haven't time to stay and talk. And oh, Claire, the days! They're so wearily *long*!"

Claire murmured tender exclamations of understanding and pity. A pained conviction that Sophie was no better made her shrink from putting the obvious question; but Sophie did not wait to be asked.

"Oh, Claire," she cried desperately, "it's so hard to be patient and to keep on hoping, when there's no encouragement to hope! I'm not one scrap better after all that has been tried, and I've discovered that they did not expect me to be better; the best they seem to hope for is that I may not grow worse! It's like running at the pitch of one's speed, and succeeding only in keeping in the same place. And there are other arthritics in this ward!" She shuddered. "When I think that I may become like *them*! It would be much easier to die."

"I think it would often seem easier," Claire agreed sadly, her thoughts turning to Cecil, whose trouble at the moment seemed as heavy as the one before her. "But we can't be deserters, Sophie. We must stick to our posts, and play the game. When these troubles come, we just *have* to bear them. There's no hiding, or running away. There's only one choice open to us—whether we bear it badly or well."

But Sophie's endurance was broken by weeks of suffering, and her bright spirit was momentarily under an eclipse.

"Everybody doesn't have to bear them! Things are so horribly uneven," she cried grudgingly. "Look at your friend Miss Willoughby, with that angel of a mother, and heaps of money, and health, and strength, and a beautiful home, and able to have anything she wants, as soon as she wants it. What does *she* know of trouble?"

Claire thought of Janet's face, as it had faced her across the table in the refreshment room, but it was not for her to betray another's secret, so she was silent, and Sophie lifted a spray of pink roses, and held them against her face, saying wistfully—

"You're a good little soul, Claire, and it's because you are good that I want to know what your opinion is about all this trouble and misery. What good can it possibly do me to have my life ruined by this illness? Don't tell me that it will not be ruined. It must be, in a material sense, and I'm not all spiritual yet; there's a lot of material in my nature, and I live in a material world, and I want to be able to enjoy all the dear, sweet, natural, human joys which come as a right to ordinary human beings. I want to *walk*! Oh, my dear, I look out of these windows sometimes and see all the thousands and thousands of people passing by, and I wonder if a single one out of all the crowd ever thinks of being thankful that he can *move*! I didn't myself, but now—when I hobble along—"

She broke off, shaking back her head as though to defy the rising tears, then lay back against the pillows, looking at Claire, and saying urgently—"Go on! Tell me what you think!"

"I think," Claire answered slowly, "that we are bound to grow! The mere act of death is not going to lift us at once to our full height. Our training must go on after we leave this sphere; but, Sophie dear, some of us have an extra hard training here, and if we bear it in the right way, surely, surely when we move up, it must be into a higher class than if things had been all smooth and easy. There must be less to learn, less to conquer, more to enjoy. You and I are school-mistresses and ought to realise the difficulties of mastering difficult tasks. Don't look upon this illness as cheating you out of a pleasant holiday, dear—look upon it as special training for an honours exam.!"

Sophie smiled, her old twinkling smile, and stroked Claire's hand with the spray of roses.

"I knew you'd say something nice! I knew you'd put it in a quaint, refreshing way. I shall remember that, when I am alone, and feel courage oozing out of every pore. Two o'clock in the morning is a particularly cheery time when you are racked with pain! Claire, I asked the doctor to tell me honestly whether there was any chance of my ever taking up the old work again, and he said, honestly, he feared there was none."

"But Mrs Willoughby—"

"I asked that, too. He says he quite hopes to get me well enough to go to Egypt in October or November, and that I should certainly be much better there. It would be the best thing that could happen if it came off! But—"

Claire held up a protesting hand.

"No ifs! No buts! Do your part, and get better, and leave the rest to Providence and—Mrs Willoughby! It's her mission in life to help girls, and she'll help *you*, too, or know the reason why. The truly sensible thing would be for you to begin to prepare your clothes. What about starting a fascinating blouse at once? Your hands are quite able to sew, and if you once got to work with chiffon and lace the time would fly! You might write for patterns to-night. You would enjoy looking at patterns."

When Claire took her departure half an hour later, she left behind a very different Sophie from the wan dejected-looking creature whom she had found on her arrival.

Hers was a happy nature, easily cheered, responsive to comfort, and Claire had a happy conviction that whatever physical handicaps might be in store, her spirit would rise valiantly to the rescue. A winter in Egypt was practically assured, since Mrs Willoughby had privately informed Claire that if nothing better offered, she would send Sophie at her own expense to help in the household of her niece—an officer's wife, who would be thankful for assistance, though she could not afford to pay the passage out. What was to happen in the future no one could tell, and there was no profit in asking the question. The next step was clear, and the rest must be left to faith, but with a chilling of the blood Claire asked herself what became of the disabled working women who had no influential friends to help in such a crisis; the women who fell out of the ranks to die by the roadside homeless, penniless, *alone*?

Chapter Twenty Seven.

Surrender.

It was a very limp and exhausted Claire who arrived at the farm that evening, and if she had had her own way she would have hurried to bed without waiting for a meal, but the kind countrywoman displayed such disappointment at the idea that she allowed herself to be dissuaded, sat down to a table spread with home-made dainties and discovered that she was hungrier than she had believed. The fried ham and eggs, the fresh butter, the thick yellow cream, the sweet coarse bread, were all the best of their kind, and Claire smiled at her own expense as she looked at the emptied dishes, and reflected that, for a person who had professed herself unable to eat a bite, she had made a pretty good sweep!

The bed was somewhat bumpy, as farmhouse beds have a habit of being; there was one big ball in especial which took many wrigglings to avoid; but on the other hand the sheets smelt deliciously, not of lavender, but of lemon thyme, and the prevailing air of cleanliness was delicious after the smoke-laden atmosphere of town. Claire told herself that she could not expect to sleep. She resigned herself to hear the clock strike every hour—and as a matter of fact after ten o'clock she was unconscious of the whole world, until her breakfast-tray was carried into the room next morning.

After breakfast she had another nap, and after lunch still another, and in the intervals wandered about the farm-yard, laboriously striving to take an interest in what really interested her not at all. Hens seemed to her the dullest of created creatures, pigs repelled, cows were regarded with uneasy suspicion, and sheep, seen close at hand, lost all the picturesque quality of a distant flock, and became stupid long-faced creatures, by no means as clean as they might be. Milking-time aroused no ambition to experiment on her own account, and a glass of foaming new milk proved unexpectedly nauseous. Sad as it was to confess it, she infinitely preferred the chalked and watered edition of the city!

Indoors things were no better, for the tiny sitting-room stood by itself at the end of a passage, cut off from the life of the house. It was spotlessly clean and the pride of its owner's heart, but contained nothing of interest to an outsider. Pictures there were none, with the exception of portraits of the farmer and his wife, of the enlarged photograph type, and a selection of framed funeral cards in a corner. Books there were none, with the exception of a catalogue of an Agricultural Show, and a school prize copy of *Black Beauty*. Before the second night was over Claire had read *Black Beauty* from cover to cover; the next morning she was dipping into the catalogue, and trying to concentrate her attention on "stock."

As her body grew rested, Claire's mind became increasingly active. It was inevitable, but the second stage was infinitely harder to bear. For the first hours after her arrival her supreme longing had been to lie down and shut her eyes; but now restlessness overtook her, and with every fresh hour drove her more helplessly to and fro. She went out for long walks over the countryside, her thoughts so engrossingly turned inward that she saw nothing of the landscape on either hand; she returned to the house and endeavoured to write, to read, to sew, only to give up the attempt at the end of half an hour, and once more wander helplessly forth.

The good countrywoman was quick to sense that some hidden trouble was preying on her guest, and showed her sympathy in practical fashion.

"A bit piney-like, aren't you? I seed from the first that you was piney-like," she said, standing tray in hand on the threshold of the little parlour, her fresh, highly-coloured face smiling kindly upon the pale girl. "I always do say that I pities ladies when they has anything on their minds; sitting about, same as you do now, with nothing to take them off theirselves. A body like me that has to keep a house clean, and cook and wash, and mind the children, to say naught of the sewing and the mending, and looking after the cows and the hens, and all the extra fusses and worries that come along, she hasn't got no time to remember herself, and when she gets to bed she's too tired to think. Now if you was to have some work—"

Claire's face brightened with a sudden inspiration.

"Will you give me some work? Let me help *you*! Do, please, Mrs Corby; I'd be so grateful. Let me come into the kitchen and do something now. I feel so lonely shut off here, all by myself."

Mrs Corby laughed, her fat comfortable laugh.

"Bless your 'art, you can come along and welcome. I'll be proud to have you. It ain't much you know of housework, I expect, but it'll do you no harm to learn. I'll find you some little jobs."

"Oh, I'm not so useless as you think. I can brush and dust, and polish, and wash up, and I know a good deal about cooking. I'll make a salad to eat with the cold meat—a real French salad. I'm sure Mr Corby would enjoy a French salad," cried Claire, glancing out of the window at the well-stocked kitchen garden, and thinking of the wet lettuce and uncut onions, which were the good woman's idea of the dish in question. "May I make one to-day?"

Mrs Corby smiled with a fine resignation. Personally she wanted none of them nasty messy foods, but there! the poor thing meant well, and if it would make her happy, let her have her way. So Claire collected her materials, and washed and mixed, and filled a great bowl, and decorated the top with slices of hardboiled eggs, and a few bright nasturtium blossoms, while three linty-locked children stood by, watching with fascinated attention.

At dinner Claire thoroughly enjoyed her share of her own salad, but the verdict of the country-people was far from enthusiastic.

"I don't go for to deny that it tasted well enough," Mrs Corby said with magnanimous candour, "but what I argue is, what's the sense of using up all them extras—eggs, and oil, and what not—when you can manage just as well without? I've never seen the day when I couldn't relish a bit o' plain lettuce and a plate of good spring onions!"

"But the eggs and the dressing make it more nourishing," Claire maintained. "In France the peasants have very often nothing but salad for their dinner—great dishes of salad, with plenty of eggs."

"Eh, poor creatures! It makes your heart bleed to think of it. We may be thankful we are not foreign born!" Mrs Corby pronounced with unction, and Claire retired from the struggle, and decided that for the future it would be more tactful to learn, rather than to endeavour to teach. The next morning, therefore, she worked under Mrs Corby's supervision, picking fruit, feeding chickens, searching for eggs, and other light tasks designed to keep her in the open air; and in the afternoon accompanied the children on a message to a farm some distance away. The path lay across the fields, away from the main road, and on returning an hour later, Mrs Corby's figure was seen standing by her own gate, her hand raised to her eyes, as though watching for their approach. The children broke into a run, and Claire hurried forward, her heart beating with deep excited throbs. What was it? *Who* was it? Nobody but Sophie and Cecil knew her address, but still, but still— For a moment hope soared, then sank heavily down as Mrs Corby announced—

"A lady, miss. Come to see you almost as soon as you left. She's waiting in the parlour."

Cecil! Claire hardly knew if she were sorry or relieved. It would be a blessing to have some one to whom she could speak, but, on the other hand, what poor Cecil had to say would not fail to be depressing. She went slowly down the passage, taking a grip over her own courage, opened the door, and stood transfixed.

In the middle of the hard horsehair sofa sat Mrs Fanshawe herself, her elaborately coiffured, elaborately attired figure looking extraordinarily out of place in the prim bareness of the little room. Her gloved hands were crossed on her lap, she sat ostentatiously erect, her satin cloak falling around her in regal folds; her face was a trifle paler than usual, but the mocking light shone in her eyes. At Claire's entrance she stood up, and crossed the little room to her side.

"My dear," she said calmly, "I am an obstinate old woman, but I have the sense to know when I'm beaten. I have come to offer my apologies."

A generous heart is quick to forgive. At that moment Claire felt a pang indeed, but it came not from the remembrance of her own wrongs, but from the sight of this proud, domineering woman humbling herself to a girl. Impulsively she threw out both hands, impulsively she stopped Mrs Fanshawe's lips with the kiss which she had refused at parting.

"Oh, stop! Please don't! Don't say any more. I was wrong, too. I took offence too quickly. You were thinking of me, as well as of yourself."

"Oh, no, I was not," the elder woman corrected quietly. "Neither of you, nor your friend, my dear, though I took advantage of the excuse. You came between me and my plans, and I wanted to get you out of the way. You saw through me, and I suppose I deserved to be seen through. It's an unpleasant experience, but if it's any satisfaction to you to know it, I've been *well* punished for interfering. Erskine has seen to my punishment."

The blood rushed to Claire's face. How much did Mrs Fanshawe know? Had Erskine told her of that hurried interview upon the station? Had he by any possibility told what he had *asked*? The blazing cheeks asked the question as plainly as any words, and Mrs Fanshawe replied to it without delay.

"Oh, yes, my dear, I know all about it. It was because I guessed that was coming that I wanted to clear the coast; but it appears that I was too late. Shall we sit down and talk this out, and for pity's sake see that that woman doesn't come blundering in. It's such an anti-climax to have to deal with a tea-tray in the midst of personal explanations. I'm not accustomed to eating humble pie, and if I am obliged to do it at all, I prefer to do it in private."

"She won't come. I don't have tea for another hour," Claire assured her. "And please don't eat humble pie for me. I was angry at the time, but you had been very kind to me before. I—I enjoyed that first week very much."

"And so did I!" Mrs Fanshawe gave one of her dry, humorous, little laughs. "You are a charming companion, my dear. I was a little in love with you myself, but— Well! to be honest, it did not please me that my son should follow my example. He is my only child, and I am proud and ambitious for him, as any mother would be. I did not wish him to marry a—a—"

"A gentlewoman who was honourably working at an honourable profession!" concluded Claire for her, with a general stiffening of pose, voice and manner; but Mrs Fanshawe only laughed once more, totally unaffected by the pose.

"No, my dear, I did not! It's very praiseworthy, no doubt, to train the next generation, but it doesn't appeal to me in the present connection. I was thinking of my son, and I wanted him to have a wife of position and fortune, who would be able to help his career. If you had been a girl of fortune and position, I should have been quite ready to welcome you. You are a pretty creature, and much more intelligent than most girls of your age, but, you see, you are not—"

"I have no money but what I earn, but I belong to a good family. I object to your saying that I have no position, Mrs Fanshawe, simply because I live in lodgings and work for my living!"

Mrs Fanshawe shrugged with a touch of impatience.

"Oh, well, my dear, why bandy words? I have told you that I am beaten, so it's useless to argue the point. Erskine has decided for himself, and, as I told you before, one might as well try to bend a granite wall as move him when he has once made up his mind. I've planned, and schemed, and hoped, and prayed for the last dozen years, and at the first sight of that pretty face of yours all my plans went to the wall. If I'd been a wise woman I would have recognised the inevitable, and given in with a good grace, but I never was wise, never shall be, so I ran my head up against the wall. I've been through a bad time since you left me, my dear, and I was forgiven only on the understanding that I came here and made my peace with you. Have I made peace? Do you understand what I mean? That I withdraw my opposition, and if you accept my boy, you shall have nothing to fear. I'll make you welcome; and I'll be as good to you as it's in my nature to be. I'll treat you with every courtesy. Upon my word, my dear, as mothers-in-law go, I think you would come off pretty well!"

"I—I—I'm sure—You're very kind..." Claire stammered in helpless embarrassment; and Mrs Fanshawe, watching her, first smiled, then sighed, and said in a quick low voice—

"Ah, my dear, you can afford to be generous! If you live to be my age, and have a son of your own, whom you have loved, and cherished, and mothered for over thirty years, and at the end he speaks harshly to you for the sake of a girl whom he has known a few short months, puts her before you, finds it hard to forgive you because you have wounded her pride—ah, well, it's hard to bear! I don't want to whine, but—don't make it more difficult for me than you can help! I have apologised. Now it's for you—"

Claire put both arms round the erect figure, and rested her head on the folds of the black satin cloak. Neither spoke, but Mrs Fanshawe lifted a little lace-edged handkerchief to her eyes, and her shoulders heaved once and again. Then suddenly she arose and walked towards the door.

"The car is waiting. Don't come with me, my dear. I'll see you again."

She waived Claire back in the old imperious way against which there was no appeal. Evidently she wished to be alone, and Claire re-seated herself on the sofa, flushed, trembling, so shaken out of her bearings that it was difficult to keep hold of connected thought. The impossible had happened. In the course of a few short minutes difficulties which had seemed insurmountable had been swept from her path. Within her grasp was happiness so great, so dazzling that the very thought of it took away her breath.

Her eyes fell on the watch at her wrist. Ten minutes to four! Twenty minutes ago—barely twenty minutes—at the end of the field path she had looked at that little gold face with a dreamy indifference, wondering only how many minutes remained to be whiled away before it was time for tea. Even a solitary tea-drinking had seemed an epoch in the uneventful day. Uneventful! Claire mentally repeated the word, the while her eyes glowed, and her heart beat in joyful exultation. Surely, surely in after-remembrance this day would stand out as one all-important, epoch-making.

And then suddenly came a breathless question. How had Mrs Fanshawe discovered her retreat? No address had been left at Laburnum Crescent; no address had been given to Janet Willoughby. Cecil was in her mother's home; Sophie in hospital. In the name of all that was mysterious and inexplicable, *how had she been tracked*?

Claire sat bolt upright on her sofa, her grey eyes widened in amaze, her breath coming sharply through her parted lips. She thrilled at the realisation that Erskine's will had overcome all difficulties. Had not Mrs Fanshawe declared that she came at his instigation? And where the mother had come, would not the son follow?

At that moment a shadow fell across the floor; against the open space of the window a tall figure stood, blocking the light. Erskine's eager eyes met her own. Before the first gasp of surprise had left her lips, his strong hands had gripped the sill, he had vaulted over and stood by her side.

"I sent on my advance guard, and waited till her return. Did you think you had hidden yourself where I could not find you? I should have found you wherever you had gone; but as it happens it was easy enough. You forgot that you had forwarded flowers to your friend in hospital! She was ready enough to give me your address. And now—*Claire*"—he held out his hands, gazing down into her face—"what have you to say to me now?"

Instinctively Claire's hands stretched out to meet his, but on the following impulse she drew back, clasping them nervously behind her back.

"Oh, are you *sure*?" she cried breathlessly. "Are you *sure* you are sure? Think what it means! Think of the difference it might make! I have no money, no influence; I'd be an expense to you, and a drag when another girl might help. Think! Think! Oh, do be quite sure!"

Erskine's stern eyes melted into a beautiful tenderness as he looked at her troubled face. He waited no longer, but came a step nearer, and took forcible possession of the hidden hands.

"It is not my feelings which are in question; it is *yours*. There has been no doubt in my mind for months past. I think you know that, Claire!"

"But—your career?"

"I can look after my own career. Do you think it is the straight thing to suggest to a soldier that he needs a woman to help him in his work? It's not as a soldier I need you, but as a man. I need you there, Claire. I need you badly! No one else could help me as you can!"

Claire's lips quivered, but still she hung back, standing away from him at the length of her stretched arms.

"I've no money. I'm a—a school-mistress. Your friends will think—"

"I am not considering what my friends will think."

"Your mother thought—"

"I am not asking you to marry my mother. Mothers of only sons are hard to please, but you know as well as I can tell you that the mater is fond of you at heart, and that she will grow fonder still. She had her own ideas, and she fought for them, but she won't fight any more. You mustn't be hard on the mater, Claire. She has done her best for me to-day."

"I know! I know! I was sorry for her. Sorrier than I was for myself. It's so hard that I should have come between you two!"

At that Erskine laughed, a short, impatient laugh.

"Oh, Claire, Claire, how long are you going to waste time in discussing other people's feelings, before you tell me about your own? Darling, I'm in love with you!—I'm in love for the first time in my life. I'm impatient. I'm waiting. There's no one in the world for me at this moment but just yourself; I'm waiting for you to forget every one but me. Do you love me, Claire?"

"You know I do! You know I do! Oh!" cried Claire, yielding to the strength of the strong arms, and resting her head on the broad shoulder with an unspeakable rush of joy and rest. "Oh, but you don't know how much! I can't tell you—I can't put it into words, but it's my whole heart, my whole life! Oh, every *thought* has been with you for such a long, long time."

"My darling! My own sweet, brave little girl! And my thoughts with you! Thank God, we shall be together now. We have had enough of separation and chance meetings. There must be an end of that. You'll have to marry me at once!"

This was rushing ahead with a vengeance! Claire shook her head, with a little laugh sweet as a chime of joy bells.

"You ridiculous—boy! I can't. It's impossible. You forget my work. There's all next term. I couldn't possibly leave without giving notice."

"Couldn't you! We'll see to that. Do you seriously believe that I'm going to let you go back to that drudgery, and kick my heels waiting for four months? You don't understand the kind of man you are marrying, my lass!"

Claire loved the sound of that "my lass," loved the close grip of the arms, the feel of the rough cheek against her own. For a few minutes neither spoke, too utterly, completely absorbed in each other's presence. To Claire, as to Erskine, a four months' delay seemed an aeon of time through which to wade before the consummation of a perfect happiness, but it seemed impossible that it could be avoided.

"Miss Farnborough would never let me off. She would be indignant with me for asking."

"I'll tackle Miss Farnborough. Leave Miss Farnborough to me!" returned Erskine with so confident an air that Claire shook with amusement, seeing before her a picture of her lover seated *tête-à-tête* with the formidable "Head," breaking to her the news that one of her staff intended to play truant.

"It's very easy to say that. You don't know her. She thinks everything in the world comes second to education."

"What if she does? I'll agree with her. You're the most precious darling in all the world, but you can't honestly believe that there aren't a thousand other mistresses who could teach those flappers as well, or better! Whereas for *me*—well! it's Claire, or no one. I'll throw myself on the good lady's tender mercies, and ask for your release as a favour to myself, and I bet you anything you like that I succeed. Miss Farnborough was a woman before she was a school-mistress. She'll set you free all right!"

"Perhaps—perhaps possibly at the half term."

"Rubbish—the half term! We'll be married and settled down before we get near then... Where will you go for our marriage, Claire? To Mrs Willoughby? I'm sure she'd be willing."

"No!—no!" Claire marvelled at the obtuseness of men; at the utter unconsciousness of this particular man of the reason why Mrs Willoughby's house should be the last one on earth from which his marriage should take place. And then in the midst of these questionings, to her own surprise a sudden pricking of tears came to her eyes, and she cried sharply, "I want mother! I must have mother. She must come home. She'll come at once, when she hears—"

"We'll cable to-day. That will be best of all. I'm longing to meet your mother, and you ought to have her with you, little lass! Poor, little, lonely lass! Please God, you shall never be lonely any more."

"Ah, Erskine darling, but the *other women*!" Claire cried, and there was the sharpness of pain in her voice.

From within the shelter of her lover's arms her heart went out in a wave of tenderness towards her sisters who stood apart from the royal feast; towards Cecil with her blighted love, Sophie with her blighted health, with the thousand others for whom they stood as types; the countless hordes of women workers for whom life was a monotonous round of grey-hued days, shadowed by the prospect of age and want. From the shelter of her lover's arms, Claire Gifford vowed herself to the service of her working sisters. From the bottom of her heart she thanked God for the year of work which had taught her to *understand*.

The End.